DETROIT'S GOT SOUL

Marc Humphries

iUniverse, Inc.
New York   Bloomington

Detroit's Got Soul

This is a work of fiction. All of the characters, names, incidents, organizations, and dialogue in this novel are either the products of the author's imagination or are used fictitiously.

iUniverse books may be ordered through booksellers or by contacting:

iUniverse
1663 Liberty Drive
Bloomington, IN 47403
www.iuniverse.com
1-800-Authors (1-800-288-4677)

ISBN: 978-1-4502-3225-8 (pbk)
ISBN: 978-1-4502-3226-5 (ebk)

Printed in the United States of America

iUniverse rev. date: 6/7/2010

Author's Note

This book is a work of fiction. References to real people, events, institutions, and organizations are intended only to provide a sense of authenticity. All other characters and dialogue are all drawn from the author's imagination and not to be considered real.

The real Detroit St. Martin DePorres existed from 1968-2005. In 2005, the Archdiocese of Detroit closed all of its inner-city Catholic schools in Detroit. Detroit's Got Soul is, in part, a tribute to all those dynamic teachers, staff, and administrators, especially principals Joseph Dulin and Sunbeam Hughes – because they cared so much. The fictionalized basketball matchups are not intended to take away from the great high school teams of that era such as Northwestern, Mackenzie, Pershing, Cass Tech, and Catholic Central, among others. And there were dozens of organizations and hundreds of people who battled against police brutality and the police unit STRESS in Detroit. This story does not intend to minimize their efforts as they were heroic.

Acknowledgements

There are numerous people to thank who have made a contribution reviewing early and final versions of this manuscript, including participants of the Sterling Brown Writer's Workshop in Washington, D.C. and participants of the Writer's Center Workshop in Bethesda, Maryland. Thanks so much to my editors and reviewers for their tireless support and fine-tuning including Rachel Frier, Charlynn Spencer-Pyne, Michelle Simms, Patricia Liske, Gretchen Roberts-Shorter, and David 'Hump the Grinder' Humphries.

Special thanks to Joseph Dulin, Ben Holloway Sr., and Carlos Cortez for sharing their invaluable insights and experiences of the 1960s and 1970s in Detroit. And thanks to my wife Gwendolyn and my girls: Erica, Shakenya, Imani, and Niya.

For my parents, Bill Humphries III and Dolores Comeaux-Taylor

The Period: 1963 to 1972.
The Place: Detroit, Michigan

CHAPTER 1 -
Bloody Friday (March 1963)

MIKE WATERMAN BOUNCED IN HIS CHAIR and waved his hand frantically to get Sister Sarah's attention. With about five minutes before the school bell rang, he had to go to the boys' room, bad. The girls giggled.

"Sister Sarah, can I have a hall pass for the bathroom?" Mike blurted out. Sister Sarah looked at the clock, then peered over her spectacles.

"We have less than five minutes before school lets out. You will have to wait. Who would like to wash the board today?" Mike squirmed in his seat. "George, I mean Michael, will you please be still? You are disrupting the entire class."

Without further hesitation Mike jumped up from his seat and ran down the hall to the boys' room. Mike made it to the stall in the far corner.

"Ahhh, just in time."

A white high school kid stood at the urinal near the door. He was the only other person in the boys' room. The radiator clanged so loudly that neither of the boys heard the restroom window being pushed open by some teens from Central High School.

"Hey white boy," one of the teens yelled.

A tall Negro teenager spun the white boy around from the urinal and landed a solid right fist to his nose. The boy instantly buckled and fell limp to the floor. The teen shouted to his partners, "Let's kick some Catholic school ass." Mike stood at the urinal at the opposite end of the boys' room and watched several, perhaps a dozen of neighboring Central High School boys stream in through the basement windows of his school. Mike froze, but the Central invaders weren't paying any attention to him, maybe because he too was a Negro like them or maybe because he was just too little.

He felt a strong gust of wind against his back as he made the sign of the cross and began to recite, "Our Father, who art in heaven, hollowed be thy name, thy kingdom come . . . " The school bell rang and broke his focus. He thought, *Daggit, I better get Jon-Jon and Denise.* Once in the hallway, Mike saw Central High School boys everywhere throughout Visitation, a combined Roman Catholic elementary and high school that Mike and his siblings attended. The hallway turned into chaos as the Visitation students began coming out of their classrooms.

"Where they at, where they at?" The Central boys' yelled while running through the hallway and peering into classrooms. The Visitation kids were screaming like mad.

"There they go," someone pointed to several white high school football players wearing letter jackets, coming down the steps. Their eyes became as big as silver dollars when they saw the Central boys.

Mike scurried down the narrow, dimly lit, navy blue painted hallway, dodging students, some black, and some white, who ran in every direction. Some of the kids ran back into their classrooms.

Others took off down the long corridor towards the church.

Mike Waterman was just eight years old in the third grade. He was searching for his six-year-old brother Jon-Jon, his seven-year-old sister Denise, and four schoolmates. They usually walked home together. In the chaos he saw his best friend DeAngelo who was standing in front of his siblings and schoolmates.

"Let's go," Mike cried out.

There was so much chaos and confusion that Mike couldn't see the door to get out. Mike led everyone into the boys' restroom, including Denise and her friend Sharon. Right behind them, the Central high teens dragged in two Visitation football players and tossed them into the toilet stalls. The white kids were far outnumbered by the Central high teens and they offered little resistance. Their pleas for help rang over the noisy radiators.

One of the Central teens said, "You tell your friends they best not say one more word to our girls. No more bitches and ho's. You hear me. Say it. Say it."

"No more whore . . . , the white boy moaned.

"Say it louder."

"No more . . . "

"That ain't good enough, sucker." The Central boy dunked the boy's head in the toilet, then, bounced it against the back wall. He punched the boy so hard that his head hit the side of the stall. Blood squirted out from the boy's forehead and streamed down the wall.

"This shit better not happen again," the Central boy warned.

Mike wondered where all the teachers were. He and his friends were trembling, their backs pressed against the wall trying to disappear. But there was nowhere to hide.

"Let's get outta here," DeAngelo shouted.

As they headed out of the restroom towards the exit door, Mike saw that Father O'Brien and several lay teachers were running down the stairs screaming at the Central High School boys to leave the building.

"Get out of here now. Get the hell out of here," Father O'Brien yelled. Mike, his siblings and friends finally made it outside, where the situation was not much better. White Visitation students were running like crazy, trying to escape the onslaught. Books and papers were blowing in the wind. It looked like half the Central student body was outside at Visitation. If the Central students weren't fighting, they were watching.

"I can't see, I can't see," said one white guy on his knees with his hands over his blood-covered face. "Where are my glasses?" he moaned.

"Here they are cracker," said a Central High student as he crushed the glasses under the weight of his black army boots. He then began to kick the white kid in his ribs. Denise, whom Mike, his brother, and parents called Lil' Sis, couldn't help herself as she instinctively ran over towards the assault.

"Don't kill him. Let him go," Lil' Sis cried.

The Central teen with a menacing look that could even be seen through his dark shades asked, "What the hell you care, you a black Catholic or something?" Mike jumped in front of Denise to protect her. The Central High teen faked a punch towards Mike and the other kids, then backed off laughing. Mike, Jon-Jon, Lil Sis and the four schoolmates scattered through the school parking lot and ran down 12th Street towards home. They didn't stop running for nine blocks. With a strong wind at Mike's back, he felt like he could fly. Mike ran so fast that the houses, stores, and trees were a blur. Mike led the group with DeAngelo on his heels. Lil' Sis trailed behind them. Mike didn't realize as he headed towards home that Lil' Sis had suddenly tripped and dropped her school bag. Paper blew in the air, pens and pencils rolled on the sidewalk. Lil' Sis stopped to gather them up. Sharon stayed back to help her. All the boys kept running. As Mike got closer to home, shouts from his mom, Rose Waterman, rang out.

"Where's Denise? Where is your sister? Where's Sharon?" Rose cried out. Mike saw fear on his mother's face as she stood on the porch. Her cinnamon-brown skin glowed brilliantly in the afternoon sun. Rose Waterman – petite in size - spoke with authority. Her perch on the front porch allowed her to see all the way down the block. The boys who were all together looked back and saw that Denise and Sharon were not with them. Denise and Sharon were still on 12th Street picking up paper, pens, and pencils blowing in the wind. Mike ran back to get them.

"Say, Lil' Sis, come on. Let me help you gather these things up." Denise was crying. She was furious as she threw her school supplies in her book bag. Sharon helped her up.

Denise cried, "He didn't have to do that. He didn't have to do that to him. He wasn't doing nothing."

She kept crying, burying her face in her hands. Sharon put her arms around Denise. Mike took Denise by the hand and grabbed her book bag from her.

"We don't have to run now. Nobody is after us. There's no reason to cry. We'll tell dad and he'll deal with this," Mike comforted her. Denise stopped crying. She wiped her face with the back of her hand, and they began to walk home. Jon-Jon, DeAngelo, Luke (Sharon's older brother) and Brother Bear walked back to meet them.

"Shit," began DeAngelo, still breathing hard, "Shit, Sis you almost got us all killed. You feeling sorry for that white boy."

"She's just like daddy, always tryin' to help somebody. But man, we can't be running from these public school dudes," Mike burst out. "They ain't even after us. They jumpin' on white boys. Why we running anyway? I ain't running no more. I don't give a darn if they after me, I ain't running ever again."

"I heard white people are moving anyway," said DeAngelo. "They can't take it. Too many niggers in the neighborhood, and they can't think straight. And man, Darren told me the Central boys were looking for some football players that was bothering Diamond Jim's sister. One of them fools grabbed her on the butt and called her a 'ho. You can't mess with Diamond Jim's people and get away with it. Anyways, my brother told me that when they run out of white kids to beat up, they gonna come after our Catholic school asses."

"But, tell your brother Darren, we ain't calling nobody hos and grabbing no girls butts."

"It don't matter," said DeAngelo.

"I still ain't runnin'. And I thought it was about the championship game with Central tonight," said Mike.

"Why come they don't cancel the game after this shit? Who's gonna go now?" asked DeAngelo.

"I'm going, we're going. My father's gonna take us. Y'all wanna ride with us?"

"I'll let you know," DeAngelo said, while he and the other boys trailed off towards their homes. Denise ran straight in the house, not stopping to say a word to her mother standing on the porch.

"Mom, can you get dad on the phone?" Mike asked.

"Wait a minute, first sit down and tell me what's going on."

"Mom, there was a big fight at school," Mike began. "Central invaded our school. They came in through the bathroom windows."

Mike and Jon-Jon were seated at the breakfast nook table while Mike told his mother what happened. Denise and 'Mama E,' Rose's mother, were resting on the couch in the family room. Rose sat on a stool inside the kitchen and faced the boys. She had been preparing their supper and had already arranged an after-school snack.

"Why?" asked Rose. She stood up and reached inside the fridge for the pitcher of iced tea. Pouring the boys tea, she said, "Before I call your dad, I want to know why this happened."

Fidgeting in his seat, Jon-Jon said, "Mom, I think somebody, one of the football players felt down Diamond Jim's sister and called her a 'ho, I mean whore, you know."

"What did the teacher's do when they saw all this commotion?"

"They didn't know what was going on at first, then, they chased them out." Rose grabbed the phone and dialed Frank's number.

"Frank, the boys got something they need to tell you."

"Dad, there was a fight at school. Central dudes were up there beating up every white boy in the high school."

"Are you kids okay?" Frank asked.

"We're fine," said Mike. "We're fine, everybody's fine. We ran out the school and ran home through the middle of it all. We saw some kids getting beat up pretty bad. Lil Sis is still upset. She tried to stop one of 'em and almost got us all killed. The Central dude almost jumped us. He had a knife, I saw it Dad, I saw it myself."

"Where's Denise?"

"She's on the couch with Mama E."

"Okay, I'm going to make some calls to see what's going on. Put your mother back on." Mike handed the phone to his mother.

"Frank, Denise is traumatized, poor child. She went straight for the couch. Okay, Okay, see you soon."

Mike could overhear the anxiety in his dad's voice.

"Your Dad is going to leave work early and call the archdiocese to find out if they canceled the game."

~ ~ ~ ~ ~ ~ ~

It was a beautiful spring afternoon, sunny and about seventy-five degrees. A strong breeze blew through the windows carrying the aromatic scent of their spaghetti and meatball supper to every corner of their spacious home. Mama E and Denise lay on Mama E's favorite couch, it was green and covered with plastic. Mama E threw a pink blanket beneath them and another pink blanket over them. She held Denise and stroked her hair. She told her that it was okay and that Denise had nothing to worry about. Mike noticed that whenever Denise felt nervous or scared, she cuddled up with Mama E, and talked to her. Mama E always had a great story to tell to Denise.

Within thirty minutes, Frank was home. When he walked into the house, supper was on the table and the aroma of the spaghetti and meatballs enveloped him. Frank wore a grey sharkskin suit and white shirt. His navy blue tie still hugged his neck. Frank's chocolate-brown African features were a striking contrast to the light-colored suits he often wore. The boys, Frank and Rose sat in the breakfast nook since the table was already set when the kids arrived home from school.

"Hey love, sure is good to be home, and sure smells good in here. Been a rough week. Where's Denise? Is she doing better?"

"She's sleep on the couch, all curled up with Mama E. She had a fall and scrapped her knee. I cleaned it, it's not bad. What did the archdiocese say about the game?" Rose asked.

Before answering Frank walked over to Denise and kissed her on the forehead and smiled at his mother-in-law. He walked back to the kitchen. He loosened his tie, sat down, and leaned against the bench.

"They aren't going to cancel the game tonight," Frank said.

Mike hoped for that answer.

"You're kidding, right?" asked Rose as she carried the bowl of meatballs to the table. "Don't you think they should after what happened?"

"There'll be an army of police down there, Rose. It'll be alright. They plan on having extra police and security inside and outside the field house," Frank said, leaning forward trying to sound convincing.

"Honey, I think you should call Father O'Malley and see if he can get the archdiocese to call this thing off." Rose untied her apron and pulled it over her head. "I don't have a good feeling about this game." The family clasped hands while Frank led them in prayer.

"Bless this food, oh Lord, which we are about to receive, from our bounty, through Christ our Lord, amen." Frank paused for a moment. "The archdiocese won't change their mind. You know they won't. They're just like a bunch of donkeys when they got their mind made up. Do you know how important this game is to them? The Catholic league lost the last three years."

"Oh my God, is it that important Frank?"

"Dad," Mike interrupted. "Are we still going to the game?"

Rose glanced up. Frank was silent for a second.

"Of course we're going son," Frank assuredly responded.

Jon-Jon said, "Mom, these meatballs are the best ever. You got some special recipe or somethin'."

Rose laughed, "Thank you baby." Then she stared at Frank.

"They are delicious, Dear. Right Mike?" Frank responded.

"The best, Mom."

"Rose, who really knows what caused the invasion? Father O'Malley, (Visitation's Pastor), and people at the Archdiocese of Detroit acted totally dumbfounded about it. Mike said it was about the game. Then Jon-Jon heard it was about some stupid kid talking bad and feeling down Diamond Jim's sister. I don't know much about Diamond Jim except he's some local hoodlum, but if it was my sister I might want to go upside the boy's head too."

"Frank, what are you saying?" Rose asked.

"What I'm saying is that you stand up for your sister. She's not going to fight a bunch of boys by herself."

"But you don't go raid a whole school to do it," Rose responded.

"No, you don't. They went way overboard, way overboard."

Rose glanced at her watch. "I think you all better get going if you must go."

"Yeah mom, we must," said Mike. "This is the big game. At the Big House."

"Well, I hope y'all ain't the only three down there."

"Mom, half the city's gonna be there. School riot or no school riot. Most people probably still don't even know what happened. Dad, can DeAngelo and Luke ride with us? Bear can't go. He got music lessons or something."

"Sure, tell them to be down here in five minutes."

Mike called Luke and DeAngelo right away to invite them down to the house for a ride to the game. DeAngelo and Luke's parents didn't hesitate in letting their sons go to the game as long as they were in the custody of Mr. Waterman. The boys' parents told Mike that they trusted their kids with his dad. And because of Frank's involvement with the Atkinson Ave. Block Club, he seemed to know many of the neighbors pretty well. Mike felt good about his father being so well-liked by his friends and their parents on the block. After all, his dad was a successful insurance salesman.

CHAPTER 2 –
The Big House

THERE WERE HUNDREDS OF POLICE AT the University of Detroit Field House – The Big House. Scout cars were everywhere. Police were on horseback and had their billyclubs drawn. They were prepared for a showdown. When Frank and the boys entered the field house, there was a modest and quiet crowd from Visitation, but people were still coming in. Central's side was packed.

Visitation had only two Negroes on the team. The high school was still about ninety-percent white, while the elementary school was about fifty-percent Negro. Central High School was nearly all Negro. Visitation had become a major sports powerhouse. And it had one of the best coaches - Michigan high school basketball coach of the year–Jake McCoy, nickname Mac. Mac built up quite a basketball empire at Visitation. It took him ten years to do it.

The game got off to a good start while Visitation fans kept entering. By the second quarter, the Visitation fans began to show more excitement. Central fans were making quite a ruckus, trying to be intimidating. During the game Mike reacted just like his father: Frank jumped, Mike jumped, Frank clapped, Mike clapped, Frank hollered, Mike hollered. Mike idolized senior guard Ray Miles, one of the two Negroes on the team. He knew his father wanted him to play like Ray one day. During many backyard basketball sessions with his dad, Mike felt he'd better learn this game of basketball or his dad might lose his cotton-pickin' mind.

Visitation played well in the first half. Down by only three points at half time, Ray Miles had ten points, five assists and two steals, Mike counted. And every time Ray would do something good, his father would stand up and holler, then, look at Mike and give him a nod of approval. Visitation's two big guys, Dick McMann, whom everyone called Big Boy, and Tom Sullivan, nicknamed Tree Top, were both six feet eight inches tall, who looked like football players, pounded the boards during the first half. Big Boy and Tree Top led the Catholic league in rebounds. The Central team had stringy, lanky guys, none who were taller than six feet three inches tall. Visitation's domination of the boards often gave them two or three shots at their basket. But the Central players were a lot quicker, which allowed them to make fast breaks and carry out a good full-court press.

By half-time, the Visitation team looked tired. Mike even felt tired as he stood up, sat down in a synchronized rhythm with his father. Jon-Jon, Luke and DeAngelo cheered along but didn't show nearly as much excitement as Mike. The Visitation cheerleaders took the floor. Mike joined in singing his favorite cheer V-I-S-I—T-A-T—T-A-T—I-O-N, what's that spell, the cheerleaders called out, VISITATION, VISITATION, VISITATION, the crowd hollered back.

When the second half started, the Visitation bleachers were full. Mike pounded the bleachers with his feet right along with the others. Visitation began to press, trying to play the run-n-gun game that Central had perfected. The game stayed close as the teams traded leads. Near the end of the fourth quarter, Visitation pulled ahead by five points. With a minute left, Central had the ball. They nearly sprinted down the court, made a 20-foot jump shot, and drew a foul. The Central crowd pointed to the Visitation fans and shouted, "YOU, YOU, YOU, YOU, YOU." The shouts were deafening. The bleachers vibrated. Mike couldn't hear what his father said. Frank pointed to the clock. There was less than a minute left. But Mike could see the nervousness on the faces of many Visitation fans. Mike even felt butterflies in his belly. His body tightened. He glued his hands to his head while the Central player stood at the free-throw line. Central made the foul shot–a three-point play. The Central crowd roared. Now, down by two, they pressed Visitation, stole the ball, and made another basket. In ten seconds, Central tied the game. Out of frustration, Mike flopped down in his seat and pounded one hand into the other. Frank laughed. The other boys looked at each other with intensity written over their faces. The Central crowd was on its feet. Visitation called time out with forty seconds left in the game. On Visitation's next possession, they slowed the game down for a final shot. Ray Miles fed Sullivan the ball at the foul line. He turned towards the hoop, then, drove inside the lane for a lay up. The officials called a foul on Central. The Visitation crowd was on its feet yelling, stomping and clapping.

"The game might come down to free throws. He gets two shots," said Mike's Dad.

"Two shots," said Mike turning to his friends and brother. With ten seconds on the clock, Tree Top Sullivan, the 6' 8" center, stepped up to the line. He took his time bouncing the ball. He missed the first shot. The Central fans cheered wildly. He bounced the ball again, bent his knees, and let the ball go. He made the second shot. Visitation fans let out a thunderous roar. Down by one point, Central called time out. Someone hurtled a bottle from the Central stands; it burst on the court. The crowd went silent. The police moved in and took up positions on both sides of the arena. It took workers ten minutes to clean the glass off the court.

Central took the ball out near half court. Visitation pressed, but no fouls were called. With five seconds left, the Central guard drove in the lane trying to draw a foul. He got knocked to the floor as he threw up a desperation shot. He missed. The officials didn't call a foul. The buzzer rang - game over. Visitation was the new city champion. The Visitation fans leapt from their seats and screamed with excitement but no one ran on the court. Led by their cheerleaders, they stayed in the stands and ended with their victory chant: "V-I-S-I T-A-T T-A-T I-O-N. Visitation. Visitation."

The Central crowd looked stunned and became very, very quiet, but then suddenly they began to shout, "FOUL, FOUL, FOUL, . . . "

Tension filled the air. Police hustled across the gym and formed a double line in front of the Central fans.

Over the loudspeaker, the announcer said, "All Visitation fans, please exit to your right. Visitation fans please exit to your right. Central fans will exit on their right following the dismissal of the Visitation fans." Boos rang out from the Central side of the arena and ricocheted through the tightly-packed arena.

"Jesus Christ, the announcer would have to rub it in. He would have to do it," said Frank.

"Do what?" asked Mike. Mike could not hear his father's response as the thunderous chants from the Central fans grew louder. "YOU, YOU, YOU" drowned out the announcer as he tried to direct the crowd. Police in full riot gear now placed themselves three deep in front of the Central stands. This deterred Central fans from crossing the court. When Mike, his friends, and Frank exited the field house, Mike noticed that the police presence was not as beefed up outside as it had been inside.

"Dad, look," Mike pointed.

A couple a dozen Negroes, presumably Central fans, gathered outside about three hundred yards from the field house, past all the police barricades, crouched near some bushes. These kids rose and ambushed five white guys who were leaving the game. Mike overheard one of the white guys say, "I'm not going to take this shit from you."

"You kids keep walking, I want to see what I can do to stop this," Frank said. Mike and the others decided not to keep walking but watch the melee instead. Frank could not easily penetrate the crowd. They attacked the five white guys as Frank kept trying to fight his way through the crowd. But Central fans blocked him as others pounded and pounded the five white guys. Mike, Jon-Jon, DeAngelo, and Luke stared motionless. Then, in a loud voice, someone hollered.

"I got the pipe, I got the pipe."

Frank let out a scream, "nooooooo." The crowd scattered. Three of the white guys ran across an open field profusely bleeding; with their shirts ripped off, they ran for their lives. The attackers scattered in the other direction. The entire attack seemed to last only thirty seconds. When the police arrived, the other two boys lay bloodied in the grass. They appeared lifeless. An ambulance soon arrived and then sped the boys to Henry Ford Hospital. Mike led his brother and friends over to his father's side. The police asked Frank his version of the story. He told the police what he saw, however, he was unable to give them a description of the attackers.

"Did you kids see anything?" an officer asked.

"No, they didn't see anything," Frank spoke up in a forceful tone.

"Were these attackers from Central?" asked a motorcycle officer wearing knee-high boots.

"I'm not sure, maybe," Frank responded.

The motorcycle officer began to holler in Frank's face, "They were Negro, right?"

"Yes."

"They were from Central, right?"

Remaining calm, Frank responded, "I don't know."

"We need to get your information. You're a witness."

When the Waterman family arrived safely at home, Rose had the news on the television. One of the two boys who were rushed to the hospital died. The other survived in critical condition.

"Frank, we know the families of the two boys from church. Oh my God." Rose hugged Frank tightly.

"I tried to stop it, but couldn't get through the crowd. The police are going to call me in as a witness," Frank said.

"Did you see who did it?"

"No."

CHAPTER 3 -
The Aftermath

MIKE FELT THE TENSION AT SCHOOL. He heard that members of Visitation Parish and people in the Catholic community stormed up to the Archdiocese of Detroit to express their outrage to Cardinal Beardum over the murder after the game. They asked the cardinal why the game was held in the first place and why wasn't there better police protection. Visitation Parish and much of the Detroit Catholic community flooded the archdiocese with phone calls and letters, while Mike witnessed the police, especially the notorious Big-Four, a Detroit police unit, which consisted of patrol officers and detectives, pull over Negroes driving in the neighborhood. He'd heard stories about their brutality. The Big-Four, who cruised around Central High School in their black Chrysler 300 Sedan, responded to this murder and school invasion in a worse way than they did two years prior when a Negro was mistakenly accused of striking a white woman on Woodward Avenue, Detroit's main street. They stopped Negroes on Linwood Ave. and LaSalle Blvd., without probable cause, beat them up with their billyclubs, and threw them in the back of squad cars; and then meted out even more brutality once the alleged perpetrator, who had not been informed of his alleged crime, was taken into custody at the police station.

Every day since the murder someone at school asked Mike if his dad really saw who did it. Mike got annoyed with the semi-interrogation and would sometimes scream – "hell no!" There was a sudden coldness after Sunday Mass. Some of his parent's white friends seemed more distant. Rumors swirled around the school and church that Frank refused to I.D. the murderers.

Parents continued to flood up to the headquarters of Cardinal Beardum in protest. They forced a meeting to express their outrage. Mike heard after Sunday Mass that many whites were planning a mass exodus out of Detroit.

The Detroit Common Council and the mayor of Detroit hurriedly set up public hearings that following week to find out what led up to the violence and why the police were unable to prevent the school invasion and subsequent killing.

There was a lot of tension in the community between Negroes, who had been moving into the area around 12th Street since the 1950s, and whites, who had been living in the neighborhood since the 1920s when many of the homes were built. The neighborhood was changing, and the Catholic Church refused to recognize this change and the racial tension it spawned.

The Archdiocese of Detroit and the Detroit mayor's office set up a High School Sports Commission to investigate the incident. They were charged with reporting back within thirty days. Frank testified before the Detroit Common Council and the High School Sports Commission and talked about the issue regularly with Rose at home. Frank talked about how Central High School girls told their story about regular harassment while walking home from school.

Frank told Rose at dinner one night about the testimony of Central High's principal, Dr. Charles Jones. He admitted that some of the hoodlums who invaded Visitation were Central students, but he distanced himself and his students from the murder. He told the commission that he didn't know if the kids who attacked the students after the game were Central students, and he also pointed out that there was no evidence yet that proved that the perpetrators went to Central. He went on to say that the police were arresting many of the kids in the neighborhood, threatening them with jail or a beating if they didn't provide them information on the murderers.

As the sports commissioners continued to listen to testimony from Central and Visitation students, Mike got wind of more rumors. This time the neighborhood kids were suggesting that his dad cooperated with the police in identifying the perpetrators.

Mike could see that his parents were being drawn close together during this ordeal – always hugging and kissing. They gave each other that long embrace like the kind you give someone before or after a long separation. Mike didn't detect any animosity between them. Rose would constantly tell Frank that they would get through this. Mike saw her praying the rosary every day. At dawn she could be seen with the door open in the bedroom on her knees. In the afternoon, when the Mike and his siblings returned from school she answered the door with the rosary in her hand.

The sports commission reported back to the mayor and common council in a matter of days. They concluded that the violence was racially motivated.

13

They recommended that playoffs between Catholic and public schools no longer be permitted in the city. They announced that there would be a public school league champion and a Catholic school league champion, and that was that.

For two weeks following the murder, Frank had been called down to the 13th police precinct almost daily. Mike heard his father talk warily of the police and once said the he'd never experienced anything remotely close to what he'd been going through lately.

Mike saw his father often come in late, looking tired but always trying to put on a happy show: asking the kids how their day went; swinging Denise over his head; or joking with Mama E about hitting the numbers. She played daily. Frank would hug Rose tightly, then sink into the large chair in the living room, pull off his tie, remove his shoes, and put up his feet on the footstool. One night while Mike was helping his mother clean up the kitchen, he felt his father's frustration.

"Rose, the police are squeezing me to I.D. several of the boys they brought in for questioning. And I kept telling them I didn't recognize anyone. I did *NOT* see their faces. They've gone as far as saying that I must be trying to protect the killers. They've already beat up some of the kids they took in for questioning."

"But Frank, we know the dead boy's parents. Did you tell them that?" Rose switched on the mantle lights over the fireplace, then, dimmed the bright overhead lights.

Mike felt a knot in his stomach. *The police were going to arrest dad, he thought. Maybe he's gonna rat-out somebody. Some of the people in the neighborhood already think he is. Shoot, I better watch my back, Mike thought.*

For several weeks following the murders until summer break, the police had nearly camped out at Central High and at Visitation located three blocks away on 12th Street and Webb Ave. to watch Visitation students leave school. Frank complained at home that he was being followed by plainclothes policemen. Denise and Sharon continued to walk to school with the boys and were largely unaffected by the rampage through the neighborhood, which was primarily directed towards older Negro males, or the remarks about their dad, Frank. They moved about as if they were in some kind of protective bubble.

"They want to charge about a dozen kids with murder, attempted murder, aggravated assault and battery, you name it. The police are all over Central High, and as we can see, all over the neighborhood trying to get information," said Frank.

"We need to talk to Father O'Malley," Rose demanded.

"For what?"

"To tell the police you are telling them the truth."

"No, no, no, no, no, I ain't in no trouble yet. I'm just fed up with the police bully tactics."

"Well Frank, they can't do anything if you don't know anything."

"Oh no?"

"What?" Rose asked.

"They will kill our Negro behinds as easy as waking up in the morning."

"Then we need to talk to Father O'Malley."

A few days later during dinner, Frank looked exhausted. The family was crowded in the breakfast nook. Mike opened a window letting some cool air in.

"The police got the nerve to insist that I cooperate with them. I told them everything I know."

"Dad," Mike interrupted. "People in the neighborhood think you've been squealing to the police. I told everybody that we were all there and couldn't see nobody. We just heard the screams."

"Mike, look here, this squealing thing doesn't bother me. A boy was killed, another nearly killed and we know their parents. We go to church together. We know what they are going through. You think I'm worried about what those kids are saying. Son, Jon-Jon, Denise, I want y'all to hear me good. It's what the police are doing that bothers me the most. They are telling people in the neighborhood that I'm cooperating with them, telling them everything, then telling people at the parish that I'm not cooperating at all. They're looking for a weak link trying to get someone who does know something to talk. They're lying to people about your dad so they can get an arrest and conviction."

"Frank, you have to stop talking to the police. Do we need a lawyer?" Rose asked.

"The damage is already done, but it's over for me. I'm through with it. The commission and the council are done with me, and I'm done with them. And the police too."

By mid-April, the severely-injured boy recovered enough from his injuries to talk to the police. He identified one of the Negro teenagers in a lineup – a fifteen-year-old junior high school dropout who last attended Durfee Junior High School. After being pummeled by the police, he ratted out three others involved in the melee.

They were arrested and by the end of the year convicted of second degree murder.

Chapter 4 –
The Neighborhood

THE WATERMANS LIVE IN A NICE neighborhood, full of life, and loaded with children. Mike once counted over 50 kids under the age of 18 on his street alone. Some children were playmates of the Watermans, but others were too young to go beyond their front porch. There were parks, schools, and libraries nearby. They lived on Atkinson Avenue, a street with single-family brick homes, tall elm and maple trees providing a canopy cover over the street, and beautiful lawns.

Frank and Rose purchased the house between 14th Street and LaSalle Boulevard after Frank took a job offered to him by an old college friend, Jerry Drumbrowski, at Statewide Insurance Company. He had previously sold insurance for the city's only Negro-owned firm, Peabody, Ltd.

The Waterman's home was beginning to take shape. When they bought the two-story, five-bedroom, brown brick house just two years earlier, in 1961, the basement was unfinished and the house needed a paint job inside and out. Frank and Rose did the painting. Frank borrowed a neighbor's ladder to paint the exterior second floor and attic trim. They purchased a couple of small step ladders to paint the interior. Rose hung new curtains and, after going through three different contractors in two years, they finally got the basement finished. Frank purchased new carpet for the entire house and new kitchen appliances. He kept the grass maintained with the help of his two sons. Mike and Jon-Jon would also cut lawns for several neighbors and clean garages for extra money.

The neighbors were always concerned about their lawns. Every year the block club had a lawn competition. Mowing, weeding, and trimming were standard practices on weekends. Some of the neighbors went beyond the call of duty and had professional landscapers come in regularly to perfect their lawns. There were plenty of flowers on the block. Rose and Mama E would plant up a storm: they planted three dozen rose bushes, mostly in the backyard, as foot-high starters. The rose bushes were now nearly three feet high. It was a great pastime for both of them. Denise spent most of her time watching everyone else work in between trying to do cartwheels on the front lawn. When you walked or drove down Atkinson Ave., it was the most beautiful sight in the city. The roses, tulips, petunias, and daisies in rainbow hues could be seen from one corner to the other. In the fall, Frank would supervise many of the neighborhood children as they burned leaves curbside in front of their houses.

Youthful energy filled the air. Mike had enough playmates to go around. Their house soon became 'hood central' because of the way Frank and Rose would accept the kids into their home. This easily became a reason to elect Frank block club president in 1964. Frank would frequently invite the kids to go to the beach and on picnics at Belle Isle Park, Kensington Park, and even as far as Point Peely in Canada.

Because of past housing discrimination in Detroit, this neighborhood was home to Negroes from all walks of life. Everyone from medical doctors and ministers to factory workers and school teachers; even big-time numbers men. It seemed to Mike that people lived well.

Two school teachers who lived across the street from the Waterman family were middle-aged women, very neat, and sharp. They always drove new cars. One owned a Buick LaSabre, the other a Ford Galaxie 500. A Baptist minister lived next two doors on the left, the Rev. Willie Boykin, an impeccable dresser. He stood about 6'6", had a reddish-brownish complexion and wavy silver-black hair always slicked back. He looked like he could've played football in his younger days and always drove a new Thunderbird. Every year he would trade his year-old car in for a new one. A family of musicians lived two doors on the right: a harpist, a trumpeter, a pianist and a vocalist. They had their own family band. A family of twelve had just moved in next door. A few doors away lived the sister and mother of the well-known Rev. Albert Cleage Jr., who founded the Shrine of the Black Madonna, AKA the Pan African Orthodox Christian Church. They would open service declaring that Jesus Christ was the Revolutionary Black Messiah. Rev. Cleage promoted Black Power and pride throughout the city of Detroit and was becoming a very powerful force in Detroit politics. The Watermans met him at a block club function in their home when he was in the neighborhood organizing for the Freedom Walk — a prelude to the 1963 March on Washington. The Detroit March was also to serve as a 20th anniversary remembrance of the 1943 race riot in Detroit and to be in-sync with the anti-Jim Crow marches in the South. There was

Dr. Les Woods, a widowed retired physician and part-owner of one of the few black-owned hospitals left in Detroit, who lived near LaSalle Blvd. He'd been one of the first blacks to move on the block. Plenty of factory workers lived on the block — Detroit was an auto factory town. Then there were the numbers men. The number two dealer in the city, Luke's dad, Joe Tucker, lived on Atkinson Ave. too. The top numbers man lived around the corner on Edison Ave. — Justice "Big Man" Williams, who stood six feet ten inches tall. These men dressed up like they were going to church everyday, with their Stetson hats, alligator shoes, and silk and wool suits.

Atkinson Ave. sat in a district of homes called the Boston-Edison area, known for their old large brick homes and even a few mansions. Many of these homes were those of former automobile executives and other business leaders in Detroit back in the 30s and 40s soon after these homes were built. Now, they were kept up by middle-class black families.

While the neighborhood was growing more beautiful, 12th Street, one block away, was still 12th Street. It was full of activity, day and night. There were bustling businesses during the day. There were clothing, furniture, grocery, and liquor stores, restaurants, bars and pawn shops. Most of the store owners were Italian and Jewish. Negro customers would often complain about the poor treatment and poor quality merchandise at the white-owned stores. There were a few Negro merchants: Bill's Records, Stagger's Hardware, Booker's Party Store on 12th & Taylor, and Perry's Drugs and Photo Studio on 12th and Atkinson. At night, there was the smell of pimps and whores who worked the street, the hot tamale man wheeling his cart up and down the street while local and national jazz artists worked the Chit-Chat Lounge — the place to be.

CHAPTER 5 –
Mojo and Mama E -1965

MAMA E HADN'T UTTERED A WORD all week since the killing of Malcolm X. The day after he was killed, she passed a note at the dinner table that read *I'm in mourning*. She stayed holed up in her room until dinner. She didn't go out, didn't play the numbers, didn't do nothing.

Her quiet solitude was in stark contrast to a neighbor named Mojo Johnson. Mojo was about 40 but looked 60 because of long hard days at the plant. He was stout — built like a football fullback —with light brown skin. He kept his hair short and nappy. He lived with his mother and her sister down the block. Both women lost their husbands in an auto accident when they were returning from a fishing trip.

Mojo pulled his Volkswagen hatchback up to the corner where Mike, Luke, DeAngelo, Jon-Jon and Brother Bear were congregating the night after Malcolm was murdered. It was dark and cold. "Get in," Mojo yelled. The boys looked at each other confused but without fear because they all knew Mojo from his backyard parties that he invited the kids to. He loved to play music by Muddy Waters and John Lee Hooker. They squeezed into his car. Mojo had the only Volkswagen hatchback Mike had ever seen – a rarity in Detroit. "They killed him, dammit. They killed him," Mojo said, nearly screaming as he sped off. He drove to the end of the block at Linwood, where Atkinson was cut off by Sacred Heart Seminary. When he stopped, he looked at Mike who sat in the front seat. "He's dead." He then looked at the boys in the back and screamed, "He's dead." He turned the car around, then gunned the engine, and sped up the street driving as fast as the car would accelerate, then came to a screeching halt at LaSalle Blvd. He then sped off again. Mojo Johnson started crying. "Malcolm's dead. They killed him, dammit. He's dead." At

14th Street he hit his brakes hard, sending the boys in the back nearly through the front window.

"Slow down, my man," cried Brother Bear.

Mojo took off again. He sped to 12th Street, then jammed the brakes, again burning rubber in front of the stop sign. "What we gonna do?" he asked to no one in particular. "What the hell we gonna do?" He turned the car around again and headed back down the street. This time as he sped down the street he barely stopped at the stop sign. He barely looked for oncoming cars. He kept going all the way back to Linwood. Mojo continued his erratic driving and rage about Malcolm X's murder for another five minutes. To Mike, it seemed like forever. Mojo finally pulled up into his driveway and buried his face into the steering wheel and continued to cry. "You kids go home, get outta here."

"That crazy fool like to got us killed," complained DeAngelo.

"What we gonna do now?" asked Jon Jon.

"About what?" replied Mike.

"Malcolm X's murder."

Luke replied, "Call the gotdamn FBI, that's what."

"They probably killed him," said Jon-Jon.

Mike put his hands on his head. "I can't even think straight. Mama E done gone quiet, Mojo done lost his mind, and all I want to think about is our last game next week. We're playing for the championship next week. Just leave me alone."

Mojo's behavior reminded Mike of how Kathy Smith went crazy after the announcement of John F. Kennedy's assassination. After the principal made the announcement, he asked the students to bow their heads for a moment of silence. Instead, Kathy jumped out of her desk, flung the door open and screamed hysterically up and down the hall for the next five minutes.

Mama E said she loved Malcolm. She talked about how she loved what the Nation of Islam did in the community, cleaning up drug addicts and visiting prisoners. She once said that Malcolm X and Elijah Muhammad, founder of the Nation of Islam, would work things out. Mike didn't understand why Mama E was into all this stuff. They were Catholic. He remembered when Mama E got them all worked up over the Freedom Walk down Woodward Ave., had the entire Waterman family marching behind Rev. Martin Luther King, Jr., Rev. C. L. Franklin, and the Rev. Cleage. That was the most people Mike had ever seen in one place. The *Michigan Chronicle* reported that as many as 300,000 people walked that day in Detroit – just two months before the March on Washington.

Then, a few months after the March on Washington and after John F. Kennedy was killed, Mama E almost tripped out when Frank's Brother, Uncle

John, came by the house at Christmas and told her he was going to join the Army before he got drafted. Mike heard Mama E tell his mom and dad that John would be nothing but canon fodder if he was sent to the civil war in Vietnam, where the communist- supported North Vietnam was fighting the U.S.-backed South. Mama E said U.S. involvement in Vietnam was not justified. Uncle John left for the Army anyway, in June, 1964. Mike saw the television reports on the war starting up in Vietnam. Mike knew he would miss Uncle John: his jokes and his card tricks. His uncle had an endless supply of "white man, colored man, and Chinese man" jokes. *When would Uncle John get back?* Mike wondered. Mike wondered if Uncle John died in Vietnam, would he freak out like Kathy or Mojo did. Mike loved his dad's brother, John. After a week of quiet mourning, Mama E told the family that she was okay now.

CHAPTER 6 –
Ball Games -1966

AFTER TWO YEARS OF CATHOLIC YOUTH Organization basketball, Mike's excitement about basketball grew more intense as he watched the historic NCAA championship showdown between the University of Kentucky and the all-Negro lineup at Texas Western. DeAngelo, Luke, and Brother Bear watched the game with Mike, Jon-Jon and their dad. In anticipation of an upset, Mike cut up paper to make confetti. When the game was over and Texas Western began to celebrate, Mike dumped confetti everywhere – all throughout the house. He ran up to Lil Sis's room, barged in and littered her and her room with confetti. He shouted that the game was like David versus Goliath, "David versus Goliath . . . " Mike said. But after basketball season, something new was on the horizon, Mike was introduced to baseball.

In April 1966, a nineteen-year-old neighbor named Larry Driver recruited Mike to play baseball. Spring hadn't quite set in yet. The temperature was near freezing, and the ground was still hard on the playing field at Central High School, twelve blocks away, where the team practiced. Some of the boys donned coats at practice. Mike wore his thermals to stay warm.

The boys voted George Harris captain. George was the oldest and seemed to know everyone in the area around Central High. By mid-May, Mike settled into a five-day-a-week practice routine, with games on Saturdays. About thirty kids came out for the team, the Green Sox. But, by the time the Green Sox played its first game, only fifteen of the boys had stuck it out. Coach Larry did not have deadlines or cutoff numbers. Whoever wanted to play could play. His only rule was you had to come to practice. Larry, who lived near the Waterman's house, had a commitment to the neighborhood and made all the boys feel welcome. Mike didn't care who came out or when they came out for the team because he felt that he earned his starting position at shortstop. He also backed up DeAngelo in right field.

Frank Waterman volunteered as General Manager and chief fundraiser for the team. And Frank delivered on his promise to outfit the team before the first game. Statewide, the insurance firm for which Frank worked, sponsored the team. When Frank delivered the uniforms, the boys' eyes sparkled. The brand new, ivory-and-green-lettered and striped uniforms looked too new to wear.

"Treat them like your Sunday best." Frank smiled.

Everyone broke out in a hearty laugh. Bright faces lit up the diamond that day. Even the water boys got uniforms.

Big G joined the team a week later. The boys talked about Big G like he was the second coming. Big G stepped up to the plate his first day of practice and cracked five home runs back-to-back, all off Luke, the team's leading pitcher. After each swing, Luke followed the ball overhead and said, "Daaamn."

Coach Larry snapped, "Luke, you must be sleepwalking out there, boy. Your fastball looks tired man, I mean tired. Can somebody pitch to this boy?" asked Coach Larry, scanning the field.

Coach put Big G at first base because he had long arms and legs, and a long reach, even though his back was short. He stood nearly six feet tall. He caught or trapped everything thrown his way. Big G was fourteen and going to Northern High School in the fall. He lived on the corner of 12th Street and Gladstone Avenue.

After that practice, Big G started to walk to practice with Mike, DeAngelo, Luke, and Jon-Jon. The boys played in the twelve–to-fourteen age bracket. Mike was thirteen. But Jon-Jon was only eleven, too young to play, so he asked the coach if he could keep the batting statistics for the team.

"Of course," Coach Larry told him. Jon-Jon's stat work helped Coach Larry keep up with each player easily. Jon-Jon even started taking notes on what each player did before he swung the bat, and how many seconds it took them to run to each base.

About one-quarter way through the season, Willie came out for the team. Mike knew Willie from the newspaper headquarters on Linwood and Clairmont Avenue. They both had paper routes. The summer of '65 Willie got a paper route with only thirty customers. But Willie would regularly show up two, even three, hours late every day for two weeks. Eventually the station manager fired Willie.

Coach Larry tried Willie at second base, but Willie kept wandering off into the outfield. Then coach put him in right field, but he played either too deep or too shallow. Willie paced the field like he had to pee or something.

After several errors, the coach finally asked him to help as an assistant manager. Willie agreed, and this really meant that he became the new water boy. He enjoyed his new role.

Larry's twenty-two year old brother, Dave, who attended law school at Detroit College of Law, invited the boys who were on the baseball team to help him sell bumper stickers at Detroit Tiger home games. He operated a silk-screening machine in his parent's garage where he made all kinds of fancy colorful bumper stickers supporting the Detroit Tigers baseball team. He asked the boys if they wanted to make a little extra money selling the bumper stickers before and after the games. Everybody's hand went straight up in the air. Big G responded "Hell yeah . . . " then said "oops" and covered his mouth, trying to show respect for Dave and Coach Larry, both young adults.

During the summer of 1966 Mike felt like he was in heaven, playing baseball and going down to Tiger Stadium to sell bumper stickers before and after the games. Mike and his teammates mixed right into the hustle. *"PEANUTS, SOUVENIRS HERE!"* And the roar of the crowd gave Mike goose bumps. Mike had just as much fun outside the stadium as inside when he occasionally attended a game with his Dad or friends, especially with Big G. Mike and Big G walked to Tiger Stadium once for a twi-nighter, a double-header night game, that lasted until 1 o'clock the next morning. Mike and his teammates grew closer and played better as a team. Their baseball season ended on a high note as the team won their last four games. They went from a 4-4 record to 8-4, tied for second place in their six team league. Mike could not wait for next summer to come.

CHAPTER 7 -
Summer of '67

MIKE KEPT UP HIS PAPER ROUTE. He added new customers almost weekly. By the summer of '67 he had 120 customers, double the number he started with. He needed two grocery carts to deliver the thick Sunday paper. The papers were dropped off on the corner of 12th Street and Taylor. Mike and Jon-Jon would get up early enough to see the rats making their final rounds, scavenging through the litter. Some people in the neighborhood called these rats horse-rats because they were so big and bad. These are rats that would rise up on their hind legs and snatch your last pork rind without asking. Mike always thought he could put a saddle on one of those bad boys and ride it, they were so big.

Mike and Jon-Jon ventured up to 12th Street on a regular basis where Mike bought all of his favorite Motown 45s at Bill's Records, and occasionally picked up hardware supplies at Stagger's. Mike remembered his first visit to Bill's Records in 1964. Bill himself came over and greeted Mike and Jon-Jon, and said, "Here's my card, young fellas. Every time you buy a record here, we'll punch a hole in it and, after you buy ten records, you get one free. Deal?" They shook on it.

By 1966, Mike had collected well over one hundred 45s. On many hot summer afternoons, after he searched for records, Mike would make his way to Booker's Party Store for a quart of the coldest orange juice he ever tasted. "Y'all must keep this stuff in the freezer," Mike said to the clerk once.

Early on one hot and muggy Sunday morning, Mike and Jon-Jon headed towards 12th Street to retrieve their papers, Mrs. Robinson called out to them. "Don't you boys go down there, they rioting," she shouted from her bedroom window. Mike and Jon-Jon looked up at her. She lifted the screen up and stuck her head outside. She had a head full of rollers.

"What?" asked Mike, sounding confused.

"Go home. They rioting on 12th Street. Go home," Mrs. Robinson repeated.

"Our papers are up there ma'am."

Mike and Jon-Jon continued to walk to the corner of 12th and Atkinson to get a look for themselves.

Mike heard the loud clanging of metal security gates that were locked in front of most storefronts. "Look at this!" said Mike, stunned.

"What are they doing?" Jon-Jon asked.

"Looks like they're breaking into stores."

Dozens of people swarmed on the corner of 12th Street and Clairmont, in front of Parker Brothers Clothing store, one block away. The clanging of the security gates became louder. Broken glass lay scattered in the streets and glistened under the street lamps just as the early morning stars retreated in the sky. The air was very still and thick with humidity. At nearly five o'clock on this July morning there were so many people out and about that it felt like noon. Mike couldn't take his eyes off the crowd for several minutes. This was like being at the drive-in movies, he thought.

"What's that?" Jon-Jon asked, pointing to the crowd.

"What's what?"

"That thing he's carrying."

Mike tried to zero in on the images that moved about him in the dawn.

"Looks like a bat, I don't know. He's swinging it like a bat. Oh, that's a . . . " The loud crash of broken glass at Parker Brothers Clothing made Mike pause. "That's a car jack, dammit," Mike cursed. "We can't get our papers. I ain't going down there."

Mrs. Robinson had come out of her house. She was middle-aged. She stood on the porch, her pudgy frame clad in a nightgown.

"I told you boys to go back home." She seemed annoyed that the boys had not heeded her warning earlier. As the boys passed her house headed back home, she muffled, "Thank you. I don't want to have to tell your daddy."

The boys were quiet on their slow march down the block. Mike knew that his Sunday newspaper delivery was the biggest and most financially rewarding enterprise he had. Jon-Jon interrupted the silence.

"Well, maybe they can bring the papers to us."

"Yeah, maybe," Mike responded, sounding irritated.

The boys sat on their front porch talking about baseball, trying to erase what they had just witnessed. They still hoped that they would get a delivery of newspapers or a call from the station manager.

The 1967 summer league baseball season was about half over, and Mike was delighted that his skills at shortstop had improved immensely. Mike turned to Jon-Jon and said, "Maybe I should play more right field, be the next Roberto Clemente."

"Maybe you should practice batting more if you want to be the next Roberto Clemente. Your batting stinks," said Jon-Jon. It's only .225. Why don't you practice hitting more? Mike, you gonna be like Ray Oyler maybe, definitely not Roberto Clemente."

"Man, give me a break. I'm getting better. And besides, Coach spends more time on defense."

"Tell him you wanna hit more."

"Tell Coach? Just tell him. Right."

"Yeah, ask him. You know what I mean."

"Jon-Jon, you just do the paperwork. I'll do the hitting. And hey, I ain't gonna be no Ray Oyler. Now, his batting stinks, and he's been playing all his life."

"How did he even make it to the pros?" Jon-Jon asked.

"Because he's the best damn shortstop in the game."

That round-faced, orange ball of fire climbed over the treetops and houses, and stared down at the boys. It seemed to say, "Today is gonna be one hellava hot day."

"Let's go in the house. It's almost seven o'clock," Jon-Jon suggested. Mike glanced at his watch to confirm Jon-Jon's estimation. Mike felt good that he and his brother shared an interest in baseball.

On Sunday morning the boys usually got home around seven o'clock, after delivering Mike's papers. Mike would usually jump in the shower, then, get dressed for 8:30 morning Mass at Visitation.

Frank and Rose were early risers, but Mama E and Denise were laggards on Sunday morning because they usually stayed up late watching movies and talking. They often opted for a later service. As the boys made their way upstairs, Frank was coming out the bathroom, clean shaven, wearing beige suit pants and a black silk tee shirt. He had been making good use of the weight set he had purchased several months ago. Mike noticed no fat on his dad's sculptured 5' 10" frame. They were about the same height.

"Dad," Mike began, "they rioting on 12th Street. They pulling down the gates . . . "

"Wait a minute. What did you say?" Frank cut Mike off and finished wiping his face with a wet towel.

"They having a riot up on 12th Street," Jon-Jon repeated.

"A riot?" Frank looked at them in disbelief. "A riot, uh," he said.

"I couldn't get my papers. There were about two hundred people on the corner of 12th and Clairmont."

Frank let out a long sigh. "Jesus Christ. I don't believe it. Honey," Frank called out to Rose. "Cut the television on, the boys say there's a riot on 12th Street. Maybe there's something on the early news. I can't believe this." Frank sounded bewildered. "Your mom and I were out at the Chit-Chat Lounge last night. I'll be darned."

"Frank, here it is, come look," Rose called out as she put the finishing touches of makeup over her cinnamon-brown complexion. A reporter stood in front of Hitsville, USA, the home of Motown Recording, on W. Grand Blvd., about a mile from the scene.

"A melee erupted after the police raided an after hours club, also known as a blind pig, on the corner of 12th Street and Clairmont in the early morning hours," the reporter said. "As we understand it, the police made several arrests this morning, but there are no police on the scene now and hundreds of people have gathered on 12th Street. There is looting and vandalizing taking place as I speak."

The phone rang, breaking their fixation on the news report. Mike hurried to answer it.

"Hello, Mom it's for you." He disappointedly gave up the receiver to Rose.

"I thought it was Mr. Wallace calling about my newspapers. We couldn't get to the papers. It looked too dangerous," Mike told his father.

"Frank, Delli's on the phone. Delli Tucker was Luke and Sharon's mom. She got a call from Mrs. Matthews who's all in a panic saying that she has no food in the house and wondered if the grocer would be open today with this rioting going on."

"Rose, Sweetie, can I please talk to Delli? We need to check on our neighbors to see if they need anything. This riot could spread," Frank stated. Rose handed the receiver to him.

"Hi, Delli, how you doing this morning? Good. Would you mind putting our block club phone tree into action and make a list of supplies people might need? Try to deal with their essentials. Then ask to see if we can get some drivers to go to the A&P in Highland Park and get the stuff. Yeah, I know people may not want to go out but ask anyway."

Mike knew that his dad, who was the block club president, would bend over backwards to help his neighbors, especially the elders. And his dad always said that he could depend on Delli because she knew everybody.

"Dad, can you go and see about my papers?"

"I was thinking about taking a walk down the block to assess the situation. You want to go with me?"

"Frank, can I see you for a moment?" She pulled Frank inside their bedroom, then, shut the door. That didn't prevent her voice from escaping.

"You have two sons, Frank, and a daughter. Now, I don't expect you to ask Denise to go anywhere near that disturbance up there, but ask Jon-Jon if he wants to go. He is Mike's helper."

"Rose, it's Mike's paper route . . . "

"Ask him anyway. You got to start including him in things."

"Even a trip through a war zone?" Frank sarcastically responded.

Rose said the rest with her beautiful marble-shaped eyes embellished with black eyeliner. Frank knew what that look meant.

"Okay," he acquiesced.

Mr. Waterman, Mike and Jon-Jon headed toward Linwood Avenue, three blocks west of where the early morning raid took place. Linwood Avenue was home to the Nation of Islam's Muhammad Temple #1; the Shrine of the Black Madonna, Rev. Cleage's politically active church; Sacred Heart Seminary, a four-by-two block Roman Catholic colossus; and Rev. C. L. Franklin's New Bethel Baptist Church. Mike and Jon-Jon were quiet. Frank was whistling in a low tone. Mike looked at Jon-Jon shaking his head.

"What is Dad doing whistling when these people out here going crazy?" Mike whispered to Jon-Jon.

"Dad, why are you whistling?" Mike asked laughing.

"To keep cool. I always do it to keep cool." Frank paused, then said, "Boys, our people need help."

"What kind of help?" Mike asked.

"Our people got to learn how to use the system to get ahead."

"So why are they rioting?"

"Life for many Detroiters has been like living in a pressure cooker. Think of it as a pot of boiling water with the lid on tight. It's gonna explode sooner or later. The police, they're running amok on Negroes. You remember what happened after the championship game in '63?"

As they arrived on Linwood, Mike heard the crash of glass at the grocery and liquor stores just ahead. A small crowd of about two dozen people erupted with a big cheer. Some of the looters had on what looked like their church clothes. Broken bottles littered the street and sidewalks. Old beer and whiskey stench emanated from the streets. Mike, his Dad and Jon-Jon watched as people carried boxes of liquor and beer down the street. Some tossed the boxes into their cars while others ran up the street to their nearby homes. The streets were crowded as if people were enjoying a Christmas Eve shopping spree. People were running in all directions with grocery carts loaded with food. The looting took on a carnival-like atmosphere. It reminded Mike of the TV game show Supermarket Sweep where winning contestants would have so many seconds to plow through a supermarket loading up their baskets with as much food as possible. Frank led his sons south down Linwood carefully side-stepping the looters. There were no police in sight. Mike spotted Willie.

"Willie, what you doing, man?"

Willie was pushing a grocery cart loaded with food taken from a Chaldean grocery store that had been ransacked.

"Hi, Mr. Waterman. Hey Mike, Jon-Jon," Willie greeted them with a beaming smile.

"Your mother know you . . . ?" Frank asked.

"Mr. Waterman, I know this don't look good, sir. But she sent me out here. All we got is kool-aid and salad dressing in the fridge. This is just like Supermarket Sweep." Willie made an about-face with his cart and ran toward his house on Clairmont near Linwood. Frank shook his head. The boys laughed. The Watermans walked seven blocks before they turned up Pingree Avenue towards 12th Street. On 12th, the Watermans watched trucks back up on the sidewalks and haul off entire bedroom sets. People plundered pawn shops. Hats, shoes, fine knit shirts, and shadow-striped suits were being flung into cars. Mike felt the crunch of shattered glass underfoot as he watched boxes of jewelry fall from overloaded arms. Several boxes of rings hit the ground directly in front of him. Frank and Jon-Jon didn't notice as the rings bounced from their boxes and landed at Mike's feet. He bent down and scooped up a couple of the rings and shoved them in his pocket. When they arrived at 12th Street and Taylor, there were no newspapers to be found. They headed home. They had been gone about an hour.

Mike, Jon-Jon, and Frank walked through the front door. Rose, now ready for Sunday Mass, was still watching a special report on the disturbance. The reporter was still near 12th Street and W. Grand Blvd. because Mike could see Hitsville, USA in the background. Rose looked at Frank with tears in her eyes.

Frank said, "We got us a full-scale rebellion on our hands. We're tearing up our own community."

"What a shame," said Rose. She hugged Frank tightly. "I'm so happy you're back. I was getting nervous. Oh, the man called. Mr. Wallace, the newspaper manager, he said he'll bring the papers by the house later today."

"Hear that, Mike. You'll get your papers later today," Frank hollered out.

Rose walked into the kitchen, pointing to the oven. "I got breakfast ready."

"Baby, you are so sweet. Thank you dear."

"I'm so worried, Frank. They just showed the police on T.V. gathering up on 12th like they're going to war. I think people are gonna get killed out there. You think we should be going to church this morning, maybe the ten o'clock Mass?" Rose asked.

"This thing is too close to home. Let's stay put today so we can monitor the situation. I'm gonna go over to the A&P before things get totally out of hand. Delli's compiling the list of what some of the neighbors need." The phone rang, interrupting Frank.

"This phone's been ringing off the hook since you left," Rose said.

"Mike, telephone," Frank yelled.

Mike answered the telephone and heard DeAngelo's voice on the other end.

"Hey DeAngelo. What's the deal?" Mike asked.

"Let's go up on 12th man. Darren just got back with tons of shit. New suits, shoes, man."

"I heard the police were moving in."

"Not yet, Darren just walked in. He said there weren't any police around. Meet me at the alley." Mike grabbed some trash pretending to be taking care of his chores. He headed for the alley. The boys often used the alleys to travel when they didn't want to be detected by neighbors. His mom and dad were so engrossed in discussing the riots that they didn't notice him leaving. When he got to the alley, he stuffed the trash in the large garbage container and ran to the corner. He saw DeAngelo running up the alley.

"Let's go," said Mike.

They ran up the alley toward 12th. They turned on 12th Street and got down as far as Blaine Avenue, six blocks from Atkinson. DeAngelo seemed to not be fazed at all by the crowd and the looting. He acted like he was at the State Fair.

"Let's check out the pawn shop," said DeAngelo.

"Man, I don't care."

"Looks like they left some watches," DeAngelo noticed. DeAngelo went behind the counter and took what few watches were still left. "These ain't bad." DeAngelo held up the watches to the light. He laughed and said, "It's ten o'clock."

Then someone shouted, "The police are up the street and coming fast." People scattered. People ran wildly, grabbing anything they could carry. Mike saw a few cars roll by overloaded with stereos and televisions. Mike thought, *people just don't care. They're taking everything.* He could see the police in the far distance in full riot gear walking from W. Grand Blvd. towards Clairmont. They were still several blocks away. But it didn't matter, he watched as people hauled ass outta there. One woman slipped on some glass, broke her fall with her arm, and cut herself. Mike ran to help her up. "I'm cool," she said. She rose quickly, brushed herself off, wiped the glass from her arm, shifted around her tight-fitting skirt, twisted her blonde wig to the front, then started running again like nothing happened. Mike knew that this was crazy, and he was in the middle if it. The boys ran back the same way they came. They turned at the alley and started walking.

"How many watches you get?" Mike asked.

"Four," DeAngelo said with a big Cheshire cat grin.

"Give me one."

"Here man, take two. We'll split 'em. Give Jon-Jon one. It's like a souvenir." Mike pulled a ring from his pocket and gave it to DeAngelo.

"Here's a souvenir I picked up earlier this morning. Give it to your girl friend or somethin'." The boys were less than fifty yards down the alley when they heard a car hit its brakes. Two young men jumped out the car with boxes and bags in their hands. They ran into the alley and stuffed the boxes and bags into empty trash cans. The boys pressed their backs against a garage wall and watched. The men hopped back in the car and sped away. Seconds later, another car stopped. A man got out with shoe boxes in his arms. He found an empty trash can and stuffed the boxes in it. He hurried back to his car and took off.

"I think we hit the jackpot," DeAngelo cried out. The boys ran back up the alley to loot the loot. DeAngelo wanted to carry away the entire trash can. But Mike sounded more pragmatic.

"Let's not take the neighbors' trash can," Mike insisted. "Let's just take this trash off their hands." Mike grabbed the boxes and bags of clothes out of one can, while DeAngelo snatched three boxes of shoes from the other. The boys ran back to safer ground with their loot. DeAngelo took some of the clothes with him while Mike stashed a few bags of clothes and boxes of shoes in his garage.

"The governor is calling up the National Guard," Frank announced later that evening as the family sat around the television in the family room. "And they imposed a dusk to dawn curfew."

"Dad, I heard the police were out of control and beat some people up last night."

"Like I said earlier, they been outta control. They think they got free rein in the Negro neighborhoods. Police brutality has got to stop," said Frank.

"Stop how Frank? How is it going to stop when they run everything?" Rose asked, searching Frank's eyes for an answer.

"Well, maybe that's just it. We gotta start running something. We need to get more Negroes on the police force. Get some Negroes in political office. Listen to it out there." Frank walked to the front door.

"Where are you going?" Rose asked.

"Mike, Denise, everybody come over here and listen to this," Frank beckoned. Denise didn't move. Mike and Jon-Jon got up and walked to the door. Frank snatched open the door.

"Listen to this," he hollered over the screaming police sirens and fire trucks. "Listen to this madness. This is madness! You hear that?" Jon-Jon started crying. He didn't seem to handle it too well.

"Honey," Rose began, "the news says that the firemen are being shot at and they refuse to put out many of the fires."

"The whole damn city is going up in smoke," Frank yelled.

That night the Waterman family went to bed to the eerie sound of automatic weapons firing and the wail of sirens.

Denise and Jon-Jon cried themselves to sleep.

CHAPTER 8 –
Detroit on Fire

AFTER BEING INDOORS MOST OF MONDAY, Mike and his partners persuaded their parents to venture out to Central High School to check on their baseball practice field. On Tuesday morning, Mike, Jon-Jon, Luke, DeAngelo and Brother Bear gathered at the Waterman's house and headed down LaSalle Blvd. towards Central High. Mama E asked Mike to pick her up two bean pies from the Nation of Islam Deli on Linwood, across from the playfield.

"Well, I'll be darned," said Mike as they approached the playfield. They all looked at each other and said in unison, "There goes the neighborhood."

Central High's playfield and school complex had become a National Guard headquarters. Sentries were posted around Roosevelt Elementary School, Durfee Junior High School, and Central High, the three schools that comprised the school complex. The boys could see choppers taking off and landing. Tanks, armored personnel carriers, and jeeps were lined up waiting to be dispatched.

"We can kiss the rest of this season goodbye. The city is burning out of control anyway," Mike added. They heard the sound of prayer in Arabic ring out at Muhammad's Temple #1 on Linwood, directly across the street from the playfield and now the National Guard's encampment.

"Almost forgot. I got to get Mama E a couple of bean pies," said Mike. They entered the Nation of Islam's deli next to the mosque. Several dark-skinned Negroes wearing starched blue uniforms and baseball-like caps that had FOI, which stood for the Fruit of Islam, stenciled on the front, milled about the deli. Mike knew from Mama E that the FOI stood for the Fruit of Islam. Mike always felt good when he went to the deli because everyone who worked or purchased food there was so polite. "Yes sir, no sir, yes ma'am, no ma'am," is what he often heard. Behind the counter prominently displayed were two pictures, one of a young Elijah Muhammad, and another picture of a crescent moon. On top of a refrigerator was a copy of *Message to the Black Man* written by Elijah Muhammad. The newspaper, *Muhammad Speaks*, rested on a stand beside the checkout counter. Mike bought three large bean pies. Mike smelled the honey-nutmeg aroma of the pies - a real treat to the senses.

"Humm, these pies smell so good. They must be fresh," he said.

"Yes sir," said the middle-aged female clerk, "baked early this morning."

As he and the boys headed home, Luke blurted out, "They killed Malcolm X. The Black Muslims killed Malcolm X."

Mike gave Luke a look of no confidence.

"No, they didn't. The government killed Malcolm X. Mama E's a Malcolm X expert. She said the government did it, and blamed the killing on the Black Muslims."

"I think the Black Muslims did it. He crossed them and they killed him. Point blank," Luke added with a tone of finality.

"Luke, you believe anything man. I think Mama E is right. The FBI or somebody like that did it," Mike said.

"Any of y'all ever been inside the Mosque?" DeAngelo asked.

"Naw," the other boys replied.

"Darren went once and said they got a poster of a Negro man hanging from a tree with a sign over his head that reads 'strange fruit,' DeAngelo motioned with his hands. Then they asked him to join the Lost Found Nation."

"Lost-found what . . . " Luke interrupted.

"Yeah, you lost in America and you get found through Islam or something like that. Darren tried to explain it to me."

"Yeah, Mama E been up in there, and she ain't told me about that," contested Mike.

"Well, you told us she don't talk about it when she goes," DeAngelo continued. "And you gotta get searched, from head to toe."

"Well maybe we should go one time and see for ourselves," suggested Mike.

"Shit," said Luke. "I ain't going nowhere. They don't believe in God. They believe in Allah."

"Same thing as God, Luke," said Jon-Jon.

"Allah ain't God. Don't sound like God to me, it's not the same as the Father, Son and the Holy Ghost," Luke challenged.

"So Luke," interrupted Mike. "Since when you so damn godly. You don't even go to church."

"Fuck you, Mike."

"Fuck you back," Mike said.

"Mike, you don't know shit," screamed Luke.

Jon-Jon who hadn't said much the whole time spoke up in a commanding tone. "Why don't all y'all just be quiet. We're in the middle of a riot. Baseball season's over. And people out here getting shot and what not, and y'all don't even know what y'all talking about. We all need to just go in the mosque and find out for ourselves. When you enter, they say 'Assalamu alaikum,' my brothers. Y'all supposed to say 'Wa'alaikum as salam.'"

"And what's all that mean?" asked Luke.

"'Peace be unto you.' And y'all say '*and unto you*,'" Jon-Jon responded.

"Jon-Jon knows what he's talking about. He be listening to Mama E, too," Mike added.

The boys continued walking quietly down LaSalle Blvd. They kept walking past Atkinson Ave. and headed toward LaSalle Gardens to see what was going on. Any illusion of peace and tranquility along beautiful LaSalle Blvd. shattered in Mike's mind when he saw a bullet-ridden mansion on the corner of LaSalle and Blaine.

"What the heck happened there?" Mike asked to the group. No one answered. Plumes of smoke rose on the horizon on the left and right. 12th Street and Linwood were burning. They turned around. Just as they were heading home, Mike heard one of the neighbors say that someone just firebombed the grocery store on the corner of Atkinson and 12th Street. Frank and one of the neighbors, Rev. Willie Boykin, the pastor of the church on the corner of Atkinson and 12th Street, were walking to see about the fire. Mike took the bean pies into Mama E, and then hurried out to follow along with his father and Rev. Boykin. The other boys stayed back. He caught up with his father and fell in beside him. Mike knew that his father and Rev. Boykin didn't know each other too well but were always cordial. He heard that Rev. Boykin helped start the block club several years ago but became inactive because of his church activities.

Rev. Boykin turned to Mike's father and said, "Hey Frank, I heard that you were taking good care of the neighbors, running grocery errands to the A&P. Everyone appreciates that. Most of the neighbors are scared to death and don't want to leave their houses.

"Yeah, with a lot of support, I think we took care of everyone who needed supplies," Frank responded.

"That's fabulous Frank. How's the life insurance business?"

"Great."

"You still work for Statewide?" asked Rev. Boykin.

"Yeah," Frank responded.

"Are there any other blacks on staff?"

"No. I'm the only Negro."

"That's a good start," said Rev. Boykin.

"And they're trying to bring in more Negroes."

"Good, let me know if we can help at the NAACP. We've been asking these companies to find and hire more qualified black folks."

Rev. Boykin changed the subject. "This rebellion is serious Frank. I received a call from one of my church members, and she told me that her son was inside that blind pig when it was raided. Now, her son is laid up at Henry Ford Hospital with his head split open. The young man said it all started when the police wanted to arrest a partygoer who appeared to be drunk in front of the club. Then when members of the crowd offered to take the man home, the police insisted he be arrested for disorderly conduct. Then a shouting match ensued and the police decided they were going to arrest everybody. That's when things got out of hand. I heard the police were brutal. And, just a minute ago, Rev. Cleage called and told me there was a massacre at the Algiers Motel on Woodward Ave. and Euclid. The police shot five black men who were unarmed in cold blood. We're gonna ask for an investigation right away."

"Who, the NAACP?" Frank asked.

"Yes, the NAACP. As you know, I'm an official with the Detroit Branch. Why don't you join us Frank?"

Before Frank could respond, they reached the corner. Mr. Perry, a Negro store owner, stood very distraught. There was not a fire truck in sight as Perry's Drug Store, the Chaldean-owned supermarket, Newport Foods, the new cleaners and the bike shop went up in flames. They watched from the church steps across the street. The businesses burned and burned. Mr. Perry watched from the corner as his drug store burned. He also owned other businesses, including a photography studio across the street from the fire. His other storefronts were boarded up with the words "SOUL BROTHER" written in huge letters across the front of them. Mr. Perry was talking out loud about why there were no fire trucks at the scene. He was visibly shaken. His voice trembled. Mike watched. Mr. Perry cursed. Thick, black smoke billowed upwards to the sky. The fire's intensity sent beads of sweat rolling down Mr. Perry's forehead. Flames shot out the front of the drug store. Glass shattered onto the street. The stench and smoke overwhelmed them.

"We got to go inside or head back," Frank said.

Nobody moved. Two of the church deacons held hoses that were connected to the side of the church. They began to water down the roof. Everyone looked saddened while watching. Finally, the entire row of stores was reduced charred frames and rubble. Mike looked into the watery eyes of men standing there helpless. Mike held in his grief and tears. On his way home, Mike saw a convoy of army jeeps, tanks, and armored cars move slowly down 14th Street. Mike felt the ground shake beneath his feet.

CHAPTER 9 –
Jesus is Black!

TWO WEEKS LATER AT VISITATION'S SUNDAY Mass, the Waterman family was among the many families looking for answers. Mike heard his father's anguish the night before pounding the wall and talking to his mom about how he wanted to help rebuild Detroit. He said, "I'm searching my soul, Rose, searching for what I can do to put this city back together."

Before Mass, many of the families had been milling around on the sidewalk in front of the church. Mike, Jon-Jon and Denise waited out front with their parents. Mike observed the adults shaking their heads at each other and talking about how sorry they were for all kinds of tragedies they'd experienced in the past two weeks. Everyone seemed to know someone who was either arrested, beaten, or shot, or knew of some neighborhood store owner's shop's being looted or firebombed. Mike thought about Big G, who's house was burned down because it was right on the corner next to the storefronts that burned. Big G, too, was gone. Bill's Records- gone. Mike felt the sadness that loomed over the parishioners. The mood was solemn and the music emanating from the church was even more solemn.

Mike perked up when he saw Luke and Sharon get out of their parent's car. Luke's mom Delli got out wearing a white silk pants suit and straw hat. She walked over to Rose Waterman who couldn't be missed wearing her bright orange, gold-trimmed, loose-fitting dress. Her matching scarf tied around her head like a bandanna flowed down her back. Delli spoke to Rose, briefly, then got back in the car with her husband. They drove off in a hurry. "Luke, we over here, man," Mike said.

"What's happnin' my man?" asked Luke. "Hey Jon-Jon, hi Denise. Y'all heard from Big G?"

"Ain't nobody heard nothing," said Mike, rubbing his hand over his head.

"Yeah, I saw his house still smoking, even felt the heat, furniture and everything up in it."

"Man, that's messed up man. I mean that's a shame, we don't even know where he is. I wonder if baseball season's over."

"Hell yeah, the season's over, Mike. You seen the field lately? It's fucked up big time. And, oh yeah, to make it worse, Coach Larry is moving. His whole family's pullin' up to northwest Detroit."

"He can still coach, can't he?"

"Man, be for real. And, besides, half the team don't even feel like playing no more. All people talking about is what they copped in the riot. What's his name got five color TVs."

"Who"?

"What's his name . . . you know, George, our team captain."

"Well, all these old folks talking about is rebuilding Detroit and giving kids more to do."

"Then, get your dad to help redo our field."

"Man, I don't feel much like playing neither. Think I'm gonna wait 'til high school to play again." Mike wanted to forget about how the rebellion impacted his baseball season.

"Uh-oh," Luke interrupted, "there goes that fine-ass Christina. Wasn't you talking to her?"

"*Was* is right."

Mike hadn't seen Christina in weeks – ever since they got caught skipping out of mass one Sunday morning and kissing in the corner of the basement cafeteria. Father O'Malley cut the lights on to set up for the typical after-mass juice and donuts. He caught the two red-handed as Mike was working on his tonguing skills. Father told them that as long as they came to church every week, he wouldn't tell their parents. *Mike thought, blackmail like a mug.* But that might be better than their parents finding out.

Christina's parents breezed by everyone outside as if they were trying to catch a bus. They nodded hello to people while Christina gave Mike a tight-faced smile, making it clear she recognized him but had to keep going. Christina's mother and father looked teary-eyed. Mike heard that Christina's brother Greg, who was only a year older than Mike, had been arrested for firebombing the Chaldean party store on the corner of Linwood and Cortland, a block from where they lived. He later got a thorough beat-down by the Big-Four when they caught him trying to flee.

All three sets of Visitation's tall dark brown and heavily varnished doors were open. The dark brown brick structure, built in 1940, sat back from the road a good 30 feet. The extra large sidewalk made the front of the church a natural gathering spot.

Upon entering the church, you could see a wide staircase leading up to the church lobby, and another set of stairs leading down to the basement cafeteria and multipurpose room. The church had balcony seating for about 50 people. The balcony housed the brand new pipe-organ. Mr. Dunlap, the church's masterful organist, would, on a typical Sunday, lift any spirit and carry it straight to heaven with his magical musical vibrations.

But this was not a typical Sunday. The July heat spilled over into August, and the giant fans in each corner of the church tried desperately to make a difference. Visitation was a small-to- moderate-sized church by Catholic Church standards. But that smallness gave it an intimate feeling. As people started to fill up the pews, Mike noticed how colorful people were dressed, as if to say we are still a beautiful people, no matter how much burning and looting and shooting went on for the past two weeks. The sun's rays hit the new stained glass windows in a way that gave off a mystical aura. Father O'Malley never failed to mention the new stained glass windows and how the sacrifice of the parishioners made them possible. All the candles were lit on both sides of the altar, and the pungent fragrance of frankincense hung like a misty cloud throughout the church. Mike noticed more Negroes in church than he ever saw at 10 o'clock Mass.

Father Thom Kelly, the new, young, barrel-chested priest who walked on his toes, said the Mass. He was an understudy to Father O'Malley. Father Kelly's voice during the homily suddenly snapped Mike from a daze.

"And someone painted Jesus black," Father Kelly said. He pranced back and forth, barrel chest stuck out while his hair bounced off his head to its own rhythm. "They painted Jesus black to let Detroiters know, let the world know, that things are different. Things are changing, brothers and sisters. Someone painted Jesus black – coal black – not brown, not tan, no, Jesus Christ is black. And the priests. What did we do? One of the seminary students said to me it caused quite a stir. He went to the Monsignor at the seminary and said, 'They forgot to paint the feet. The feet are still white.' And Monsignor said, 'Well, go buy some black paint. What the hell are you waiting for?' They finished the job. Our giant statue of Jesus, the Christ – right on the corner of Linwood and Chicago Blvd.- is black and beautiful."

The new young priest fresh out of the seminary himself seem to relish in the thought of the paint job on Jesus. And the fact that the seminary was somehow able to flow with the times.

After Mass, Frank was downstairs chomping on a donut and talking to Ted Wilson, a long-time parishioner who served on the usher board with Frank and had put five of his seven daughters through Visitation High School. Mike delivered some juice to the two men, his mom and Mrs. Wilson, who stood nearby talking. Mike hung around his dad to listen in on the conversation.

Frank said, "Now that Sacred Heart Seminary is so liberal, I'm going up there this week to persuade them to open up the seminary to the community, mainly, that gym and giant playfield." Sacred Heart's massive playfield stretched a block in each direction and the Archdiocese of Detroit maintained it well. "The first thing I'll tell 'em," Frank continued, "is to take down that barbed wire. Why lock yourselves up from the community? You're not in prison."

"Not only that," added Ted, "we can start right here by opening up the Visitation Recreation Center to the community."

"Good idea," said Frank as the two men slapped palms.

Mike noticed some angry expressions on the faces of a couple of elders walking towards them. Mr. Stu Jackson, flailing his arms like a bird in flight, expressed outrage. "What the hell was that all about? Jesus is black? Who does he thinks he is? Ain't been out the seminary two months and wants to tell us about who's black."

Frank laughed while sipping on his juice.

Ted chimed in. "Call the cardinal, Stu. Call Pope John. They got to be red as a beet."

"He'll be back white tomorrow," said Stu. "White folks ain't gonna have it. Probably Rev. Cleage's people did it."

"Think so?" Frank asked. "Things are changing, Stu . . . "

"Oh, Frank, you gotta know better. Negroes are not gonna get away with this."

"Negroes want change, gentlemen. If the pope flew in and painted it white tomorrow, it would be black again the day after."

"What the hell, Frank. You men take care, we're gonna get out of here." Stu turned around flailing his arms again.

"Frank, how long do you think Father Kelly's going to last around here sympathizing with Negroes so openly?" Ted asked.

"He can stay forever if it was up to me."

"Good seeing you and the family. Ted extended his long lanky arms and patted Frank on the shoulder. "Glad y'all are safe. Man, we right in the belly of this beast."

"Good to see you all too, Ted."

"Look, we're all going to Howard Johnson's for brunch, wanna join us?"

"Not this time, but thanks for the invitation. We're doing our own

Howard Johnson's at home. I'm the chef today. I got my special flapjacks on tap. We'll get together some other time."

"Sure, I'm off for two weeks. Then it's twelve hours a day for the next six months. This plant's gonna kill me one day."

How 'bout some handball tomorrow night?" asked Frank, as both men played often at Visitation Recreation Center.

"Dad," Mike interrupted, "Luke and I are going to walk home, and I wanted to stop by the bakery on the way. Mom said it was okay."

"Okay, bring a few jelly rolls home for your dad."

"Can Jon-Jon go?"

"Where is Jon-Jon? Haven't seen him since church let out."

"He's right here, Dad." Jon-Jon emerged from behind a pillar next to Mike and Luke. Jon-Jon had removed his clip-on tie and pulled his shirt out of his trousers. Frank rolled his eyes.

"How many times have I told you, son, not to undo your clothes in public. Just because church is over doesn't mean it's time to play. Now go in the restroom and put yourself back together, then come back and see me."

"But Mom said . . . "

"Don't 'Mom' me boy, do as I said."

Rose overheard the exchange and rushed over to calm Frank down.

"Frank, please don't make a scene. We got enough to deal with. Jon-Jon is just being a boy."

"Jon-Jon will not look like a tramp in public."

"I told him he could remove his tie, not his shirt, his tie, okay. I thought the boys were leaving soon. Sorry."

"No need to apologize for Jon-Jon. He knows the rules. He shouldn't have even asked you."

"Can this be over now, Frank?"

Frank caught Rose's deep-setting eyes and responded, "It's over, Sweetheart."

Jon-Jon reported back to his dad with his shirt tucked in and tie back in place and gave off a salute like a soldier standing at attention. Frank dismissed him.

"Boy, get outta here. Just stick with your brother. See y'all at the house. And, oh, Luke, you and Sharon are joining us at the house for brunch."

While walking down 12th Street, Jon-Jon followed Mike and Luke mainly because the sidewalk could only accommodate two people to walk side-by-side. The few stores on 12th Street, from Webb Ave. to Boston Blvd., were still boarded up with the words "SOUL BROTHER" printed across in bold black letters. Kelly's Corner - Mr. Kelly's, malt shop - the Collingwood Bar and Lounge, and Sal's Five & Dime on the corner of 12th and Calvert had reopened for business. They had survived. But Mike could still smell the burnt storefronts from seven blocks away.

Suddenly out of the blue, Jon-Jon belted out, "And Jesus Christ is black - coal black," mimicking Father Kelly.

Luke cracked up and said, "Coal black!"

"Y'all crazy with all this black stuff," Mike said.

As the boys came closer to Scott's bakery, near the corner of 12th Street and Clairmont, almost directly across from the former blind pig where the rebellion began, the wafting of fresh glazed donuts gave Mike's nose some needed relief. Mr. Perry was hosing down the sidewalk in front of his boarded-up photo studio that survived. "SOUL BROTHER" in huge black letters still graced the plywood boards. "Good morning, boys," he said.

"Good morning Mr. Perry," the boys responded.

The bakery survived too. The bakery survived because Mr. Scott - nicknamed Scotty - sprayed painted the words "SOUL BROTHER" on his boarded up windows. He saw Mr. Perry do it to save his photo studio, so he must've figured it could save him, too, even if he was white. It worked. But the bakery's owner had taken his "SOUL BROTHER" boards down and put fresh donuts in the windows. While Mike headed inside, Luke and Jon-Jon decided to walk to the corner just to look again at the devastation on 12th Street.

"Ah, that smells good," Mike said as they entered the bakery. And then Mike noticed for the first time a very beautiful girl behind the counter serving up donuts. *Who is this fine young lady?* Mike thought. She reminded him that there was still life after the death and destruction on 12th Street. When 13 year-old Mike came in, she winked at him.

"Hey, cutie," she said softly, looking Mike dead in his eyes, "get what you want." Mike looked puzzled. He ordered a dozen donuts for home. She gave him two dozen. "Yeah, they're yours - on me." Mike said thanks while keeping his eyes fixed on her.

Before he left, Mike asked, "How old are you?"

"Seventeen, too old for you, but you still cute."

"You sure are a fine young lady. What's your name?"

"Renee, and you?"

"Mike." To Mike, Renee seemed like the last glow of light on 12th Street. The Detroit landscape had changed forever.

CHAPTER 10 –
The Bakery

MIKE MADE REGULAR VISITS TO THE bakery during the fall, and became friends with Renee, a high school senior. They mostly engaged in small talk, but Mike enjoyed every minute of it. He started his own donut hustle at school. He sold the extra donuts Renee gave him. He looked at Renee as a big sister, *at least for now,* he thought. But, later, maybe when he was older, a senior in high school, he would take Renee to his prom. That is, if she didn't get married to her 19 year-old boyfriend. The Tuesday before Thanksgiving Mike headed down to the bakery to fill the big donut order for tomorrow – the last day of school before the holiday.

After about three weeks of Indian Summer, it had suddenly turned cold. A Canadian wind bore down on the city. Clouds danced across the evening sky. Twelfth Street looked like a scene from a World-War II movie. Hollowed storefronts and burned homes still stood for several blocks. The awful odor of charred wood emanated from the gutted storefronts. When Mike crossed 12th Street, he barely noticed the billboard just erected on the corner where Mr. Perry's drug store once stood.

As Mike approached the brightly lit bakery, the sugary smell of fresh-baked donuts washed away the foul stench of burnt buildings. Once inside the bakery, the feeling of freshness overcame him. The brilliant white walls made the place feel new. The glass counters were so clean you could literally walk right into them if not for the donuts. The glazed donuts looked like scintillating gems in a jewelry store. A large calendar hung on the wall with days of the month crossed out. Renee, busy behind the counter, greeted Mike with a big smile. She had on her usual glazed-coated white apron, and a tight-fitting black turtleneck sweater. Her jet black hair was tucked neatly under her hair net. Her unibrow was trimmed but apparent. Before Mike could say a word, Renee spoke up from behind the counter. "How are you tonight, Mike? What do you have for me?" she asked.

"It's good to see you." Mike ran down the list. "Half-dozen jelly, a dozen glaze, uh, here take a look . . . " He handed Renee his order sheet. Renee started counting, nodding her head, "Uh-uh, uh-uh, okay, looks like six dozen. Is that about right?"

"Yeah, that's right."

"Well little brother, this is it. The bakery is closing tomorrow. Scotty's moving to Southfield, somewhere around 10 Mile Road and Northwestern Highway."

"What, way out there? I don't get it."

"Business is down, way down, and Scotty is still baking like he did before the riot." Then Renee said in a whisper, "Maybe he thought his customers were coming back," as she continued to place Mike's donuts neatly in the boxes she had set out. Scotty was a short round man with uncombed sandy brown hair and a bushy moustache. He'd owned the bakery since the mid-1950s. Mr. Scott spoke with a heavy Canadian accent and was usually in the back surrounded by tall donut-filled racks. Mike noticed the tight space in the back as he peered through the archway that separated the front and back of the bakery.

"Renee, I can't get out there, 10 Mile Road and whatever," Mike said with a sad look.

"Boy, get that sad look off your face."

"But you're leaving just like that."

Renee stopped moving and stood still. "It'll be alright, little brother. I'll give you my number and we can stay in touch. I'm not going to be working at this bakery forever anyway. You know I'm graduating in June." Renee focused back on packing the boxes. "Look at all these donuts left over. This is the afternoon batch. They are not selling. We either give them away or throw them away."

Mike thought, *no more Renee. After all, it wasn't about the donuts, it was all about Renee's special glow.* When he dealt with Renee, Mike often thought about some of the things his father would say during their basement workouts. In between pumping iron and doing sit-ups his father once said, 'Women are like flowers, so treat them gently. Give a woman the right nourishment and watch her blossom, just like a flower. And if she's a good, hardy perennial, you will see her again.' He believed his dad. At thirteen, Mike was handsome, 5'11", 170 pounds and muscular because he loved sports. He looked older and was bigger than most boys his age. For a second Mike almost lost his composure, but kept his cool. "Renee, I come up here only because of you, not the donuts. To see you and that beautiful smile." Renee blushed highlighting her evenly balanced dimples and perfectly white teeth. "See what I'm talking about. Your smile is like sunshine to me."

"Why, thank you, dear," said Renee as she took each of the three boxes of donuts and fitted two side-by-side into a large shopping bag, then set the third box in a separate bag.

Mike unbuttoned his double breasted navy pea coat and leaned forward against the counter. He noticed the book *Native Son* opened up. "Is that your homework back there?"

"Yep, got this book report due for my black lit class. They call it black lit now. Last year people called it Negro literature."

"Black, you black, I ain't black." Mike held his pecan-colored hand up against Renee's black turtleneck sweater. "Do I look black?"

"We're all black, Mike. I'm black."

"Girl, you about as high-yellow . . . "

Renee cut him off. "I'm still black, Mike."

"The word is Negro, Renee, Neeegro. Your sweater is black, that donut is black, there are black crayons. How're you gonna to call yourself black?"

"Negro is what our enslaved ancestors were called." Renee looked a bit confused, not really knowing what else to say. Finally she said, "Well, the course is called Black Literature, and we read books by some famous writers like Richard Wright, Ralph Ellison, Langston Hughes, Zora Neale Hurston, and many others. Have you read anything lately?"

"I always read. It's mandatory in my house."

"Like what?" Renee asked.

"Like *Mad Magazine* and *Sports Illustrated*. I read them cover to cover."

"Oh yeah." Renee closed her eyes for a second as she seemed to recognize a familiar song on the small red portable radio she'd turned down low on the counter next to the book. "Oh, I love that song. That's Smokey. I love Smokey."

Mike recognized the tune also. "*Second That Emotion*, right?"

Renee untied her apron, pulled it over her head, laid it on the stool beside her, and came from behind the counter. She said to Mike, "The bakery is closed but . . . " Renee walked to the door, reached for the closed sign and flipped it over, then bolted the door. She took off her hairnet and flung it behind the counter allowing her glossy jet black hair to drape across her back. "Would you like to dance, my little black brother?"

"Right here?" asked Mike.

"Right here."

"I, I don't know how to dance. And the word is Negro. I'm too cool to dance. I play ball, girl."

"What!" Renee said in disbelief. "You're about to go to high school and you can't dance? I don't believe it. You'd better get hip. Let me show you this slow dance. Follow me. It's a three-step." She led Mike, pressing gently against his body. Her breasts were much larger than he'd thought after only seeing her from behind the counter with her apron on. She had a perfectly curved body, soft as a pillow. She was wearing black fluffy house shoes.

"Why are you wearing those bedroom slippers?" Mike asked.

"They're the most comfortable shoes in the world." Renee struggled to lead Mike across the floor. "You got to move your feet, Mike. You got bricks in those shoes or what?" Renee moved Mike's feet with her feet to get started.

"Won't the owner say something?"

"No, my work is over for the night." The owner came from the back of the shop to collect the remaining unsold donuts. He shook his head and laughed.

"Now what do you call this?" he said in a heavy Canadian accent. He didn't even wait for an answer as he laughed his way to the back.

"Dancing lessons for Mike," said Renee. Mike was holding on tight to Renee hoping she would comment on his muscular physique. They made eye contact. "Mike, you got to relax, you're as stiff as a board, with stone feet. Just relax. It's 1-2-3, okay?" Smokey's crooning seemed to put Renee in a very relaxed state of mind, even though she continued to struggle with Mike's stiffness. "You're going to need more practice, my little brother."

"That's alright, I'm more into sports anyway. When I go to high school I'm playing football, basketball, baseball, and track."

"What high school are you going to?" She asked.

"Visitation. Ever heard of Jeff Dillon or Harry Lane?"

"Uh, no, can't say that I have."

Mike stopped. "You never heard of Jeff Dillon? He's only an all-American in football and basketball. That's my goal, all-American. I want my varsity sweater to be covered in medals and stripes. Then college, then pro."

Renee gave Mike a rather empty stare, then said, "Good luck with that. Tonight is my night, Mike. Butterball Jr., my favorite disc jockey, is playing all my favorites songs."

"You don't believe me, do you?"

"I do believe you, Mike, but you do have a little way to go. High school first. Let's dance to this." Curtis Mayfield was blowing his latest single, *People Get Ready*. As Mayfield's voice was oozing out the speaker, Renee walked over to the radio behind the counter and turned it up. "If the three-step is too difficult, we can try the two-step." Renee pulled Mike closer and they rocked back and forth, not moving much.

"This is easy," said Mike.

"But not as much fun."

"Just holding you close to me is fun. Are you going to college?" Mike asked.

"Of course, I applied to three schools to study nursing. Mercy, Olivet, and Ferris State."

"You really want to be a nurse? When I get banged up on the football field, can I call on you?" Renee didn't answer. She seemed to be in deep thought.

Then she said, "Yeah, Mike. You know, Mike, my brother just got back from Vietnam, and all I can remember is him telling people that it was not a pretty picture. It was just something, I'm not sure what exactly, but I want to help people, and that's why I want to be a nurse. So, yeah, I'll be there to stop the bleeding, reattach your head or whatever else happens to you on the football field. The truth is, I may be away while you're on your way to all-Americanism, and then you'll probably go far away to college yourself." Butterball Jr., WCHB's nighttime DJ, went into an up-tempo mode.

"Get up, everybody. Get on your feet and dance to the beat," he said.

Mike said, "You know, Jon Jon imitates all the DJs in Detroit. He walks around the house rhyming and talking just like them. One day it's Ernie D, then it's Butterball Jr., and then Al Perkins. He gets on my sister's nerves."

"Your brother is nice. I like him. Hey, let's dance to this," said Renee. Mike watched as Renee danced alone from one side of the bakery to the other. As the lyrics called for, "Lets do the shing-a-ling,", "Do the jerk," "Get on up." Renee flowed effortlessly from one dance to the other, then she started to do the twist – all the way down to the floor. Mike egged her on.

"How low can you go?" Renee reached for Mike's arm. She snagged a piece of his jacket and pulled him down to join her. Mike started to twist. When they both stood up, she had his hand and started swinging it, twisting together.

The baker came back out to retrieve his last tray of donuts but stood there watching them for a few seconds. Then offered. "Mike, you got a great teacher."

"I'm hip. Renee, you should go to school for dancing."

"Dancing is just for fun. I want to help people get well." Renee glanced at her watch. "My ride will be here soon."

"Your boyfriend?"

"Yep."

"What's he do?"

"He's at the plant right now, Fleetwood Assembly."

The DJ kept his up-tempo roll going as he said, "It's time to be cool, real cool, and do the jerk, Coo-ool Jerk, Cool Jerk." Renee was still dancing, now doing the bunny hop, acting silly. The baker started flicking the lights off and on,

"Party's over. Time to go, eh," he said. Mike danced along with her. Mike snapped his fingers and sung along with the song. Then Mike said.

"Renee, Renee, Renee."

"Mike, Mike, Mike," she said back, laughing.

Renee finally slowed down and walked back behind the counter, wiping the perspiration from her forehead.

"Alright Scotty. Whew, I thought I was at a house party for a second. Mike, I want to give you this newspaper to read." She fumbled through her large leather handbag, spilling some things on the counter. She pulled it from the bottom.

"The Black Panther Party Community News?"

"Yeah, I've been doing volunteer work with them at a neighborhood elementary school. They have a free breakfast program, and they're trying to get a chapter at my school." Without saying another word, Mike rolled the paper up like he would to throw it, then stuffed it into his back pocket. "And here's my number." Mike reached for the piece of crumpled up paper. "I'll see you later, Mike." Then to Mike's surprise, she gave him a gentle peck on the lips. He tasted her sweet, succulent lips and felt her warmth.

"You know, Renee, I thought dancing was for sissies. But I had a good time." Mike remembered hearing that phrase a few years ago, but now he thought that if dancing was for sissies, he wanted to be the biggest sissy in Detroit.

Renee put on her full-length leather coat and a black beret on her head and said, "Happy Thanksgiving, brother. We have a lot to be thankful for."

Mike let himself out and, with his two extra large bags, he darted across 12th Street. He turned around for one last look. He put the bags down and couldn't decide if he wanted to button up the pea coat, still feeling the warmth of Renee. He saw a 1966 silver deuce and a quarter - Electra 225 - pull up to the bakery. Renee came out and jumped into the car. Scotty followed her out and climbed into his own Chevy station wagon parked directly in front. The brightly lit bakery was dark now. Before Mike turned around to head home, he once again looked at the huge billboard-sized sign just erected on the corner of Atkinson and 12th Street.

It read, "The Future Home of Rosa Parks."

CHAPTER 11 –
Detroit's Calling (Fall 1967)

FRANK'S CALL FOR A FAMILY GATHERING after Thanksgiving dinner came as no surprise. Mike had to admit that the house was as busy as a Greyhound bus station since the rebellion. There were several block club meetings at the house. City officials, ministers, and politicians — those running for public office — all stopped by for a visit. Rev. Boykin introduced Frank and Rose to many of the city officials and politicians. After the other guests left, Rev. Boykin and Dr. Woods, often stayed and told stories. Frank and Dr. Woods drank scotch and soda while Rev. Boykin preferred Vernors Ginger Ale. They always picked out a few of Frank's jazz LPs for easy listening on the family's new hi-fi. The trio loved sax men like Dexter Gordon and John Coltrane.

Mike and his siblings quietly observed many of these meetings, and ran errands or acted as hosts for the guests. Mike remembered one pleasant visit from Rev. Boykin not long after the rebellion. As Mike brought a bucket of ice into the living room for his Dad and Rev. Boykin, he overheard a cordial and straight forward Rev. Boykin.

"What do you think about my idea, Frank? You see, the city is putting thousands and thousands of dollars back into urban renewal-money into all kinds of community programs right now. That old school building just past Dexter Blvd. I told you about, it's been vacant for the last couple of years. The city would like to refurbish it, turn it into some type of community facility, something for the kids. The pressure is on them. The city needs somebody with your leadership to come in and run this place."

Mike remembered his father looked stunned. "Reverend, the only thing I'm leader of is our block club, and secretary of Visitation's usher board."

"Doggone-it Frank, that's perfect. I'd like to put your name forward

50

to the common council's search team as our choice for director of this new youth initiative."

Mike heard on several occasions his dad express that something had to change. He'd heard most adult men express their outrage with the city's handling of the rebellion, the massacre at the Algiers Motel, and the police treatment of Negroes in general. Frank and Rose sat down after dinner that evening after the Rev. Boykin pitched his proposal.

"We have three beautiful children," Frank said, "a nice home, a nice job, a nice ride. Damn, we're a regular Ozzie and Harriet television family. But Rose, I feel there's another calling for me. The city and the federal government are talking about putting three million dollars in the neighborhood right now for community service programs for young people. Some of that money is going to go towards rebuilding this vacant school for a community service program for people in the area, like a Boys' Club. They may be on to something here. We could have youth basketball and baseball leagues, and we could have meetings in this place. This could be a second home for many kids. Right now we need a bright spot in this burned-out community. Detroit needs a bright spot. This may be a new leaf for us all, a new leaf, Rose."

"Frank, you're giving up a good career with Statewide. You're putting everything at risk," said Rose, her arms folded. "Everything."

Later, Mike saw his father up around midnight sipping scotch and listening to some Coltrane on the turntable. Mike dug Coltrane too. He often listened to his dad's albums such as *Blue Trane* and *The Believer*. Mike also liked listening to Dexter Gordon and Charlie Parker.

In early November, after Frank accepted the position as director of the yet-to-be-established City Club, Mike overheard a rather heated exchange between Frank and Dr. Woods. Rev. Boykin tried to keep the peace between the two men. After a few rounds of scotch, Dr. Woods leaned his wiry small frame against the sofa, making himself look at home. "Frank, you must've been tired of being the token black at Statewide."

"Token," Frank said as he reared up from a restful position on the sofa. "Oh, no, I never was a token."

"Frank, you were the only black on staff for six years. And there were none before you."

"That didn't make me a token. I may have been the only Negro at Statewide but I can assure you they are going to bring some more in. They want the Negro dollars."

Rev. Boykin interjected, "Frank broke new ground Doc. You're going to see more of this real soon. Black folks are going to start getting hired for positions they qualify for. Black accountants will be hired as accountants, not janitors. You know Frank's father's story."

"Yes, I'm well aware of Frank's father's story. I knew Frank's father. He was the accountant for our hospital and several other black-owned hospitals after he threw his janitor's bucket down at Woolsworth's department store."

"Well Doc," said Frank, "I wasn't just some Negro face in the place. I wasn't on display." Frank then pulled his trousers up over his knee showing his black hosiery, leaned over towards the Dr. Woods, and said to him as if he were closing an insurance sale, "I don't carry nobody else's water, nobody's water boy. Isn't that what they called my father at Woolworth's — a water boy. He threw his bucket alright, damn near hit the manager upside the head. Well, I busted a hump at Statewide and brought in more money than the entire staff. Doc, I made the company and myself some damn good money."

"I didn't mean it like that, Frank," said Dr. Woods, as if to back off the remark that Frank took as an insult. "I mean you are held up to the media or other institutions like the NAACP to say, see, we hire black folks, we are not prejudiced."

"And we love to see more black faces in more places," said Rev. Boykin.

"You see Doc," Frank was about one inch from Dr. Wood's face. "You don't understand. The regional manager, Jerry, Jerry Drumbrowski, my supervisor is an old college buddy of mine. We were in class together, we double-dated together, we ate together. This man is not looking at race. He's not looking to score points with anyone."

"Well, Frank", Dr. Woods came back. "Then you must've taken them financially to the mountain top."

"Doc, I simply did what I love to do. Yes, I have asked some Negroes to join the company, but they turned me down. They felt they would be isolated, especially in social circles."

"Then maybe that's why it makes more sense to build up our own companies. Like we did with black-owned hospitals in Detroit," said Dr. Woods.

"Now Doc, I'm with Rev. Boykin on this one," said Frank.

"But we need our own Frank, our own!"

"Frank," Rev. Boykin chimed in, "the Doctor just hasn't seen much progress in his lifetime. We're just coming out of Jim Crow, even here in Detroit, Up South. And Frank, carry water for God."

Frank paused. "Uh huh, now that I can do." Frank realized that the conversation with Dr. Woods wasn't going anywhere. Frank glanced over his shoulders and caught Mike's face peering through the glass doors. He pulled back from Dr. Woods, got up, started laughing and headed for the door with an empty bowl he used for ice. "Mike," he said, as he opened the door still laughing, "these elders, jeez. Hey, can you get us some more ice?"

"Sure, Dad."

Frank returned to the living room, sat down and changed the subject. As Mike refilled their glasses with ice, Frank said. "I'm taking this position with City Club because I think I can make a difference in re-making Detroit. I'm convinced that we can re-make this city. And working with our young people may be just where I need to be."

"Absolutely, Frank, they need you; we all need you."

~ ~ ~ ~ ~ ~ ~

After Thanksgiving dinner, the taste of turkey was still in Mike's mouth while they were huddled into the family room for the grand announcement. They had a clear view of the backyard from the room. The room was intimate and warm. There were several book-filled shelves, a small black and white television, Mama E's green sofa against one wall, and a love-seat against the other wall, just enough room for the ever-growing Waterman family. Mama E had decorated the room with colorful pictures, many she bought up from her home in Louisiana, painted by people she knew, and then a few painted by several well-known local artists like Carl Owens and Jon Lockard. Beautiful images encircled the room. Several small lamps with decorative shades were neatly arranged around the room.

"I see a rose," said Denise who pointed to a rose as she looked out of the back window. "Right there."

"Where, honey?" asked Rose.

"See, right there, Mom. There's another one. One red and one pink. Can I pick them?" Denise stood up and headed outside with scissors before anyone could even respond.

"A rare Indian Summer rose in the month of November. The girl knows what she wants," said Mama E. Once outside, Denise just stood there; she looked as if she forgot where the roses were located. Mama E tapped the window to get her attention. "Over there," she said very slowly, then pointed to the red rose. Denise twisted her slender neck almost 180 degrees and brushed back her long brown hair, to catch a glimpse of the red rose. She stood next to the three-and-a-half-foot-tall bush and clipped the red rose. Denise looked back towards the window and held the rose up as if to say, this one's for you, Mom. Then she swiftly walked over to the pink rose bush and clipped the lone blossom and gestured to Mama E, to show that the pink rose was for her.

Before Denise could get back in the house, Frank tried to get Jon-Jon's full attention. Jon-Jon had his face buried into the Black Panther newspaper Mike brought home from the bakery. Jon-Jon wore dark glasses and a black-hooded sweatshirt with the hood pulled over his head.

"Jon-Jon, son, please, put the paper down. And I noticed at dinner you still hadn't gotten your hair cut. Why not? I told you to go yesterday." Jon-Jon pulled his hood off to show off his neatly trimmed two-inch natural hair style.

"I want to get a natural look, Dad."

"Son, we don't live in the bush. You will have a neat hair cut around here."

"This is neat. I got it trimmed."

"Get it cut – tomorrow!"

"But everybody's wearing a natural now."

"Who? I haven't seen them. You look uncivilized, right out of Tarzan."

Denise returned with roses and broke up the conversation.

Frank said, "Those are beautiful, Denise."

"Mom, this one is for you, and Mama E, this is for you. Just want to let you know how thankful I am for both of you. And the dinner today was the best ever."

"Ahhh, dear," said Rose. "You are such an angel."

"She sure is," said Mama E.

"Your dad has an announcement to make, and I want you all to listen up," said Rose, helping Frank to get the family focused.

"Are you running for president, Dad?" Jon-Jon jumped in.

"Son," Frank started, "what does it take for you, what is it, Jon-Jon? And take those sun shades off, you're not outside." Jon-Jon slowly removed the glasses.

"Dad, it's just a question. You told us that no question is a dumb question."

"Just hold your questions until I'm finished. Your father is not running for public office, but I am taking on a new position as director of the brand new City Club Youth Center. It's located just on the other side of Dexter Blvd. So, I'll be leaving Statewide at the end of January next year. City Club is slated to open in May or June 1968, just in time for the summer."

Mike said, "We knew something was up, Dad, all those people parading through the house talking about making Detroit new. Especially Rev. Cleage and that man running for judge. Those two are the whitest Negro men I have ever seen."

"Negroes come in all shapes, sizes, and colors of the rainbow," said Frank. Rose sat quietly, leaning toward Frank, giving off body language that she was in total support of Frank's decision. But Mike remembered hearing all the verbal battles between his mom and dad over the career move. They argued about giving up his lifestyle, his great position with the company, not to mention the potential salary increases and bonuses. Rose looked as if she'd rested her case and was at peace. Mike reflected on the past for a second. The fun-filled company picnics, the annual Christmas party, the family get-togethers.

Mike spoke up. "Well, I guess I won't be seeing the Drumbrowski's anymore." Mike had a friendship with Mr. Drumbrowski's daughter Becky over the years. Denise called her bad-Becky because she acted too fast.

"Oh, we'll see Jerry and his family again. But it might not be the same."

"I got basketball to think about anyway," said Mike. Jon-Jon put his face back in the newspaper, and Denise fidgeted in her chair as if she was trying hard to say something to her dad.

"Can I get a job there?" she finally asked.

"I don't see why not."

"Daddy, you're the greatest."

CHAPTER 12 -
City Club

THE FAMILY PILED IN THE 1966 Fury III with room to spare. Three adults in the front, three kids in the back. The four doors made it easy to get in and out. The ride over to City Club lasted no more than ten minutes. Frank took LaSalle to Chicago Blvd. to Petoskey, and right across the street from Don Bosco Boys Home the new City Club building lay abandoned and neglected. As Frank pulled into the parking lot Mike noticed the rusted gutters hanging from the roof and heard the sound of crushed glass under the tires. The once-bright pinkish colored bricks were dulled by the dirt smudges throughout. *The windows could use a serious washing*, Mike thought. Frank parked at the rear entrance. The parking lot was littered with trash and full of chuck-holes. The field out back, big enough for a football field, was overgrown with weeds and the hoops on the basketball court looked like they were hanging by a single screw.

The building for City Club was the old St. Jude - the former K-12 Catholic School - closed by the Detroit Archdiocese in 1963. The city purchased the building two years ago with the intention of turning it into an adult learning center but changed its mind after the riot. And despite the city's assurances everything worked, it took Frank five minutes to find the right keys and another five minutes to find a working light. "Well, this is it, what do you think?" asked Frank, smiling at Rose. A musty funky odor hung heavy in the hallway. The building had unusually wide hallways that formed a horseshoe shape. At the front door sat an empty glass display case. The sky blue walls still had some shine to it but the white tiled floors were scoffed and worn.

"Let's have a look around," said Rose laughing. "You have got your work cut out for you."

"Yeah, they're going to be busting down walls, rewiring the building, putting in new equipment, new tile and paint, the works," said Frank.

"And the field, don't forget that huge field out back. Frank what have you got us into? And what about the plumbing? Does the little girl's room work?" Rose gave Frank one of those looks, head tilted down, eyebrows arched up.

"Well, the city says the building is in 'good structural condition' so we should have running water." The wood floor gymnasium installed by the archdiocese in 1960, was still in good shape and was about the only thing that could be used right away.

"More than a job isn't it? You and Mama take a look around. We got a gymnasium at one end and the multipurpose room at the other." Mike and Jon-Jon tagged along with Frank as Denise went with the two women. Frank and his two sons went from room to room, Frank taking notes as he checked door knobs, windows, and bathrooms. Within ten minutes the kids left their parents and were instead racing through the hallway. A few minutes later, they all met in the extra large kitchen at one end of the multipurpose room. "What are you going to do with all this kitchen?" asked Mama E.

"Don't know yet," said Frank.

"Dad, can we go outside?" asked Denise.

"Go." The three kids raced out of the building, then from the parking lot to the other side of the field.

Mike, running, led his siblings through the knee-high grass littered with pop cans, beer bottles and candy wrappers. Denise, pulling up the rear shouted, "Watch out for the snakes."

Mike came to a sudden stop, then said, "Girl, ain't no snakes in these grasses." Then after looking on both sides to be sure, he took off running again. Now Denise was on Mike's heels while Jon-Jon lagged behind. When Mike reached the basketball courts he saw three full courts painted on the asphalt. There were lights towering above the courts that were once used for the Catholic high school league. A couple of the lights dangled from their sockets. Mike looked around, turning 360 degrees placing his hands on his hips.

"This is a damn disaster. How is dad gonna resurrect this place?" Mike posed to his siblings.

Without hesitation Denise said, "Dad can work miracles."

"No, Mom's the one," said Jon-Jon, she works all the miracles in our house. She be on that rosary constantly. It's like whatever she asks for she gets."

Mike cut Jon-Jon off, "Hey y'all, let's play horse until dad and them get ready to leave. We can use these pop cans."

"Mike, you'll play basketball with anything. It's hard for me to pretend

57

this pop can is a basketball," Denise protested. She lifted a Faygo Red Pop can out of the nearby grass and handed it to Mike. "Here you go, my brother." Mike threw up a hook shot from the free throw line. He put enough force on the shot that it banked off the backboard and fell through the hoop. Jon-Jon looked at Denise and said "Uh, you go next." Denise picked up the can and threw it grunting, while the can fell far short of the rim. Jon-Jon ran up to the can, picked it up and banked a layup and caught the can on its way down then threw it at Mike. Mike pretended to bounce the can on the court, went towards the corner, then spun back towards the middle and went in close for a reverse layup. He banked it again against the backboard and it fell through the hoop. "Next!" Mike hollered. Denise took the can and drove in to attempt a reverse layup but froze when she got close to the basket. Jon-Jon called traveling, motioning his arms like a referee. Denise turned around with her back to the hoop and threw up the can. It went in hitting nothing.

"Look, they're leaving," said Jon-Jon. Mike could see his father searching the grounds for everyone else.

As they left the lot, Mama E didn't waste any time talking about her interest in something at City Club for seniors.

"I know it's a youth center, Frank, but the seniors in Detroit need so much," said Mama E as they drove home.

CHAPTER 13 -
Visitation Era Ends

FRANK PLACED THE PHONE BACK ON the receiver and said to Rose, "That was Father O'Malley on the phone. He asked me to represent Visitation at an emergency parish summit this Saturday morning at the archdiocese downtown. Be his eyes and ears."

"You can't do everything, Frank. You've been working overtime getting the City Club ready for its grand opening. Can someone else go instead?" asked Rose as she washed her hands in the kitchen sink. She had been in the backyard preparing her flower-bed for spring planting. Frank stood in the kitchen pouring a glass of cold water. He handed it to Rose.

"I don't think so, baby. I signed up for a two-year stint on the Visitation Parish Council. Still got over a year to go."

"There goes our Eastern Market morning. What's this summit all about anyway?"

"Don't know. Father O'Malley didn't say." Frank grabbed another tall glass and filled it with water for himself.

"That's strange. Father didn't tell you?"

"He said he didn't know himself, but all the parishes need to be represented. Some kind of announcement, I think."

"I bet Father O'Malley knows."

"So what? He ain't tellin'," said Frank.

"I don't get a good feeling about this," Rose said as she undid her full-length apron.

Maybe Cardinal Beardum would be giving out awards, recognizing the increased outreach in the parish communities since the rebellion, Frank thought. But at the moment Frank was working to keep the City Club on track for its

June opening. He had enough on his mind to be thinking too much about the summit.

"How's the garden this year?" Frank asked, absently.

"Well, I've encroached on just about all the play area in the yard. Think there may be enough room to teach Denise how to do cartwheels. But eventually, I want to put a picnic table and a couple of lawn chairs back there. And you are going to see more roses this year than ever . . . guaranteed!!"

~ ~ ~ ~ ~ ~ ~

Frank got up at about 7A.M. on Saturday, didn't bother to fix anything to eat and instead hurried out to pick up Ted Wilson, who had been invited to attend as a Visitation Board member. As they drove together, Frank quizzed Ted about the summit.

"Frank, I'm told that the priests were sworn to secrecy on this," was the only response he received.

It took Frank about ten minutes to snake his way through Detroit and into the downtown area. The two men arrived in time to indulge in a breakfast buffet provided by the archdiocese: eggs, pancakes, sausage, biscuits, coffee, juice, and donuts.

"What do you think, men, they fattening us up for the slaughter?" Frank joked to a small group in the buffet line. They all laughed. Frank loaded up on scrambled eggs, polish sausage, grits, toast and jam, then grabbed a orange juice and joined Ted and a couple of parishioners from St. Cecelia at a table near the front of the large cavernous hall. The six large crystal chandeliers that hung from the high ceiling gave the room an upscale ambiance. The food was good and hot as the group engaged in small talk as they focused on their plates.

Frank panned the room while chewing and noticed that all the predominately inner-city black Catholic schools were represented. Just when most folks had finished eating, Father Richard, Cardinal Beardum's top assistant, gave everyone a warm welcome, then introduced Cardinal Beardum to the group in attendance.

"Ladies and gentlemen, your courage is admired and your leadership has been invaluable to the Detroit Diocese," Cardinal Beardum said as he opened the meeting. "And though we've been faced with tough decisions recently, your work is not over." Those beaming smiles that had been radiating throughout the room, those beaming smiles that were at the breakfast reception just minutes ago, all began to fade. "I want to acknowledge your commitment myself – that's why we are gathered here today – and I want to further encourage you to fight for truth and justice wherever you land."

Suddenly there was rumbling among the group.

"Wherever we land?" exclaimed Jose Gonzales of Holy Redeemer High.

"What is he talking about?" another voice in the audience demanded.

"The Archdiocese of Detroit," Cardinal Beardum continued in a very stern tone, "has decided to suspend operations at ten of its inner-city high schools and all twenty of its elementary schools. The parishes will remain open and continue their services for now."

A loud collective groan bellowed throughout the room.

"How could you?" said Tom Davis, a middle-aged gray-haired teacher from St. Cecelia High. He stood up as if to challenge the decision. "We have kids about to graduate."

Cardinal Beardum raised his hand for silence. "Ladies and gentlemen, we still have the University of Detroit High, Catholic Central, and Immaculata that will remain open for now. There is still plenty of opportunity for your children to receive a Catholic school education. And there is plenty of time to pursue a transfer, because I have asked the schools to extend their deadlines for next fall's admission."

The rumblings got louder. Carl "Curly" Cornell, chairman of the Visitation school board, stood up to address Cardinal Beardum.

"Now, Cardinal Beardum," Curly began, glancing back to see if he had the group behind him. "With all due respect, sir, that is entirely too many schools to close at once." Curly, 55, stout, with a head full of curly hair and a Hershey chocolate complexion, had been an active Visitation Parishioner since 1950. He had already put two sons through Visitation and had one more son who would be a senior in the fall. The Harvard-trained lawyer and real-estate professional began to argue his point. "There are, as I understand it, over five hundred students at each of these high schools you would like to close. That's over five thousand predominantly Catholic students. Five thousand, sir!"

"Curly." The Cardinal raised his hand for quiet. "Curly, that's five thousand students and we don't know how many are Catholic. Many of these kids – and I am certain that you would agree – many of these kids would feel perfectly at home attending a nearby public school. Let's face it, Curly, the schools are broke. The buildings are in disrepair and we simply must consolidate our schools. If you were in my shoes you would do the same thing."

"Sir." Curly remained standing. "With all due respect, sir, consolidation is one thing and outright closure is another. The church's mission is to serve the needy, and it must replace its parishioners because of white flight."

"White flight?" Cardinal Beardum fired back. "Don't lecture me! This is not about race."

Frank felt the hostility now building in the room.

Sam Jones from East Catholic High School jumped up and cried out, "Then what *is* this about?"

Jack Johnson, the principal from St. Leo's, rose to speak. "The schools are too black and too poor. We should've seen it coming."

"Now just a minute, Mr. Johnson," the Cardinal interrupted, with his signature raised hand. "You must remember our discussion last year." Cardinal Beardum was adept at remembering names and faces and could remember events better than anyone Frank knew. "We discussed the fact that the Detroit Diocese could not carry the schools that were in the red much longer. This is purely a financial decision."

Curly cut him short, reasserting himself like a courtroom lawyer and looking around the room for nods. "This is contrary to the mission of the Catholic Church. Sir, I think your proposal, while it may have some merit based on some of the schools' financial circumstances, does not square with the overarching mission to recruit and retain new Catholics in the spirit of Christ. Financial conditions should not override the principal foundation of the church's existence. If we need a subsidy – fine. If the subsidy comes from outside Detroit – then so be it!!" Curly exclaimed.

"And where do you think this imaginary subsidy would come from, if not from Detroit, Curly?"

"Rome, by God, Rome! What they pay for chalices in a year alone could underwrite a couple of schools."

"Hear, hear!" the group erupted behind Curly.

"Curly!" The Cardinal looked pink-faced and near the boiling point. "Don't get in over your head on this. This is not an easy decision for us. This is not easy . . . but now that you know our decision is made . . . "

"Wait just a minute! We are surely not lap-dogs either. I think some consultation would have been appropriate," Curly interjected.

"This is not a democracy," Cardinal Beardum fired back. "Don't get confused – I take the heat for the situation in Detroit. The buck stops here. However, I do understand your concerns."

"No," Curly interjected again, still on his feet. "No, I don't believe you do. We are saying unequivocally – and I don't think I speak for myself alone – we are saying that your decision to close as many as ten high schools and *all* the elementary schools is far too drastic." He paused, then continued. "I suggest we take a fifteen- to twenty-minute break, please. Let's cool down and get back together. Sir, I may have a counteroffer for you to consider."

"Curly, this is not a negotiation."

"Cardinal Beardum, please give us 20 minutes. Is that too much to ask?"

"Okay, let's reconvene at 10:30."

"Thank you," Curly responded politely, and turned to face the others. "Ladies and gentlemen, I would like to conference briefly. We can stay right here." Frank glanced behind Curly and noticed the Cardinal and his entourage leaving the room.

"Got to give it to you, Curly, you stood right up to him," said Ted.

"Enough already." Curly waved the comment off. "This is not about me or about standing up or whatever. This is about saving some of these schools for our children. We simply cannot allow this to be the final word. Here's what I have in mind: we can fight to consolidate the ten high schools into three. The elementary schools are going to be much more difficult to save."

"Which three high schools get saved?" a voice in the audience rang out.

"The ones with the best facilities and the most capacity to absorb additional students." Curly launched into an explanation of how the three schools could serve the students of all ten of the former schools. The group was caught so off guard by Cardinal Beardum's announcement that they felt compelled to hear Curly out. No one else had a plan. "I'll need a consensus on this," Curly said, nodding to the others. "If there are any problems, let me know now so we can get through this."

"We need more than a few minutes, Curly," said Mrs. Jones, the principal from St. Cecilia. "These closings have long-term implications. The archdiocese should've thought things through better than this. They are simply telling us what they are going to do."

"Let's see what you got; it's worth a shot," said Frank. "What else do we have?" After about fifteen minutes, the group agreed that since Curly had a plan in hand that seemed reasonable, they would support it.

Father Richard, the cardinal's aide, soon peered out from the door to the cardinal's office. "Curly", he called, waving Curly over, "Cardinal Beardum would like to have a word with you." Curly eagerly rushed over to the office door.

Frank followed. "I want to go with you. Do you mind?" Curly hesitated for a moment, frowning, then said, "Okay, come on."

"Come on in," Father Richard beckoned, and led them through the maze of bookcases back to the cardinal's desk, talking all the way. "The cardinal regrets that he has another engagement he must attend to. Something has come up. Come right this way, gentlemen."

Then out of nowhere the cardinal appeared. "Curly, and . . . "

"Frank. Frank Waterman with Visitation." Frank extended his hand and Cardinal Beardum shook it and said, "It's good to meet you Mr. Waterman."

"I need to attend to some urgent matters. Do you have something for me to look at"?

"Yes, I do."

"Leave it with Father Richard. He will brief me." Cardinal Beardum proceeded to leave through the side door which led back to his office. Curly handed Father Richard the proposal.

Father Richard began softly. "Curly, I think we know what you want. You've expressed it on more than one occasion. We may be in a position to give it to you. The cardinal wants to meet with the Visitation Board in a few days. We may be able to save one school and pursue your vision – our collective vision – of a prep school for inner-city kids. Just like we talked about – a model for the city – we want the high-achievers. Cardinal Beardum has the highest standards, you know. Oh, Curly," he added, almost as an afterthought, "as Chair of the Visitation Board, are your fellow board members behind you?"

"Absolutely," Curly answered without hesitation. "You mean Cardinal Beardum shares my vision?"

"You better believe it!"

"Good, then we may have something here." Curly sounded even more excited. "Let's see, how about next Saturday evening around seven?"

"Cardinal Beardum will be there," Father Richard responded. Curly was all smiles.

On the way back to the group, Frank asked, "What on earth was that all about?"

Curly stopped in his tracks and turned to Frank. "Trust me on this, Frank. I know what I'm doing."

"Curly, you've already been talking to them about this."

"That's right, I have. We'll save at least one." As the two re-entered the meeting room, Curly put on a big smile.

"Cardinal Beardum liked the proposal. He said he will make his final decision next week. An emergency came up and the cardinal had to leave. Ladies and gentlemen, this meeting is adjourned. Thank you all for your invaluable input and your patience." Ted and Frank both confronted Curly as they began to walk to their cars.

"What happened to the cardinal?" asked Ted.

"He had an emergency. I don't know exactly what, but he said he wants to meet with our board and parents next week, Saturday evening, April 6, at seven o'clock."

"You said he liked the proposal. Does that mean three schools?"

"Ted, like I told Frank . . . just between us, we'll be lucky to get one".

"One?"

"Yeah, let's hope it's us. See you next Saturday."

Frank said, "Three schools, not one. We're gonna fight for three."

"Like I said, Frank, we'll be fortunate to get anything. Don't be so naive. We can sell them on an inner-city prep school for high-achieving Negroes."

"Yeah, and what about everybody else?" said Ted, as Frank and Ted climbed into Frank's Fury III. Curly didn't respond.

Ted continued, "Curly got something up his sleeve. Maybe he's buying up some old archdiocese property for pennies on the dollar, who knows."

"Naw," said Frank, "Curly got this big idea about having a inner-city prep school on par with Brother Rice or Country Day."

Even though Frank had known Curly for the past eight years, both as active members of Visitation's usher board and through the PTAs and other social functions, he didn't really know Curly. After a long silence as Frank headed down the ramp of the John C. Lodge Freeway, Ted spoke up.

"Didn't see it coming, Frank, didn't see it at all."

"Didn't see who coming? Curly, or Cardinal Beardum?"

"Both."

"Well, Curly had said that the school board was in his corner for this prep school idea."

"We don't know a damn thing about it. But the problem is that over half the board will do whatever Curly says. He'll get on the horn tonight and line up support just like that." Ted snapped his fingers.

"We still gotta fight for three schools, man. There's East Catholic for the east side, Holy Redeemer downriver, and Visitation in the middle. Those are the three we need to save. We need to make some phone calls of our own."

Ted agreed.

Frank broke the news as soon as he saw Rose. "How can they do that?" Rose said furiously. "How can they? How *can* they?" She started pacing through the house. "I won't let this happen. Frank, what can we do?" Frank mentioned to Rose the upcoming meeting next Saturday. "I know what. I'm gonna call and invite every Catholic in Detroit to that meeting on Saturday!!"

CHAPTER 14 -
Visitation Board Meeting (April 1968)

FRANK AND ROSE SAT UP LATE that night in the living room discussing the fate of Visitation and other Catholic schools in Detroit. They sat next to each other on the sofa closest to the fireplace. The early April weather was still cold enough for Frank to light a fire. He had lit the birch logs already in place. Rose poured them a cup of tea. Frank had never seen Rose so furious. He knew why. He knew Rose was set on sending all her children to Visitation where Mike could excel in school and sports, Denise could join the cheerleading team and Jon-Jon would come out of his shell. Frank knew that Rose did not want to let her children down. They both heard Mike often tell people that when he got to Visitation he would star in every sport they offered. If the school had a squash team he would play.

"The boy got big dreams," Frank once said. And Rose often expressed her feelings to Frank several times about how he pumped Mike up about his athletic prowess and what would happen if Mike didn't realize his goals and dreams of being "all-everything"— making pro or the Olympics. How would Mike's fragile ego handle a let down, Rose would ask Frank. Frank responded to her concern. Frank told her, "the boy can dream big, come-on Rose. You know the saying, reach for the stars and you may fall among the clouds, fall among the treetops or something like that. Mike knows."

Rose replied, "Not the way that boy talks. He's obsessed."

Once Frank got the fire going good he sat down across from Rose who was sipping tea.

"We have to keep some of these schools open, Frank, the kids are looking forward to going to Visi. I'm going to make some phone calls. I also think if people called up to the archdiocese, Cardinal Beardum might get the message." Frank reached into his briefcase against the wall and pulled out the parish directory and handed it to Rose.

"Ted is going to drop off the school directory."

"Great, and maybe we can get some names and numbers from the other school principals. They need to be in on this too," said Rose.

Frank leaned back into the cushy sofa. His eyes met Rose. "You are the most wonderful woman in the world." He leaned against her and hugged her tightly, kissed her, then said, "Girl, you still light my fire." They rolled off the sofa onto the carpet in front of the fireplace. They continued kissing passionately while the fire burned brilliantly beside them.

"I love you, man."

Rose laid on top of Frank, pressed her head into his chest, then fell asleep.

~ ~ ~ ~ ~ ~ ~

Later that week, when Frank came home from a visit to City Club, Rose was on the phone with Mrs. Williams, principal of St. Bridgette. Rose's voice trembled. "Oh my God Frank," said Rose. "Mrs. Williams said Dr. King's been shot, they think he's dead. Oh God, no." Rose's voice sounded worse. "Where are the children. Mama, where are the kids?" Rose shouted. Frank started up the stairs but met Mama E coming down holding a transistor radio tuned to WCHB.

"The kids are upstairs playing cards," she said. Mama E continued down the stairs. News reports spread like wildfire. There were reports of riots in Chicago and Washington, D.C. The phone rang. Frank stepped in the kitchen to answer it.

"Frank, it's Rev. Boykin, ministers in Detroit are fanning out throughout the city with the men in their congregations to prevent looting and bloodshed. I'm heading over to Dexter and I'd like you to join us."

"You bet I will, and I'll bring some men with me." Frank picked up Ted and Stu from Visitation's Usher Board. Frank spotted several ministers and community leaders gathered on Dexter and Joy Road, many holding white candles as a sign of peace. They split up and walked north towards Davison Ave. stopping at each corner to talk to several angry residents. Detroit remained mostly quiet but experienced some minor looting that night and for the next several days. And despite the pain Rose expressed about the murder of Dr. King, she steadfastly continued to make calls in order to have a packed house for the upcoming meeting and announcement on the school closings.

~ ~ ~ ~ ~ ~ ~

The night of the meeting with the school board members, parents and Cardinal Beardum, Frank felt the uneasiness in the room. People were still talking about Dr. King's assassination and what he meant to civil rights and the community. There was a large turnout. Some of the parents from other parishes on the archdiocese's "hit list" received a call about the special meeting and showed up.

One of the parents from St. Leo stood up before the meeting was called to order and expressed her rage. "We cannot allow all our schools to be shut down just like that. We should demand they combine all these schools into three or four and not just shut the entire system down."

"The schools are becoming too black for them, that's all," shouted another person in the audience. "I'm from St. Cecelia and we don't plan to take this lying down."

Frank heard the commotion inside as he and Ted stood in the lobby exchanging pleasantries about each others families before Ted changed the subject abruptly. Ted looked strained and sounded tired as he continued to work twelve hour shifts at the auto plant. "Frank, are you aware that the archdiocese is here tonight to cut a deal. Curly told me that he sold the cardinal on saving Visitation."

"Just Visi?" asked Frank.

"Just Visi. But check this. Curly told us after the meeting last Saturday that the cardinal would consider saving three schools. Curly's happy. We, the Visi board had a short pre-meeting just a little while ago and he started in about why we need an inner-city prep school – an inner-city Brother Rice, he said. That's his angle, Frank."

"But that's not a done deal, is it?"

"Oh no, hell no!! He doesn't have a majority on his side."

"What's not a done deal?" asked Robert James, a St. Agnes parent who stepped into the lobby from the auditorium.

"We're talking about the consolidation." Ted responded.

"I heard it's over for us at St. Agnes. The priests all got letters about the closings. They won't tell us much else. Some official announcement is coming down. I thought that's what this meeting must be about. Our board representative told everybody they may save three of the high schools. None on the school board approved the way this is coming down but I don't know how we are going to fight it."

"We're fighting by doing what we doing tonight, said Frank."

"I hear ya Frank. Where the heck is the little boys room?" asked Robert.

"Down the hall to the left," pointed Ted. "This meeting is getting ready to start." Cardinal Beardum and Curly enter the auditorium from the side door next to the parking lot. Curly wasted no time starting the meeting.

"Good evening, ladies and gentlemen. Tonight we are honored to have with us Cardinal James Beardum of the Archdiocese of Detroit to make a special announcement." Curly then stepped back from the podium. The cardinal entered the overcrowded room and seemed impressed but also looked overwhelmed. He began slowly.

"Before we get started, I would like to ask for a moment of silence in honor of a truly remarkable man, the Rev. Martin Luther King Jr. I am deeply saddened by his death." Complete silence fell over the room. Then Cardinal Beardum began, "I read your proposal." The audience applauded. The cardinal raised both hands for quiet. "I read your proposal with great delight. I am impressed with the interest in maintaining the schools and your belief in the Catholic Church. We have a solution I believe will work. A merger can work but we'll have to go with two schools not three. We think Visitation should be the site of one and East Catholic the site of the other because of their proximity to adequate transportation facilities, the recreation facilities, parking, and classroom space." Frank and Rose jumped for joy. Ted even joined in with his much cooler demeanor. Most in attendance stood on their feet clapping; several hooted in satisfaction.

"Yes, I knew we'd get something out of this" said Frank, "I knew it."

The parents, board and others appeared pleased about saving at least two schools.

Cardinal Beardum continued, "I understand you already have a name for the consolidated schools" He looked to Curly. Curly gave him a nod. "St. Martin DePorres would be located here and St. Benedict the Moor will be the new name of East Catholic."

"Two Black Saints!" Rose exclaimed. "Two Black Saints."

The cardinal told the audience of the challenges they faced but he felt everyone was up for it. He concluded his remarks by reminding everyone of their commitment to God and service to the poor.

~ ~ ~ ~ ~ ~ ~

After Cardinal Beardum and the crowd departed, Frank sat in on the outgoing Visitation board meeting. Father O'Malley announced that the current board at Visitation would be dissolved while the new board would expand from seven to eleven members and Curly Cornell would continue as chairman with a new four-year term. That night Father O'Malley also announced that Ted would be in charge of the search team for a new principal. Ted told Frank that he'd been tapped by Father O'Malley in advance of the meeting if Cardinal Beardum accepted the merger. And Ted had done some leg-work in finding a suitable person.

"Jim Dunham is the man we need in here!!" Ted said emphatically.

"Jim who"? asked the others.

"Jim Dunham. He's a young brother who works over at the Catholic Relief Services. He was the assistant principal at Blessed Sacrament Elementary School before they closed it down. He's young, energetic, and enthusiastic, and highly qualified. He's the best person for this job."

The small group gave a collective sigh of relief.

CHAPTER 15 -
City Club Grand Opening — June 1968

IT SEEMED TO MIKE THAT EVERYBODY from the neighborhood came out to celebrate the opening of City Club. Young mothers and fathers pushing infants in strollers, grandmothers grouped together walking the halls admiring the fresh look in the neighborhood. Frank stood at the door for over an hour shaking everyone's hand that came in. "Welcome to City Club. If you would like a tour, you can sign up and wait in the room to the right. If not, you can make your way to the multipurpose room where we have refreshments. Take a left at the end of the hallway." Rose and some others in the neighborhood volunteered to give tours of the building. Mama E joined several others as hostesses in the multipurpose room. The Mayor of Detroit, Jerome P. Cavanaugh, arrived with his entourage, several members of the Detroit Common Council were already milling around. The Governor of Michigan, George Romney, flew in for the occasion.

Jerry Drumbrowski brought his entire family, except Becky. Mike stood at the door as the two men greeted each other. "What a surprise," said Frank as the two long time friends gave each other a warm embrace.

"Great to see you Frank. How's the family?" asked Jerry.

Mr. Drumbrowski smiled at Mike and said, "Becky couldn't make it, she's visiting her grandmother in Maine."

"Oh," said Mike.

Frank rallied everyone into the auditorium.

The official program was short. The Mayor milled around from room to room, apparently very pleased with the work Frank Waterman and his small staff put into the restoration and reopening of the building. The mayor and Ernest Browne, member of the Detroit Common Council, made short laudatory comments. Mayoral candidate for next year's election, Richard Austin, the first Negro mayoral candidate in Detroit praised the community for coming together and helping City Club staff to turn this abandoned building into a new jewel of the neighborhood.

~ ~ ~ ~ ~ ~ ~

Before the Waterman family left the building, Mama E caught up with Frank.

She said to Frank, "I know you got your hands full with the City Club and you got things pretty much how you want it, but I was wondering if we could build an extension to this nice facility to serve as a health clinic mainly for seniors. That way we could help give our elders that need check-ups and what not a place to go when they can't get all the way to Henry Ford Hospital and the like." Mama E stepped into the middle of the hallway, then walked back into Frank's office where she had cornered him, faced the window looking out to the field and said "Right here Frank. Put the extension right here so that it can extend out to the field."

"I love it. Let me give that some thought," said Frank.

At the end of the day, as the three Waterman children stood alone in the lobby entrance, Denise said, "See, Dad really can work miracles, I told you."

"Mom did it," Jon-Jon insisted.

"No, it was Dad," said Denise.

"Mom."

"Dad."

"Girl, Mom be on that rosary, Dad just put in the elbow grease."

CHAPTER 16 -
Keys to the Castle -
June 1968

FRANK KNEW THAT HIS WORK AT City Club was about to be much more demanding. If last week's grand opening was any indication of what was to come, he knew that he would be looking at wall-to-wall kids for the rest of the summer. But with Frank and Rose intent on sending their own kids to the newly-created St. Martin DePorres High School, he would try to somehow remain active in the school's affairs. Frank, still on the parish council, felt obligated to see the process through. He was confident that the team made a good choice in hiring Jim Dunham to lead the school.

Frank offered to drive Ted Wilson and Jim Dunham to the rectory so that Jim could sign the contract agreement between the church and the new school with Father O'Malley, the long-time Visitation priest. Father O'Malley, near 60, had a head of gray hair, and stood about 6'5". He was assigned to Visitation about 25 years ago, in 1943, after completing his studies in his hometown, Boston, then Rome. His big interests were Latin and European history. Father O'Malley's younger assistant, Father Thom Kelly, was out of the country on a mission to Central America. As the three men approached the rectory, Mr. Dunham asked, "Is this my swearing-in ceremony?"

"You got it," Ted laughed. The rectory was located directly across the street from the church and school campus. The rectory's front yard was well maintained by one of the parishioners. Bright yellow tulips lined the sidewalk leading to the front porch. A couple of lush green ferns hung on the porch in front of a dingy old sofa. The well-manicured lawn complemented the bright red bricks and fresh white paint around the trim.

Father O'Malley's 1966 Ford LTD, with bucket seats, was parked in the open garage as was Father Kelly's 1963 Falcon. They were greeted by Paul, who attended the former Visitation High School and worked as an assistant to Father O'Malley. Paul's skin looked red, as if he'd spent a lot of time in the sun. Frank recognized Paul from the recreation center where he worked as a lifeguard.

"Hi, Paul," said Frank. Ted pulled open the screen door. "We're here to meet with Father O'Malley."

"Come right this way, gentlemen. He's expecting you." Once inside, the aroma of fresh-baked cookies greeted the senses—a sweet tooth's dream. Paul escorted the men past the small, intimate living room and into the spacious dining room. The large overhanging crystal chandelier hung about head level providing ample light. The deep burgundy carpet contrasted well with the ebony dining room furniture. The oversized end chairs looked like something out of a medieval European castle. Curly Cornell was already waiting, sitting at the far end of the table with his pen and paper at the ready.

Ted opened the conversation. "Jim, you remember Curly Cornell. Curly's the new board chair of St. Martin DePorres. He'll serve a four-year term with the option of running for a second two-year term after which he'll step down automatically. Other board members like me are elected to either a three-year term or two-year term." As the two men extended their hands to shake, Curly interrupted.

"It works like this, gentlemen. We have staggered terms for the board members, five two-year terms, and five three-year terms. We'll be able to keep our continuity and bring in some new voices this way. Have a seat, Jim, Frank, Ted. Father will be with us momentarily. Would anyone like a soft drink? The men nodded in favor. "Miss Kathy, can you please bring us a Vernors?" Miss Kathy, a frail, elderly white woman near eighty, kept the place immaculate. She'd been living at the rectory for the past four years, ever since one of the parishioners found her sleeping in the church. She was widowed at seventy and lost everything she had. Miss Kathy delivered a pitcher of Vernors and a tray of cookies. The men thanked her graciously.

"Damn, Curly, you got clout," Ted said with a cynical laugh.

"Gentlemen," Curly reasserted himself in a serious tone, "Father's on the phone with the cardinal. Cardinal Beardum has taken a keen interest in this experiment. We must not disappoint him."

Frank thought, *what the hell is this man talking about – an experiment –* as he noticed the other men with puzzled looks on their faces. Father O'Malley entered the room as if he had just finished a race.

"Good afternoon, gentlemen." He welcomed each with a hearty handshake. "Sorry to keep you all waiting. We have so much tragedy right before our eyes. Dr. King and now another Kennedy boy taken from us. Such a tragedy. We're having a special memorial service this Friday night for those who want to attend. I said mass at the Kennedy family church once," Father O'Malley reflected. "Well. Ted, Frank, good to see you and Mr. Dunham. What a pleasure to have you on board. We look forward to your leadership at the school. The kids certainly stand to gain."

"That's why I'm here," said Mr. Dunham. "And you can call me Jim."

"The cardinal and I were just discussing the school. We need to go over a few details before we give you the keys to the castle," Father O'Malley said, laughing. You've been hired, as you know, for a five-year term, renewable of course."

"Yes, I'm very excited about that, and I appreciate this opportunity to help our young people develop their whole selves. We have great facilities here. But, I noticed the sign on the church still reads Visitation, while the school sign reads St. Martin DePorres," said Jim Dunham.

"Of course, of course," said Father O'Malley, "You're wondering what the hell is going on here. Well, here's how it works. The church will remain Visitation and continue to serve its function for all those long-time parishioners. They wouldn't go along with a name change. Now, as stated in the contract before you, the school will rent the church as needed."

"And we get the recreation center, right?" asked Jim.

The Visitation Recreation Center was the crown jewel in the neighborhood. Built in 1959, it had been meticulously maintained. It contained a 2,000-person capacity gym, an Olympic-sized swimming pool, an eight-lane bowling alley, four handball/squash courts, ping-pong tables, a pool room, a lounge, and several meeting rooms. Father O'Malley said, "The recreation center belongs to the church, as you well know, and will be leased to the school."

"Wait a minute, the school, the school has to pay to use its own gym? This doesn't add up," Jim protested. "Father, how can the church rent to itself?"

"Look, the church is already making the school available at no cost. We're still paying for the construction of the center." Frank rolled his eyes and leaned back and looked over to Ted.

"Father, I've been a parishioner here for nearly eight years, and none of this makes sense to me. I thought we were all one unit." said Frank, puzzled.

"We are one unit. And the church is bending over backwards to keep it that way, I assure you." Curly fidgeted in his chair and looked uncomfortable with the level of tension over the use of the recreation center. He spoke up.

"Gentlemen, understand the difficult position you are putting Father O'Malley in. He said the church is bending over backwards. We should be damn thankful!" he added. "And the school board already approved it. Ted, you look surprised."

"Who sets the rate?" Ted asked.

"Ted, that's out of our hands. You know that. It's done downtown," said Curly.

Jim jumped back in the conversation. "How can the school afford this? We have the lowest tuition in the diocese."

"The terms are spelled out in the contract. You've got three months before your first payment," Father added. "Sure, I would love to give you the keys and say go for it. The neighborhood needs it. But, somebody's got to pay for the water, the lights. Let's face it. The parish is shrinking, our revenues are down. And look, many of these old parishioners want to keep things the way they were. They don't understand change. They're not comfortable with this new black thing."

"Yeah, it's a new black thing," Jim Dunham fired back, "and we're in the middle of a rev—," Curly cut him off.

"We have a lot to get through today, Jim we still have a ways to go."

"Okay, what's next?"

"Next," Father continued, "we have provided the school with several teachers who are nuns and priests. They are all very qualified. One doctorate, and a couple have their masters in education. On page three, you'll find that you can hire and fire the lay teachers. You and the board will go through the applications, but as principal, the ultimate decision is yours. Read over the contract, and as soon as you sign it, the keys are yours." Curly immediately distributed another document.

"This second document is the curriculum guidelines," Father O'Malley said. "There is some flexibility, but as we know the archdiocese has high standards." Father O'Malley then exited the room through the swinging door connecting to the kitchen. The men overheard him thanking Paul for the freshly-baked cookies. "Paul I wouldn't know what to do without you."

Jim read each page, then passed them one at a time to Frank, who did the same for Ted. "Haven't you seen this"? Frank asked Ted.

"No, only Curly has seen it." Curly was lurking in the hallway, not quite out of sight, but not in the room with the other men.

"Only the chair was privy to these details before now," Curly said.

"Curly," Ted said, "come on man, quit this sucking up. You're acting like the class pet or something."

"Do you want my job, Ted? You want my job? You know how hard I have worked here at the parish. Now with the new school, we have a chance to prove to the whites that we can handle our own affairs. We can develop our kids to compete at all the universities throughout this great nation. We can get these kids into the Harvard's, Yale's, and Princeton's — on their academic merit. No, not everyone, but for those who aspire, we can push them with our honors program – as you will read about in the contract document. The honors and college prep program at St. Martin DePorres will be second to none in a few years. Black Catholics will have their place in the sun."

Curly began to sound like he was arguing before a jury. Mr. Dunham looked up from the contract, then back down. He signed it, then leaned back with both hands behind his head and said to Curly Cornell, "I've looked over this curriculum guide, Curly, and it's right out of Brother Rice Prep or Catholic Central."

"Top shelf isn't it?" Curly boasted. "We want St Martin DePorres to be that shining light – up from the ashes of 12th Street, like a Phoenix rising . . . " Ted snapped his fingers.

"Yo, Curly, snap out of it, man. Mr. Dunham is the expert on education here. He's been doing this for what, eight, ten years?"

"That's right," Jim added, "and we don't need all this to be great. Latin, classical music lessons, an orchestra. You all hired me to give these kids the very best education they could get, and they will get that." Father O'Malley returned to the room before Curly could respond.

"Do we have a deal, Mr. Dunham, uh Jim?"

"Yes, Father, we got a deal." They shook on it.

"Then here are the keys to the castle."

"Oh, one more thing," said Curly. "Here's the book for uniform selection." He handed Mr. Dunham a catalog of uniforms as the men got up to leave. "I circled my choices, so let me know what you think."

Frank headed for the door as he heard Father O'Malley say to Paul, "Show the men out Paul. Then you and I can go for a drive. I'm going to teach you how to drive a stick yet." Paul appeared from the kitchen all smiles.

"Mr. Waterman, Mr. Wilson, and Mr. Dunham, right this way."

Frank said, "See you Sunday, Father." Frank knew he would see him again at Sunday Mass and after mass for fellowship over coffee and donuts. Ted thanked Father O'Malley for his time and commitment, then turned to Curly and said, "You got this all figured out, don't you?"

"Yes, I do. I have to, because that's what it takes. Mr. Dunham, call me tonight so we can finalize the uniform selection."

"Okay, and the books?"

"You got that information in your packet, too. Work with your assistant principal, Sister JoAnna. I believe you two will meet tomorrow."

"Yeah, that's right".

"Thanks, Paul. Will we be seeing you this fall at St. Martin DePorres?" asked Frank.

"Uh, no sir, I'll be attending Brother Rice Prep next year. I'll be on their swim team."

"Oh, okay, well, good luck." Curly walked to the back of the rectory where he parked his new 1967 Chrysler Newport. Frank, Ted, and Jim climbed in Frank's Fury III.

"Let's stop at the Collingwood Bar," Ted recommended.

"We need to talk some things through. I can see right now that Curly wants to ramrod this shit down my throat, and that's not what I signed up for. Has anyone else looked at this?" Jim asked, as they rode over to the bar.

Jim flipped through the catalog. "Hey, look, maybe Curly helped save the school from closing, but he don't own it. St Martin DePorres is not Catholic Central. Black people - yeah, I said black - black folks are on the verge of a revolution, man. I ain't gonna ask them to walk around dressed like some white suburban kids wearing penny loafers, white shirts and blue slacks."

"But the kids need a uniform," Ted asserted. "It's part of the archdiocese dress code."

"That's right, a uniform, not any of these uniforms. We have to set our own standards." Frank found a parking space almost directly in front of the bar on the corner of 12th Street and Collingwood. The bar's large picture windows were boarded up and freshly painted a dull brown. They had been boarded up since the riot, with SOUL BROTHER written boldly across the front for protection. The front looked recently cleaned. The three got out and made their way to a corner table in the dimly lit lounge and bar. A waitress was there to greet them.

"Hey sister, you wearin' that natural," Jim commented. She smiled back bashfully,

"Hi, I'm Bonnie, can I get you all a menu?"

Ted asked the others what they were drinking. They all ordered a round of the locally brewed Stroh's beer.

Jim seemed mesmerized by the waitress's brown-glazed glow and almond-shaped eyes.

"Jim," snapped Frank, "how the hell are we gonna make these finances work? And tell us what you think it'll take to make a solid curriculum for our kids? You're bringing some great credentials to the table – a double masters in educational psychology and secondary education."

"First," Jim paused, then spoke slowly, "I want to let you know how humbled I am to be given this opportunity. I am not going to squander my time. These kids need to be challenged. And we must have high expectations. But the same ol' shit is not going to work. Can you dig it? And the finances. We'll have to pull some rabbits out the hat, man. We're starting off with a huge load on our shoulders. We'll need to talk in more depth about the finances —

maybe tomorrow. But as far as the uniform goes, we'll go with dress shirts, ties and hardsole shoes for the boys, skirts – knee level, and white blouses for the girls. No sneakers and no jeans. It'll be real cool, believe me."

"And what about the curriculum?" Frank asked.

"Right, I'm really gonna need y'all on this one. I'm struggling with this Latin requirement. Is that an archdiocese rule?"

Bonnie brought over a tray of drinks, gave each one of the men eye contact and a smile as she placed the glasses on coasters.

"Would you like to see the menu?" she politely asked again, still smiling as she reached for the menus under her arm.

"Ted?" The men looked to Ted for direction because he was a regular.

"The wings are outta sight."

"We'll go with the wings, all of us," said Frank.

"Great, I'll be right back."

"Gotta have wings to fly." Jim added.

CHAPTER 17 -
The Bar-B-Q

MIKE FELT RESTED EVEN THOUGH HE'D been up since 5 A.M. to do his paper route. He stayed up to mow the grass. That afternoon, the Watermans were hosting a big Independence Day cookout. Before Mike started to mow, he oiled between the wheels just as he'd always done. He hitched up the bag to catch the grass clippings. He filed the blades a week ago and knew they were still sharp.

As Mike started to mow the grass he could not help but notice his parents on the front porch laughing while having coffee and donuts. He wondered what on earth was so funny. They were on their way to Eastern Market to pick up a few last-minute supplies. The grass wasn't very high so Mike adjusted the blade so he wouldn't cut it too close. He pushed the mower evenly as the blades cut the grass like a hot knife through butter. Cutting the grass had become so routine he daydreamed while doing it. He clicked on auto-pilot. Mike started thinking about seeing Ted Wilson's daughters. He had seven. But who knew which ones would show up. Five had already graduated from Visitation, two were college graduates and three in college. One of the girls, Robin, the youngest, would start St. Martin DePorres with Mike and another would be in her junior year.

Mike finished the front yard before the sun could rise above the nearby houses and trees. Thank goodness, because it had been pretty darn hot lately, near a hundred degrees. Mike checked his yard work by walking across the street and standing on his neighbor's porch. He panned the entire front. "Beautiful," he said aloud, "simply beautiful". He wanted his lawn to have that manicured look, like so many of the neighbors. He especially wanted to please his dad who had a knack for perfection.

Now the back, he thought. There was much less cutting to be done in the back – only the grass between the rows of rose bushes. As Mike walked to the back, he saw Jon-Jon stumbling out the house, hair uncombed, like he just woke up. "Wake up boy. Dad said he wants you to get the grills out and make sure they're clean."

As Mike cut and edged the strips of grass, he wondered whether 'bad ass' Becky and her family, the Drumbrowski's, were coming. They usually did. Their families had been doing this Independence Day cookout together for five years now – not long after Mike's dad started working for Becky's dad, at Statewide Insurance. Mike liked Becky and Becky liked him. At least that's what she told him. But that's about as far as it got. Mike never forgot the severe reprimand he received from his mother after going on a hike with Becky at the company picnic two years ago. He'd never heard his mother issue such a stern warning or seen his mother look so afraid. She said that she thought the worse. Maybe they had run into a couple of white men who didn't like Mike walking with this white girl. Maybe they got caught kissing or something and some crazed white boys, maybe in a drunken stupor, got jealous and decided to mete out some punishment on Mike. Rose met them both before they got back to the picnic site. She told Becky to keep going; she wanted a word with her son. As soon as Becky walked out of earshot, she looked sternly at Mike and told him in no uncertain terms, never to let this happen again — goin' off with a white girl, especially out here. This is Klan Country she told him, even though the picnic site was right outside Detroit in Brighton, Michigan. "White men have strung up black boys by their private parts just for looking at white girls. Do you understand? Remember Emmitt Till." She went on to say, "I pray every day that you children are not a victim of their ignorance. And I've told you before, the Klan is rampant throughout the police department - everywhere. DO YOU UNDERSTAND ME?" She demanded an answer. Mike remembered how meekly he responded as if he were some kind of baby, "Yes Mommy."

"Yes, Mommy what?"

"Yes, Mommy I won't go off with Becky like this again." His mother blew an obvious sigh of relief.

~ ~ ~ ~ ~ ~ ~

Mike saw Becky only once since then, at the company Christmas party. He told her they should remain friends even if all they did was talk on the phone. "You mean that you'll never come out to our farm and chase me through the cornfields," she joked.

Mike wiped his brow and said, "No cornfields, Becky. You still think it's funny my moms told me I'd get hung by my privates just for looking at you wrong." Mike heard a sniffle. Her eyes welled up with tears.

She said, "You know my dad looks at your dad like he's a brother. Did you know that?" Her voice cracked with emotion.

"Well then I guess that settles it. What I look like chasin' my cousin through the cornfields. What if I catch you, then what?" Becky just looked teary-eyed, then she let out a wail and walked off. Mike didn't know what to think because he'd never seen anyone well up with tears over him. Then to ease her pain he hollered out, "I'll call you, I promise." Becky kept walking without even turning around.

Later that morning Mike walked over towards the garage, noticed it had been thoroughly cleaned out, then watched his dad place a slab of marinated ribs on the large grill he kept in the garage. Jon-Jon had cleaned it off and set it near the rear of the driveway near the alley. Frank had all his supplies laid out along with the two smaller grills he used for hamburgers, hot dogs and heating side dishes. His cooking order was always the same: ribs first, then chicken and Polish sausage. He put on the hot dogs and hamburgers when he figured folks were hungry.

Mama E made the sides - collards and candied yams - the kind that made you foam at the mouth once you came in contact with the scent. Rose supplied the desserts. Her specialty was pecan cake. This incredibly tantalizing cake could leave you toothless in ten years. She prepared it to look similar to brownies. She got the secret recipe from Mama E. Rose told her children that one day she would pass it on to Denise just as her mother – Mama E passed it on to her.

Jon-Jon set up his turntable and speakers inside the garage. He turned the mike on and went straight into his DJ 'thang'. His new JBL speakers were booming. "I want y'all to sit back, relax and enjoy some bar-b-que today cause I'm gonna be kickin' out your favorite Motown hits. My name is Jon-Jon the Music Man, live at the Waterman Palace. Don't be shy, there's plenty of good food to give you a natural high. You gotta try the candied yams," said Jon–Jon, while laughing. "And there's plenty of drink to fill your tank. We got the ping-pong tournament goin on beyond the grill, checkers and dominoes set up along side the house. And anyone for darts – head to the basement. The limbo contest starts at noon. We got something for everyone." He put on the Jr. Walker and the AllStars' hit song *Roadrunner*.

~ ~ ~ ~ ~ ~ ~

As Mike watched his dad turn over the ribs, Frank said, "Your mother thinks you'll have a heart attack if you don't get to play football and how you 'bout to eat us outta house and home." Mike, now six feet tall and going into the ninth grade. "She had me crackin' up on the porch this morning. Your mom thinks I got you on a special diet."

"Only the Joe Weider powder," said Mike. Then he added, "And the weights. Dad, football practice starts August 15th, I got five weeks to be ready to face the heat, the coach, and all that competition out there."

"I know, your mother never thought you would play football; maybe basketball or even baseball.

But lately we noticed you've been talking all about DeAngelo's brother Darren and his football playing days with the West Side Cubs, a Detroit Pop Warner Little League team, Visitation, and Michigan State University. I know he's filling your head up and you look up to him. And I understand Darren's former coach from the West Side Cubs is now St. Martin DePorres' new head football coach. That means that St. Martin DePorres has got the best coach in town." Frank flipped the ribs over once again using both hands, a long fork in one and a large clasp in the other.

The heat from the grill made Mike's forehead bead up with sweat. He pulled the wash cloth from his back pocket, poured some water on it and wiped his forehead cooling him off. Mike wanted to play for the West Side Cubs before he turned fourteen but was always over the weight limit.

"Dad, I want to play college, then pro." Dreams of being the next Paul Warfield and catching that long touchdown pass flashed through Mike's head.

"Yeah, I want you to play college ball too and if you want to dream big and think pro, ain't nothing wrong with that either, but you got to learn geometry first, understand?"

"Yeah," said Mike. "I got to learn those angles to the endzone."

"Ha, I'm thinking more like when you finish playing ball you better have some skills under your belt so you can put food on the table. Remember that. I want you to do well but don't get too cockeyed about it. There's more to life than football and basketball."

Mike looked up and saw the Wilsons coming up the driveway and into the backyard. Robin, the youngest, 14, Ronnie, 16, and Rhea 19 strode in like a walking rainbow with their yellow, purple and orange short sets. All three of the girls were tall, with long beautiful dark legs that glistened in the sun. Rhea wore her hair in a natural while the younger two had their hair parted in the middle, curly locks hanging down each side. Mike knew he would be seeing a lot more of Robin and Ronnie at school in the fall. The Wilsons made their way into the yard to mingle with Rose, Mama E and a few neighbors including Delli. The Wilson daughters stood together like they were posing for a Miss Universe pageant. Mike hollered back to Jon-Jon. "Play some Temptations – *Ain't too Proud to Beg."*

Jon-Jon played Mike's request then walked up beside him and said. "My beautiful black sisters." Jon-Jon nudged Mike on the shoulder and said, "There's that bad-ass Becky comin' up the driveway with her family." Becky and Mike acknowledged each other at a distance with a smile and a wave, but Becky turned into the yard where everyone was gathering and talking. Jerry Drumbrowski reached for a beer in the cooler, then headed back to the grill to talk trash with Frank. The boys greeted Mr. Drumbrowski and shook his hand.

"So Mike what you gonna do about Becky?" asked Jon-Jon. Mike watched her in her white summer dress as she sprung into her natural flair and started conversing with the Wilson girls.

"Man, we're finished before we got started, thank Mom for that. Becky's over me anyway."

"Oh, wasn't it about getting strung up by your wee wee?" Jon-Jon asked.

"Yep, Mom freaked out. But I ain't given up my wee wee." Mike grabbed his crotch. Then said, "Bump that. But check this, our families are best friends but no dating. Thang is, we all like family, Sharon, Becky, the Wilson girls, shit even the bakery girl, Renee. Ain't that 'bout nothing."

Jon-Jon said, "I hear ya bro., but I got to keep the rhythm and the flow. I got some Smokey, Marvin, and some Gladys Knight and the Pips, then I'm gonna get real funky and play some Parliament, *Testify.* Later, brother."

"Later."

"Luke, what's the deal?" Luke walked in with his pockets full, looking like a squirrel that gathered nuts. They gave each other the black power shake. Mike learned it after the rebellion last year: A regular shake first, then a grip around the thumbs, then another regular shake, then a grip with the fingers. Shaking hands became a new art form in the hood, very unlike the standard handshake.

"Hey man, I got cherry bombs, hammer heads, M-80's." Luke displayed his cache of Independence Day fireworks. Mike and Luke loaded tennis balls with the bombs and tossed several of them down the alley, then returned and ate plenty of the ribs, sweet potatoes, and pecan cake. After getting full on food and fun the families headed down to the Detroit River for the evening fireworks.

"Me and all my sisters," Mike said to Luke.

"Yeah, no shit," said Luke, They slapped palms and laughed.

CHAPTER 18 -
Boys to Men

"GET UP MIKE," SAID FRANK. IT was already seven o'clock in the morning. Football practice began at eight. "It's time to play with the big boys," said Frank.

Mike rolled over with a wide grin on his face knowing he couldn't wait. But Mike also felt butterflies in his stomach. He tightened his stomach muscles, raised his legs six inches off the bed, then raised his torso to make a V-shape with his body. He pounded his stomach muscles the way Darren had showed him. He pictured the butterflies turning to eagles.

Mike bolted into the hall towards the bathroom, "Dad, gotta call the fellas. Man, I can't wait. Yes!!" said Mike flapping his arms like wings. "This eagle is ready to fly." As he entered the bathroom, Mike looked into the mirror and repeated the advice his dad gave him last night. The words were still fresh on his mind, *"Son, your internal compass must guide you and help you navigate through the treacherous waters. Just like the elders once told you, it's a minefield out there and sometimes you do nothing but lay your foot down in the wrong place at the wrong time . . . "* This eagle's 'bout to navigate, Mike thought.

DeAngelo and Luke showed up at the Waterman's house like clockwork. Once on the practice field, Mr. Taylor, the new head coach began checking in all the tryouts.

"Okay, step up, how many of you have been accepted to St. Martin DePorres? Let's see your registration. Got to be registered to practice." Mike couldn't wait until the moment came. Playing for Coach Taylor, what a dream. Coach Taylor, who towered over the boys, looked them up and down and said quite bluntly, "Let's see your registration." Mike and Luke produced their crumpled up slips of paper. But DeAngelo didn't have his paper work.

"Where's your paperwork Son?"

"Well," DeAngelo began nervously, "well Coach, well my parents, my folks, aren't sure yet. They'll decide today. I know they'll say yes."

"Son, see me after you register for school. Ain't nothing I can do. I ain't even supposed to look at you. Everybody else get in line for drills. All y'all is, is fresh meat to me, now gimme ten laps. Two by two, that's right find somebody to run with." Mike paired up with Luke.

"Man, what's up with DeAngelo?" asked Mike. "I thought he was coming to DePorres."

Luke said, "I heard his father say he wasn't thinking about sending him to no Catholic school like they did Darren. His mom was all for it just like she was for Darren, but his father told DeAngelo he wasn't nothing but a sissy for going to Catholic school all his life and wouldn't amount to nothing."

"What!! His father's a drunk. Look at Darren." exclaimed Mike. "We can go toe-to-toe with any public school in the city. I'll put money on it."

Luke said, "Oh Mike, toe-to-toe in what, b-ball? Football? Fighting? Or are you talking about a spelling bee? How're we gonna prove we can go toe-to-toe? We don't play the public school league anymore. Ever since that white dude got killed, man we don't even scrimmage against the public schools. This is Coach Taylor's first year and he's just getting started."

"But we got all the top Catholic schools right here," explained Mike, who felt like he was coming into his own. He stood a lean six feet, 185 lbs. His dream was to break all school records in as many sports as he could. Wow! Wearing medals and stripes all over his school sweater would be cool. Just like his heroes at Visitation used to do. Mike laid on the grass after his first practice thinking of the days when Alan Akers and Jeff Dillon used to walk the halls with an arm full of stripes and all sorts of medals dangling from their varsity sweaters. Alan and Jeff were state champs in the long jump, the 440, 880, the mile relay. Stripes for all-state, all-American, in football, track and basketball. *I can see it now*, Mike thought to himself.

"Get up, boy, you're killing the grass," Coach Taylor shouted, "I know you ain't tired after a few wind sprints. You ain't seen nothing yet".

Mike hopped up, "I was just thinking . . . "

"Thinking, you ain't got time to think, go get on the bus, we're heading back to the locker room."

"But my dad is over there to take me back," Mike said.

"Son, your dad left you here with me. And don't forget our Saturday night unity sessions, we're gonna go over some plays and get acquainted with one another." Mike already felt like one of the fellas.

During the bus ride back to school, Coach Taylor stood up to speak to the players: "This is gonna be our first year as St. Martin DePorres, but that doesn't make any difference to me. I was selected to coach because I had a great record with the West Side Cubs football club and I presented the best overall program for the school. My program is about winning. It's about making winners out you boys. Winners not just in the game of football but in the game of life. I love to win. I love to win and I hate to lose. I like a good game, I like a clean game but I want us to come out on top. You've got to give 120 percent if you want to play for me, not 99 not even 100 percent. You've got to stretch, you've got to go beyond the call of duty. That's what I expect. And I will send your butt home if I think you're cheating. All right, repeat after me. I love to win."

"I love to win." The entire team shouted back.

"I love to win, and I hate to lose."

"I love to win, and I hate to lose."

"We can't lose."

"We can't lose."

"With the stuff we use."

"With the stuff we use."

Mike joined in with the team chant . . . "win, win, win, win, win . . . "

Coach Taylor allowed DeAngelo to ride back on the bus with the team since Mr. Waterman had basically dropped the boys off and went on about his business. DeAngelo rarely showed any emotion but today he was nearly in tears.

The coach, still standing facing the boys said, "St. Martin DePorres WILL be a powerhouse. Not because we have the best raw talent but because we got the best coaches, we got the best fundamentals and most importantly we're gonna play with the biggest heart." Mike felt a tingling down his spine rubbing elbows with the varsity players.

~ ~ ~ ~ ~ ~ ~

The next two weeks were brutal under the hot summer sun. Practice went from a week of twice a day to a week of three practices a day. After the morning practice which ended at eleven o'clock. Mike had enough time to walk home, eat a light lunch, gush down some Gatorade, then pass out for about an hour. He returned for an afternoon skull (strategy) session that went from two until four o'clock. An evening session of full contact followed from four-thirty until six-thirty.

Mike buried his face in the grass during one of the morning sessions. Just ten more seconds, he thought, just enough time to catch a second wind. Mike took a deep breath and tried to forget the aches and pains of full contact football. Mike knew he had to get up and get back to the huddle despite the pain he felt from the hard tackle delivered by senior strong-safety Jason Tyler. Mike made the catch and held on to the ball. *This should go a long way towards proving myself as varsity material,* he thought, as he struggled to get up. He pulled himself up and ran back to the huddle. Sweat dripped through his helmet and ran down his face and into his eyes. Mike reached for the only dry patch of jersey, tucked deep into his pants, to wipe his face. He pulled off his helmet and wiped his forehead dry. He caught Coach Taylor glaring at him. Mike quickly placed his helmet back on his drenched head. Mike felt a quick, but short term relief.

"Okay," the coach whispered in the huddle, "give me a 99 2X Slant."

"On one, break," said the quarterback. The defensive back played Mike close. The second and third team offense, which Mike rotated into, was working against the first team defense. "Ready-set," the quarterback barked out, "hut." Mike remembered to take one quick step forward. The defensive back tried to jam Mike into his own players. Mike slanted right away. The quarterback faked to Mike and threw the ball downfield instead, because the defense read the play perfectly. Then out of nowhere — BAM!! Mike felt like he was hit by a freight train. Mike's guts might as well have ended up on the grass next to him. He curled up like a baby in the womb.

"You can't waltz up in here boy. I'm the new 'night train', said the senior all-conference linebacker, Bruce Lightfoot, referring to Dick "Nighttrane" Lane, an all-pro cornerback of the Detroit Lions.

One of the coaches yelled out, "Do we need to call 911 or what? Are you still with us son?" Mike rolled over to his side, he staggered up, then stumbled over to the sideline where everyone else headed. He held in his tears and pain. Mike remembered his fathers words to *be strong and never cry in public.*

"That's enough scrimmage for today, line up for wind sprints." Mike pushed himself during the final wind sprints, making noises and ugly faces trying to finish near the front to impress the coaches. On the last sprint Mike dived across the finish line trying to beat the fleet-footed senior wide receiver Jack Adams — an early pick for all-state track in the 100 and 220 yard dash. Big Jeff, the starting defensive end finished last. He could barely walk. He grabbed his gut, bent over and started hacking. He stopped and coughed up globs of blood then fell forward and hit the ground like a giant oak tree.

An assistant yelled out, "Somebody call me an ambulance."

"We ain't got time for that," said Coach Taylor. "I want y'all to lift him into the wagon and get him down to Henry Ford emergency right now. Shit, do a 100 miles an hour if you have to." Several of the assistants went into action right away bringing the station wagon over to where Big Jeff collapsed, while other coaches kept the players back.

"Give the boy some air," one coach screamed out. The defensive coach

Mr. Walters opened the back hatch and laid down the middle seat providing a bed for Big Jeff. They struggled to lift the 300-pounder into the wagon and get him stable. One of the coaches stayed in the back while one rode in the front with the driver.

"Call his parents when you get there," said Coach Taylor as he handed one of his assistants the players personal emergency information. "Take some water." Everyone on the team watched in quiet disbelief. "Think I've seen enough for one day," said Coach Taylor. "Everybody on the bus."

On the ride back to the school Coach stressed the importance of keeping oneself hydrated, drink water or Gatorade he said over and over. Mike felt at ease when Coach told everyone with reassurance that Big Jeff would be alright. Then he started ranting about diet and how teens drink too much pop. He told the team to throw the pop and the chips away and eat plenty protein foods like eggs, sausage, Wheaties, and oatmeal. Then at the end of the ride to the locker room he said with a solemn face, "I don't ever want to see what happened today happen again."

As they were getting off the bus, Luke, who seemed to be doing alright on the junior varsity team, told Mike that he decided to quit.

Luke said, "Man, I can't take this. You see what happened to Big-Boy Jeff? Shit, that big motherfucker went down. I'm through with this shit, done Mike. I'm 'bout to throw my guts up on this damn bus. I'm done." Mike kept walking off the bus without saying a word.

CHAPTER 19 -
St. Martin DePorres (The Big DP)

THE INSIDE OF ST. MARTIN DEPORRES, the old Visitation building, must've been scrubbed from top to bottom because the school looked cleaner than Mike had ever seen it. Mike smelled the fresh blue and gold paint as he walked down the crowded hallway. St. Martin DePorres looked and smelled different than the old Visitation. Even the fire escape ladders shined like new. There was not a single piece of trash or broken glass in the parking lot. Signs were posted: "Take Pride – Keep Your School Clean." Mike especially liked the giant eagle, freshly painted above the principal's office with the words, "We Are the Mighty Eagles." The tile floors looked spit-polished. Mike thought, *this doesn't even look like Visitation.* Everything seemed different. Volunteers repainted the restroom, where Mike witnessed the school invasion five years earlier, sky blue with a navy blue trim. They put new stall doors in place. And instead of windows, artwork covered the now-bricked off windows. Murals graced many of the hallways. Mike heard that a team of college and high school artists were asked to design and paint the murals throughout the school. Mr. Dunham accepted offers from several area colleges and universities - Mercy, Marygrove, University of Detroit, and Wayne State University - to paint the murals. The Detroit Institute of Arts along with some local black artists helped finance and oversee the project. One wall read SOUL BROTHER! SOUL SISTER! along with images of a black man and woman. Another mural read Right On! with a picture of a man giving the Black Power salute. Another mural had images of Detroit's Motown recording artists, yet another showed an eagle in flight pulling a rope of people holding on upwards into the sky and out of collapsed buildings with the caption above it that read "Out of the Ashes — We Rise."

Mike had never seen so many happy people. The new teachers, white and black, priests and nuns, showed so much enthusiasm it seemed infectious. The school's senior class dressed in stylish clothes since the dress code only consisted of shirt and tie, slacks, no jeans, and hard sole shoes. Mike thought they looked cool with their short and long sleeve gabardine shirts, solid color ties, silk and wool slacks, complemented with polished Florshiem or Stacy Adams shoes. Some even wore gators or lizards. On the other hand, the girl's options were limited to navy blue skirts and white blouses. Mike felt good about his own collection of fine clothes from downtown Detroit's Broadway and Woodward Avenues.

The school books were so new that you could still smell the glue that bound them together. Mike had eight classes including two in physical education: one required physical education class and another elective called *Fundamentals of Football*. Mike looked forward to the regular stuff like math, science, English, history, French, and social studies. The teachers seemed to be dead-serious about school work even though the teachers loved to talk sports with the students. By the second day, Mike brought home an arm-load of books for homework, mostly reading assignments.

With all the assignments, Mike wondered if high school was going to be tough. He wondered about making new friends. And most of all, Mike wondered, *where on earth did all these fine young women come from?*

CHAPTER 20 -
Are the Eagles 'Gonna' Win It?

"DON'T FORGET, THE PEP RALLY'S AT two in the gym," said Todd, the senior tight end and captain of the team. "Everybody's fired up for our first game."

After social studies class, Mike rushed over to the gym for his first big event. He made varsity, the only freshman to make it. When Mike made it through the gym doors he could see the cheerleaders out on the floor dancing and waving their pom poms to the rhythm of James Brown's *Say it Loud, I'm Black and I'm Proud.*

Todd called Mike. "Come on up here Mike, you sit with the upperclassmen, the big dogs. Shit, you off the porch now baby. Ain't no turning back." The students were rocking back and forth to the beat. Mike felt that this was just the beginning of great things to come.

"I can't believe this man. This is hip. For a Catholic school this is hip," Mike said.

"Boy, this is hip for any school. We got the baddest cheerleaders in the world," Todd said. "Most of us been through this before, these pep rallies, at St. Teresa, but every year it gets better. And this year with the merger and Coach Taylor, man, the adrenaline is flowin'. Hey man," Todd continued, as he hollered over the music, "I'm grooming you for captain."

Mike smiled. The chant changed from 'Say it loud, I'm black and I'm proud' to 'say it loud, we eagles are proud.' Mr. Dunham ran in the gym as if he were a Las Vegas entertainer. He grabbed the mike and fell right in line with the chant. Soon he motioned to the DJ to turn the volume down.

"The eagle flies this Friday." Friday night we're gonna fly high. Everyone got quiet. Then Mr. Dunham belted out in his booming voice, *"Are the Eagles gonna win it"?* And the students replied,

"Hell yeah!"
"Are the eagles gonna win it?"
"Hell yeah!"

The call and response lasted a minute. Then the cheerleaders did a dance routine to the Temptations hit song *Get Ready*. When their dance routine ended, a tall brother with a eight inch Afro hairstyle, everyone called Bongo Bob, jumped from the stands with bongos in hand and played some African rhythms. The students went wild and the cheerleaders danced to the beat. People were falling all over each other to see.

Jim Dunham interrupted, "Yes, let's bring this spirit to the game Friday, let's bring this spirit to the game." He allowed the flow of enthusiasm to continue for the next few minutes.

Coach Taylor, who stood in front facing the football team, said to the team in a low voice, "You got to bring ass to kick ass, you got to bring ass to kick ass." As the students settled down, Mr. Dunham spoke in a very calm tone.

Mr. Dunham said, "These boys have been working their tails off, I've been to a few of their practices. They've come together in such a great way under the leadership of Coach Taylor and his staff. Last year, these boys played for several different schools. They played against each other but now we're one. And we have one goal - to do our absolute best. Tomorrow night, let's show Detroit, let's show the world what we're made of. Okay, okay, let's introduce our boys so you know who's under those big hard hats." As Coach Taylor went through the roster, Mike felt the butterflies, just like he'd felt the first day of practice. When Coach Taylor called his name, Mike felt his legs nearly give out as he stumbled down the bleachers to the team lineup along the gym floor.

"Hear we go, brothers and sisters," said Mr. Dunham. Mike felt the rush of his life, the adrenaline was flowing.

Coach Taylor was at the mike now. He spoke slowly, "One game at a time, one win at a time." Now the coach and Mr. Dunham were in harmony. "One game at a time, one win at a time." Coach Taylor turned towards the team and began his favorite chant, "I love to win" then the whole school responded with a thunderous roar,

"I love to win."

"I hate to lose," the coach said.

"I hate to lose," the school called back.

"We can't lose."

"We can't lose."

"With the stuff we use."

"With the stuff we use."

Then out to the middle of the gym came Bongo Bob, playing his bongos, and getting the students all riled up in a wild African dancing frenzy. Then, the student body turned its attention towards the cheerleaders.

"Let's introduce this year's super cheerleaders," Mr. Dunham said. The cheerleaders had left the gym to make their grand entrance. The cheerleaders made their entrée back into the gym to the sound of Curtis Mayfield, *We're A Winner.* The music rang out over the public address system as the elegant looking cheerleaders walked in with all their poise and grace, and afros leaping into outer space. Mike knew that he was part of something big.

"These ladies look like royalty!" Mike said to Todd.

"They are royalty." They slapped palms and shook their heads in agreement. The pep rally ended at three o'clock, just in time for school dismissal. Mike had never experienced this level of intensity and enthusiasm. He left the gym with goose bumps on his arms. As some of the football players filed out, all Mike could hear was which cheerleader belonged to whom. Mike didn't express any interest in any particular cheerleader. He was in such awe of the celebration he had to remind himself he made the varsity squad and tomorrow he would be playing on special teams - the kickoff and kick return teams, punt teams. Tomorrow night he'd be part of something special at McCabe Field under the lights.

The Eagles won that night, 21-20. They beat Sacred Heart of Livonia.

CHAPTER 21 -
The Ice Breaker

MIKE'S CLASSMATE BILL, PLANNED A HOUSE party on Saturday after the first game to celebrate the opening of the season and serve as an ice-breaker party for all the new freshman students. Bill and his main man, Duane, another freshman, were the party hosts.

The party that night was full of energy as the football team won the game by one point in the final seconds. Before Mike could get all the way into the basement party room, he heard a voice call out. "Pssst, pssst, come over here, Mike," said Duane. "Come here, my brother. Congratulations, y'all did it. We got our first victory."

"Thanks, my man," said Mike. The two classmates gave each other the black power handshake.

"Hey Mike, got something I want you to check out." The music of Sly and the Family Stone's *Sex Machine* played in the background. Sly Stone's hit *Sex Machine* caught everybody's attention with the new electric guitar sound. The basement was packed. Mike felt the energy of the crowd rocking the joint. "You ever try this shit?" Duane held out a bottle of Boone's Farm Strawberry Hill wine. Before Mike could answer, Duane said, "My brother, let me pour you a cup." Duane had a way of making everyone feel special. He had a gift of gab and a voice that could match the smooth silky voice of Eddie Kendricks of the Temptations. Mike froze in place. He didn't know whether to keep going or indulge his curiosity. Duane sat on a stool in what looked like a closet. It looked big enough for only two people. Mike entered the tight space and accepted the drink.

Sounding nice and proper Duane said, "Let's toast to you making the varsity football team your freshman year. What a great accomplishment my brother! You're the only freshman on varsity."

Duane finished off his second bottle. They drank. And they drank some more. The two were drunk. Mike felt pretty loose. And Duane was laughing at everyone that walked past. Mike fixed his eyes on the beautiful women coming and going from the basement but did not say a word. But when one sister stepped in like the Queen of Sheba, her striking beauty mesmerized Mike. Her afro hairdo sparkled under the dimly lit hallway. Her long beautiful legs said, "*watch me now.*" Mike's eyes ran from her three inch heels up to her tight fitting "hot pants."

"Now that's royalty," said Mike. He thanked Duane for the wine.

"You get a buzz?" Duane asked.

"I'm buzzin', my brother," said Mike, already out of earshot. As he followed her royal-highness to the packed party room, he said, "Good lookin, hey girl, I'm talkin' to you." She turned with a smile. Mike seen her in school but did not know her name.

"Hi, I'm Mike."

"I'm Lo . . . ," Before she could finish her name Mike kissed her. And she kissed him back. His tongue made contact. Wow, I'm already kissing her royal-highness and don't even know her name. He took her hand and pulled her through the thick crowd that bounced to the rhythm of the Funkadelics hit song, *I Bet You*. Bill had decked the basement out in black-light posters. Most noticeable were the signs of the Zodiac sexual postures poster.

"Check that out Baby, a pose for every sign." Mike didn't know much about girls or what made them tick, but in this instance all his inhibitions seem to fade after the Boone's Farm wine kicked in. He said whatever came to his mind. He moved his new-found friend to the far corner of the room. "What's your name again?" Mike asked.

She said very slowly, "Lo-la. Like Lo-la Falana." Mike remembered seeing a picture of Lola Falana in *Ebony* magazine once.

"And you just as fine." he said. He gently pressed her back against the wall and kissed her again as the beat slowed to a Smokey Robinson and the Miracles tune. Mike did a slow dance grind with Lola in the corner. He pressed her harder against the wall and she pressed back. Long before the song ended, Mike got the hardest he'd ever been and felt like he was bustin' out of his pants. Then he thought about how she kissed him – the wettest kiss he ever tasted. *Is this the shape of things to come,* Mike thought.

He imagined what she would look like on a throne. Her purple and white hot pants set contrasted with her dark black-velvet skin. She sparkled as magnificent as a moonlight-rainbow — a moonbow. Against the dark backdrop of her midnight complexion she glistened of purple and blue diamonds, skin as smooth as silk, her eyes like almonds – fixed and penetrating — inviting. Mike wondered how close he could get. This beautiful young lady, Lola, his Queen of Sheba, intrigued Mike, to say the least.

CHAPTER 22 -
Sweet Lo-la

THE MONDAY MORNING WALK TO SCHOOL had a little more edge. By the time the group of students got to 14th Street and Calvert, the group had grown to a dozen. While Mike attended St. Martin DePorres, Jon-Jon and Denise now went to Durfee Junior High on LaSalle Blvd. next to Central High. On their way to school, the Watermans would usually meet the Nelsons on Edison Ave., the Clarks on Longfellow Ave., the Williamses on Chicago Blvd., and the Washingtons on Boston Blvd. Luke stopped the group at Calvert and 14th Street.

He said, "Y'all just wait just a minute, I got something to say, I gots to tell you the story about Dolamite I just learnt the other day." Luke had a mental storehouse - an arsenal - of jokes. He had just as many white man, black man, Chinese man jokes as Uncle John. And he must've learned comedian Rudy Ray Moore's entire album collection he'd overheard at his daddy's parties. On the block, Luke would often get in a joke-telling frenzy. Everybody's favorite was the Signifyin' Monkey. Luke told it with such animation you would think he was on a nightclub stage. Luke continued. "I want y'all to take a real good shit and screw your wigs on tight, 'cause I'm fittin' to tell y'all about a bad rascal called Dolomite. From the moment Dolomite was born, he slapped his pappy's face and said from now on I'm runnin' this place. At the age of two Dolomite was drinking gin, at three he was eatin' the bottles they came in . . . " By now the group surrounded Luke. He took center stage. A few more students who were on their way to Central High joined the crowd. " . . . now they let Dolomite outta jail when he turned thirteen. They said Dolomite we gonna make you an offer, that is, we got you a job in Africa if you promise to leave us alone and never come back to San Antone. He took the job in Africa kickin' lions in the ass to stay in shape, then got sent to Brazil to wrestle steers, but got ran out because he screwed a she-elephant 'til she broke down in tears . . . "

By the time Luke finished he had the group in tears laughing.

With Mike and his mellows less than a block away from the school, a group of students from Central and St. Martin DePorres - who were wearing Black Panther buttons, bullets hanging around their necks, and their signature black berets - handed Mike, Luke and the others fliers.

"Brothers, and sisters join us at Kennedy Square for a Free Huey P. Newton rally." Newton, the founder of the Black Panther Party for Self Defense, had been jailed for over a year for allegedly slaying a police officer. "Speak out against this Gestapo government who wants to silence our leader by keeping him in solitary confinement. They want to shut down the voice of the people. We won't be quiet. And we demand that black studies be taught in the schools now!"

"What's this?" asked Luke as he grabbed a flier.

"Free Huey, brother."

"Man, don't you know who I am?"

"No brother, who are you?" The Panther brother asked in a deadly serious tone.

Luke said, "I'm Dolamite, when I was two I was drinking gin, when I was three I was eating the gotdamn bottles it came in." Mike and his boys broke out in laughter. Luke continued to clown. "Just got back from Africa where I had a job kicking lions in the ass to stay in shape and you want me to march down to Kennedy Square. Let me read this. What's the deal, my man?"

The Panther brother said, "Black power, my brothers and sisters, that's the deal, black power."

Then another young man said, "Don't be afraid. Stokley Carmichael, a leader of the Student Nonviolent Coordinating Committee, said, 'Don't be afraid of black power. Black power, black power.'"

Mike said, "Right on." Then held his fist up, and thought, *this is Renee's thing.*

Luke raised his fist and said, "black power."

A Panther sister handing out fliers said, "Join us at Kennedy Square. All Power to the People."

The group kept walking. Mike pushed the flier in his pocket without reading it and began to daydream about Lola. The first thing he would do is ask for her phone number. He knew he would see Lola in homeroom class as soon as he got to school. And he did. There she was avoiding eye contact with him. Lola avoided Mike all day, but at the end of the day as Lola stood at her locker and gathered her books, Mike walked over to her and said, "Why you avoiding me like that?"

"Like what."

"You won't even look at me."

"I'm embarrassed. You embarrassed me at the party, kissin' me and I barely even know you." Mike took a step back.

"I'm sorry you felt embarrassed, but everything just happened so fast, you were looking too gorgeous, I couldn't help myself."

"Well you better help yourself. I mean, you're a football player, and you're gonna have a lot of girlfriends."

Mike said, "I don't have any girlfriends now."

"Right, not now. In a week I'll be a distant memory."

"Can't I call you at least?"

Lola swung her locker closed and sat her book bag down. "I should hit you over the head with this bag, boy."

"And then give me your number."

"I'll give you my number and won't hit you this time. I suppose a call won't hurt. But don't call me after eight during the week. My mom will kill me."

"Oh, you sweet soul sister," said Mike. He couldn't believe he uttered those words. "My soul sister," he said again. Lola headed down the hallway to meet up with her girlfriends.

The football players at St. Martin DePorres were treated like kings by the other students. Mike liked the attention but Mike's dad warned him about how stardom can be fleeting.

Frank relayed his own story to Mike of wrestling when he attended University of Detroit High School where he was loved and admired by the teachers and students. His grades were superior. It was all good until he suffered torn ligaments in mid-season during his senior year. He couldn't help his team at city or state championship matches. He fell out of good graces with his fellow students and teachers. He was no longer the *knighted one- Sir Waterman, as Frank's fellow students called him.* Frank told Mike how he would have lost his scholarship if it wasn't for his father fighting for him. He nearly flunked out his final semester because of the new harshness he received from the priests. The idea of fleeting stardom stuck in Mike's head ever since.

CHAPTER 23 -
School Protest

ON THEIR WAY TO THE SCHOOL office that same morning, Frank Waterman and Jim Dunham walked through a small group of DePorres students gathered on the corner with students from Central and Durfee. The two men had just finished breakfast at Kelly's Corner, located at 12th Street and Webb. The two men agreed to meet every Monday morning for breakfast to talk about fundraising for the school. In the midst of the black power movement, high school and junior high school students were voicing protest over everything from police brutality to course curriculum.

Back in the office, Mr. Dunham peered through his window shades and said, "The natives are restless and we won't be able to contain them much longer." Frank got up to look across the street at the crowd near Kelly's Corner. The Black Panthers were selling their papers as were members of the Nation of Islam.

Sister JoAnna, assistant principal, joined the two in the office to discuss the school's curriculum. "Sister Jo, the kids are tired of the same old lies," said Mr. Dunham, as he turned away from the window. "I told y'all that from the get-go. And here we are trying to go along with the Detroit Archdiocese edicts."

"There are standards Mr. Dunham," said Sister JoAnna.

"How many times have we heard that before? Is that some sort of excuse not to make change," said Mr. Dunham. "And whose standards anyway?"

Frank said, "What are you saying, Jim?"

"What I'm saying is that we can create our own black studies curriculum and have it accredited."

Frank looked puzzled. "You think we can?"

"Of course we can. We'll still have the math, science, religion, and English but for social studies and humanities and other social sciences we will integrate more about the civil rights struggle and the new black power movement. There's already tons of information on the subjects. A whole body of knowledge is being omitted – just plain ol' left out. And it's my job, our job, to include it. Ain't nobody else gonna do it for us. Frank, this is what I was talking about at the Collingwood Bar, man. The archdiocese can't ramrod us like that. What do they know about the needs of our people." Mr. Dunham pulled up the blinds and pointed over to the group of students and said, "These kids ain't havin' it!"

"Who's gonna teach this Black studies, we got the staff?" Frank asked.

"We got staff who've read and studied Marcus Garvey and the United Negro Improvement Association movement, Elijah Muhammad and the Nation of Islam, Frantz Fanon, Dick Gregory, Stokley Carmichael, the Student Non-violent Coordinating Committee, Huey P. Newton and the Black Panther Party."

"And don't forget W.E.B. DuBois and the NAACP," Sister JoAnna added. "And the great work of Thurgood Marshall."

"Of course, Sister, of course," said Mr. Dunham.

"This sounds a bit militant, don't you think?" said Frank.

"Not at all. Not if we're preparing the leaders of tomorrow," said Mr. Dunham.

"Well, Jim, all this stuff is new to me. I'm not the educator like you two, I'm your friend, your supporter . . . "

"Frank", Jim cut him off, "you got to trust me on this. Sister, are you familiar with those people I just ran down?"

"Well, not everyone but I did read the *Autobiography of Malcolm X* and *Soul on Ice* in grad school last semester. They were hot items."

"Where was this?" said Frank.

"Wayne State."

Frank asked, "Was it required reading, Sister?"

"Yes it was."

"Then it can be required here."

"Well Frank, the smart thing to do is to introduce the material in various ways. I'll draft a plan and present it to the board. And maybe we can have something in place by December. I'll call Ted tonight and get on the board agenda and let him know we want to discuss curriculum changes. The next meeting's about a month away."

The next day members of the Black Panther Party for Self Defense circulated flyers throughout the school calling for a walk-out Friday. The protest flyer read:

His-story — full of lies
No More Lies
Walk out on Friday to support a Black studies program.

CHAPTER 24 -
Mama E & City Club

MAMA E TOLD ROSE SHE TALKED to Frank about adding a medical wing to City Club. She told Rose that her friends, other elders along with herself, needed a place they could go for regular check-ups. Mama E told Frank she would raise the money if necessary. Frank told Mama E, it was necessary.

Mama E said to Rose, "You know, I see our community out here buying fish, buying whiting fish and bean pies from the Black Muslims like it's goin' outta style. We could sell the same thing at Friday night bingo at Visitation. We could sell sandwiches and dinners and slices of pie. We could make just as much money as we need to make. I think we could do it in a matter of months." Mama E continued, "I know it, I see it. We love this whiting, we love bean pies. We can do this."

"Mama, how much do we need to raise?"

"Frank said that adding a medical wing would cost $300,000, but we need to raise 25 percent, which is $75,000. The Upwards Detroit Foundation will match our share, then the city will match that."

Rose tilted her head down at Mama E and said, "We come up with $75,000, Upwards Detroit kicks in $75,000, and the city kicks in $150,000."

"That's the math, sugar. But the only trick is we got to raise our share first."

"And you think we can sell $75,000 worth of fish and bean pies?" asked Rose.

"I know we can. We can buy the bean pies at wholesale prices from the Black Muslims. They will sell us as many as we want. I know the people up there. Abdullah Muhammad's a friend of mine. Frank knows him too. He will sell us the bean pies. As for the fish, we buy it, then fry it, sell it up as sandwiches and dinners with potato salad and green beans. We could even sell them right out of this house."

"Wait a minute Mama. Frank, I don't think he's going to go for that. But I like the bingo night idea and maybe even after church. We can set up a booth after church and on bingo night and sell fish dinners. I think we can do it. But I don't know about right out the house here Mama. So, how many bean pies will that be at two dollars a pie?"

"We'll pay two dollars per pie then get eight slices at fifty cent per slice, we double our money. And we can get ten, two dollar sandwiches from a five dollar box of whiting. After supplies we'll still make over ten dollars on every box of fish. You do the math, you tell me how many pies and sandwiches we'll need to sell."

"A whole lot, Mama, that's how many."

"Hey, listen Rose, the other thing we can do is have talent shows. There's so much talent in this city. I think we can have talent shows every so often just to showcase the up and coming young talent. We can invite Berry Gordy - founder and president of Motown Records - and his people, and some other record labels, like Mr. Wingate around the block. They can send some of their scouts. We know these kids need the exposure and we can give it to them and we can raise money at the same time. These kids love to perform. They love to be on stage. Of course, we can do it at City Club. We'll ask Frank. And we also have to ask Father O'Malley about bingo night."

Rose said, "I think Father O'Malley will go for it because right now all they've got is popcorn and pretzels for Friday night bingo, I know we can do better than that."

It took less than a week for Mama E and Rose to start their fundraising campaign selling bean pies and fish sandwiches at bingo night every Friday in the church hall, that doubles as the school cafeteria.

Mama E said, "Honey, we're gonna do whatever it takes."

~ ~ ~ ~ ~ ~ ~

When the kids heard Mama E say that she will do whatever it takes, it reminded them of when their mother told them that Mama E did what it took to keep them alive against the KKK one night back in their home down in Sugarville, Louisiana. Mama E said, "I had to do what I to do."

CHAPTER 25 -
Mama Two-Gun

MAMA E WAS ALWAYS TELLING STORIES. The kids loved to ask her about her life. One time when Mike and Denise were very young they asked her what happened to her husband: "What happened to Grandpa? Where is he?"

"Well," she began, as if she had been expecting the question to come at any moment. "I'll tell you what happened. 'Way back down in Louisiana, your grandpa, Papa Jack, had been complaining about the low prices he was getting for his sugar cane. We had 160 acres of cane down there; we were farmers. Your Grandpa decided to take his cane elsewhere — to a farmers' co-operative — because the whites weren't giving him the price he knew he deserved. Now, he had been doing okay for a while because the white men didn't believe him at first. But when they saw what he was doing—"

"Hold up, Mama E," Denise interrupted. "I heard you had run off a bunch of Ku Klux Klan one day."

Mama E continued, "Honey, I'll get to that; let me tell you the whole story. Your mama was only about ten years. Well, at any rate, the Klansmen did try to burn our house down. They did try to run us out of town because your Grandpa took his sugar cane to the co-op. They told him not to take it to the co-op. He could only sell his sugar to them. Now, you know that wasn't right. At any rate, the night riders came one night. The night riders were so cocky about coming to run us out of town that they even warned Pa they were coming."

"What's a night rider?" Denise interrupted again.

"That's the KKK, honey. They used to ride horses. But they had no idea, see, my Dad, your Great Grandpa Zeke, was a hunter. He hunted everything: squirrel, rabbit, deer and duck. He taught your Grandma how to shoot. When he died he left me with darn near an arsenal. Now listen to this, children, Papa didn't even know about it because your Grandma never did like to hunt. I always kept the guns hid. Never went hunting and never told Papa Jack about the guns until that night. Papa was thinking that if he called a couple of the town ministers to stay up with him and stand outside waiting in a peaceful fashion they wouldn't be able to sneak attack his family and they might not shoot three unarmed men for nothing. This is, oh, about 1943, I think. So your Grandma overheard his plans with the ministers. And she bust that bubble fast. I told him, your Grandpa, I said, 'who do you think you're dealing with? These men may be businessmen or sheriffs by day, but by night these men have nothing but hatred for us. These men are coming to make an example out of you,' I told him.

'Stay out of this mess, Elli,' your Grandpa told me.

I said, 'How on earth am I going to stay out of this when I have two children here and we expecting uninvited guests tonight?'

Your Grandpa in his loud booming voice said, 'The ministers and I are going to handle it. You and the children stay inside.'

I said, 'Jack, I'm not going to stand by and watch you die; I ain't no fool. Come in here and let me show you something.' Now Papa Jack looked at me in shock as if he was saying what does this woman have to show me? Your Grandma took him by the hand and took him into the bedroom, and she got down on her knees and bowed her head and said, 'Dear Lord forgive us for we know not what we fittin' to do. Give us the courage to fight these crackers and protect our family.'

As your Grandma went under the bed, Papa said, 'Wait now, Elli. We're not going to hide under no darn bed. I am not a coward.'

'Coward,' I told him. I stuck my head up under the bed and opened the secret hatch in the floor. And I could hear Papa Jack saying, 'Elli, now what you doin', woman? Get from under the bed.' He could hear me pulling up the floor-board. 'Come on, Elli, now what you got to show me?'

'Just one minute, just a minute.' And I threw a rifle from under the bed.

'Holy smokes!' Papa Jack jumped back like it was a snake.

Then I threw out a shotgun, then another and another. Two rifles, three shotguns, two pistols and a box of ammo, a big box. 'And don't ask me where I got it,' I said to him.

'Elli, what we gonna do with this?'

'While you three standing out there, we gonna be inside, guns loaded, at the ready, that's what.'

'You think I want to get caught with these loaded guns, Elli? We'll all go to jail.'

'Well, that's better than being dead, that's all Elli got to say,' I told him. It must have been about eleven o'clock that night when your Grandma Elli finally came back outside. I saw the men under the big tree singing spirituals. When they finished singing I jumped in and said, 'I love that song. Wasn't that the song they sang for little Bobby Joe's funeral?'

'Yes it was, Elli. We sang it,' Papa Jack said.

'But why y'all singing it now?' your Grandma Elli asked them. 'This ain't no funeral. Look, gentlemen, I hate to break up y'all's party but I was thinking that Rev. Mike over there goes hunting. You go hunting, don't you?'

"Yes I do, ma'am, but what—" Your Grandma didn't even let him finish. I just said, 'Come inside with me.'

'Elli,' Papa Jack shouted back at me then, 'this ain't the time nor the place. We're not afraid of these demons. They will not make animals out of us.'

And Rev. Mike said in a very sincere tone and solemn voice, 'we'll confront them with our head up and with God on our side.'

'Rev.,' I said to him, 'I like what you said, even how you said it, but there comes a time when you've got to face reality and this reality is that these Klansmen are coming here tonight to kill them some Negroes. That's putting it nicely. They ain't comin' to negotiate. Look, I ain't trying to bust y'all's bubble, but I'm going to need somebody else inside with me to watch the back of the house. We've got two rifles, three shotguns and two pistols in there. You two men that stay out here need to carry one.'

Papa didn't even want to look at me. Your Grandma Elli felt that deep down in his heart, he knew he was going to have to fight to save his family. He didn't want to accept that he might even have to kill someone. Now, he always believed that he could persuade the opposition to be reasonable. After all, he made it this far. He thought he was well-liked in town. Yeah, people smiled at him, and sometimes call him 'Sir' or 'Mr. Truth.' I told Papa that they like you if you ain't rocking the boat. He went along for so long.

'I did what I had to do,' he snapped at me.

'And you did it well,' I said. 'We just taking this whole thing to another level now. We are talking about economic independence. You are one of the biggest cane growers down here and you cut off the white man from his source of supply.'

Well children, this talk back and forth with us went on for about an hour. It was not much past midnight and you could hear the cars coming; we saw headlights.

'I'm heading inside, Papa,' I said. Rev. Mike said, 'I'm right behind you.'

'You chicken poop,' your Grandpa said.

'Don't be crazy, Jack. You talk to them; we got your back.'

'Yeah! Yeah! Yeah!' said Grandpa.

Your Grandma told Rev. Mike that we couldn't let the Klan get close enough to firebomb the house. Rev. Mike took up the position on the side of the house. We could see more than ten cars coming. Papa started waving a white flag as he walked out to the road from the house. He beckoned them to stop, like this, holding both hands up like this.

'Stop, let's talk, let's talk,' he told them. Then he saw them speeding up.

'Jack, get behind the tree!' Rev. Mike yelled. 'They ain't stopping; they're coming for us, brother.'

So Papa dashed behind the tree. Just then, bam, bam, bam, shots rang out. Papa got hit in the arm. He got behind the tree. Your Grandma waited for them to get close enough. They began piling out. One of the Klansman called out: 'Jack, get your black behind out here, boy. That's a perfect tree up there to swing from, boy.'

Your Grandma Elli was inside the house, and guess what, that's right, I started firing their behinds right up. Ka-Pow, Ka-Pow! They scattered and returned fire. I just kept shooting. And before they knew what hit them, there was two of them laid out on the grass. I kept shooting. Rev. Mike went to check the back; he was ready but he wasn't shooting. Some in the mob fired back from behind the cars as the others started piling into them. Rev. Mike watched as a few others tried to reach the house. Rev. Mike then came from behind the house and fired off a few rounds. We heard a holler. Then we saw a couple of cars move out.

One of the Klansmen said, 'We got a few casualties, Bob. Three been hit.

Papa yelled, 'Bob, how many people have to die?' Three more cars left. Bob didn't even have his white sheet over his face. He just knew they were coming to burn the house, hang Papa from a tree and they didn't care if they were seen 'cause wasn't nobody suppose to live.

'We'll be back, boy, we'll be back for you,' Bob threatened. They all piled in their cars and left, throwing the wounded in the back seats.

Papa ran back into the house, screaming, 'we did it, we beat them.' Then he came to himself and we started packing.

Papa said, 'they gonna put together a bigger mob, we got to get out of here, we've got to leave through Heavensville,' where a black doctor removed the bullet from Papa Jacks arm. It took us all of ten minutes to pack, we left without incident. Unfortunately, for the rest of the black folk in town, the sheriff and the mayor didn't want a race riot like people had experienced all over the South back then, so they helped contain a mighty hostile white crowd. Another thing they didn't know was which Negroes had guns. Well, that's how Grandma got her nickname, Mama Two-Gun. Your mother gave me that name; she saw Mama with two guns in her hands. She said, 'Mama Two-Gun, Mama Two-Gun.' That's just how she saw it.

Now, you must remember we left town but eventually the law caught up with us. Papa drove non-stop to Detroit and we laid low with his brother for weeks. Well anyway, to make a long story short, we were caught by the FBI, sent back down to Louisiana and they put Papa on trail. They didn't know who did the shooting. They thought it might have been Papa. He told me to keep my mouth shut about what really happened. Papa Jack protected me. Your Grandpa loved me so much. He was not going to let me go to trial and face attempted murder charge. Well anyway, there was a mistrial because some of the folk on the jury actually believed it was self-defense with Papa getting shot and everything. Well, the mayor and the sheriff were eventually run out of town behind this incident. Now, do y'all understand why your Grandma loved Mr. Malcolm X so much?"

Mama E spoke in a hushed tone. "You've got to defend yourself and your family, baby. If we don't, who will? Who will?" She asked this not rhetorically, but as though she were really expecting to hear an answer — then proceeded without receiving one. "Ain't nobody advocating overthrowing the government. I support nonviolence in a non-violent situation, but we have to defend ourselves."

Mama E continued, "So, after the trial and everything, we eventually lost the land and that was so devastating to Papa. We stayed in Detroit after the trial and that's what broke his heart. What he loved doing so much was no longer a part of him: working the land, being by the river. Things he loved to do he could not do anymore. He could not return to Louisiana. He suffered—suffered mentally, and barely survived in the city. He worked for the factory, made decent money, but he had no heart left, no will to live. Then one day they found him outside the plant suffering from a stroke. That was it, he died before the ambulance arrived. Poor Papa, his heart broke, it was devastating. I was devastated. He thought he could save his land and his family without a fight. He saved his family but we lost the land. He loved me so much. I miss him. I'll never forget Papa Jack."

The children looked on shaking their heads in disbelief. Jon-Jon and Denise jumped up from their sitting position on the floor and hugged Mama E. Mike just closed his eyes and shook his head.

CHAPTER 26 -
Frank, John, and Methadone -
Fall 1968

FRANK DROVE SOUTH ON WOODWARD AVENUE as he headed for the Greyhound bus station in downtown Detroit to pick up his brother John. John had just received an honorable discharge from the Army. Frank knew his brother had changed from being the class clown and academic slacker to a person who seemed much more serious about life and very studious. The two exchanged numerous letters over the past four years. In the letters, John told Frank he wanted to study politics at Wayne State University when he returned, then maybe get a master's degree in history. He never said what he wanted to do but he thought teaching would be interesting. He told Frank the auto assembly plant nearly killed him before he left, working all that overtime. He said it was good money but he might be dead before he turned forty.

John also told Frank about all the devastation that he'd seen in Vietnam. Mostly, the trauma his fellow soldiers suffered after returning from a mission. When John was in Vietnam he spent almost all his time maintaining and repairing vehicles to go in the field. He told Frank in a letter how men would come back from the jungle with their heads "all fucked up" from all the killing. Many soldiers had gotten strung out on heroin before they returned home. Frank asked him how he managed to stay clean. He said to Frank, 'just smoked that boo, baby, mary-jane - referring to marijuana. That's all I needed.'

Frank explained to John he, too, had gone through a change. Frank told John of the tough decision he made to leave Statewide Insurance to run City Club.

Frank gave John a tour of Detroit before dinner at the Waterman's home, then later that night dropped him off to stay at the apartment near Wayne State University he shared with a couple of brothers whom he'd met in the service. "We're all gonna make Mike's last game, you want to join us . . . swear that boy gonna make all-state next year . . . " said Frank.

"You got it," said John.

~ ~ ~ ~ ~ ~ ~

Frank and John got together regularly after his return. Once Frank picked up John from Big Man Williams' house around the corner. John jumped in the car talking, "See those two Caddies in the back. A 1950 and 1952 Fleetwood. The old man asked me if I could fix 'em, both of 'em. Mama E told him how I knew how to work on old cars and trucks. He said he didn't trust anyone to work on them. Well, anyway they're running now. I did it as a favor for Mama E. Hey Frank, it's like I owe her. She told me how she prayed the rosary for me everyday while I was in 'Nam. Must be why I'm still alive today,' bro."

Frank laughed as he drove off and said, "Boy, you are something else." During the drive, John kept harping to Frank about the horror of the drug addiction that so many servicemen had picked up. Frank wondered whether John too, was addicted. He seemed secretive about so many things. Frank doesn't dare ask him, but John was persistent about Frank starting a methadone clinic at the City Club. He said that methadone could be a stop-gap measure, like a substitute that would help get rid of the heroin addiction.

"Frank, check this out, the government would pay you a gazillion dollars to set up this methadone program in your building, I'm telling you. All you got to do is go down and meet with federal officials, downtown Detroit. They're looking for places to put these clinics."

Frank said, "Well, John if the problem is so huge, why don't they have better oversight over the military personnel?"

"Look, look, look, Frank, you don't understand. When you're over there, overseas, the military is looking away, they're doing whatever they can do as long as these brothers on the frontline keep fighting. They don't care what else they do. This here military is so desperate they just look the other way or they got their hands out looking for a cut. These brothers are getting strung out left and right. This is a way you can help, this is one way you can help."

"I hear you John, I'm just thinking, man, we're already about to bust out of the space we're in. I promised Mama E we'd build a medical wing for health screening. We're really pushing it, but if we get enough money to hire some people to run it, then it could work."

"Frank, you made the right choice to do the City Club man, I mean, bro., you knew you had to do more in your neighborhood. Man, I come back here and there's no more 12ᵗʰ Street, you know. I've been gone for four years and look what's happened in America. Malcolm X gets assassinated, King's assassinated, 12th Street burnt down to the ground. You had a rebellion here, 45 people dead and all I could do is hear about it while I'm over in 'Nam fixing trucks. I'm shocked to see this, my city devastated like this. And now more devastation with this massive, massive influx of heroin. The heroin's coming in mighty pure, Frank. It's cheap and it's pure. And some of these young brothers are picking up on it. You better even watch your kids, you better watch your son and these kids in high school, you don't know what they doing."

"Oh John, you're sounding just . . . , you know, too paranoid, man."

"Paranoid my foot, bro, have you been down to the high schools? Do you know what these kids . . . see, these kids are getting militant and the government can't take it, they can't take it Frank. They're pumping this stuff into the neighborhoods man. Tell me what these police doin' all in the neighborhood. You think they don't know where it's coming from? They're giving it to us. Dig it, Frank, they can't stand these young folks like me coming back from Vietnam with their heads on right, they can't take it. Bobby Seale and them telling the police to back off. These white folks can't take it, brother, and that's why you see this heroin on every corner. You got more dope houses than churches."

"Oh, John."

"Frank, there are more dope houses than churches, man."

"How do you know so much, how do you know so much, John?"

"Dig it Frank, you've got to get involved with this methadone, I mean that's the only hope for some of these people, man. They're coming back, they're bringing the stuff back. It's available, it's accessible and if you want to save your people, you'd better get with the methadone."

Frank said, "You're talking about the government being the enemy and you're telling me to go get with the government to set up a methadone clinic."

John said, "Tell me of a better way. You ain't seen the devastation yet, it's just beginning to happen. We at the beginning stage. If you want to wait two more years, you'll be begging for something, anything. I say get it now, cash in on it now. At least you'll get some more monies pumped into your community club program. You'll be able to hire more people, I guarantee you. Anyway, check this out, listen to this poem on the radio by James Brown, I can't believe they playin' it, *King Heroin*, I memorized it." John recited the poem as it was being played over the radio: "I came to this country without a passport,

Every since then I've been hunted and sought.

My little white grains are nothing but waste."

John spoke over the words.

"Soft and deadly and bitter to taste. I'm a world of power, and all know it's true, use me once and you'll know it too.

I can make a mere school boy forget his books, you hear that Frank, I can make a world famous beauty neglect her looks."

John stopped for a moment and said, "See that bro. it can take us all down . . . a schoolboy forgets his books and a beautiful girl forgets her looks. A girl will sell her body for a hit . . . " The poem continued . . . "I'm financed at China, run in Japan, I'm respected in Turkey and legal in Siam. I take my addicts and make them steal, borrow, beg then they search for a vein in their arm or their leg."

John said, "Now dig this part, heroin's waiting at the gate. Don't be afraid, I'm not chased . . . " John suddenly fell silent as James Brown finished the poem.

Behold, you're hooked, your foot is in the stirrup,
And make haste, mount the steed and ride him well,
For the white horse of heroin will ride you to hell . . .

"Now Frank, what you think about that?"

~ ~ ~ ~ ~ ~ ~

Later, at the Waterman house, Mike had busted his butt all week and was lying down on the upstairs hall floor when Jon-Jon hollered out, "It's on Mike, Mike." Mike had asked Jon-Jon to wake him up for the Olympics 220 yard dash. Mike did not want to miss this big race. All week after football practice, the players and coaches had been talking about rumors of a protest if John Carlos or Tommie Smith won. The Watermans watched with excitement as the John Carlos and Tommie Smith took first and third place then gave the black power salute during the National Anthem - they raised their fists with a black glove on after winning medals in the 220 yard dash.

CHAPTER 27 –
One More Devil's Night, Please.

By late October, the St. Martin DePorres Eagles were 5-2 with one football game remaining. The team maintained second place all season. And since the first place team was undefeated, a win would not get the Eagles into the playoffs. They had to win the division title to make the playoffs.

Mike moved up to second team wide-receiver and would occasionally carry in plays. The senior wide-receiver who played ahead of Mike broke his thumb during a late season practice.

All week the coach emphasized playing for pride and ending the season with a victory. Coach Taylor said, "Keep your heads up high. Given your new circumstances, you did damn good."

At least, that was the coach's public stance to the players and parents. Rumors floated through school that coach wanted to get more players from the West Side Cubs, those who had some football-playing experience before they got to high school. The West Side Cubs had a winning tradition and the players had a great desire to win. He wanted to bring that desire to win to the DePorres' football team.

Mike heard that in private Coach Taylor complained about the whiny, cry-baby attitudes of some of the older players, especially the seniors. And even with the respectable won-loss record, Coach Taylor complained that DePorres wasn't even close to competing with the Public School League or class A Catholic schools like Brother Rice, for that matter.

During the last week of practice, two seniors who were first string starters — neither of whom had received recognition for possible all-conference honors or scholarship offers from colleges—came into the locker room and threw their helmets the full length of the locker room against a set of lockers.

Both started cussing people out indiscriminately. They used every variation and combination of motherfucker, goddamn, and bitch until assistant Coach Walters rushed in the locker room, and blew his whistle to a deafening pitch. He must have heard the commotion from outside. The sound nearly burst Mike's eardrums.

"Shut up!" the coach started screaming. "You two punks just shut up, you couldn't bust a grape at full speed all year and now you want to act mad, take it out on the school's equipment. This is not your shit to tear up! You wanna act tough, get mad, do it on the field. Marshall, look at you, boy. You got potential. You're six-two, over 200 pounds, you're anybody's all-star man, but you got no heart. You're out there playin' patty-cake. If you lookin' for the Wizard of mutha-fuckin' Oz, you're in the wrong place. This here is the real deal. And you, Deon, you choke in the tight. A cold glass of water and a hot piece of pussy . . . boy, you'd choke to death."

The locker room erupted with laughter.

"Shut up, everybody! Just shut the fuck up. I don't want to see either one of you two mistreating this school's equipment again. And that goes for everybody in here. The coaches, your parents, the school, everybody sacrificing for y'all, everybody. Don't disrespect what we're struggling so hard for. Don't do it!!"

At this point nobody in the locker room wanted to brave a hearty laugh, so all that was heard was a bit of giggling. When Coach Taylor came in with team captain Todd McDonald, Coach Walters immediately briefed Coach Taylor on what had happened.

"Marshall, Deon, come here. I want three hundred push-ups right now, with your hats on."

"But coach," Marshall spoke up. "I need to leave right away. My mother's waiting."

"Your mommy's waiting." Coach Taylor mimicked Marshall. "Mommy's waiting to change her baby's diaper."

"Naw, Coach, it ain't like that. I need to . . . "

"Mommy's baby. Did she bring your bottle too? Let's go tell mommy about her baby boy having a temper tantrum and tearing up the team's equipment. Let's go tell mommy. Where's your stroller? Anybody seen Marshall's stroller?"

By now the teammates couldn't hold it in any longer and were out of control with laughter. Marshall nearly broke down in tears from the humiliation.

"Tell you what, mommy's baby. You go 'head on. We got three more practices. I want my 300 pushups everyday until the season's over. That's three on Tuesday, three on Wednesday, and three on Thursday. Now get outta here." Marshall finished getting dressed and left quickly. "Deon, why don't you get outta my face, too." Deon left soon after Marshall, without taking a shower or even buttoning his shirt.

Coach Taylor had spit forming on the side of his mouth. "Gonna tear up the team's equipment cause you frustrated ain't no college scouts lookin' at you? Well team . . . " Coach Taylor turned towards the players in the locker room. "Ignore that bullshit. That's why these two ain't captains. Gentlemen, it's been a helluva ride this year. We got a lot to build on for next season and quite frankly, I'm lookin' forward to it. I know what it's gonna take. We gotta knock that softness outta ya. If you want to act soft at home, at school, I don't care. That's your business. But don't bring that soft sissy shit up in here. This game ain't for no softies."

This temper tantrum display was the first Mike had ever seen from these two teammates. *Maybe the coaches did think they were a bunch of cry-babies,* Mike thought on his walk home. *And this was no way to end the season.*

~ ~ ~ ~ ~ ~ ~

Before Mike could sit down for dinner that night, he got a phone call from DeAngelo. "Tomorrow's Devil's Night, remember?"

"Can't do it, man. I got too much goin' on," said Mike. The thought of another Devil's Night, after last year's narrow escape from the hands of several homeowners who had ambushed Mike and DeAngelo, gave Mike butterflies. Only DeAngelo would want to do it again.

For many years, Mike and DeAngelo had engaged in what had become, on the night before Halloween, their Devil's Night ritual of overturning neighbor's trash cans in the alley. Many kids did this and similar antics throughout Detroit. Others, feeling bolder, would throw eggs at city buses or soap up car windows. Mike always thought it was pretty harmless stuff, and viewed it as child's play. After all, now he attended high school.

Mike's most cherished memory of Devil's Night was when he, DeAngelo, and Luke hid on top of Mike's garage roof, waiting for other kids to come tearing down the alley to tip cans. Mike and his mellows were armed with B-B guns. They opened fire on the group just as the other kids started tipping cans. The intruders, probably no older than twelve, did a hurried about-face, screaming and crying. DeAngelo got so bold as to hurl a couple of bottles at the kids as they dashed away.

Then last year Mike and DeAngelo were ambushed by several adults just a few blocks away. *Thank God the men were too slow to catch us,* Mike remembered.

"Let's quit while we're ahead," Mike suggested. Mike remembered how they'd had to fake the older men out in the alley to get past them, then had outrun the rest of the homeowners for nearly ten blocks. Mike had insisted then that he'd had enough.

But DeAngelo didn't let up. "Look Mike, we've been partners in this for the last four years. I just want to go out with a bang. We can do Boston, Glynn and, Calvert. There's a lot of loose trash cans in them alleys."

"Can't do it, man. I'm done," Mike resisted.

"Mike, man, you think you too good. You act like one them e-lites or somethin'." DeAngelo had to get in the last word and was probably trying to guilt trip Mike. Mike hung up the phone, then thought, *that chump.*

The next day, after returning home from practice, Mike got a phone call. "Hello, Mike. This is Angela Parker, DeAngelo's mother."

"Hi, Mrs. Parker."

"DeAngelo's in the hospital Mike. He's down at Henry Ford Hospital and would like to see you." Mrs. Parker's voice started to crack. "He was attacked by a Doberman last night when he was walking home from the store."

What the heck—the store? Mike thought. *Walking home from the store, my butt.* Mike knew he'd been caught tipping cans.

"How is he, Mrs. Parker?" he asked.

"Much better now, but he got bit up pretty bad. Can you please go and see him?" Mrs. Parker's voice trailed off as she started crying. Mike said goodbye, then hung up the phone.

Before going down to the hospital Mike checked in with his dad who was cleaning up the pile of ashes from the leaves that he burned a couple of nights before. Mike walked up to his dad and said, "Dad, DeAngelo's in the hospital. I'd like to run down there and see him tonight."

"What happened to him?"

"Got attacked by a dog. He probably had to get rabies shots. He's okay though."

"Man, that sounds serious. What, the dog just attacked him?"

"Mrs. Parker said he was walking home from the store and a Doberman attacked him."

"Now who in the world would let a Doberman Pincher out to roam the streets. What do you think happened?" Before Mike could answer, his dad asked him to hold the large trash bag open to pour a shovel load of leaf ashes. Mike looked into the bag and saw the looted clothes he and DeAngelo recovered during last year's rebellion.

"Dad why are my clothes all burned up with these leaves?"

"Those are yours son? I thought they were trash. Why were they in the garage in this trash bag? You and DeAngelo got them off 12th Street didn't you?"

"Naw, we found them in the alley."

"Well, they looked like trash to me."

Mike's heart sank. He'd only taken one sweater from his stash but planned on wearing the new clothes later during the year. Mike felt like crying, but held it all in.

Dad, I'm gonna go see DeAngelo. I'll catch the 14th Street bus to W. Grand Blvd., then walk to the hospital from there." After Frank loaded the ashes into the bag. Mike left for the hospital.

Mike made it to Henry Ford Hospital in less than thirty minutes. Arriving at DeAngelo's bedside, he stared at his friend who was out cold, and laid back in his hospital bed. Tubes were running in and out of his arm, nose, and mouth. DeAngelo's brother Darren sat alone in a corner of the room. Mike nearly started crying but again held it in, looking at Darren.

"What's happenin', my man?" Darren asked, then looked down at his shoes.

"I'm doin' alright, Your mother told me what happened. So I came as soon as I could."

"DeAngelo got fucked up this time. You should be happy as hell you didn't go with him."

Mike plopped on the chair next to Darren and put his head between his hands, then looked up at DeAngelo's still body.

"Damn, he looks froze. So Darren, what really happened? He looks like a dead man breathing."

"Dead man breathing. You're a trip. Yeah, Mike, he's still breathing, and they think he'll live," said Darren with a wry smile. "Somebody let the dogs out on him. But seriously, Mike, he'll be alright. He's just asleep. Looks like shit though, don't he?"

CHAPTER 28 -
Drug Education

IN GENERAL, MIKE LIKED HIS TEACHERS at St. Martin DePorres High School. One in particular stood out to him among the others. Mr. Ludwig, a short and chubby man with an infectious smile who regularly wore wrinkled shirts and brown khaki pants, taught health studies. He couldn't have been over thirty, and was full of energy. He joked with student-athletes and told them that if they didn't make it in the professional ranks, there were opportunities in the sports industry as health and fitness professionals, such as sports trainers or physical therapists. And for those who didn't care for sports, they could find something rewarding in the field of health education.

Once, early in the school year, Mr. Ludwig proclaimed how much he loved Detroit and the Detroit Tigers. "I love Detroit, I love my Tigers," he said. "They're winners, and that makes us all winners. Detroiters are winners." He kept the class lively and most of Mike's classmates showed their eagerness to learn.

At one point in the semester, Mr. Ludwig decided to try the shock-you-away-from-drugs approach. He had brought in about a half-dozen people in the past two weeks to tell the students the real deal about illegal drugs, everyone from ex-cons to former heroin addicts. At the end of the second week, he told the class he had a 'rather poignant' movie to show. Mr. Ludwig swore that the movie he was about to show would 'knock your socks off' and make the class never, ever want to even see illegal drugs, let alone try them.

The movie, Poppy, took the class on a journey back to China's opium dens. It told the story of two families, one family living in poor rural conditions and another living as middle class urban dwellers. Both men in the movie seemed to be happy family men while at home, but after work hours they slipped into areas where opium was smoked. Over a period of a few weeks, both men spent less time at home and more time smoking opium.

As the class watched, the movie's sound kept going in and out. Ned, the student audio-visual expert in the classroom, stopped the movie to make some kind of correction. He restarted the movie, and not long after there was a rap at the door. Mr. Ludwig answered, opening the door only slightly to keep the light out of the classroom. A senior classman named Jack stuck his head inside the door and called one of Mike's classmates, Norm, to the door. Jack then turned and explained to Mr. Ludwig that he needed to see Norm just for a moment.

Norm got up and hurried to the door, reached into his pocket, handed Jack something, and then hurried back to his seat. Jack turned and left without another word. Mike and his classmates continued to watch the men in the movie deteriorate into full-blown heroin addicts. The men neglected their jobs, their families, and themselves.

Minutes later, there was another knock at the classroom door. This time Curtis got up and followed Mr. Ludwig to the door. Curtis took something out of his pocket and gave it to a senior classman named Rich. Rich left and Curtis returned to his seat. There was another rap on the door. Mr. Ludwig turned the lights on and told Ned to stop the movie.

"What the hell is going on here?"

"They want to watch the movie, that's all, Mr. Ludwig," said Norm. When Mr. Ludwig opened the door this time, standing outside was a tenth grader named Wil, who Mike knew from his Visitation days and who was in the same grade as Curtis and Norm.

"You want to watch the movie, too?" Mr. Ludwig asked.

"Yes. Can I?" Wil came into the classroom and took a seat in the back with Norm and Curtis.

"Gee whiz," said Mr. Ludwig. "We ought to be charging admission. Okay, Ned, start it up again." Just as the movie resumed playing, Nick, another tenth grader, came in without asking. Mr. Ludwig gave no protest. "Come on in and have a seat," he said.

Next thing Mike knew, Norm, Curtis, Wil, and Nick were gathered in the back of the classroom around Norm's desk. Mike turned around to see the quartet huddled, each with a playing card in his hand. Mike noticed that it looked as if they were trying to conceal something.

Mr. Ludwig silently watched the movie with the rest of the class, without looking to the back of the room. As the movie came to a close, about thirty Chinese men were huddled in a small room, smoking opium. The filmmakers flashed on the family farm to show that the crops had wilted and died. The filmmakers next showed the urban family searching for food, to no avail.

Meanwhile, Norm and his boys had opened the little red caps that contained heroin onto an album in full view for anyone looking. Norm made a nice-sized pile of heroin. They gathered around the desk and started to snort the stuff, right there in the classroom during the drug education movie. And that's how Mike and his classmates really learned about drugs, watching—in full view—his classmates doing the hard core stuff.

The movie was nearly over; the two Chinese fathers were now together and in quite a nod, nearly dead, as they laid on the floor of the opium den. Mr. Ludwig didn't seem to see anything going on in the classroom but the movie.

All four of the tenth graders, still huddled around a desk fell into a nod. Following the movie, Mr. Ludwig said, "Wake up." They stumbled out of the class and into the hallway.

As Norm and his partners stalked off, Mike reflected that he didn't like what he had seen. He had a hard time reconciling the teacher's words of enthusiasm—"we're all winners"—with his classmates' idea of drug education. Mike was to learn later that Norm and Curtis were not only using it, they were dealing horse throughout the whole school in the fall of 1968.

~ ~ ~ ~ ~ ~ ~

And yes, Detroit's World Series victory gave the city a shot of much needed adrenaline.

CHAPTER 29 –
What - No Latin?

AT THE ST. MARTIN DEPORRES' SCHOOL Board's second meeting in early November, the Board voted eight to three in favor of including Black Studies within the History and Literature curriculum. Jim Dunham couldn't get the board to approve a separate Black Studies program. Instead, they voted to revisit the question of a separate Black Studies program at the end of the school year. Meanwhile, the English and History departments would propose and then prepare the expanded curriculum.

Jim and the students were proud of their victory. Curly Cornell seemed to be devastated. He'd had no idea that the board would swing against him. Up until then, members of the board had given him nothing but positive feedback on his vision for an inner-city prep school. In fact, the school had just received an anonymous educational grant to develop college prep courses. Jim told the board he would use the grant to develop honors classes in math and science but continue to work towards a strong Black Studies program. Jim described to the board that the issue was that Curly thought it was either be like Brother Rice or die. Mr. Dunham explained, they could develop an honors program and be black at the same time.

Frank Waterman attended the meeting as a non-voting parish representative. All of the merged schools also had at least one non-voting representative who could attend the meetings. Frank remembered how smooth Jim had acted when he had briefed him and Ted before they reached the boardroom.

Jim Dunham had said, "Only a handful of kids, about five, signed up for Latin. It's an elective, and thus, not required. I've dropped the course from the curriculum."

When the men entered the room, the first thing they heard was Curly's loud exclamation: "How could you drop Latin from the curriculum?"

Frank Waterman had no idea that Jim already had most of the board in the palm of his hand. Curly's small block of support for Latin had been out-maneuvered. Curly's support came from two of the elderly white board members who were long-time parishioners and left over from the Visitation days. The other eight members: two nuns, two priests, and four lay members, including Ted, were solidly behind Jim and his proposal to move towards a Black Studies program. Ted's support for Jim had been unwavering from the giddy-up. He wanted Jim Dunham to succeed, as did Father O'Malley and several others on the board. Jim's proposal seemed to be too radical for Curly and his backers, and Curly called Jim Dunham's ideas a disservice to the community.

During the meeting, Curly, as chair, didn't want to relinquish the floor, and stood at the head of the table. He tried to filibuster Jim's proposal and prevent a vote. Finally, Ted stood up to challenge him.

"Curly, we all can appreciate your wide knowledge of parliamentary procedure and your concern over school repairs, but we all know why we're here tonight. So cut the crap and move on with the vote to incorporate the Black Studies program."

Ted's interruption was exactly what Jim needed to stop Curly's show of arrogance. Jim didn't want to have to do it himself. Ted, though, had been around the parish for nearly as long as Curly, and had put more children through the school. Even though Ted had admitted earlier to Jim and Frank that he didn't know much about a Black Studies program, he knew that a new day was dawning in America and he wanted his kids and the kids at St. Martin DePorres to receive the very best education they could get.

Although it was November, the air in the room felt like that of a steamy July night. The radiators clanged loudly while the board met. Curly looked exasperated as beads of sweat streamed down the sides of his cheeks. He kept dabbing his forehead with a handkerchief. The pits of his blue-stripped shirt were soaked. For the first time he was speechless.

"Hey Curly, we're goin' over to the Collingwood Bar for drinks. What the heck. You want to join us?"

"No, go and enjoy your celebration gentlemen. I have other matters to attend to," Curly replied curtly. Ted extended his hand for Curly to shake. Curly took it and gave Ted, then Frank and Jim, a firm handshake. He then threw some papers into his briefcase and began to leave.

Frank put a hand on Curly's arm to stop him and said, "Curly, it's for the kids, man. It's for the kids. They'll need it. Hope there're no hard feelings."

He stepped a bit closer to Curly and continued. "C'mon man, join us for a beer. We're all on the same team. We're all fightin' for these kids."

Curly took a step back, pulling his arm away. "I don't think you have any idea what it's going to take for these kids to make it out here," he said. "You have no idea."

Jim said, "Curly, these kids are not you, man. This is a new day and they need new tools. They ain't you. What you talking 'bout was then, and this is now, baby. It's a new day!"

"Goodnight gentlemen," Curly shot back. Then he closed his briefcase and abruptly left the room.

As the trio walked over to the bar, Frank asked, "How did we do it so fast?"

Ted explained, "A couple months ago, Curly turned off a few of his supporters when he kept coming back to his theme of *'proving to the whites'* that Negroes can tackle the rigor of prep-school academics. Curly's stuck in the 50s, trying to prove to white people that blacks are worthy, getting permission from white people . . . basically following the white man's lead. In other words, if the white man says it's okay, then it must be okay But because of your leadership, Jim, others on the board probably felt the surge, the juice, of the Black Power movement. They honed in on how best to empower black kids, which is perhaps not to mimic white people."

At the bar, Frank, Ted and Jim settled in around their favorite corner table, not too far from the juke box. They ordered the usual: a pitcher of Stroh's beer and hot wings. The bar had branded their wings "Soul Wings," steeped them in the sweetest-tasting barbeque sauce on the planet. The atmosphere in the bar was lively; the owners had recently put in two new pool tables, and the juke box had all the latest hits. Jim got to see Bonnie, his favorite hostess, and the men, did in fact, toast to victory.

"Here, here," Ted toasted. They all stood up and clanged their glasses together while Marvin Gaye's *"Pride and Joy"* played on the jukebox.

CHAPTER 30 -
Varsity Ball

MIKE'S TRANSITION FROM FOOTBALL TO BASKETBALL got off to a rocky start. Mike tried to stay focused on his quest to make varsity basketball. He'd been playing CYO ball since the fifth grade and had gotten pretty good at the pivot position. But he also knew that basketball talent saturated St. Martin DePorres and his right middle finger still felt sprained since the final football game.

His quest for varsity basketball was short-lived. After about two minutes of tryouts, Coach Freddie Ray. asked Mike to go one-on-one with a junior forward named Steve. Steve taunted Mike, saying, "I'm gonna teach you some manners, young blood." Mike didn't stand a chance; within moments, he got stuffed on twice and had the ball stolen from him once.

Mike was promptly demoted to junior varsity tryouts, though he didn't fare too well at the junior varsity level either. Hordes of aspirants were going out for the team. Mike noticed at least three very good centers, two tenth graders and one junior, all of whom must have been over 6'4". Mike, at 6'1", hadn't really thought of playing forward, let alone guard. Mike wasn't so sure that he was ready for this level of competition. After about twenty minutes of half-court scrimmaging, during which the junior varsity coach rotated in many players, Mike got about five minutes of action.

The freshman coach, watching on the sidelines, called Mike over to the side of the court and made him an offer. "Mike, I want you to be my first team center. You got what it takes to start at that position in freshman ball right now. You'll get plenty of playing time and that's what you want your first year." Seeing Mike's initial dismay, he added: "Only a very few freshmen will make the J.V. team and none are going to make this varsity team. What do ya say, Mike?"

Mike knew the answer.

"Sure, of course I'll be your center."

When Mike entered his house with his gym bag over his shoulder, the rest of his family had just started eating dinner. Mama E's famous gumbo could not wait. Mama E didn't make gumbo often but when she did, the gumbo was special. The occasion didn't matter. The gumbo became the event.

Just the thought of gumbo erased Mike's memory of his most recent basketball experience where Mike felt like a puppy in a sea of big dogs.

Anyway, the smell of gumbo in the air somehow gave Mike comfort, like a security blanket. Mike heard the chatter over the size of the portions Jon-Jon was taking. As he entered the room, Frank called out to him.

"Boy, get in here and tell everybody how varsity basketball practice went. And don't worry, the food is still hot. We just sat down."

Mike tossed his gym bag on the foyer floor and hung his coat on the hook. Before Mike sat down, he announced sullenly, "Didn't make varsity."

"Why not?" asked Frank, in an unusually stern tone.

"My finger is still bothering me. It hasn't been right since the last football game. Remember, I sprained it."

"Sure, son, we remember. Was that the only reason, was that it?"

"No," Mike replied as he sat down with the family. "The competition's too thick. These ball players comin' from all over the city . . . "

Frank patted his son on the arm and said, "Forget about it, son, and enjoy this great gumbo your grandma made. We already said grace. Bless your food and dig in." Then Frank asked, "You make J.V.?"

"No, I'm playing freshman ball this year."

"Damn it, boy," Frank said, with a hard-nosed demeanor. Then he leaned back in his chair, laughed, and added in a low tones, "Well, son, then you be the best freshman on that team."

Mike bowed his head to bless his food and thought that he'd better say a prayer for his father before he had a stroke about his basketball future. After his silent prayer, with his head still down, Mike took a spoonful of gumbo.

"Mike, keep your head up." Rose chided him. "When is your first game?"

"First Saturday in December. We play on Saturday mornings at about 9 o'clock."

"Well, we'll be there with bells on," Rose said, then looked at her husband Frank.

Mike finished his gumbo in silence, then retreated to the basement study to call Lola. *What on earth am I going to tell her?* he wondered. *Just tell her, 'I got the axe'?*

He called Lola and told her.

Lola said, "You didn't make the team."

"I didn't make varsity," said Mike. "I made the freshman team."

Lola laughed. Mike felt embarrassed. "Well," she said, "at least you made freshman. I mean, you just a freshman anyway."

"If my finger wasn't hurting so bad, I woulda made varsity. Know what I mean?"

"With your finger hurting so bad, you should feel good that you'll be playing."

Mike asked, "You goin' to the game Friday?"

"Of course. The eagle's flyin' high." said Lola laughing. "You know me and Steve are goin' together."

"What? Naw, I didn't know," said Mike. Steve, the 6'5" junior starting forward, was St. Martin DePorres's premier player and preseason pick for All-Metro. Mike thought, *damn, he kicked my butt on the court and took my girl, my "Moonbow."*

"Yeah, we hooked up last week, at the junior-senior party. You remember . . . at his house?"

"Yeah, I remember freshman weren't invited."

"Except the girls."

"Shit. I mean, shoot. Sorry."

"You going to the game, Mike?"

"I'll be there. Suppose to be goin' with my partner DeAngelo, who goes to Central, his brother Darren, and his cousin from Mumford High School. You know, Darren was an all-American when he played football for Visitation."

"Didn't know that."

"Yeah. Anyway, we goin'. DeAngelo's cousin—you know, the one I told you about, from Mumford High?—yeah, he wants to do this thang with the National Anthem."

"What are you talking about? He wants to sing it?"

"Something while they playin' it. Something like what John Carlos did."

"Mike, who is John Carlos? I don't know what you're talking about. Y'all not gonna start any trouble are you?"

"Naw, naw, naw, nothing like that. I hope not, anyway. But I really don't know."

"Mike, it's getting late, and I got to finish my homework. But thanks for calling," Lola said sounding as if someone was rushing her off the phone.

"You gonna come see me play on Saturday mornings?"

"What? What time?"

"Nine o'clock."

"Doubt it, that's early for me on Saturday. That'll be like going to school."

"Don't you get up to watch TV or do some chores?"

Lola burst out laughing. "My chore on Saturday is sleeping."

Mike felt frustrated, and was about to respond with a sharp retort when Lola said, "Got to go, Mike. See you in school tomorrow."

"See ya," said Mike, then he hung up the phone. Mike held his right hand in front of him, felt his finger throbbing, and said aloud, to no one in particular, "This finger is killin' me."

CHAPTER 31 -

...And the Rockets' Red Glare...

MIKE GOT THE APPROVAL FROM HIS parents that he could ride with Darren and DeAngelo to DePorres' first game at Catholic Central High School. Luke went along too. Darren would pick up Davis, DeAngelo's cousin, along the way. Mike wasn't sure what they were going to do except sit on the opposing team's side of the gym and disrupt the playing of the National Anthem.

Davis, a senior at Mumford High School, was supposed to lead whatever it was they were going to do. As soon as Davis got in the car he said, Y'all ain't getting scared, are you?"

"Should we be scared?" replied Mike.

"Hope not, but y'all got to deal with the repercussions, that's all. What we fittin' to do just ain't gonna blow over. Y'all strong enough? All power to the people!" Davis raised his right, gloved fist. Mike didn't care for all this tough talk, especially after football season, during which he felt he had proved he was tough. Darren, driving the car, didn't even react to Davis's tough talk. Darren had told Mike and DeAngelo earlier that he was going mainly to watch their back.

Mike said, "Man, look, I don't expect it to get me kicked out of school or nothing. What did y'all do at Mumford, and what happened when y'all did it?"

"What happened? What happened?" Davis replied, laughing. "Didn't *shit* happen, that's what happened. Nobody said shit!!" But we just did it once at the last football game up at Henry Ford High."

"Maybe . . . maybe they just don't know what to say yet, or how to say it," Mike responded.

Davis said, "Maybe, but we got more white folks here tonight."

"What we supposed to be doin', anyway? I don't even know," Mike mumbled.

Davis explained to the group that they were just not going to stand and would continue to carry on a conversation during the National Anthem. "That's all," Davis said, then laughed.

When the athletes from Catholic Central and St. Martin DePorres finished their warm-ups, they returned to the benches. Then, a voice boomed over the loudspeakers, "Please rise for the National Anthem."

Mike noticed that Mr. Dunham and his father arrived just before tip-off and sat next to Mr. Ted Wilson on the top row near center court. *I hope he don't see me*, Mike thought.

Everyone in the gymnasium stood up to honor the Star-Spangled Banner except Davis's group - Mike, Luke, DeAngelo, and Darren - who sat on the Catholic Central side of the gym. They remained seated and began talking. After a few moments they started horsing around, and talking loudly in the stands. They were purposely being disruptive. Davis talked the loudest.

Loud enough that those around him could hear him above the loud music and singing, Davis shouted, "This song doesn't deserve our attention." Stares of anger turned towards the boys. Their angry red-glare looked redder than any rocket Mike could imagine. "Yeah, that's right," Davis continued. "Y'all may get upset, look crazy, but what y'all gonna' do?" Everyone else stood in stony silence.

In the meantime, Mr. Waterman's brother John got wind from Jon-Jon of what was gonna go down. Jon-Jon had told Uncle John that Mike and DeAngelo were planning to do something during the National Anthem, maybe a protest but wasn't sure. So Uncle John showed up with three of his college buddies just to watch their backs. After the National Anthem, Davis's group, Uncle John and his buddies, retreated to the St. Martin DePorres side of the gym.

~ ~ ~ ~ ~ ~ ~

On Sunday morning, Jim Dunham called Frank to talk about the national anthem incident. He told Frank that Curly Cornell had insisted he call an administrative staff meeting, first thing Monday morning. Frank had a personal interest to be there. He talked to Mike to hear his story, and learned from Mike that the boys had planned the prank. Frank dismissed it as nothing more than a boyhood prank, but advised Mike not to do it again, then repeated several times, "You'd better stay focused."

When Frank arrived at the school for the meeting, Curly was already in a rage. Sister JoAnna was there too. Curly said, "The archdiocese is hot and they are breathing fire down my neck. They want you to make an announcement tomorrow morning, Mr. Dunham, that you will not tolerate inappropriate behavior during the Star-Spangled Banner, at home or away games." Mr. Dunham sat down, clasped his hands behind his neck and fixed his eyes on Curly, who was pacing the floor in Jim Dunham's office.

Jim said, "Look folks, it's not a crime and it's not harming anyone to talk during the National—"

"Jim," Curly burst out, "you're not condoning this disrespectful behavior, are you? These kids need to be expelled."

"Expelled? You want my son and Luke expelled?" asked Frank.

"Hold up Frank," Jim interjected. "Curly, back up man. I'm not condoning it, but what about their First Amendment free speech rights? They aren't making any threats. They weren't using any foul language . . . "

"But it's provocative, Jim."

"To whom? White people?"

"It's an assault to all Americans, and as the principal of this school you should condemn it. And Frank, this isn't personal."

"Now, c'mon, Curly. It's personal for me," Frank reminded him.

"Look gentlemen," broke in Jim, standing up and taking a step toward Curly. "I've thought about this action long and hard over the weekend, and what I would like to do is this: talk to the students and let them know what people are saying."

Curly broke in. "And then what?"

"Then come up with a fix. For example, let's play Kim Weston's version of 'Lift Every Voice and Sing,'- the James Weldon Johnson song also known as the black national anthem. That's how some colleges - addressed it. This has happened at several black colleges Howard, Fisk, Southern," said Jim.

He sat down again looking more relaxed.

"But those colleges play both," said Ted. "I heard that they played both. That way people are attentive to both the black national anthem and the national anthem."

"That might work at home games," Sister JoAnna chimed in, "but I don't see it happening at the other schools. I heard that parents at Catholic Central plan to press the archdiocese for disruptive behavior or disorderly conduct expulsions if it happens again."

Jim said, "I believe in expulsions as a corrective measure, but I don't want to hear about expulsions for talking during the National Anthem. That is utterly ridiculous, in my book. This is not the military. And this is not a police state — Curly!!" Jim stood up, looked Curly in the eye as he voiced his sudden idea. "We could do away with the National Anthem altogether at the home games and just play 'Lift Every Voice and Sing.'"

"There is no song requirement at the games. It's all optional," Ted pointed out.

"We could even ask the cardinal to discontinue the practice," added Jim.

"Why?" asked Curly. "Why should they? We need to respect their wishes. This has been going on for years."

"And they should respect our wishes," said Jim.

Curly walked up close to Jim, looked him in the eye, and said,

"I think you need to make a decision here. Who's running the place? You, or the kids? Frank, we may not see eye-to-eye but this situation can get outta hand." Curly glanced at his watch. "I need to be at an Open House in fifteen minutes. You all should be able to figure it out. If you don't, next time it won't be me in your office. The archdiocese will send an envoy."

"I'm trembling, Curly," Jim called after him. Curly exited the room with surprising grace, leaving the other men standing still.

"Come on Jim," Ted chided. "This is a serious matter. Cut the crap."

Jim said, "Frank, you go to the games at Tiger Stadium, Cobo Arena, don't you? When they play the National Anthem, aren't some people buying beer, going to the john . . . ?"

"It's overblown, Mr. Dunham," said Sister JoAnna, "but it still requires a response. You need to say something about it."

"I will. We have a pep rally this Thursday . . . "

"Sounds wonderful! I need to get back to the convent. I'll see you gentlemen tomorrow," said Sister JoAnna.

Ted, Frank and Jim waited until sister JoAnna left, then resumed their discussion.

"Ted, Frank," Jim began, "We got bigger fish to fry here, man. This National Anthem issue is small potatoes."

"What do you mean?"

"I mean we got real problems here. We got heroin. One of the teachers found some red caps in the boy's room."

"He found heroin?" asked Ted in a naive manner.

"He found some empty red caps that heroin comes in. Not only that, this teacher has a pretty good idea of the users and the dealers."

"Dealers?" Alarmed, Frank leaned forward. "You got to be kidding me on this."

"Now were talking expulsion," said Ted.

"Not so fast, Ted. We're talking about a much bigger problem, much deeper. Kicking students out of school may not be necessary to solve the problem."

"But Jim, sometimes you got to get rid of the troublemakers."

"I look at counseling first. Straight-up talkin' to these kids and using our counselors. We have counselors for a reason," said Jim.

"But these kids will just deny," said Frank.

"That's okay They'll start thinking about it, at least, if they know we're hip to what's going on," said Jim.

"Let's say we just tell the parents," Ted suggested.

"That's next," Jim reassured him, "if the kids continue to screw up. The last resort is the police."

Frank said, "And Curly wants to have a cow over kids talking during the National Anthem."

CHAPTER 32 –
The Halftime Show

ON THIS NOVEMBER NIGHT, THE WEATHER was colder than a bull's ass in Montana. An earlier-than-usual cold winter frost had set in.

Mike, Jon-Jon, and Luke entered the gym of St. Martin DePorres High School about ten minutes before the varsity's first home game tip-off. They searched long and hard for seats. The school's first home game drew a huge crowd. The hardwood floor, freshly finished with a glossy wax, looked new. The eagle painted in the middle of the court looked elegant, and the blue and gold trim painted around the gym emanated brilliance. During the introductions of the teams, floodlights shined brightly down over the floor like spotlights at a play.

Mike, Jon-Jon, and Luke sat at the far end of the gym on the lower benches. Just before tip-off, Bongo Bob and three other upperclassmen started playing bongos and congas. The cheerleaders had worked on a routine to the African rhythms. After the summersaults and splits they all did a routine facing the DePorres crowd dancing and swaying their hips to the beat of the bongos and congas.

After playing Kim Weston's rendition of "Lift Every Voice" to a standing ovation, a DJ, put on the Star-Spangled Banner. Some visitors and a group of Black Panthers who attended DePorres promptly rose and walked out.

"Ain't you gonna leave?" Jon-Jon asked Mike.

"For what?"

"To protest."

"Man, look. Dad told me to be cool, or else," said Mike.

"Or else?" said Jon-Jon.

"Right. Or else I'd be lookin' for a different school."

Jon-Jon's Afro hair style had grown to three inches and the high school girls, including Mike's classmates, called him a little cutie. Just before the second half began, Lola introduced herself to Jon-Jon as a special friend of "your big brother." Lola wandered off, and Mike told Jon-Jon he would meet him back in the gym. After hanging around outside the entrance to the gym, Mike then cornered Lola in the lobby before she returned to her seat.

"I want you to be my girl," Mike said, leaning toward her. Lola's deep, dark complexion made Mike think of the midnight sky, mysterious dark matter. Mike felt the explosion of his passion pulling him in to explore that deep dark space. *The infinite possibilities . . . ,* he thought, *will she open the door to infinity . . . ?*

Lola shrugged and took a step back. "But I'm taken," was all she said. Mike just shook his head; he'd thought he would at least give it a try. "I still want you to be my girl."

Lola strode off and Mike went back into the gym to take his seat.

Facing the DePorres crowd, the cheerleaders were doing a routine with hips swaying, afros bouncing. They formed a circle and let each cheerleader briefly perform on her own inside the circle. The sound of congas punctured through the dense sweat of emotion. The rhythm was pronounced. Mike, Jon-Jon, and Luke stood up and bounced to the beat. Mike felt all of his soulful spirit bubbling up from somewhere inside. He tried to forget about Lola. The conga players drummed with such intensity, never losing form, never missing a beat.

The DePorres crowd stood up and began to chant, "DePorres, DePorres." Soon it became a contest between one end of the gym and the other, to see which end could shout the loudest. "DePorres, DePorres." The chant rang on.

The cheerleaders ran along the boundaries single file, then formed two rows—one facing the other—at the back door leading to the locker rooms. The varsity players emerged wearing shiny gold uniforms with royal blue letters. The conga players kept their rhythm.

Once the players were into their warm-up, the cheerleaders belted out before the crowd, "Are the Eagles gonna win it?"

And the DePorres crowd answered back, "Hell yeah!"

"Dag," Jon-Jon said. "The cheerleaders are smoking and the congas are on fire. I want to play like that, Mike." Mike looked at Jon-Jon in amazement, his eyebrows raised.

"Maybe you can play with them one day," Mike responded gently, patting his brother's back.

"I sure want to."

During school, Mike had met Bongo Bob, who was only a tenth grader but led the group of conga players. Mike introduced Bongo Bob to Jon-Jon after the game.

"Maybe y'all can play at next week's freshman game," Mike suggested.

Melvin, a senior, said to Mike and his brother. "Man, I won't be getting up at eight to play. How 'bout you, Timmy?" Timmy just shook his head, indicating that he wouldn't be there at that early hour either.

"Where can I learn to play like you?" Jon-Jon asked Bongo Bob.

"Go down to the African Drum and Theatre Troupe, up on Dexter and Davison. They'll teach you bongos, congas—you name it, they'll show ya."

Jon-Jon didn't waste anytime convincing his mother he had found his new thing. It wasn't being a radio DJ. Jon-Jon had said he changed his mind. He didn't want to become the next Butterball Jr., the hottest DJ in Detroit. Jon-Jon wanted to drum.

~ ~ ~ ~ ~ ~ ~

That Saturday morning, Mike entered the locker room on a natural high after scoring twelve points in his team's victory over Our Lady of Sorrows. Then, seemingly out of nowhere, Duane started talking trash to Mike.

"Man, why ain't you wearing a fro yet?" Duane heckled.

"Thinkin' about lettin' my hair grow out," Mike retorted, then added: "Jon-Jon got a fro."

"Your little brother is ahead of you, man. What you waiting on?" Duane asked with impatience in his voice. "Look at my 'fro. It's already six inches tall. Remember, two years ago people was just talking about it. Now, we doing it. Everybody's wearing a 'fro. After the rebellion, man, Pops and all my brothers just said, 'Fuck this shit. We going natural. We showin' our black pride.' My ol' man took me to a rally about six months ago down at Kennedy Square and all the brothers and sisters down there had a 'fro. You got to get yours, my brother. Let your hair grow. They got this special comb," he continued, "an afro-pick. This one here I got is the Picel-Pick made by this dude right here in Detroit. You can even get one o' these picks at the Chaldean stores."

"What you doing tonight besides wearing an Afro?" Mike asked. "You still chasing that tenth grader, Michelle, tryin' to jump in those pants?"

"Chase?" Duane laughed. "I ain't got to chase no more. I mean, these girls see me with this Afro and they automatically fall for me just like that." Duane snapped his fingers, then laughed. "No shit!"

"Just like that?" Mike asked.

"Yeah, brother, just like that. But oh, yeah, my brother, you got to have the required reading in your back pocket. *The Autobiography of Malcolm X.*"

"What?" shouted Mike, surprised. "All I need is an Afro and a book by Malcolm X and I'm straight?"

Duane said, "Yep, you'll get all the poon-tang you want. I swear. It's nation time, my brother."

"You know, I got to ask my folks," said Mike. He really had no idea what else to say. No one except Jon-Jon was wearing an Afro in his household. Even Uncle John wore only a small fro.

At home, Mike looked in the bathroom mirror and began to practice. "Dad, look, I'm gonna let my hair go natural," he spoke aloud to the mirror. "I bought the special Picel Afro Pick and some Afro Sheen." Then, in a lower voice he also said, "And the girls will love it." *Naw, better not say that.* "Ummm, will it help me get better grades? Of course it will. This Afro makes me think better. Okay, it's about Black pride, and Black is beautiful, right? That's it!!"

Ever since football season had ended, Mike had kept his middle finger wrapped daily during basketball practice. One day his finger would feel as if the pain were going away, but then a week later it would throb continuously, keeping Mike in pain for hours. His dad brought him some over-the-counter pain medication but insisted that he go see a doctor after the season.

Once, when Mike woke up screaming, his father thought it would be necessary to check into the emergency room. Mike told him that he must've laid on it in his sleep.

"The pain's going away, Dad." Mike couldn't keep a straight face, but managed to speak between clenched teeth, "It's just a sprain."

"We need to get you x-rayed, boy," his father replied.

"It's not broke."

"Let's see you bend it." Mike grimaced as he barely bent his middle finger.

"See?" Mike tried to smile. He worried that if his finger were broken or badly damaged, he could be out of commission for weeks. He did his best to reassure his father, and vowed silently to continue playing through the pain.

Near the end of basketball season, Mike's academic performance had been pretty solid, tackling the demanding homework assignments but not quite making the honor roll and entrance into the highly coveted National Honors Society. The teachers demanded so much: reading, writing, and algebra. And they had high expectations. He didn't have the time for anything but school work and practice during the week.

He realized that there were many smart kids at the school. None of the other athletes made the honor roll either, and anyway, three-fourths of the honor roll students were female. Mike shrugged as he told his mother, "I got A's, B's and a couple of C's."

"One too many C's," his mother Rose replied. But you can be on the honor roll if you want to, Mike. You got to want it just as bad as you want football and basketball."

Mike looked at her with his head cocked to one side. "Yeah, I know," was all he said.

Rose went on: "I mean, a C in English because you didn't get a paper typed and the teacher couldn't read it. Now that's uncalled for."

"Mom, you sound just like Sister Mary, telling me all the time that I can do better than this." The subject was dropped.

By late January, Mike had completed his freshman-year football and basketball seasons. In basketball, he played the position of center in every game, and averaged twelve points and ten rebounds per game. He felt better about his football future than he did about basketball because he felt that there were dozens of more talented basketball players than he - where he would need to fight to keep his center position on junior varsity - but in football, Mike thought that he would be a starter at wide-receiver next year.

Mike hadn't spent much time with his father since school had started. They rarely lifted weights together anymore. Mike knew his father was stretched thin and would occasionally see him at City Club some evenings. Frank worked six days a week—that was his norm. He insisted that Sunday was a day off, no matter what. He went to church, and then took the family on a Sunday drive, often to Belle Isle or Canada.

In the late evenings when Mike lifted weights in the basement, he would see his father tucked away in the study surrounded by paperwork. One night he overheard his mother talking to his father. Rose told Frank, "You already work six days . . . ten, twelve hours a day, Frank. Leave it there. Stay late, but leave it there. And you need to keep Sunday free – all of it!" Frank looked too exhausted to argue. Rose continued, "I heard you tell John that you couldn't make the Black Power Conference later today."

"Yeah, I know, after Mike's game I'll be at the Club all day," Frank said. "But we're going to the Shrine of the Black Madonna tomorrow afternoon to catch many of the same speakers. They're speaking after service."

CHAPTER 33 -
Black Power Conference -
March 1969

FRANK KNEW THAT EVEN THE COLDEST Detroit winter couldn't freeze the fires of resistance that swept through the city in 1968 and 1969. The Shrine of the Black Madonna, Rev. Cleage's church, played host to the follow-up presentations for Saturday's National Black Economic Power Conference at Wayne State University. Sunday afternoon at the Church gave the main speakers from the day before another chance to present their specific proposals for developing economics in black communities across the country. The event at the Shrine also included some who didn't speak at the conference.

Before the speeches were made, the church's Black Christian Nationalists strode in, clad in black and red. The choir belted out the song *Like a Bridge Over Troubled Water*.

Frank and John arrived during the singing and just before the featured speakers began, and sat near the rear of the church. The church was filled with black men and women, in their twenties and thirties. The attendees talked about the impending black political revolution in America, black political power.

At first, Frank didn't recognize anyone he knew but he eventually spotted his neighbor and friend, Reverend Boykin, mingling near the front. The program was about to start and Frank thought he would speak to Rev. Boykin after it was over.

The first speaker, Jim Foreman, a former SNCC organizer, emphatically called for reparations - a payment to the descendents of slaves. He cited his demands that were contained in the Black Manifesto he had prepared and delivered at the conference the previous day. He explained that the money he demanded for the reparations could be used immediately to set up cooperative organizations - businesses owned and operated by their members - throughout the country. Foreman's Black Manifesto demanded money from churches to be used as seed money to start the cooperative businesses.

Another speaker and keynote speaker at the conference, Robert S. Browne, an economist, presented an analysis of separatism - the partitioning of specific states - at least five states for black people in America. He spoke on the people's right to petition the United States for specific states for residence in an independent nation.

John nudged Frank and said, "That's right, brother. Partition the United States, just the way Pakistan was created from India."

"This is astonishing," Frank replied. I don't agree with it but it's still astonishing."

When the speakers had finished, the audience began to chant "Free the land!" and "Black power!"- continuing for nearly five minutes. A spokesman for the Republic of New Africa, the RNA, a newly formed organization in Detroit, called for a plebiscite, or a vote, for blacks to determine for themselves where they want to be citizens - in Ghana, the United States, etc. The RNA's call for reparations exceeded by far what Jim Foreman had demanded. Their plan proposed that people of African-descent would need enough money to re-establish themselves wherever they decided to live.

Pan-Africanists spoke about the need for a United States of Africa, and called for Africans in the Americas to link up with Africans on the continent in the struggle for liberation against racism and oppression.

Frank felt a sense of urgency, just like he did after the 1967 rebellion. The speakers' messages were urgent. Frank got the sense that these young folks who spoke were not going to wait for permission, and would not wait for the folks downtown to get around to making policy changes. Speaker after speaker made it clear that the black people represented a force. Frank knew that things were changing. He knew that Richard Austin, a black man, had recently kicked off his campaign, and spoke at the City Club grand opening, to become mayor of Detroit. These were important developments to Frank.

Frank had been completely unaware of the intellectualism that had been a part of this new black *thing*, this dynamic Black Power movement. These young folks were not just yelling and screaming for change, but had instead become voices of passion and intellectual rigor.

"Reparations sure make sense," said Frank to John. He had never experienced anything like it, and was moved by the speeches he heard and by the passion of the crowd.

During Robert Browne's talk, John whispered to Frank with a tone of awe, "This is the black revolutionary intelligentsia."

The conference gave Frank new fuel for the fired passion of shaping City Club as not just a recreational center, but a center for change in Detroit. Inclusion of a senior's health clinic became paramount maybe even a 24-hour drug treatment and prevention program. Frank wanted to talk these ideas over with his staff.

~ ~ ~ ~ ~ ~ ~

While Frank drove him home, John had a point he wanted to make.

"Frank, man, when I came back from Vietnam, I made a pact. I'd been involved with the RNA for the last few weeks. I'm talking about the Republic of New Africa. As you heard, they're fighting for reparations and five states in the South."

"John, five states!" Frank replied, exasperated. "I heard that talk, man. We're fighting for survival right here and you're talking about five states in the south. We're talking about survival. I understand where they're coming from, we need reparations but we're so overwhelmed with the problems right here in Detroit, I can't think about the south right now. We've still got the south moving up north looking for good factory jobs. What am I supposed to do?"

"Keep up the struggle, my brother," John said quietly. He said no more.

~ ~ ~ ~ ~ ~ ~

At home one quiet afternoon on March 29, the phone rang, and Frank answered. "Hello?" His brother John was on the other end.

"Frank," John growled into the phone, "the police shot the place up! They shot inside New Bethel Baptist, Rev. Franklin's church, man. They had women and children up in there, hiding under the pews."

"Slow down, brother," Frank replied, reeling from the news. "Did anybody get hurt?"

"Not seriously."

"Were you inside?"

"No, was on my way," said John.

"Why did they shoot the place up John?"

"Man, the police are outta control. I heard that a pig got shot in the area earlier. I don't know the whole story. But, man I know I'm 'bout sick and tired of this shit."

Frank leaned back into the recliner chair, and wiped his face from top to bottom with his hand. Pressing the receiver against his ear, he said slowly, "We got to change the face of this police force. We need accountability. Nobody got shot in the church?"

"Nobody, but they took all of 'em, even the children to jail. Judge Crockett and Judge Del Rio got most of the people released from jail, thank God. There's gonna be some rallies all across the city." He paused. "Hey, Frank. I want to organize one at City Club. Is that cool?"

"It's cool."

"We need power, Frank. That's why your boy Richard Austin gotta win."

CHAPTER 34 -
Confronted -
Spring 1969

MIKE KNEW TRACK FROM A DISTANCE only. He had gone to a couple of Catholic School Invitational meets to watch, but he had no idea what type of training he would need to get himself in shape for track season.

Mike's late winter practices were certainly a sign of things to come. Track practice made basketball practice seem like a walk in the park. Coach Montgomery pushed his runners until they dropped. Then he'd back off a bit, but just a little. The track team ran stairs, indoors, during late winter and early spring training until the weather warmed up. The runners would start in the school auditorium below the church, then sprint to the opposite end, climb four flights of stairs to the church balcony, then race back down. The stairs seemed to separate the weak and meek from those serious about running.

Sometimes, while the team was running inside, the building's heat would be on. The sweltering temperatures were brutal. Mike wiped the sweat from his brow with a small face towel he kept tucked halfway into his shorts. He used that towel every day, because if the sweat rolled down his face and into his eyes it would burn like mad.

Coach Montgomery paced the auditorium like a caged tiger, occasionally growling. "Pick your knees up, knees up! Run those stairs with authority, son." Coach unleashed some choice words if he caught someone slacking. "If it's too hot in the kitchen, then get the hell out." "You got to pay-to-play, baby. If you run for me, you got to run to win." Coach Montgomery had been part of a winning program when he attended Florida A&M. He certainly acted as though he knew how to turn kids into winners.

Well, so much for the CYO philosophy, Mike thought. CYO philosophy focused on team spirit, character building, and good old' fashioned Christian values: such as faith in God, honesty, and integrity. Those CYO principles had been driven home since his elementary school days. *The coaches at DePorres probably believe that too,* Mike thought, *but what comes out of their mouths is the will to not only win, but to dominate.*

Mike's first encounter with the stairs made him see stars. He got dizzy. "I need air," he wheezed, huffing and puffing. "I'm getting dizzy." But instead of quitting and going outside, he continued to push himself, trying to make a positive impression.

Soon enough, his fatigue started to get the best of him, and was clearly visible to the coach.

"Step outside, son, and walk it off," said Coach Montgomery. Mike bent over with his hands pressed on his knees. "Walk, son, walk! Don't bend over like that. Keep walking."

The air outside felt great to Mike. The chill didn't matter. He walked around the school parking lot for a few minutes, until the stars disappeared, and he felt prepared to go back inside.

Before he could get back in line to do more stairs, the coach called him over. "Son, before you hit those stairs again, I got to tell you that you ain't gonna get in shape in one day. But you keep pushing hard, you keep coming back, and I'll get you there."

Mike thought he'd quickly do one more set of stairs, then stop for the day, but his legs ached as he kept climbing. They felt like tree trunks, and he climbed the staircase slowly. With one more flight to go Mike stopped running altogether and walked to the top, then ambled back down to the auditorium.

When he arrived in the auditorium, he was feeling pretty good about his first day. He had heard what Coach had said, and knew that he needed time to get into his best shape. He kept walking slowly across the auditorium while he took his sweat-drenched t-shirt off. He had long since given up trying to keep the sweat from his eyes, and headed to the boy's room to wipe his face. At the sink, Mike turned on the cold water and stuck his head in the sink for more relief. *Oh, yeah, now that's what I need,* he sighed.

By now Coach had ordered everyone to take a break. "Shit, take a break, everybody take a break," Coach said, laughing. "Lookin' good, lookin' good. After the break we'll do some starts, and then call it a day. Y'all lookin' good, but you still got a long way to go. And some of y'all play football and basketball, so you should be in better shape than what I see."

During quick starts, a sophomore named Roland Johnson complained, "I need a break, coach."

"One more, Johnson, then break." Johnson did one more at less than half speed and kept going out the door. Coach threw up his hands and said, "Well, if y'all can't cut the mustard, let the door hit ya where the good Lawd split ya. And that goes for everybody."

~ ~ ~ ~ ~ ~ ~

Heading home after practice, Mike met Luke at the door leading out to the parking lot. As the two rounded the building they were met by about twenty-five boys who were gathered in the school parking lot, evidently waiting for someone or something. Mike and Luke were taken by surprise, but Mike immediately recognized the others as Captain Z's boys, part of a crowd headed by that well-known neighborhood thug.

"Where did all these fools come from?" asked Luke.

Petey Bones, one of Captain Z's main henchmen, was out front, wearing his fake Bosalino hat cocked sideways. His hair looked like a dried out "doo" that turned orange. He spied Mike's new jacket, and looked Mike up and down. Then, as if in slow motion, Petey Bones flipped out a 6" blade and raised the shiny steel tip to Mike's throat.

"Give me your jacket," Petey Bones demanded. Mike nervously searched the group for help as he felt the sharp tip of the steel blade on his throat.

Mike spotted T-Man, whom Mike knew from his former baseball team, among Captain Z's boys. T-Man was pacing the lot, sporting a fresh set of silver-colored brass knuckles. He gave Mike no sign of recognition or greeting.

Mike drew his eyes level with Petey Bone's. He still didn't move, but shook his head signifying "no." When Petey Bone's didn't respond immediately, Mike eyeballed T-Man, then called out to him.

"Hey, T!"

In response to Mike's prompting, T-Man waved off Petey Bones. Out of nowhere, Don, another one of Captain Z's henchmen, grabbed Luke by the collar, then let him go. The two quickly marched away.

Once out of sight, Mike slammed his gym bag to the ground. He was furious about the assault.

"I'm not down with this, man. We got to do something," said Luke. Luke wanted to seek revenge.

"Yeah, we gotta do something. I don't know what, I just don't know. There's too many of them."

"Catch one by himself," said Luke, as he hit his fist into his palm. Mike kicked his gym bag out of frustration.

CHAPTER 35 –
Rose in the Garden

MIKE WOKE UP EARLY SATURDAY MORNING, despite his sore and tired legs from yesterdays track practice. He couldn't miss his favorite show, ABC's Wide World of Sports. Before he turned on the television, he paced the room slowly, trying to relieve the tension in his legs. After some minutes, he stepped up to the family room window and watched as his mother, Rose, took a handful of mulch and placed it firmly around the base of the rosebushes. He saw Jon-Jon lay out about a dozen bags of mulch around the yard. He watched as his brother slit each bag with a box cutter, then, open the bags wide to make it easy for Rose to get the mulch. Rose had evidently enlisted Jon-Jon to help her mulch the bushes on this cool March Saturday morning. Usually, Jon-Jon would be inside with Mike. Calmed by having watched his family, Mike turned on the television to watch ABC Wide World of Sports, but kept glancing out through the family room window.

Mike noticed that Jon-Jon still stood next to his mom as if he were waiting for instructions. Taking Jon-Jon's stillness as his cue, he rapped on the window to get his brother's attention. Jon-Jon glanced over at Mike. Mike beckoned him to come inside, pointing to the TV and mouthing to Jon-Jon that Wide World of Sports was about to come on.

They never missed the beginning of the program, and looked forward to hearing the commentator say " . . . the thrill of victory and the agony of defeat . . . " It was exhilarating to watch a skier crash into a snow bank and tumble over a rail. Every time they saw the opening, it was as exciting as seeing it for the first time.

But Mike realized that Jon-Jon didn't budge and continued listening as Rose was talking. Mike wondered what the heck Jon-Jon had gotten himself into when he started to help their mother mulch the bushes. Mike remained standing, half watching the TV and half watching what was going on outside.

When Denise and Sharon showed up in the backyard, Mike rapped harder on the window. He wondered if they were trying to turn Jon-Jon into a girl or something. *Did he prefer to plant flowers now, and maybe join the cheerleading team when he got to DePorres?* Jon-Jon held up his index finger and signaled to Mike to wait a minute. Then he turned away again to focus on what Mama E and Rose were saying.

Denise and Sharon had a cartwheel practice session scheduled. Mike remembered overhearing the two girls last night. Rose left a grassy walkway wide and long enough for the girls to practice cartwheels. The two girls spent hours rehearsing routines, working on new cheers. They were going to try out for the DePorres cheer team over the summer. Sharon had already spent the night with Denise twice this week. The two girls lit up the household with their silliness and never-ending pranks on Jon-Jon. Sharon's playfulness, good looks, and gentle charm attracted Mike and sometimes made him wish Sharon were his main squeeze instead of his play sister. But because of his respect for his sister's friends, he kept his distance, always playing the role of a brother and good friend. He knew one day Sharon would be in the center of *Jet* magazine.

Mike rapped on the window again in frustration, waving Jon-Jon inside. Mike opened the window, then pushed up the storm window and called out to Jon-Jon. "What are you doing, man?"

"I'll be in. Just a minute."

Mike gave up trying to coax Jon-Jon inside. He sat down to enjoy the show alone. Mike had noticed that Jon-Jon's enthusiasm for sports had shrunk over the past few weeks. He'd taken up playing congas last winter and played regularly with Bongo Bob. Jon-Jon also spent hours making disc jockey tapes.

While still watching ABC Wide World of Sports, Mike could hear Denise and Mom in the backyard talking about cheerleading. They finished weeding and mulching around the rose bushes, then sat down on a large white metal chairs, pulled off their gloves, and admired their work. The rose bushes now stood four feet tall.

"Mom, we got five months to practice cartwheels before tryouts this summer. And, you promised you'd help us."

"Then girls, you better take note." Mike watched as his mom did cartwheels in the backyard. He stood up and walked to the window to get a better view, ignoring the TV for a minute. Rose did two perfect cartwheels, then, on the third try she fell hard on her butt. She just sat there both hands on the ground and laughed. The girls joined in. Jon-Jon helped his mother up and over to a chair.

Mike found it hard to concentrate on the sports program without Jon-Jon. Before the show ended, Mike went outside to see what the rest of his family were up to. The girls did cartwheels and splits while Jon-Jon leaned against the fence and talked to his mom. Once in the backyard, Mike could hear the conversation.

"I like that way you laid out the backyard. It's peaceful back here. This is nice. Mom." Jon-Jon's voice suddenly changed to a deeper, more serious tone. "Can I paint your statue of Mary black?"

Rose said, "Oh, my God. Tell me you're not serious."

"I'm serious Mom. Jesus is black, and so is his mother."

"Jon-Jon, listen. Color is not important."

"Then it's okay."

Rose hesitated for a few moments, then said, "It's okay, Jon-Jon, it's okay."

CHAPTER 36 -
Football Practice -
Summer 1969

MIKE NEXT SAW THE GIRLS DO cartwheels, backflips, and splits at his first
football practice in the summer of 1969. While the football teams practiced
in mid-August, the cheerleading teams held tryouts. Denise, Sharon, and the
rest of the cheerleading hopefuls-Mike referred to them as the finest girls in
the world - were on hand, trying to capture a spot on one of the coveted teams.
And they captured a lot of attention from the players during their tryout.

During a "skull session" before practice, during which Coach helped the
teammates get their heads in the game, Coach Taylor said, . . . "and keep your
minds off the fine china. I got a number of complaints about the coaching
staff using female body parts to describe some of y'all. So from here on out we
just gonna refer to anything female as 'fine china', China, China doll, goin'
to China, can you dig it? Then Coach expressed his dissatisfaction with last
year's second-place finish. He made it clear that he was not in the business of
being second-rate.

"You got first-rate coaches, you at a first-rate school, and we got first-rate
players. I'm expecting big things this year, big wins. The difference between
second-rate and first-rate is the size of your hearts. This year you will play with
heart. If you wanna play, you best find some heart. I can't give it to you. Naw,
I ain't no Wizard of Oz. You got to dig deep within. And if all you got is a
mustard seed, that's damn good enough. If you got heart the size of a mustard
seed, that's all you need."

After laps, Coach told Mike that he would be playing wide- receiver and
safety this year. And at safety he was told by defensive coach Walters that he
could "knock somebody's head off and not get arrested." After hearing that,

Mike felt a chill down his spine. *I guess that means someone could equally take off my head too, without reprimand. Should I even care?* Mike wondered. *After all, it's football.*

Football practice felt more hellish than track, and a hundred times more hellish than basketball. During basketball practice, the team spent a lot of time on techniques of passing, dribbling, shooting, and defense. Football practice, on the other hand, was brutal, even barbaric. Football circle-time was one example of this brutality. It looked more like cockfighting to Mike, from what little he'd seen about cockfighting. But everyone showed maximum exhilaration during this drill. Mike couldn't help but notice that during circle-time, the coach's eyes glazed with excitement, froth dribbling from their mouths. And the language . . . the language of football is not in anybody's dictionary. The coaches didn't waste any time breaking the wheat from the chaff.

A week later, during the first day of full contact under the morning hot morning sun, Coach called for circle-time, with a tone indicating he thought the players were all children. "Okay boys, and uh, well, some girls . . . , it's circle-time! For those who are new to the game, watch how it works." The team formed a circle and the coach called someone to be in the middle. That person was given the football and told to run in place. He then had to fend off tacklers who were called out from among the team. First, coach called one person at a time, then two, then three. And the tacklers came from all angles, leaving the ball carrier moving about in the circle trying to dodge them. Eventually, the ball carrier got blindsided by somebody. Coach told him to get up and continue.

Finally, Coach Taylor said, "Mike, it's on you, babe." Mike took his position in the circle. They came and they kept coming. Mike used his forearms with all his might to fend off the tacklers. He tasted the blood that ran down from his nose. The pain in his finger became unbearable. The coach called for the next victim. Mike was still standing, and felt a great sense of accomplishment.

After circle-time, the team scrimmaged among themselves for about thirty minutes. Many of the players were too tired and beat up to play effectively. They'd had too much circle-time.

The next morning's practice session consisted of nothing but wind sprints.

"Wind sprints," Coach called out. After yesterday's sloppy scrimmage, Coach Taylor decided had decided to postpone further scrimmage, but to punish the team because of its lack of hustle.

"Yesterday's game day situation looked pitiful. What do you think?" Coach asked with a hint of sarcasm. "You were supposed to give a hundred

percent for thirty minutes and what do we get? You look like shit. S-H-I-T!"
Coach Taylor slammed his clipboard against one of the benches. The board
crackled and snapped, instantly flying in three different directions. "You
linemen are blockin' like a pack of sissies! You might as well be holdin' hands
with each other."

Coach Taylor next directed his anxiety toward Joe Coleman, the senior
offensive tackle who stood 6'7" tall, and weighed in at 340 pounds. "Joe, what
you doin' man? You blowin' kisses at the defense. And you runnin' backs, y'all
tip-toein' through the holes like you at some ballet. Y'all ain't goin' to a damn
ballet. Y'all look too happy out here! Ain't nobody sweatin, ain't nobody mad.
The damn offense can't even get in the end zone. First and goal at the four.
Jesus Christ!" Coach was livid. "Let's line up. Shit!"

After ten fifty-yard sprints, Coach called for hundred-yard sprints. "Y'all
ain't seen nothing yet. Set-hit." Players had their hands on their knees. Mike
didn't buckle as easily. He had prepared himself better in the off-season.

"Set-hit," Coach repeated. Several players lay out on the grass.

"Get up, get up, damn it. It ain't over 'til I say it's over. Gimme some
water, somebody." One of the assistants handed Coach Taylor a bottle of
water. "Naw, go fill up that bucket over there." When the assistant came back
with the bucket, Coach carried it out to the field and poured it over one of
the players. Marcus Washington lay still for a few moments after the water
cascaded down on him. He looked like a bowling ball. He stood 5'10" tall and
weighing nearly 300 pounds. Mike wondered if the boy was dead. He finally
rose, very slowly, and began walking towards the end of the field where the
other players were lined up.

"Set-hit," Coach yelled again. "You can do it, you can do it!" he hollered.
"One more! Set-hit. One more!" he continued. "Set-hit. You can make it,
Marcus. I'm gonna run with you."

Coach Taylor ran the last five sprints with Marcus. They actually raced
the last one, laughing.

"Okay, take it to the bus. We can't carry your big ass all that way."

It was a quiet ride back to the school's locker room.

Mike felt pretty good after practice, except for his throbbing left middle
finger, a fat lip, and his still-bleeding nose. Just as Mike left the locker room
and made his way into the parking lot, Brother Bear, Luke, and DeAngelo
pulled up.

"Get in," said Luke. Mike grabbed his bag and walked over to the car.

Little did Mike know then that Brother Bear, Luke, and DeAngelo, were
as high as kites, driving through the streets of Detroit. Brother Bear pulled

his new royal blue '67 Mustang to a stop on LaSalle Blvd. at Tuxedo Ave., near Central High School.

"My friends, I got a surprise," said DeAngelo as he waved a sandwich baggie in the air. The baggie contained several small red capsules. Luke, who sat in the front, pulled at the plastic baggie and held it up.

"Hand it here, Luke," said Brother Bear. Luke handed him the baggie, holding it high in the air as if wanting to tell the world something.

"We got that white horse, raw dog, good P, five dollars a cap, five dollars a cap," chanted Brother Bear. While parked, he pulled out a mirror from beneath his seat, broke open a few of the capsules, built a small mountain of the drug heroin, and began snorting the heroin with the corner of his driver's license. "This shit's some good shit," he said, exhaling slowly. "Wanna try some, Mike?"

Mike couldn't believe it, and turned to Luke for answers. Luke said he'd started tooting P a few weeks ago, "Since I ain't playing ball no more," he told Mike. He proceeded to sniff P right alongside Brother Bear. Mike, just fifteen years old, was bewildered to find himself sitting in the car with the heroin snorting fools. Luke told him that the heroin would ease all his aches and pains. Mike watched in amazement as Brother Bear quickly finished off three caps, and Luke worked on his second.

"Hey brother, I hear this P is straight out the jungle," Luke said.

"Man, get me home," Mike said, an edge of concern creeping into his voice. "I still got practice again tonight, and . . . don't spill none of that crap on me either!"

"You always got to practice something, Luke said, egging Mike on. "Do you ever stop practicing? Here. Practice this." Luke laughed and shoved the mirror in his face. Mike turned aside and stared out the car window.

Just then the Big-Four police rode by in their large black Chrysler 300 Sedan. Brother Bear, who was clean shaven and neatly dressed in his gabardine shirt, didn't even look phased.

"They sure are rolling awfully slow," said DeAngelo.

"I don't even see them sorry-ass motherfuckers," said Brother Bear.

"I think someone called them on us," said Luke.

"Man, shut up. You paranoid or something," said Brother Bear. "Just keep it down. See, they kept going."

"They just out trying to terrorize black folks," said DeAngelo. "They don't scare me."

"Hey, man. I really ought to get home now," Mike insisted again.

Without a word, Brother Bear revved the engine and took off again. After a few minutes of driving, with everyone still quiet, Brother Bear skidded over to the curb in front of Mike's house.

"I'll be back to get you if you need a ride back to practice," Brother Bear called out the window, as Mike jumped from the vehicle.

"That's all right. I got a ride."

"Hey, man. What time the cheerleaders get off?" called DeAngelo, teasingly.

"They're done for the day." Mike shrugged. Mike wanted to say *You idiots are gonna waste your lives tootin' P.* But he just stood there nearly in shock as the Brother Bear, Luke, and DeAngelo rode off.

CHAPTER 37 -
Conflict at City Club -
September 1969

FRANK WATERMAN HAD BEEN RUNNING THE City Club for more than a year by then, with little fanfare. He had doubled his paid staff from eight to sixteen, and had built a solid core of volunteers.

One day, while on the phone, he heard a holler.

"Frank!" yelled out one of the volunteer staff. "We need you in the pool room!" Frank dropped the phone on the desk and ran towards the Club's pool room at the other end of the building. A small crowd had gathered outside around the door.

"Coming through, coming through," Frank said in a forceful tone. Immediately he noticed a broken pool stick on the floor. Once he managed to shove his way further inside, Frank witnessed a standoff. About six of the staff stood between Hunt and Darnell, two neighborhood rivals, both about eighteen years old and out of high school, who were glaring at each other with an intensity that sent a chill down Frank's spine. Frank began to whistle.

Darnell had in his hand the other end of the broken pool stick and one of the pool balls. Frank noticed that Hunt was wearing an awfully heavy coat for early September.

"Hunt, what you got up under your coat, man? Darnell, put the ball down." Frank's words fell on deaf ears. "Put the ball down! We're gonna settle this shit right here, right now," he continued.

Darnell's shirt had been ripped open and was hanging out of his pants. He turned to one of the staff and said, "Carr, you took sides, man. You took his side, man! That nigger's dead," he threatened.

"I ain't through with your little yellow punk ass," shouted Hunt, a husky, dark-skinned brother who stood about 6'3" tall with a perfectly shaped three-inch natural, glistening with an oiled sheen under the pool-room lights.

Stepping forward, Frank articulated slowly, "Hunt, give me the gun, or whatever you got under your coat. Carr, you and some of the men escort Darnell and his little entourage out the building."

"Why I got to go, Water (the name the boys at the City Club gave Mr. Waterman)? Why y'all puttin' me out?" Darnell complained.

"Darnell, I don't know what happened, baby," Frank said patiently, "but I want to see you in my office tomorrow. You got that? I want to hear your side of the story."

That seemed to put Darnell at ease, almost at home. The tension in his face seemed to relax, and he took a step back. Looking over to his boys, about a half-dozen of them still standing around, unsure of what to do next, Darnell motioned them to the door.

"Let's get the fuck outta here."

"Okay, Hunt. He's gone, man. Give me what you got."

Hunt still stood rigid, looking tough as nails. He glanced over at Carr, then over to Mr. Blue, another full-time staff worker and basketball coach.

"Carr, go make sure Darnell is out the building," Frank suggested.

Hunt shrugged, and loosened slightly. "Water, you okay with me man," he said, pulling a meat cleaver from his sleeve. "This is all I got." Hunt threw it on the pool table, then looked up at Frank with a sharp glare. "This shit ain't over."

"It's over," Frank responded, without missing a beat. "It's got to be over. What's this all about, Hunt?" Frank picked up the meat cleaver from the pool table and looked Hunt dead in the eye, then repeated: "What's this all about, that you're ready to turn this brother into sausage? Talk to me, man."

"You wouldn't understand," Hunt said gruffly, and turned away.

Mr. Blue suddenly jumped into the fray, eager to speak his piece. "It's about a woman, Frank—Darnell's woman friend, Darla. Her and Hunt had some words and she told Darnell. Then one thing led to another. It don't take much these days."

Carr returned to the room, interrupting Mr. Blue's hurried monologue.

Frank seized the opportunity and said, "Why don't y'all escort Hunt outta here? In fact, take him home, can you, Carr?"

"Yeah."

Frank turned to Hunt. "Hunt, go on home and cool off, brother. I want to stop by and see you tomorrow. At your house, in the morning. I already know where you live."

Hunt was alone at the center, but said he was cool and didn't need an escort. Carr led him out the front door, then went around back to be sure Darnell had left the area.

Meanwhile, inside the center, a volunteer photographer and known Pan-Africanist named Kwame came over to Frank, gazing warily at the meat cleaver he was still holding. "A meat cleaver," he said. "Now that's some serious stuff. Frank, let me call a neighborhood youth summit and bring these two brothers together to work this thing out. I don't want this to escalate."

As he spoke, Carr burst back into the room, panting and sweating.

"They fucked up my ride! Them little hoodlums fucked up my ride! Tires slashed, windows busted out . . . you know what I'm gonna do to that little punk?"

"Whoa, Carr," Frank said, placing his hands calmly on Carr's shoulders. "We'll deal with it. First thing, Carr, make sure you talk to your insurance company."

"Insurance? I got minimum coverage. It's gonna cost me a fortune to get my ride fixed," said Carr as he left once again, shaking his head and cussing to himself in anger and frustration.

Frank wanted to see the damage first-hand, and turned to his friend. "Kwame, let's walk out to the lot. Tell me what you have in mind."

As they walked, Kwame explained his ideas. "I want to get these brothers to come up with a unity agreement. I want to discuss the need for a united front in the neighborhood. At minimum, they can co-exist in some kinda peace-zone or safe-haven, such as in this center."

"And what makes you think they'll drop their beef?" asked Frank.

"We gotta try something, brother. We gotta try."

Frank nodded, and responded slowly. "First, I want to find out what Darnell is so pissed off about. I'll see him tomorrow."

Kwame said, "You still gonna meet with that knucklehead?"

"Of course. We got to resolve this ourselves and we got to do it quick. Look at Carr's car. We need to do him a fundraiser—a couple of them." Frank took a close look at the damage to Carr's '66 Impala. Frank stuck his head into the car through the broken window, and grabbed something off the front seat. Pulling his head back out, he turned to Kwame. "Darnell must be crazy. Here's the pool ball he left with." As Frank opened the car door, glass rained down onto the pavement. "We can't afford to lose these two." Frank smiled gently, turning the situation over and over in his mind.

Frank knew he had to move quickly so as not to let the situation escalate. He had to give Carr some assurances, not only about his car, but about his safety. He knew Kwame was reliable and wanted to keep him involved. "Kwame, go ahead and set up the summit. Make it for this Saturday. We can't waste any time."

"Thanks, Water."

CHAPTER 38 -
City Club Summit

ON SATURDAY, KWAME SHOWED UP WITH about seven brothers, all in their early to mid-thirties, and all dressed in African garb. The room was set up like a conference room: three long tables were connected in the front, and the room was filled with chairs. The PA system was on the table for the group of adults.

Darnell was there, with his own entourage of about twenty brothers. Hunt showed up with seemingly half the neighborhood in tow. In his earlier one-on-one conversations with Darnell and Hunt, Frank had gotten a sense of what happened at the center a few days before. Darnell had told Frank that the whole thing started with Hunt feeling his girlfriend's butt. Hunt said he didn't give care. Hunt was jealous and was gonna have his way.

After much persuasion, Frank convinced both young men to attend the summit.

"Brothers," Kwame said as he opened the summit, *"Habari Gani.* That means 'what's happening' in Swahilli. And what's happenin is unity, or *umoja,* my brothers. Unity in the community. So when I say *Habari Gani*—y'all say *Umoja.* Let's try it now. *Habari Gani."*

"Umoja," the audience replied softly.

"Louder," Kwame encouraged. *"Habari Gani!"*

"Umoja," the audience replied, with the slightest bit more enthusiasm.

"Thank you," Kwame continued. "For those of you that don't know me, my name is Kwame Toure. These other African Brothers before you this morning are Ahmad, Sekou, Malik, Kenyatta, Chokwe, Chimba, and Aye. We are here as an African Council. We are an African people."

By this time, the brothers in the audience were rolling their eyes and wearing enormous smirks on their faces.

"What the fuck this got to do with anything?" Darnell demanded loudly. "This ain't what Water said we was gonna be doin'."

Kwame cut him off just as the room began to stir. "Why are you here, Darnell? And Hunt, why are you here? My brothers," Kwame said, rising, "we are here in the spirit of unity. The white man is tearing us apart. He got us coming and going, got us imitating him, chasing all his materialism. We are chasing his dream for America. Brothers, his dream for America is to put you back on the plantation."

Hunt got up to square off with Kwame. "Fuck the white man, he ain't fucking me. You up there talking all this Africa shit, back to Africa, whatever—I ain't going back to Africa and I ain't no African. And I didn't come here for this bullshit," Hunt concluded.

"My brother," Kwame reached out.

"My brother. Nigger, please."

"We are here to seek a unity pact between Darnell and Hunt. This is why we came together today." Hunt's response is still negative.

"What's all this Africa talk got to do with this summit? I'm gettin' the fuck outta here. Sounds like y'all tryin' to brainwash people."

Hunt stormed out of the room, with about twenty-five people rising to follow his lead.

Darnell looked around. "Where's Water?" he asked, with increasing edge in his voice. "I ain't signed up for this. Hunt disrespected my woman and me. What's this Africa shit got to do with Hunt disrespecting me. I still got some things to settle with Hunt and Carr. This ain't over . . . my brother," Darnell added sarcastically, giving Kwame and the African Council a very sinister sneer.

Kwame looked more than frustrated. He looked embarrassed. No one said a word. They all just looked at each other while the room emptied out.

Frank had chosen to lay low in his office, until he saw Darnell and his boys leaving in a hurry. He followed them outside.

"Darnell!" Frank yelled. "Come back here, my man. We gotta talk." Darnell kept walking, throwing both arms up in the air. Frank caught up with him. "Bring your girlfriend by the office tomorrow. Hunt will be there to apologize to her in person. You gonna be there? You're not gonna leave me hangin', are you?" Frank asked again.

Darnell paced angrily with his face down, but eventually conceded. "Okay, I'll bring her. What time?"

"Ten o'clock. By the way, what happened inside? Why y'all rushing out?"

"Kwame's full of shit with all this back-to-Africa bullshit. I ain't African, and I don't give a fuck about no jungle."

"Cool it, brother. I'm about sick of your mouth. You need to be quiet and listen sometimes. Kwame is one of the most dedicated men up here. He wants peace, just like I want peace." He paused, considering how to gain back Darnell's trust. "Hey, look . . . see you and your girlfriend Darla in the morning."

Darnell turned on his heel, and he and his entourage left the premises. Frank thought about Rose's request that he not work on Sunday but he knew he had to work on this Sunday.

Hunt arrived at Frank's office early on Sunday morning. Looking through the doorway, Hunt stared in shock to see Darnell already there, talking to Frank.

"Water, what's this?" Hunt spat out. "You didn't tell me . . . "

"Hunt, shut up and get in here, man," Frank said, rising. "Close the door. We're all in here now. Now I don't know what really happened. I wasn't there. All I got is this version and that version. And if we keep on that track, all we got is your word against his. Hunt, first off, apologize to Darla. Do it. You grabbed her behind, didn't you?"

When Hunt made no movement, Frank picked up a bat from beside his desk and smashed it against the table, staring at Hunt all the while. At this uncharacteristic display, Hunt began perspiring, beads of sweat rolling up on his forehead. He looked from Darla to Frank, and back to Darla.

"Darla, I . . . I'm sorry," said Hunt.

"Good," said Frank. "Darnell, you're next. Hunt was man enough to apologize to your woman. Say something to Hunt. Tell him you're sorry. Just like brothers should. What you think this whole Black Power movement is about? You don't have to be African to act like brothers."

"Sorry," said Darnell, barely audibly.

"Darnell, that's weak, man," Frank corrected him. "That's some weak stuff. Shake hands, and don't let this shit happen again. I mean it. We got too much to lose."

The two young men looked at each other, Darnell damn near in tears. Frank could tell that Darnell couldn't believe that Hunt had apologized.

"Sorry," said Darnell, louder this time. Hunt looked hard at Darnell, as if wanting to take advantage of a weak moment. Instead, he extended his hand, and then, in a swift and sudden motion, pulled Darnell close in for a brothers' hug.

Everyone in the room stood in silence for a few moments. Finally, Hunt broke the silence and said, "Peace." Then he left the office. Darnell stayed behind with Darla to regroup from the emotion.

Frank decided to give Darnell and his girl a few moments' of peace, and left the office. In the hallway, he was greeted by about a dozen staff members who had come inside when they had seen Frank's car in the lot. Carr told Frank in a whispered voice that they'd all heard what had gone on inside, and at first had thought the shit would hit the fan.

Frank smiled softly and walked over to Carr. "Carr, go in there and ask Darnell how he's gonna pay for the damage to your car. Now, you know, I got a job for him."

Carr went inside the office. Darnell looked up as he entered, but said nothing. Carr extended his hand, and said to Darnell, "Darnell, my brother, I'm proud of you. I'm glad we got a truce. But what you gonna do about my ride? Sorry I held you back. I was only trying to save your black ass."

"I don't need your help, Carr."

"Darnell, all that damage . . . It's gonna cost me about two grand to repair it. You got to work it off or something. Darnell, Frank's got a job for you. He wants you to help with the Black Panther free breakfast program, twice a week for the next four months."

Darnell looked down, and said nothing. Carr could see the tension rising in his shoulders, and was eager to move the conversation forward.

"Darnell," he prodded.

"For Water, I'll do it," said Darnell softly.

Having finished speaking with a few other staff members in the hall, Frank re-entered his office just in time to overhear Darnell. "This ain't for me baby," he said. "This is bigger than me. Think about your families, think about the neighborhood. But hey, Darnell, I respect you, little brother. Look, Darla," he said, turning to face her. "This man must love you or something. Look at what he's doing for ya. Fighting, tearing up cars . . . and now he's gonna serve breakfast to children."

They all broke out in laughter.

~ ~ ~ ~ ~ ~ ~

Frank walked in the door just as the late local news came on. Rose turned the television down low in the bedroom. "Is that you, Frank?" Rose whispered.

"Yeah, Baby, it's me," Frank said in a tone that spoke volumes about his exhaustion. Then he let out a sigh. "Boy, boy, boy, boy, boy. There's got to be joy in the morning."

Rose whispered softly as Frank entered the room. "Now, you don't have to wait until the morning for this joy. Joy is my middle name." Frank could feel her warmth in the darkness. "Take that tight shirt off and get up here. Been waiting on you. I want you to know, Frank, that I'm with you all the way. I know what you been going through at the center. I'm with you, baby."

Rose's voice got softer and sweeter as she walked up to Frank, and gently began to undress her husband. "I love you Frank," she whispered, nibbling his ear. "I love you more than anything in the world."

"Still love me?" Frank asked, leaning his head into the warmth of hers and wrapping his arms tightly around her waist.

"More than anything," Rose said.

"More than a suitcase full of diamonds?" Frank asked jokingly. "Me or the diamonds, huh, baby?"

Rose laughed, and leaned back, pulling her face away teasingly. "Well on second thought . . . of course you, man. Money, diamonds, gold, it comes and it goes. But there is only one Frank Waterman, and ain't nothing gonna get between us."

She pulled Frank even closer and began to undress him. Kissing, then biting his ear, breathing heavy she said very passionately, "I love you Frank." Frank held her body tightly against his.

"What in the world would I do without you, Rose?"

"What *would* you do?" she asked back.

"Don't even want to think about it. Right now I'm so happy with you. Your love, your radiance, your glow . . . baby, you light up my life."

"Still do?"

"Still do, baby doll. Now more than ever." Frank pulled Rose down onto the bed.

"Oh, Frank," Rose sighed, pressing herself against him. "I'm so hot for you. It's getting hot in here, baby, and I'm just getting started." They fell asleep to the sounds of the Four Tops singing *Baby I Need Your Lovin'*.

Rose looked up, glancing at the clock, which read 3:30 a.m. She got slowly out of the bed, looking down at Frank and watching his chest rise and fall with each breath. *Poor baby*, she thought with a smile. *I know my lovin' wore him out.*

Slowly and quietly, Rose walked down the hall leading to Mike and Jon-Jon's bedroom. She cracked the door and looked to see that both boys were in their bed. *Hmmm, wonder how long they been in there.* Mike had been out that night, but the boys were always taught to check in with her or Frank before they went to bed. Rose wondered why he hadn't come to tell her or Frank he was home. Maybe he'd known better than to interrupt?

When Mama E saw Frank the next morning at the breakfast nook table, she said, "Now is the time, Frank. I want to organize a talent show, a fundraiser at the Club. The kids need a unifying event. Something all the kids in the compact schools can participate in." She paused to make sure Frank was listening. "A talent show would be perfect, because Detroit's got talent, Detroit's got soul."

Frank said, "I can go for that."

Most of the kids at City Club attended Central, Mackenzie, Northwestern and St. Martin DePorres high schools'. Frank had organized monthly gatherings of the schools principals and staff. His next move was to invite parents from all four schools to socialize and get to know each other. He called the loose-knit gatherings The Compact to reflect their intention to keep harmony between students at the different schools. The schools became known throughout Detroit as the compact schools.

CHAPTER 39 –
Detroit's Got Soul

MAMA E AND ROSE HAD BEEN doing well, selling whiting fish sandwiches and bean pies at the Visitation's bingo games every Friday night. At home late one Friday night, Mama E announced that they were making about $500 each week since they had started eight months ago. They had already raised twenty percent of their goal.

After the conflict at City Club, both Mama E and Rose had talked with Frank after dinner about the idea of a talent show at City Club. The ladies had suggested that they could invite all the compact schools to participate. Frank didn't hesitate for even one second. He'd become so involved in managing the Club that he depended on his staff and volunteers to carry out their plans once he gave them the green light. He just needed regular briefings, usually weekly.

City Club already served over two hundred kids every day, and fed another hundred at the free breakfast program, run by the Black Panther Party—all this in addition to a number of other regular activities. Frank was eager for the opportunity to extend the Club's outreach still further, to other kids in other neighborhoods.

Frank loved after-dinner discussions, especially around community affairs, business or politics. At dinner one night, after Rose and Mama E had been working all day preparing for the talent show, Mama E said to Frank, "You remember Paul Mack, don't you?"

"Sure."

Mike, Jon-Jon, and Denise, who had been preparing to leave the table and head off to their respective after-dinner activities, instead hung around to hear more about this idea for a talent show.

"Well," Mama E continued, "Paul offered his high-school jazz band and thirty-piece high school orchestra to back the performers. And his high school jazz band signed up to compete in the show. They want to rehearse with the vocal acts that sign up."

Paul Mack had been director of the city's youth orchestra for the past five years, had taught music at Wayne State University, and played in a jazz combo locally, often performing at Baker's Keyboard Lounge. Paul's orchestra included an all-female violin section that sounded like heaven on earth.

"Okay," Frank said, reflecting on this new development, "we have twelve acts that need backup." Already scheduled were five acts that featured dancers, 2 comedians, and Paul Mack's jazz band.

"I want this to help bring these kids together," Mama E went on. "I already sent invitations to local record labels, including Motown's Berry Gordy. Of course, Paul knows the Funk Brothers, who played on some of Motown's greatest hits. And Paul says they'll be there, with front row seats."

"That's great," Frank said, trying to imagine how he would make this all work. The City Club stage comfortably held Paul's thirty-piece orchestra with a good ten feet of stage left for the singers. But backstage, it was narrow and did not accommodate many acts at once. There was a side door which allowed the acts to wait outside if they choose to, or sit in the audience and wait their turn.

Frank voiced his concerns about seating capacity, but Mama E had an idea. She talked with Rose about setting up the auditorium with the round tables at the club instead of the row seating. She asked Rose and Delli to help her design a more elegant set-up.

The rounds would have red or white table clothes—neutral colors that did not represent any of the schools in the compact. Each table could seat eight. The black chairs would also provide an elegant dimension, and the tables, they decided, would each have a candle and a flower for centerpieces. Mama E expressed her satisfaction with the idea of an elegant evening for the kids as a worthwhile investment, and one they could surely afford, given the fact that she could use the place for free.

Rose was elated with the whole idea, and she and the children expressed their excitement as Mama E continued to discuss the logistics with Frank. Mama E told him that Paul knew a light and sound man who worked with him at Northwestern High School. By using friends and other connections, they could keep the cost low. Frank estimated that five dollars would be an acceptable charge for admission. Rose would collect the five dollar admission, and Mama E would keep track of the performers.

The auditorium held five hundred people in total, but the room would only accommodate forty tables. There would have to be additional long rectangular tables to accommodate the crowd at the capacity they were expecting. They decided to keep the menu simple for the mostly-teenaged audience they expected. Rose suggested hot dogs, hamburgers, fish sandwiches, fries, soda pop, and bean pie and banana pudding for dessert.

On the night of the talent show, Frank and his staff transformed the City Club into an elegant nightclub for the performances. Outside, the street lights gave off ample light along the street. The parking lot had been cleared of all debris and its lights were finally working. Frank's brother, John, coordinated security, while Carr coordinated valet parking. Frank also arranged front row seating for Hunt, Darnell, their families and a few friends.

The first act featured *I Heard it Through the Grapevine*, by Gladys Knight and the Pips, sung by a freshman girl from Mackenzie High. She sang her heart out. Outside, near the side door, Mike mingled with Luke. Mike tapped his feet and leaned against the wall outside the club. He had agreed to be the primary "gopher"— go for this, and go for that, and basically do what he was asked to do. For the time being, there was nothing for him to do, and the idleness was making him nervous. Jon-Jon came outside to join them.

Jon-Jon wore his favorite dashiki, the purple and gold one given to him by a Nigerian priest, Father Akojie, who was new to Visitation and a good friend of Father Thom. Jon-Jon chewed his gum nervously, then finally spit out the whole gob onto the grass nearby, energized by the soulful sounds streaming from inside.

Delli, headed up the kitchen detail, instructing her young volunteers on putting together fish baskets and hamburger plates. Mama E and Rose hung out near the entrance, standing and watching. The auditorium had filled up to capacity by the third act, and there were no more tickets left to sell. Frank acted quickly to have about fifty more chairs set up along side the wall, and reasoned that he could squeeze in another fifty on the other side if they needed to.

Listening from outside, Mike realized that Mama E must've put the acts in some kind of order, because just before the first break a trio of young Central girls sang The Supremes song *Come See About Me*. The crowd in front jumped up, whistling and clapping overhead. The lead singer had the crowd in the palm of her hands, and Mike thought they would bring the house down. Hunt and Darnell and their families had tables right up front, and on their lead, many in the crowd got out of their seats and danced between the tables. Mike felt electricity in the air, generated by the enthusiasm among the performers and the audience. Mike was overcome by such a powerful vibe that all he could do for that moment was feel good about what his Grandma had done.

People were crammed in throughout the auditorium, on stage, and backstage. Many were fanning themselves with their programs or with the church fans Mama E had placed at the entrance. The room temperature in the room must have registered near 100 degrees. Paul's forehead beaded up with sweat, and his white shirt was drenched.

Just before break, Mike noticed Luke pacing outside. Suddenly, it seemed like Luke made a quick decision to go inside, and he rushed over to where Mama E was standing. Mike followed.

"Let me do the intermission. I cleaned up the Rudy Ray Moore joke about Shine and the great Titanic. Honest! No cussin', I promise," Luke said.

"I'm glad you took the cussing out. But what about this part here?" asked Mama E as she pulled from her pocket an old copy of the joke Luke had wanted to perform. She pointed about halfway down the page. "What about this part right here, about some woman's panties wrapped around her nappy head? We got families here."

"I'll redo it again. I'll even leave that part out. I just want to perform. I might be a comedian one day."

"Do you have any clean Bill Cosby jokes you can tell us, Luke?"

"Uh, no. But I got a bag full of white man, black man, Chinese man jokes. And they clean."

"Okay, Luke," Mama E conceded. "Go on and tell your jokes and keep the crowd entertained during this first intermission. I'll give you ten minutes."

"Thank you, Mama. Thank you, Mama!" Luke said, bowing constantly.

"Go on, boy. And I best not hear one profane word out your mouth. And definitely no panty-talk."

Earlier in the week Mike had watched Luke flop his audition. Luke had started off cussing, and that's when Mama E had cut him off. "Luke," she said, "you know we can't have that. Too much cussin'."

"But Mama, it ain't funny with no cussin'. That's how it's told."

"Well, you're gonna have to tell it to someone else."

Knowing how disappointed Luke had been, Mike's heart swelled to know that he would be in the show after all.

Luke made his way to the stage in his brand new green and white gabardine suit, with white buttons and white stitches along the collar. He wore a pair of green gators to match.

Luke immediately got the audience. "Listen up everyone, screw your wigs on tight, tonight I'm 'bout to tell you a story about Shine and the great Titanic. One beautiful day, in the merry month of May, the great Titanic sailed away . . . " Luke started off. Luke's tone and demeanor had people laughing right away. Mike laughed too, even though he'd heard the story many times and knew the lines by heart. Somehow, Luke always made it sound fresh.

"Cap'n Cap'n, I'll have you know, there's nine feet of water on the ballroom floor. Well Shine, you gone back and stack some sacks, now we got nine water pumps to keep that water back . . . " Mike loved it that his main man was getting laughs.

Mama E and Rose set four pitchers of water and paper cups near the stage for the band. Paul gave up a big smile and said, "Water's up!" Several hearty "thank yous" rang out from the musicians as they grabbed their cups.

A short fashion show was to follow Luke's performance. Rose asked Mike to come with her backstage. Delli had taught the models how to walk, and had choreographed three short routines for the intermission. Mike checked out about a dozen students, including Denise and Sharon, dressed in African garb. The women and men were picking out their afros. Delli left the kitchen to join the group backstage. Delli sprayed Afro Sheen on one girl's hair as she picked it out. "You brothers and sisters ready?" Rose asked. "You're on in 30 seconds."

"Keep those heads up," Delli added, "and be proud. Shoot, I don't need to tell y'all that." Delli finished spraying and said, "You look fabulous girl." Mike admired the girl from Central High with her perfectly rounded six-inch afro. As DJ Bongo Bob put on the record, *Miss Black America*, by Curtis Mayfield, the girls cued up backstage.

"Mike," Rose said, "I want you to help the gentlemen to change into these clothes over here in the corner once they get off stage." Near the end of the song all of the models walked the perimeter of the stage, single-file, with their arms extended. Several of the men in the audience raised their fists in a Black Power salute. The models got a standing ovation.

Mike helped the men take off shoes, put on different shoes, and get into their alpaca cardigans. Mike and the men were on one side of the backstage partition, just beginning to change their clothes, when Mike heard his mother on the mike. The women changed into evening gowns and did an all-woman modeling act to Curtis Mayfield's song *The Woman Got Soul*.

Rose said, "That was act one, give it up one more time." And the crowd hooped and hollered. Then Rose said. "We have one more act. We're going to change the tempo just a little bit. We got a real treat in store." People whistled. Rose continued to engage the audience for another minute, then Delli motioned to Bongo Bob that they were ready. Bongo Bob played James Brown's *Hot Pants*. The audience stood in anticipation.

The men and women went onto the stage as couples in fall clothes. But about half-way through the song, the girls unhooked the dresses and skirts and revealed their hot pants underneath. Mike noticed that many in the crowd were giving dap, while others were clapping. Some hooted, some hollered. The girls broke out into a dance routine, burning up the stage, while the boys watched in amazement, joining in only after the initial shock wore off. Later, Mike found out the men had had no idea that the hot pants routine was part of the show.

The stage turned into one big party, as did the audience, as people danced at their tables and in the aisles.

After intermission, the second set featured an acapella gospel act, a magician, vocal groups singing the Four Tops and Smokey Robinson and the Miracles, a piano soloist, and a couple of dance routines.

Mama E had stacked the third and last set intentionally with what she thought would be the best performances. The first act featured Paul's high school jazz band playing *Mercy, Mercy, Mercy*. Paul had introduced his sax players as the best young sax players in Detroit – Brother Bear among them - maybe the whole country. They lived up to every bit of praise he heaped on them. Like his father, Mike enjoyed the sweet sounds of the sax, and this group featured two. Mike felt enraptured as he watched the young men play with such great intensity.

The jazz group was followed up by a dance routine to Nina Simone's "4-Women," then a poet reading an original poem called "All Power to the People", and next a singer performing Aretha Franklin's *Natural Woman*. This performance was followed by David Ruffin's tune, *My Whole World is Empty Without You*, sung by a young man from Central High, who was followed by DePorres's own Duane and his group, who performed *You're My Everything*, by the Temptations. These last two performances both brought the house down.

Then came a ninth grader from Mackenzie doing his rendition of James Brown's *Papa's Got A Brand New Bag*. His version lasted over six minutes, because of his dance routine in the middle of the song. His group had four female background singers, and the girls took turns breaking out the cape to wrap him up after he broke down to the floor doing splits. They caught him when he fell back, and they sang some mean background vocals.

Paul's jazz band played like they were the James Brown's band themselves, and danced while playing. The lead singer got the crowd on their feet like no other after doing back-to-back splits. The crowd went hysterical during his performance, and when he left the stage, the crowd begged for an encore. The band kept playing, and then the little brother came back from behind the curtain doing the camel walk. He spun around took the mike and got the audience involved. When he hollered, "Papa" the audience hollered back, "Papa." He held the mike out towards the crowd five times, then broke down to his knees while his female singers covered him up with his cape and nearly carried him off stage. The audience exploded with applause and whistles, while the band played on.

When all the acts had had their turn, Mama E took to the stage to thank everyone. She said, "Wow, Detroit's got a whole lotta soul. Let me hear you say it. Detroit's got soul." The audience hollered back, Detroit's got soul. Mama E said, "Detroit's Got What?" Detroit's Got Soul, the audience shouted. Mama E kept up this chant for another minute. Then she led the audience in voting for first, second, third, and fourth place. The crowd selected as fourth place Duane and his trio doing the Temptations' song *You're My Everything*, the third place winner went to a 10th grade student named Nancy Walker from Central High who sang *Natural Woman*. Second place also went to the Central senior named Herb singing *My Whole World is Empty Without You*. The overwhelming winner went to Mackenzie High 9th grader Tony Black who did *Papa's Got A Brand New Bag*.

As Mama E left the stage, someone handed her an envelope with cash and a note that said *"You were a hit today . . . you can pay the band."* Also, Frank had received pledges for money to help pay for the cost of the show and to build a new wing at City Club.

CHAPTER 40 -
Mike and Renee - October 1969

DURING THE PAST YEAR MIKE CALLED and talked to Renee on holidays: Thanksgiving, Christmas, and Easter. When he called her on her birthday in August she was in Chicago. She returned in September. Mike needed to see her right away. He'd asked her to type his English research paper. Mike decided to go see Renee to drop off a paper he needed typed, but he knew he had another mission. He wanted to ask her out to the homecoming dance, point-blank. He enjoyed the two-hour bus ride over to Renee's house because it gave him time to imagine Renee, her finely shaped body, her warm smile and soft breasts. After the bus ride, Mike walked another four blocks to her house. Renee's brilliant and infectious smile greeted Mike at the door. Mike could hear the radiator clanging, but that didn't take his mind off Renee. The house was warm and felt so good after being outside in near-freezing October cold. The wind chill had taken the temperature to levels far below normal. But Renee's warmth was just as intense and just as comforting. Mike thought, *she could warm me up in the middle of any cold winter night.*

"Thanks for stopping by," she said. Mike couldn't take his eyes off her. This was the first time Mike had seen her with an afro. Her natural was the curliest he'd ever seen. Mike was mesmerized as he watched her-graceful as a cat-lead him to the family room.

Renee put the brand new Gladys Knight and the Pips album on her hi-fi stereo. She blew some dust of the album, then gently wiped the needle on a white pad before lowering it on the album. She turned the volume down low. She seemed happy to see Mike.

Settling in on the leather sofa, Mike noticed on the side table a picture of Renee and her boyfriend, both clad in blue jean jackets and black berets with a "Free Huey" button on the side. Turning his attention away from the picture, Mike noticed a sizable color console television sat at the opposite end of the room. It looked new.

As Renee settled on the sofa next to him, Mike gazed again at the picture, then quickly looked back to Renee. Mike had not seen her since dancing lessons at the bakery. She looked more beautiful than he remembered and she smelled like she just stepped out of a bubble bath.

Mike wasn't sure how much longer he could keep their little brother-big sister routine going. He gradually felt a hard-on coming on strong -just being close to her. To get his mind off the idea of having sex with Renee, Mike opened the conversation.

"Well, you know why I'm here. My English teacher insists we have our papers typed. And that's fine for all the females who already took typing, but I can't type a lick."

Mike reached for his paper inside his briefcase.

"Let me see it," Renee said, leaning toward him.

Mike flipped past a couple of magazines then pulled it out and set it on his lap. He stared at the paper for a few seconds, then looked up at Renee.

"I printed as neatly as I could so that whoever typed it wouldn't get lost. It's about thirty handwritten pages. My mother told me to double-space if I was gonna ask someone to type it."

He handed her the paper. She sat with her legs pressed together so she could place the paper on her lap. She picked up the top sheet and laughed.

"You're writing about rats! Thirty pages on rats." She looked at Mike, still laughing while she flipped through the pages. "Gosh, you got tons of footnotes. This is like a college paper."

"That's what they say we need to know to get through college."

"This is going to be fun. I'll be very happy to type this for you." She looked at him, and flashed a brilliant smile. "This took you a lot of work, brother. How did you find time to do all this research and writing during your beloved football season? This is good, I'm impressed." And she really looked impressed as she laid the papers on top of the coffee table in front of them.

"I got started right away. I learned from last year that you can't wait until the last minute."

"And that's the way you got to do it in college," Renee added.

"Where you going to school now?" Mike asked.

"I'm still at Mercy. It's a great school and it's close. The work is rigorous but I love it, little brother. Next summer I'm getting a part-time job at Henry Ford Hospital, working with nurses. It's called an internship."

"Does your boyfriend go to school with you?"

"Child, please. Dean is still at the plant. He ain't goin nowhere."

Mike raised his eyebrows when he looked at Renee, wondering what she meant, wondering by the sound of her voice, *Does she think he should get out of the plant and maybe go to school like her?*

"Speaking of Dean," she said, "the Party is having a rally at Kennedy Square next Saturday." Renee got up to retrieve a flier from the bookshelf. She handed it to Mike. "Have you seen this?"

"Yeah, the Panthers at school been giving them out and posting some up. But we watch films on Saturday. Coach wants us to watch films all day. So I can't make it." Mike handed the flier back to Renee.

"You keep it," she said.

"That's okay," he insisted, embarrassed, knowing that he wasn't interested. "Jon-Jon's got one posted up on his door."

"Have you read the latest paper?"

"Naw, but give it here and I'll make sure Jon-Jon gets it." He felt he could accept something on Jon-Jon's behalf. It made him feel mature and responsible.

"Boy, you need to read it too. This is not just for Jon-Jon."

"Renee, you always trying to push this Black Party stuff on me. I mean, Black Panther . . . you know what I'm sayin'. Anyhow, Coach don't want us dealing with this stuff, know what I mean? I ain't into it. See Renee, my dad set up a breakfast program at the City Club and my sister volunteers down there sometimes. But it ain't me." He paused, then asked abruptly, "So, how much this gonna cost me?"

"What, the Panther paper?" Renee looked confused.

"No, the typing. My mom told me I need to pay you."

"Yeah, okay. Well, tell you what. I'll charge you fifty cent a page, even though I usually charge a dollar. This shouldn't cost you more than ten dollars. Probably more like seven or eight." She stopped, as if searching for words, then began again. "So, Mike, what else is it? You said you wanted to talk to me about a couple of things."

"Yeah, the homecoming this Saturday. I need a date for the dance. Um, I was thinking, would you like to be my date?" Mike asked, looking down at the coffee table.

Renee didn't respond right away, and got up instead to turn her album over. Mike's eyes followed her cat-like glide to the turntable. She bent over it, flipped the album over, and waited until the song started playing. Then she stood straight up and looked directly into Mike's eyes.

"You want me to be your date?" she said pointing to herself. "What happened to your girlfriend?" Renee asked, with a tone like a big sister. Mike thought his ship had just sunk. "Lo-la decided to go out with an upperclassman who drives. She even goes out with college dudes. And besides, she really wasn't never my girlfriend. I wanted her to be my lady. But right now we just cool."

"Just friends," Renee said, laughing. Nervously, Mike let out a little chuckle.

"Just friends."

Renee put her hands on her shapely hips, cocked her body to the side and said, "Well, Mike, then I'll just have to be your date, won't I?" She grinned. Mike let out a sigh of relief that sent Renee laughing crazily.

Mike leaned back on the sofa with his hands clasped behind his head, his eyes closed. He wished that the butterflies would fly the hell away. *What a victory*, he thought.

"You're gonna really be my date?" Mike shot forward, now at the edge of his seat. Mike felt ecstatic.

"Yeah, Mike. I can't let the future All-World go alone."

"Can you drive?" he asked, embarrassed to have to make such a request.

"I can borrow my mother's car. Just give me your address, I know how to get to Atkinson."

"It's Saturday night at nine. I'm at 2230." Mike's eyes met hers, and their gazes locked for a moment. They burst into laughter.

"Remember the bakery?" asked Mike, still eyeing Renee. "You showed me a few steps. Shit girl, I can dance now. I got rhythm, on the football field and on the dance floor. Mike stood up and play-acted catching the football, then dancing through defenders in slow motion. Renee giggled. "I'm catching me a touchdown next week. Just for you. Throw me the ball."

"Okay, catch this." Renee rolled up a newspaper and threw it to Mike. "Have you seen this?" she asked.

Mike opened the paper to see the headlines of the latest Black Panther Community News. He tensed.

"Why you always giving me this stuff? I'll give it to Jon-Jon."

"You can read it on the bus ride home."

"See, the coach don't want us involved in none of this stuff."

"Mike, he can't stop you from reading."

"This is what Jon-Jon, my Uncle John, and all them are into. This ain't me. This just ain't me. I got to go, big sister."

Mike snatched up his briefcase, stuffed the Black Panther news paper inside, and then buckled the case shut. He followed Renee to the door, but before walking out, he gave Renee another hard stare.

"You really are beautiful, my sister." Mike was thinking of her more as a soul sister, not a biological sister. *Maybe I can snatch*, he thought.

"You're beautiful too, Mike."

CHAPTER 41 -
Homecoming: Mike's Night Out

MIKE WRAPPED AN ICE-PACKED TOWEL AROUND his swollen hand. He still felt the stinging pain of his left middle finger every minute on the minute. He had taped a splint over his finger to keep it from bending, but his finger hadn't been right since a year ago when he first injured it.

Despite the agony of his sprained middle finger, and now his entire left hand, Mike managed to snag five catches, two for touchdowns in their homecoming victory over Our Lady of Perpetual Help. "Ouch!" Mike cried each time.

Mike did manage to dress himself and pick out his afro. He certainly wasn't going to pass up this opportunity to go out with Renee, no matter how much pain he felt. Mike checked himself, posed in front of the mirror, and rounded his fro while the Temptations' *Get Ready* played on his radio.

At about eight-thirty that night, Mike noticed Renee pulling her mother's Chevy Malibu into his driveway. Rose had convinced Mike to give Renee a bouquet of flowers handpicked from the backyard, since there were so many roses still in bloom. Mike had agreed, and added a box of chocolates as a gift.

"You look great, son," said Rose. "Swollen hand and all. And I can't wait to meet this nice young lady—the bakery girl—who I've heard so much about."

"You'll like her a lot, mom. She's here now."

Rose opened the French doors to the spacious living room, looked in as if to give it a final inspection, then walked into the family room where Denise and Jon-Jon were watching television. Mike didn't even wait for Renee to ring the bell. He opened the door and greeted her as she glided gracefully up the steps. She was wearing a full-length silk gown, with a string of pearls around her neck, and Mike had never seen her look so lovely, or so grown up. He hid the bouquet of roses behind his back, then exclaimed "Surprise!" and thrust them toward her. Renee blushed.

"Flowers! How sweet, Mike. These are beautiful."

"Got them right out the backyard." Rose couldn't stop smiling as she stepped inside. She cradled the roses the way a queen would. Mike ushered her into the living room to meet his family. Rose stood to greet her, and put out her hand.

"Girl, it's so good to see finally meet you. I'm Mike's mother, Mrs. Waterman."

Renee's movements were elegant. She laid the roses on the coffee table and extended her hand.

"I am so pleased to meet you, Mrs. Waterman."

Rose took her hand gingerly, nodded her head, and gave her a broad smile. "Mr. Waterman isn't home yet. Maybe you can meet him next time you stop by."

"I'd like that," she said, then added, "Mike said he picked these flowers from his backyard."

"Yes, come see," said Rose. She led Renee to the back window, momentarily interrupting Denise and Jon-Jon. Mike followed.

"It's almost too dark to see anything, but my mother and I started this rose garden in 1961 when we first moved here. Come back before they all die off and clip some for your mother."

"Be glad to."

"You're such a beautiful girl, Renee. Mike tells me that you're studying nursing at Mercy."

"Yes, I'm in my second year. And just got a part-time job at Henry Ford Hospital."

"How lovely." The two reentered the living room and sat down, Mike in tow. "Well," said Mrs. Waterman, "this is Mike's first . . . "

"Mom!" Mike interrupted quickly. Renee could hardly hold back the laughter.

"Mike's first date," Renee finished.

"Yes."

"I'll make sure he behaves himself."

"Mike's a gentleman. He better behave himself." Mrs. Waterman cast a sharp eye in Mike's direction.

Mike couldn't feel anything but embarrassed as he held his head down nearly between his legs. "Mom," he mumbled, "why you got to tell everything?"

"No son, not everything. You all have a great time. Son, you had a great game today, you deserve to go out a enjoy yourself. But remember to be back by two, got it?"

"Yes, Mom. I got it."

Renee remained closed-mouthed, without as much as a sniggle. Mike glanced over at her, knowing she no longer had a curfew. She was nearly grown.

In the car, away from his family, Mike was finally able to relax a bit. "You need gas money?" he asked as he checked her gas gauge. The tank read three-fourths full.

"No, but thanks for the offer. My dad won't let Mom's tank go under half-full. He's so finicky about that, always checking the oil. Your dad like that?"

"Just like that, exactly like that." They both laughed.

"You look so good tonight, Renee. I mean, I never saw you all dressed up before."

"Are you surprised? What, you didn't think I could come out of my blue jeans and jacket, and of course my tam, did you?"

Mike looked at her and grinned.

"But just to keep it natural, keep it black, I'll put my tam on." Renee reached into the back seat, fumbled inside her jacket pocket, and pulled her tam out. She put it on at the stop sign, and adjusted the rear view mirror to look at herself. "There," she said. Mike leaned his head back and closed his eyes for a few seconds.

"What do you mean, there?" he asked, now looking directly at her as she drove. "You can't put it down. Can't give it a rest, can you?"

"Nope, why should I? And further, don't you ever think I will put it down, as you say. You can't pick up and put down the struggle whenever it's convenient, or only if you think others are okay with it. It doesn't work that way. And that's not me, Mike."

They drove on in silence.

It took less than five minutes to get to the dance at DePorres's multipurpose room. The junior class had decked the place out in blue and gold balloons, blue and gold streamers, and blue and gold tablecloths on alternating tables. The lights were dimmed and as Mike and Renee walked in, the music of Sly and The Family Stone's *Dance to the Music* blared through the giant speakers towering on stage.

"What's happnin', black? Nice game, nice game," many of the fellow students said as they headed to a table. "What it be like, Mike? That was a great touchdown, blood," said another student. A teacher chaperone rushed over to congratulate him. Several parents, also chaperones, congratulated

Mike as he and Renee made their way through the crowd. Several students gathered around Mike and Renee to replay the game.

"Thanks, thanks," Mike said, shaking and slapping hands as his 6'3" frame towered above most of his classmates and teachers. He heard someone say, "Man, you left them defensive backs tripping over their feet like their shoelaces were tied together." Everybody broke out in laughter.

"Where you get those moves, Mike?"

"Uh, been watchin' Paul Warfield. Where else?"

"My man!"

Two senior football players walked over to Mike. They slapped palms, then, as if the two were in-sync, they quizzed Mike.

"So, who's the pretty lady?"

Mike snapped back to his senses. He could see their tongues hangin' out of their mouths like wolves as they closed in. Mike knew he had to handle this well. "Uh, gentlemen, step back, give the lady some breathing room. Meet Renee. Renee, meet Ron and Kenny, my football mellows."

"It's a pleasure, Renee," said Ron.

"The pleasure's all mine, your highness," said Kenny.

Renee simply nodded and smiled, then shook each one's hand. Mike spotted two seats at a table not far away and, placing his hand on the small of her back, led her away from the wolves. "Let's go sit down, Renee, right there."

"So, Mike, is Renee your . . . " Kenny began, but Mike whisked Renee straight to the table to get her out of range. Kenny finished his thought to Mike's back: "Is that your girlfriend, Mike?" With his back to Kenny, Mike turned around and flashed a wide grin and a wink before he sat her down at the table and out of range. Mike knew these two characters. He'd watch them snatch other fellow students' girlfriends. Once, he'd overheard them bragging about how many girls they'd snatched from other boys. It had become a competition between them, and they sometimes bet each other that they could leave the party with someone else's date. They were successful on several occasions, but Mike wasn't willing to give them the chance.

Mike had to fend off this mentality. He knew that they couldn't care less if Renee was his girlfriend. She was a female, and she was fair game.

"Mike," Renee said suddenly, shaking Mike from his daze. "I know what you're thinking, but you got nothing to be worried about. It takes two, right? I got to be just as game as they are, and I ain't game. They'll get nothing but grief from me."

Mike smiled and leaned back in his seat. *Renee is quite a lady*, he thought, and relaxed a bit. Thank God he didn't need to fight to protect his first date. Thank God!

"Renee, let's dance. I been practicing."

"Yeah, show me." They rose and moved toward the dance floor.

The DJ had the song "The Horse" on the turntable. That was perfect for Mike. He loosened up, and started slapping his legs like he would slap a horse to giddy up. Renee moved to the rhythm effortlessly. She appeared more comfortable than Mike felt, even though Mike knew more than half the people there. Mike could feel people watching him. He was the rising star for the DePorres football program, and now felt that people were watching his every move.

"Who are they?" asked Renee, pointing to two young men just coming in, dressed like twins in their gaucho suits, knee-high socks, and black leather jackets. Mike felt that every day was a fashion show for these two dudes.

"Norm and Curtis, juniors. They dealin' to the whole school." Mike knew them as a couple of soft-spoken dudes. He would often see them whispering to each other, to other classmates, even to teachers. They came across as very humble gentlemen.

To distract Renee from these two dapper gentlemen, Mike grabbed her hand and twirled her gently. She laughed and fell into step with Mike, and soon the two were dancing away, oblivious to the stares of those around them. They danced through song after song, until Renee admitted that her feet were starting to get a bit tired, at which point Mike gently led her back to their table.

No sooner had they sat down than they were approached by Norm and Curtis. The two young men stepped up to Mike's table and shook his hand. Then Curtis took Renee's hand and kissed it regally. "Your Excellency," he said. Norm looked at Mike and said, "Brother, you got a very beautiful girlfriend." He smiled broadly, and the two left the table and continued to make the rounds.

"Charming," Renee said, and blushed.

About halfway through the night's festivities, Mike saw Norm and Curtis leave. Thirty minutes later the two returned stripped down to their underwear and socks. Norm sported a purple-blue shiner under his eye and Curtis bled from his nose. They staggered into the dance hall. The crowd let out a collective gasp, and the movement and music stopped.

The music and movement resumed again just as suddenly. Several of the chaperones bolted outside, while Renee ran up to the two young men to begin providing first aid. Holding Curtis' head back, she asked some of the partygoers to give up their seats, then commanded someone to go fetch some towels and ice. Mike and several others ran outside. The two chaperones were already down the block, with Mike and several other students not far behind, in hot pursuit of the apparent perpetrators. The chaperones chased them for about three blocks, then turned around and headed back when it became clear that they had been outrun. Soon Mike and about a dozen other students caught up with the chaperones.

"Turn back, go back," they both shouted, panting heavily. "They're gone. There was about thirty or forty of 'em anyway. Go back and enjoy the rest of the party. We'll call the police."

Mike wondered whether that group was the same group that harassed him after track practice—the same group that had been known to harass his fellow schoolmates, usually after school. *T-Man would know*, Mike thought. *DeAngelo would know*.

Mike knew these confrontations could not continue, and made up his mind to go visit DeAngelo tomorrow and see whether he knew more about these trouble-makers. Mike was quick to call them trouble-makers, even terrorists, because of how one of the priests described acts of terror and terrorists who were fighting against freedom fighters in Central America. Father Thom called the right-wing hit squads in Central America "agents of terror." Father made everything seem so logical. He even accused several Detroit police officers of acting like terrorists. He had said, "there are those who foster an atmosphere of fear through terror." Those words stuck out now in Mike's mind.

Mike turned around and walked into a second wave of about thirty more students who had also left the party. They all returned together. Mike could see Renee at the "command center," giving orders and getting the boys taken care of. Both Norm and Curtis were dressed in some clothes that had been bought over from the church rectory across the street, and both seemed to be doing okay. Later that night Mike found out that Norm and Curtis had arranged to sell a couple of pounds of weed to some hooligans, whom they really didn't know. They got ripped off, big time.

The police arrived about 90 minutes after the incident. One of the parents had also called Mr. Dunham, who had stayed through the early ceremonial part of the dance and had then left. He returned quickly, and stood with the parents and police and listened to the story. Renee and Mike stood nearby. Shortly after the police arrived, Renee pulled out a notebook and pen and began jotting down notes, listening intently to what the police and the victims were saying.

One of the police officers stared Renee down, then asked, "Are you a reporter, ma'am?"

"No, sir. I'm not."

"Are you a witness?"

"Well, I was here, and I treated the two brothers who were injured."

"What are you doing now?"

179

"Observing, that's all."

Mike stepped up to Renee's side. "Okay, Renee, let the police do their job." He ushered her away slowly.

Once they were out of earshot of the police, Renee hissed, "Mike, don't ever do that to me again." Mike tensed up. *What did I do?* he wondered. Renee gave Mike a stern, pissed-off look. *She looks pissed, all right,* Mike thought, *at me and the police.*

"Mike," Renee started in. Then she stopped in her tracks. "Mike, we are trained to observe the police making stops in the black community, talking to witnesses and other types of police action, at demonstrations, and so on. As long as we are not interfering with their work, we can observe. That pig saw this tam and probably knew I was in the Party. He was trying to intimidate me, that's all. The pigs are killing us. They're tearing up the Party. You heard about the shootout last year, didn't you?"

"What!" Mike exclaimed. Mike barely remembered the shootout but hadn't heard Renee express her rage like that before. "I don't get it Renee. But then again, I ain't trying to get it."

"We're at war with this capitalistic system and the hit squads they call the police. They're not the least bit interested in solving any crimes up here. And when they do arrive, they talk to adults in our community like they're talking to children. It's pitiful. You all need better relations with these brothers around the school. You can't let them just run roughshod over y'all. If you don't stop it, they'll keep coming."

By now Mike's head was feeling fuzzy. This was exactly what Darren had been talking about when he had said *"When they run outta white kids to beat up, they'll be after our Catholic school asses."*

"You're gonna need to find somebody who knows them and who they respect," Renee continued. "Then y'all got to have a sit-down."

All Mike knew was that these 12th Street hoodlums, Captain Z and Petey Bones, were not the same as the bloods down on Dexter at the City Club, the ones who had begun to embrace some of the Black Power ideals of empowerment and social justice. Mike didn't want to deal with any of it. He just needed safe passage for himself and his siblings, so that he could focus on his ball games.

Mike leaned against the wall and said to Renee, "I ain't gonna be cannon fodder."

"Then what are you going to do, Mike?" Renee asked in a manner more exclamatory than questioning.

Mike shook his head side to side and simply said, "I don't know yet. I just don't know."

"Well, you might want to join an organization, like the Party, or the

Nation, the BCN, the RNA, or . . . " Renee seemed suddenly to draw a blank. " . . . or, or, I don't know, start your own."

Mike knew something needed to be done. But the only comment he could muster up at the time was: "I ain't got time for all that—too busy. Got practice all the time."

Renee looked at him, wide-eyed, as if in disbelief. She shook her head from side to side, and glanced at her watch. "Let's go," she said. "It's already 1:30."

Mike didn't know what to think about Renee. His first date had made him feel puny. He couldn't see himself as part of any of the organizations Renee mentioned, and he had no intention of joining the Nation of Islam, or the Black Panther Party for that matter. They arrived at Mike's house about fifteen minutes early.

"Let's just sit out front for a few minutes."

"That's fine by me, little brother. I had a good time. I'm really glad that I went with you."

"Can you drop that little brother stuff? I ain't little no more. Guess what, Renee."

"What?"

"Think I wanna go to medical school now . . . become a doctor so I can ask you to be my nurse."

"Boy, shut up," she said, giving Mike a playful push on his arm.

"Yeah." Mike leaned over and kissed Renee on the cheek.

"Call me next week, Mike. I'm almost done with your paper. Goodnight."

He got out of the car, and stood still on the porch to watch as she drove off.

CHAPTER 42 –
Mike Visits DeAngelo

SUNDAY MORNING, BEFORE MIKE ATE BREAKFAST, he headed down to DeAngelo's house. DeAngelo had moved into the attic about a year ago, and had told Mike he couldn't wait to show him. DeAngelo greeted Mike at the door, saying, "You haven't been over here since last year. Ever since that devil's night ambush went down. I still got the scars," said DeAngelo, holding up his arms. He turned and looked up the stairs. "The attic's my own little heaven. You know, away from all the bullshit below. Mom and dad still fightin' like cats and dogs. Every time she gets home, it's 'where you been?' and 'why you dressed up like that?'"

Shutting the front door, DeAngelo led the way into the house. Before Mike made it to the stairway, he noticed that the house was all decked out in various-sized statues of the Mother Mary. Rosaries were laid beside them. Mike saw the cluster of candles on a card table in the corner of the dining room. In the living room, beautiful bright red curtains hung from the ceiling to the floor.

"Hi, Mike," called DeAngelo's mother, Mrs. Parker. She surprised Mike, who hadn't thought anyone else was home. "Can you stay for breakfast?" she asked, coming into view at the doorway of the kitchen. "We hardly ever see you. You haven't disowned us, have you?" Mrs. Parker stepped out of the kitchen and looked at Mike. "Boy, look at you! You must be growing about five or six inches a year."

Mike laughed, and Mrs. Parker added, "You're a very handsome young man."

"Thank you. My mom is cooking this morning. I can't stay too long. But thanks."

"C'mon upstairs," said DeAngelo. When they got inside, DeAngelo bolted the door shut and placed a towel at the bottom of the door. "This is where I can come and do my thang and not be disturbed."

"Do what thang?"

"What you think thang, that's what."

"So what's the deal man? You dealing this stuff?" Mike scratched his head.

"Naw, I use too much," DeAngelo laughed. "How can I deal when I use this shit? I'd be snortin' up all the money."

To change the subject, Mike said, "So, how you like Central?"

DeAngelo said, "Fuck you and Central. And I know you didn't come visit to talk about Central. I heard what happened to your boys last night. Darren told me. Your boys tried to cut a deal with the wrong people. And them niggers who jumped 'em really ain't nothin' but some mercenaries, man. Hired guns, that's all."

Mike said, "I heard there were about fifty of 'em. We got to somehow deal with them. I don't know how, but we got to do something."

"Shit. You got to kill 'em, damn it," said DeAngelo as he pulled his switch blade out his pocket and jammed it into a desktop. "They ain't nobody, but they can pull a trigger."

"DeAngelo, man, I'm not tryin' to kill nobody out here. But they got to back off. I mean, like, who are they, and who do they respect around here? Who's their top dog?" Mike fired questions like a courtroom lawyer.

"Darren knows some of 'em. We all know some of 'em. Shit, you too." Mike watched as DeAngelo busted open onto an album cover some red caps of P. He piled up the P into a small mountain with a matchbook cover, then used a corner of the matchbook to scoop it up and inhaled it into his nose.

DeAngelo kept his shirt sleeves rolled up, showing his dog-bite scars that he had received from last year's "Devil's Night" romp through the neighborhood alleys. The dark scars contrasted with his high-yellow skin.

DeAngelo survived intact, but seemed as crazy as ever. He had proclaimed that night as his last "Devil's Night," and had told Mike, "That's it. No more." But Mike wasn't convinced.

As Mike watched, DeAngelo stuffed half the matchbook corner up his nose. "This here shit, this'll take all your pain away. Wanna try it?"

"Hell naw, I ain't tootin' nothin'. Keep that crap away from me, man. You need to quit."

"Oh, Mike." DeAngelo looked exasperated. "Talk to George. Remember George from baseball? He know all them fools, all of 'em. They look up to George." DeAngelo took another toot in the opposite nostril, as Mike excused himself to head home for breakfast.

CHAPTER 43 -
The Rose Garden -
December 1969

THREE INCHES OF SNOW COVERED THE top of the four-foot-high rose bushes. The bushes were in two rows, three feet apart, and formed a U-shape in the rectangular backyard. A tall trellis at the bottom of the U reached upwards to the roof of the garage which abutted the yard. A rose-covered archway greeted the visitors at the entrance to the garden. Jon-Jon's black-hued Mother Mary stood out with elegance under the cover of snow.

Looking out the family room window at the backyard Rose said, "Mama, we can sell bouquets of roses to help with our fundraising. We get so many every year. We could double our money in no time."

Mama E looked down over the rim of her spectacles at Rose and shook her head, signifying "no." "'Fraid not, baby. I got a better idea. Let's start giving the roses away. These roses have been beautiful and every year they get more beautiful. We have put so much into this. Let's give these roses to those who need some sunshine in their lives. These roses are becoming so plentiful, and they would mean so much to people, especially us females. You understand what I'm saying, don't you? Let's ask Father O'Malley about sending bouquets to the sick and shut-in of our parish. We can give bouquets to our neighbors, friends, and family. People who need a little sunshine, baby. Just like Frank needed some sunshine and love . . . and found him a rose."

" . . . And you let him keep me, right? Your sweet little rose. OKAY Mama, I get the point." Rose glanced at her watch. "It's getting late. Think we better get ready for the concert . . . "

"And our big surprise for the men."

The women had tickets to the Jackson 5 concert that night. Delli and

Sharon were also going to the concert with the Watermans'. All five of the women had retreated upstairs as they prepared to go. As the men were sitting in the living room kickin' it about Muhammad Ali's possible comeback, Mama E opened the French Doors to the living room and said, "Gentlemen, before we go to the Jackson 5 concert tonight we have a real treat for you." She walked over to the stereo and put on an album. Then she said, "One, two, one, two three, hit it. She motioned to the others, Denise, Rose, Sharon and Delli, to come down. Led by Delli they sauntered into the living room to the Jackson 5 hit *I Want You Back*. Delli played Michael Jackson. They all danced and sang to the lyrics, working the living room like center stage. The men looked delighted. Mike stood up and encouraged everyone to give the women a standing ovation.

"Encore, encore, Jon-Jon cried out, as they kept clapping. The women took a bow then Denise and Sharon did a full split and held up both hands high in the air.

Mama E said, Sorry gentlemen, the show is over. We got a date a can't be late." The gathered their things and hurried off to the Olympia Stadium for the sold-out Jackson 5 concert.

CHAPTER 44 -
Death of a Schoolmate

DUANE SHOWED UP LATE FOR PRACTICE after school. Mike detected some nervousness in Duane. Mike asked, "What's buggin you man?" Duane remained quiet while he picked his fro in front of the mirror. He waited until after practice to say anything. While the two were changing in the locker room, he told Mike quietly that he accumulated a gambling debt with some of the boys from Durfee and Central. He would pass by some of them cats on his way to school from the Dexter Davison area where he lived. He didn't quite remember why he started gambling with them in the first place. But Mike knew – Duane was Duane, ready to take on the world, especially after a bottle of wine, preferably Wild Irish Rose.

Duane is probably having trouble with the same thugs Mike remembered from after track practice last year and at the Homecoming dance whom had been known around the neighborhood as being mercenaries, hired guns. If someone needed a job done right they could see Captain Z who would orchestrate all kinds of hits: ambush, home invasion, you name it . . . Less than a week later a neighbor found Duane's body stuffed in a trash can in an alley near the school. Mike sat slumped in a chair with a ice pack on his finger. "I can barely take this anymore. My finger is killing me and my friend just got killed."

"Mike, this cannot go on, I'm paining myself," Mama E shouted to Rose and the children later that evening. "Pretty soon, they'll be no one left. Duane wasn't even sixteen yet. That's no way to die. The police are not going to stop it. And you know it. Your father," Mama E turned towards Rose, "Frank and Mr. Dunham don't even bother to call the police. Mike, you got to figure out a way to stop this killing." Mama E started crying. "Duane was a beautiful young brother. Remember the song he sang at the talent show . . . *'You're My Everything.'* The young man had a soulful spirit. And now he's gone. I'm angry. I am ANGRY. How could this have happened?" Mama E sank into the sofa with her hands over her face sobbing.

Mike thought about how his father got people together and had all kinds of enemies making peace with one another at City Club. Maybe he could do the same thing. Or maybe he should retaliate. Find out who crushed Duane's skull and stuffed him into a trash can.

The next day all Mike heard about was how the parents of the compact schools were going to get together to keep trying to build bridges. Father Thom and Father Abebe Akoji from Nigeria told students at DePorres that they decided to canvass the neighborhood promoting peace in the streets.

Mike finally called George to arrange a meeting with Captain Z. Mike wanted Darren and DeAngelo to attend. To Mike's surprise, Captain Z actually showed up, with four of his boys. During the meeting Captain Z said to Mike, "I got maybe a thousand soldiers, you got what, twenty. When you can put a thousand together, come see me, maybe then we can combine forces," he said, laughing. "Your boy just owed too many people. And when he won some money shootin' crap, he stuffed it up his nose."

"What," Mike protested, "Duane didn't use. There's no way." Mike could never accept that Duane did heroin. He was too damn good on the basketball court. How could he?

~ ~ ~ ~ ~ ~ ~

After class the next day, Miss Lilly, one of Mike's favorite teachers said, "You should attend this meeting on school security. Maybe you can give them some ideas, make a difference."

"Naw, got practice," said Mike.

"That's too bad Mike. You really can make a difference, Miss Lilly continued. Mike respected Miss Lilly, she introduced him to some interesting things like yoga and Buddhism in her world religion class. He remembered her class themes of inner peace and happiness. But Mike tried his best to stay focused on practice. The mood at school was solemn. A lot of people knew Duane and liked him.

During dinner Mama E spoke up again. She got into a rant about all the killing going on and how Detroit was becoming the nation's murder capital. "We are trying to raise this community up. What are you young people gonna do about this?" she asked Mike and Jon-Jon. "You better do something before I have to." Mike didn't know what to say or even think for that matter. *What could Mama E possibly do? What the hell am I gonna do?*

Jon-Jon said, "Hey Mike, we got to get organized. When Stokley Carmichael spoke at the anti-war rally at Kennedy Square he said – organize, organize, organize. He said, if you're not part of an organization, just shut up and stay out the way."

"Yeah, I'll have to remember that," said Mike.

Jon-Jon and Denise helped their mother clear the dinner table of dishes and food. Mike just sat there. He didn't know what he could do about Duane's death, his own safety or that of his siblings. He had to lead the way. At least George tried but the meeting with Captain Z was a joke. He thought of taking Renee's advice and join the Black Panther Party, the Nation of Islam, the Black Christian Nationalists or some other group for his own protection. He still had two more years of high school. Mike counted about a dozen fellas - at best - on the block who would throw down if necessary or at least deal with any given conflict. Another dozen or so, were too busy chasing P to be concerned and the rest still couldn't come off the porch. *What's our dozen fellas to their hundreds, Mike thought.* He quit thinking about it. *Shit, if I can just keep my nose clean like Coach Taylor said, then I'll be fine,* Mike thought.

"Dad, what can I do?" asked Mike. "Some classmates want to retaliate. But I think Captain Z might have too many boys."

"Mike, the last thing you need to do is try to retaliate. That leads to more retaliation. I'm having a meeting with the compact school principals and some parents later this week. I want you to come with me. We're gonna try to reach out to those parents of these thugs. Let them know they got help if they need help controlling these boys, their own kids. Know what I mean?"

"Do you think they'll even listen, Frank?" asked Rose.

"We'll find out. It's worth a try."

"There are so many adults afraid of these kids, it sounds a bit frightening."

"It's frightening for some, but we don't need everybody. Anyway we'll see. We get together Thursday night at the Club."

"I hear you." Rose placed a napkin on her lap and sat back down at the table and served herself a bowl of ice cream.

On Thursday, as Mike and his father headed towards to meeting, Mike still felt uneasy from his meeting with Captain Z. *What can these parents do?* Mike wondered. He walked in behind his dad into the noisy multipurpose room at City Club. It looked like a good mix of parents and school officials. After getting everyone's attention, Frank spoke for about ten minutes. He said he wanted the parents to think of themselves as a violence prevention team first, then as intervention to resolve disputes.

"We're not a vigilante group or some kind of quick strike force. We want to encourage our young people to sit down and work things out." Mike observed that some of the parents were hostile.

One said, "Frank, why you wait until a DePorres' kid got killed around here? We done had four, five murders around here in the past six months."

"Things are getting out of hand . . . ," someone shouted out.

Someone shouted back, "Things been outta hand."

"And you called the police on 'em too . . . " another voice shouted from the audience.

"Damn straight I did . . . "

"Ahh you just a rat, man . . . "

Frank quickly regained control of the meeting as it started to degenerate into a shouting match.

Frank said, "We meet monthly Bob, you know that you can come and raise the point anytime. But more importantly, this is why we as parents got to talk. You know how we came up. We looked out for each other. We had each others back, that's how we made it."

A voice interrupted, "Just call the police, man."

"The police the damn problem, you fool," said a voice in the audience.

"Wait a minute, Frank jumped in, "we got to have respect here. Nobody's a fool. Keep that name calling out of here. I ain't havin' it."

"We should've invited the police here . . . "

"They don't care, they instigating . . . "

Frank interrupted again, "This is something we can do for ourselves. We don't need the police for us to be united."

Mike observed this give—and-take for about thirty minutes then thought *maybe the parents got just as many problems as the kids do.*

"Dig this," said Frank, "I don't want y'all to leave here empty-handed, ask your son or daughter if they are facing any conflict or dispute and ask how they would want to resolve it. This compact we have is a peace-pact and it's got to work to lift us up and lift this city up." Mike saw how his dad kept the group engaged by asking more questions.

"Is there anyone here who does not believe we can stop this violence among our youth?" The group belted out a resounding "no." "Anyone think we cannot reach the hearts and minds of our young people?" Another resounding "no" from the group. "Then we got work to do." Frank passed the mike to Dr. Jones, Central High's principal. Each of the principals spoke for about ten minutes.

After the two-hour gathering and on the ride home, Mike said, "Even the adults can't seem to get along."

Mr. Waterman said to Mike, "Yeah, but this is what the struggle is all about Mike, trying to work through the tough issues, it's the struggle, not the easy."

CHAPTER 45 -
High School Frat -
Spring 1970

By the end of Mike's 10ᵀᴴ grade year at St. Martin DePorres Mike had lettered in football and track but had not played much on the varsity basketball team. Coach moved him up from junior varsity to varsity at the end of the basketball season because several players sustained injuries, and typically found a minute or two near the end of the game to put Mike in. He was the last man off the bench. But Mike was patient, knowing that half the team was made of seniors and that when they left it would give him the opportunity to play more.

One day late in his tenth-grade year, as track season came to a close, a group of friends who were not fellow b-ballers or runners called Mike over to their lunch table. Mike tuned in to Bill as he began talking about starting a high school Greek fraternity similar to the college Greek frats.

"Other schools are doing it, I tell you. Ford, Cass, U of D, they all got frats. My brother's an Alpha and he told me he's willing to sponsor us."

Danny, one of Bill's close partners, added, "And this is a sure way to attract the honeys. We throw parties, we throw parties, and we throw more parties."

"Frats do more than throw parties, don't they?" Mike asked. Mike thought he didn't need this to pull any honeys, even though he'd been working on getting past his own virginity for the last two years. But maybe, he thought, a frat could be used to form some kind of school defense club, especially in light of what had happened to Duane.

By now Bill and Danny were giving dap to each other, still talking about the honeys. Seeing Mike's pensive expression, though, Bill paused.

"What else you want, my brother?" asked Bill.

"Well," Mike hesitated a bit, then continued. "What do college frats do besides party?"

"Drink!" Everyone at the table burst out laughing.

"Bill," Mike cut him off, "here I am, me and my partners are athletes and all y'all talking about is drinking and partying. I might drink a little but damn, is that all y'all got to offer? No thanks, man. I got practice."

"Okay, Mike, hold up! They do more than that and we can do more than party. We do projects for the needy like feed the hungry, give away toys at Christmas, that kinda stuff."

Another one of Bill's partners, Samuel, chimed in. "They also help each other in school, like study for tests and shit like that. These college frats keep a file on all past tests for all classes. We can do all that too."

"And they got all the connections in the world. That's the main reason for joining," said Danny.

"So why y'all didn't say all this to begin with? What, y'all don't want to sound square? Y'all better think about what happened to Duane and be ready to form a self-defense team for the school." Everybody went quiet for a minute. It seemed like forever.

"This ain't no Black Panther Party, Mike. You want a ministry of self-defense, go join the Party. Man, this just for fun, brother."

"Let me think about it," said Mike. Later in the week Mike asked his Dad about joining the fraternity. After all his Dad had become a member of Kappa Alpha Psi while in college. Frank told Mike, "Even though this high school fraternity does not have a college affiliation it might give you an idea of what fraternities are all about. As long as you can make it an asset for you, and not a distraction, I'm with you. Go on and give it a shot, son." Mike decided to become one of the founding members.

In about two weeks the group had formed the chapter of Alpha Delta Pi. The group elected Bill president, Samuel vice president, Danny treasurer and Mike's main man, Luke, as secretary. They had two members at Cass Tech High, one at Mumford High, and one at Henry Ford High. The group created a pledge to become "their brothers' keepers" and never reveal their secrets outside the group. The core group consisted of about sixteen members.

Their first meeting took place in Bill's basement, where he held the freshman icebreaker party.

"The next order of business is to get some pledges. We should take on about fifteen or sixteen on the first go–round," Bill suggested. "We need that many in case some drop out or just ain't what we lookin' for. We may end up with eight or ten and that would be fine."

"What about a sister organization?" asked Dave.

"That'll come later," Bill responded. We'll get the women involved. We got our own sisters right here at DePorres and the sisters over at Immaculata are game."

"But they don't mix, man. It's like oil and water. I don't see that happenin'," argued Samuel.

"We'll cross that bridge when we get to it," Bill responded.

Mike had been paying attention, and getting a better understanding of what he'd gotten involved with. He asked, "So, what kind of people do we ask to pledge?"

"In most cases, they ask us."

"Okay, so what kinda people are we looking for?" Mike persisted. Bill looked over to his brother who was sitting in on the meeting as the group's advisor and sponsor.

"Good character, confidence, and loyalty—that's what we look for," said Bill's brother Dwight. "How do you think these fraternities have been able to survive all these years? You'll find out through this process who you can trust, believe me," he assured the group.

"Fine," Bill said, in an attempt to regain the group's attention. "We have two more issues to deal with. But let me recap. We have our newly elected officers; we set a date of thirty days before we begin our first line. All agreed say aye."

The group responded with a resounding "aye."

"Okay, now we need a sweater design committee and a fundraising committee."

Mike signed up for fundraising. His main man Luke signed up for sweater design. Danny and Samuel had been whispering throughout the meeting and now they both wanted the group's attention.

"We have an idea for a quick fundraiser," Samuel said, waving his hand in the air.

"Parties once a month, first one in two weeks." Danny suggested. "All that time the word will be out and we can attract our pledges."

"And we can raise the money for our sweaters," Mike added.

"Uh, not quite, Mike. We got to have the sweaters before the fist party. How else we gonna look legit?" said Samuel.

"Can we have all that in two weeks?" Mike asked.

"I think we need a mid-week meeting, to approve a design and find a sweater company," said Bill. "We need to know how much each sweater will cost and how fast they can produce 'em."

Bill's brother chimed in. "Yeah, that's right. Then you can plan your first party around that." The group voted on a $40 per person joining fee to cover the cost of the sweaters, then adjourned the meeting.

Despite the group's joining fee, the $40 per person was not enough to cover the entire bill for having the sweaters made. But by the mid-week meeting, Mike showed up feeling pretty good about getting one of his neighbors, Dr. Les Woods, to put up $200 to help cover the balance on the sweaters.

The beautiful cloud-gray sweaters had a sharp black P in the middle with icons embroidered around it. The brothers wore individualized patches on their sleeves. The sweaters arrived about two days before the first party, and the brothers decided to show them off first at Cass Tech, then at Immaculata. After dazzling the females at DePorres for a few minutes, they headed down John C. Lodge Freeway. Mike and Samuel jumped into Luke's Torino. Bill drove his father's Buick LeSabre. They stopped at Cass Tech to pick up their two brothers who were already outside handing out party fliers. But something went awry at Cass Tech on Friday. Mike didn't hear about it until he arrived at Cass that afternoon. Their two brothers MG and GM got in Luke's car. MG said "We've done enough here. Man, earlier, we had some problems."

CHAPTER 46 –
Home Schooling

ON THE RIDE OVER TO IMMACULATA, Mike listened intently as his two fraternity brothers from Cass Tech told their story. Earlier that Friday before the Fraternity's first party, they said they were getting harassed by another frat group whose members mostly attended Cass Tech High School. The two Alpha Delta Pi (ADP) brothers, known as MG and GM, said they were outnumbered twenty to two. The conflict was over a girl. A large fraternity at Cass Tech was full of pretty boys who lived pretty pampered lives, and who thought they could always get the girl. And they would crack on the ADP brothers as being rough around the edges, or ghet, short for ghetto.

But their rough ghetto style appealed to the girls. The brothers in the Cass Tech frat couldn't stand it. GM had learned later that the frat's pledges were instructed to harass and provoke them into a food fight. But at the time, they hadn't known what started it all.

MG explained, "Them dudes tried to get us expelled from school. They tried to set us up in the school cafeteria at lunch."

GM added, "So this is how it went down. Eight of the pledges surrounded us while we sat at a table full of young ladies. One of the dudes said, 'Brothers, you are not allowed in this space today.' Then another said, slurring his speech and spitting, 'we're conducting a performance — a step show. We have reserved the space. The event has been pre-approved and is sanctioned by the principal Mr. Johnson. Now please, vacate the area.'"

MG picked up the story. "So I told 'em, 'we ain't gotta vacate shit and I don't appreciate you spitting on me.' Then the brother who appeared to be the spokesman said to us, 'You've been duly warned, now vacate or else.'

"So I said, 'or else what . . . ?'" MG continued. "Me and GM got up from the table. Then we saw Donnie, the president of the frat walking towards us with two security guards.

"So I say to GM, 'man, let's get outta here. I ain't in no mood to deal with security.' Then right away, man, the president and about five of his brothers sat down and laughed in our face. They pointed at us and said to the ladies at their table, 'Those bird-brains, what good are they to you beautiful ladies?' Then the president said, 'My ghetto brothers, we ain't steppin' until next week.'"

Mike said, "They laughed at y'all?"

GM said, "The whole table minus the young ladies broke out hysterical. We didn't say a thing. Then, when the security guards walked away, Donnie scooped up a handful of jello and hurled it at us. He said, 'Have you brothers had your pork rinds today?' and laughed. Then he said, 'So ladies, whose party do you want to attend tomorrow night? The future leaders of America right in front of you, or the ghetto-bumpkins who can't even punch their way out of a wet paper bag?' We overheard that shit and headed right for his ass. Man, we were pissed."

"So I said, 'Let's get this party started,'" MG chimed in. "I ain't puttin up with this shit.' One of the girls jumped up real fast and blocked GM and said, 'It's a set-up. It's a set-up!' GM said he didn't give a damn."

"'One of the girls said, Please, please don't do anything here. The principal is looking.'

"'Then he saw the whole thing.'

"'She said, No, he just walked in. Look, I heard they set this whole thing up for you and MG to get kicked out of school. Don't do anything here.'

"I said Okay, then I hollered at him, 'Thanks for the jello, you little high-yellow bitch!'" said MG.

GM added, "The little bitch-bitch." They gave each other some dap. "Then we walked off knowing we had to do something about this. We figured if we didn't do anything about it, it would happen again."

"Then let's do something. We can't let them little e-lite punks get away with that." said Samuel.

"Next thing you know they'll think they can front us off at our own parties," Danny added.

"Feel like going back to kick they punk ass right now," GM said anxiously.

"Man, there're too many cops at the school, you know that. Ain't nothin' we can do right now," said Mike. "What you think, Luke?" Luke didn't respond.

"Tell y'all what then," began GM. "Let's promote our party right now and we'll hit the chumps the night of their party. I know where it's at."

"Where?" asked Mike.

"In Lafayette Park. I know the spot."

Lafayette Park looked like something out of a story book — a beautiful enclave five minutes walking distance from downtown Detroit. The residential complex was bounded by luxury high-rises at each end. Two high-rises in the east, along with two-level townhouses, ran parallel though the park. The manicured hedges and lawns were kept fresh by the automatic sprinkler system, a feature becoming more common even in Mike's neighborhood.

During the day, winds carried the strong odor of hops from the Stroh's Brewery located at the north end of the park. The odor would sometimes hang over the park for days. But despite that, the Park was home to some of Detroit's elite, both black and white.

The party was on the corner of Rivard and Joliet, just yards from Chrysler Elementary School. The brothers in Alpha Delta Pi hadn't bothered to case the joint but rather made a hasty decision to crash the party, find Donnie of the Cass frat, then literally whoop his ass, either inside the house or after snatching him out of the house. And if anyone tried to step in, "They'll get cracked up-side the head," as Samuel put it.

The ADP had five car-loads of brothers, altogether about thirty brothers. It was early, about 10 PM. Mike rode with Samuel, who pulled over on Rivard Street to park. The others found parking close by.

The townhouse was about one block away. Mike noticed a small gathering of mostly girls nearby and a few Cass frat boys milling around outside. MG, who also rode with Samuel, spotted the president, Donnie Washburn, outside with the girls.

Samuel coordinated the assault. "I'm gonna tell the others we spotted him. The rest of y'all stay put for now." Mike and his fraternity brothers stayed put with the windows down. They heard Samuel tell the others, "That's him out front with the girls, yeah. We're gonna go two by two so they don't see no big ass crowd marching in on 'em, know what I mean? We'll walk up to the house just like we coming to party. We'll catch him outside if we can. If he goes inside we're going in after him, kicking ass and taking names."

Samuel and Danny led about a dozen brothers in their group to the townhouse where Donnie was spotted.

Donnie didn't seem to recognize anyone until MG was about 5 yards away. "Oh, shit!" Donnie shouted, then took off running to the townhouse. Samuel led the chase. Donnie barely made it inside before Samuel and his boys were at the front door. Samuel almost ripped the screen door from its hinges, then easily pushed in the unlocked front door. The invasion was on.

The party was downstairs and the music must've drowned out the commotion taking place upstairs. Everyone was caught off guard as the ADP brothers headed downstairs for the basement. Donnie mustered up enough courage to throw a cup of punch at Samuel as he came down the stairs. The commotion soon led to total chaos. The Cass frat put up little resistance even though they had about a dozen brothers in the basement. They ran for cover but could only manage to cower in the corners as Samuel backhanded Donnie in the nose. Blood shot out everywhere. MG and GM joined in the fray, punching and kicking whomever they could. Mike couldn't believe what was happening. He picked up one of the Cass frat boys and slammed him to the floor. Mike suddenly thought, *This ain't me- what the hell am I doin'?* Everything happened so fast.

Luke said, "Let's take the liquor." Luke rushed behind the bar. "Shit, they got a gun back here, too," said Luke with a big wide grin. Before anyone knew it, Kevin, also a member of the ADP, picked up the gun. Samuel now hollered, "Anybody strapped in here? Any of y'all strapped?" The ADP brothers started patting down the Cass frat boys. Samuel retrieved another pistol.

"What y'all faggots gonna do with this?" screamed Samuel. "You bitch-ass motherfucker. Look at you. You ain't laughin' now."

MG walked up to Donnie, who was now down on his knees begging MG to leave him alone, and kicked him in the face.

Mike couldn't wait to get out the house. "Let's get outta here," he said. "I think they got the message." The brothers wanted to loot the house. Mike said, "We ain't lootin' nothing. We're leaving." The entire incident had lasted less than two minutes.

When the group returned from their stunning home invasion, there was much revelry. Kevin bolted from one of the cars just as it rolled to a stop in Samuel's driveway. Waving the stolen gun over his head, he yelled, "We kicked some ass! We whoop they asses!" Then he sauntered back to the car and gave Bill some dap.

Out of the blue Mike saw Carl Sutter, a senior at DePorres and a well-known young gangster who lived near Central. As he walked past Kevin, Carl snatched the gun and ran like a thoroughbred down the middle of the street, laughing all the way to the corner. Then he disappeared.

The ADP Brothers just looked at each other in shock, then launched into a rant at Kevin. "You chump," said Danny. "Why don't you go and get it back?"

"You go get it," said Kevin.

Mike laughed, then said, "We won't see that again. I know Carl from years ago, man, and how do you think you're gonna tangle with him? Forget it, man. You got took. You shouldn't o' been advertising it."

"That's what your ass gets," said Bill. "Hey, let's go party."

The party was a roaring success, as lively as could be. Music by Parliament-Funkadelic, Jimi Hendrix, and Sly and Family Stone dominated the turntables. Samuel put on a twelve-minute version of Maggot Brain, which had everybody staggering around wondering what planet they were on. The dollar shots went over well. They sold out of beer and wine early on then all they had left was the hard stuff: Johnny Walker Red, Black Label, Southern Comfort, and Tangeray. The Immaculata girls asked for Tequila but they had none. "Next time," Luke, the group bartender, told them. "Here, have some vodka instead."

At the end of the party only a few remained, including Mike, who counted $321. Mike promptly turned the money over to Danny, the treasurer.

Mike returned home from the party late that night. He figured it must've been about three in the morning. The house was unusually dark. No one had left a nightlight on, and Mike quietly and carefully crept up the stairs so as not to wake anyone.

Frank's voice shattered the silence. "Mike," he called out from the basement. "Come downstairs for a minute." Mike froze. "Mike," Frank called again. "I want to see you."

"I'm coming." Mike flipped the light switch to the basement but the light didn't come on. "There's no lights," Mike said, as he kept walking down to the basement.

Just as he reached the bottom, Frank snatched Mike off his feet and slammed him against the wall.

"Dad, what . . . ?"

Frank's grip on Mike's collar grew tighter. Mike's eyes got big. He began to breathe heavy. "Guess what, son. Bad news will beat you home every time. Ever heard that saying? Ever heard that?" Mike never seen his dad look this angry - his dad's face less than an inch from terrified Mike.

"What?" Mike couldn't get even muster a coherent answer. Frank pulled Mike across the room to a cardboard table.

"You talking about what, like you don't know. Here, put these on. You want to rumble, put these gloves on." Frank gestured to the boxing gloves on the table. Two pair of boxing gloves were on the table. Mr. Waterman had bought the gloves several months ago, along with a heavy bag he used on occasion. Mike was apprehensive about fighting his father, having no idea what he was in trouble for, and took his time pulling the gloves on. Frank was quicker, and didn't bother to even lace up his gloves. He landed a hard right into Mike's mid-section, then a left hook into Mike's ribs.

"C'mon, defend yourself or do *something*. Hit me. Do something!" Frank landed an uppercut into Mike's belly. "You want to rumble and tear up people's houses, let's rumble."

Mike finally got it. "We . . . I . . . I didn't do nothing. I didn't do nothing, Dad."

"You weren't with your frat brothers when they crashed that party in Lafayette Park? I got a call that you were with them. Am I wrong?" The blows kept coming, and soon Mike was balled over with his head nearly between his legs.

"Straighten up, son. You weren't there?"

"Yeah, I was there. We didn't tear nothing up. We were looking for some cats that tried to jump our brothers up at Cass Tech. They ran inside the house and we just went after them."

"Just went after them," Frank said mockingly. "Since when do you go up in someone's house without an invitation?" Mike didn't respond fast enough. "When, dammit?" Another blow landed on him.

"Never."

"Right answer, never. Let me hear it again."

"Never."

"Never what?"

"Never will I go in someone's home without an invitation."

"And what they hell are y'all doing riding down on someone anyway?"

"I'll never do that again, dad. Never ever, I swear." The blows stopped.

"You don't have to swear. Though you ought to thank God I just sprained my finger hitting you and that I'm taking the gloves off. I don't ever want to hear something like this again. I don't know all of your frat brothers but it sounds to me like you got some bad apples in the bunch."

"Yeah, well I think . . . "

"Now, I didn't ask you to rat anybody out, just like I ain't telling you my source, but I will tell you one thing. You can be guilty by association. If someone got seriously hurt, you would have been charged with assault and battery too. You can go down quickly with the company you keep, son." He was silent for a moment, and his voice softened. "Now quit whimpering and go upstairs."

Mike hurried upstairs, feeling small. He would never have even considered hitting his dad back. He knew he'd have to do double duty to get out his dad's doghouse. It was time to step up and volunteer to help his mother and Mama E with just about everything they needed help with. And back away from the dumb stuff.

CHAPTER 47 –
Party Hardy

AFTER ABOUT EIGHT MONTHS, DANNY REPORTED that the club's kitty had grown to over $3,000. In the Fall of 1970, the ADP decided to host its fifth party as a back-to-school icebreaker at the Local 75 on West Grand Blvd. near 12th Street — a popular spot for cabaret parties. The Local asked for $500 to rent the place, but the potential for income convinced the group to rent the spot.

Mike estimated that it would take another $200 for advertising and about $300 for food.

"And don't forget the DJ," Danny added. He would cost another $100. The group approved the party with the idea that the risk was worth the potential gain. Danny claimed that they could make over $5,000 in net profits.

"More than that," said Bill. "Man, we can turn ten cents into a dollar."

The group estimated that the house parties attracted about two hundred fifty people each. And the Local had much more space. "We can put damn near 800 people up in there," said Bill.

"We can't sell liquor but we can make it up with soul food dinners, pop, and chips," added Luke.

Bill let down the gavel, "the 'ayes' have it," he said, laughing. No one voted against it.

At home, Mike tried to convey the enormity of his event. Jon-Jon listened in. "So, what y'all gonna do with the money?" he asked.

Trying to look nonchalant, Mike leaned back with his hands behind his head, just like he'd seen his father do cross-legged. He said, "Don't know, but we're gonna make thousands."

"Well, maybe y'all can donate to Mama E's senior health care fund. She's out here selling bean pies and fish dinners every week."

"Yeah, maybe," said Mike. But he knew it would be a group decision, and the group wasn't thinking about sharing any of the money they raised. Mike thought about Samuel's original pitch about doing some charitable work. They hadn't done anything yet.

The brothers were sharp as tacks that night. Luke's mother, Delli, and Mike's mother, Rose, had agreed to set up the kitchen and prepare the dinner plates. Delli and Rose got the kitchen together for the busy night to come. Samuel and Danny took charge of buying all the supplies and decorations. Luke made a special spiked punch he tucked away in the corner of the kitchen- reserved only for ADP members and their special guests – typically, young ladies.

The DJ arrived early and set up his humungous speakers in the two corners of the giant hall's dance floor. Things were going like clockwork. Just as some young ladies started arriving Bill came out from the kitchen and said to Mike, "Brother Mike, can you pick up some more ice, if you don't mind? Get the cash from Danny. Thanks!" Mike promptly tracked down Danny for some money. He was with Samuel at the door.

"Danny, I need some money for ice."

"Not a problem." Danny pulled out a thick wad of bills and peeled off about eight singles for Mike.

"I think that should be enough," said Mike. Inwardly, he thought, *Damn, that's a helluva wad of money.*

The ADP had established a plan to deposit money collected at the door with Bill; both Danny and Bill would agree on the amount, then Bill would stash the dough in a small safe in the kitchen closet. Several brothers would be in the kitchen anyway helping with the food and Bill would be there for a money drop every hour on the hour.

When Mike returned with the ice he saw Bill in the kitchen. "Bill, did you see Danny's bankroll?"

"Yeah, that's the money we took out to pick up some last minute items."

"How much y'all take out?"

"Well, we spent about $1,200 for the party. I think we drew down a good chunk for emergencies."

"A good chunk? How much?" Mike pressed.

"About a grand, maybe twelve-hundred."

"Twelve for emergencies, that only leaves about $600 in the account. Man, that money needs to go in the safe. Danny don't need to be flashing that kinda money around. Somebody'll pop his little ass."

"I let him hold it. He said he'd need change on the door. He's floating between the door and the kitchen. He's making change if necessary for both. He'll be alright."

"Naw man, he's holding too much. He need to put most of that money up. That sucker's just tryin' to impress."

Mike convinced Bill to bring Danny back to the kitchen to unload some money. "You holding too much," said Mike once they were all in the kitchen.

"You should keep about $200 in small bills and that's it." Luke agreed.

"You ain't gonna need that much. Most people got twenties." Bill opened his hand. Danny looked everybody up and down and said defiantly.

"What, y'all don't trust me?"

"It ain't even about trusting you. Of course we can trust you, brother," said Mike. "I don't trust everybody comin' in here tonight. Man, they see you holding that kinda dough . . . "

"Alright, alright," Danny capitulated. *Bill did the right thing*, Mike thought as he counted out to Danny $200 in small bills. Bill put the rest in the safe, which was well hidden though most of the ADP Brothers knew where it was kept because they'd all agreed to hide it there.

Mike and Bill took turns counting the money as it came in from the door and the sale of food. After the one o'clock drop, the two had counted over $8,000: about seven grand from the door and the rest from the kitchen.

"All we got is wings left," said Delli. Delli leaned over towards Mike and said softly, "Y'all got too much money in here, Mike. I've seen that one guy, Danny, back here three times going in the closet. Now I ain't saying nothing because it really ain't my business but people go crazy over money, honey, especially that kind of money." Delli walked away and started putting dishes in the sink and throwing away trash.

Mike sat still for a moment, looked at the closet, then got up to look for Samuel and Danny. He spotted them near the door talking. Mike looked back at the closet. He felt compelled to ask Bill to check the safe. He changed his mind and went over to the safe himself. He got down low and pulled it out, then looked into the slit and saw that the money was stuffed to the brim. Mike put it back, thinking, *he didn't even have the combination*, and decided he should ask Bill for a count. The party was nearly over.

Just then, Bill walked in the kitchen.

Mike was direct. "Bill, we should take the safe back to your house now and count the money."

"Naw, man. We'll do fine right here. It'll take a few minutes and everybody will be here to see it." Mike disagreed, but didn't want to press the issue.

By now Delli and Rose had left. The kitchen looked better than they found it. Luke had saved about a quart of his jungle juice in the refrigerator for the after party. He pulled it out and stuffed it in his gym bag wrapped in a towel for safekeeping. Samuel, still at the door and surrounded by four women, moved about talking with his arms, making jokes and telling stories. He'd drunk about a quart of Luke's jungle juice by himself and seemed to feel every drop.

Danny and Bill were hunched in the kitchen corner behind the counter counting the money on the floor. Mike and a few of the brothers watched. "Man, we did it. We did it. We made bank this go-round," said Mike. Danny looked up as if annoyed with beads of sweat on his forehead. Mike held out his hand for dap. Danny gave him five. Bill kept counting. Danny looked hot but Mike felt the coldness of his hands.

"Mike, be cool for a minute, I'm still counting."

"Yeah, okay, sorry."

After a minute or two, Bill said, "We're at $9,400 and Samuel's holding about a hundred. Danny, how much you holding?"

"About two hundred." Bill stuffed the money back into the safe. Mike looked up and saw Samuel continue to carry on with the women. A man stumbled from the back of the hall holding up a bottle of Mad Dog 20/20. His shirt, unbuttoned, hung outside his pants. Mike left the kitchen and walked towards the man with a few other brothers, with Bill following behind.

Mike saw his bloodshot eyes. "Nigger, you can't have all the fun," the drunk man said, directing his remarks to Samuel. He staggered forward. "All them is your women? Who you think you is, Iceberg Slim?" The drunk reached for one of the women. She screamed.

Samuel hollered, "SOS, Brothers! SOS!" Mike reached for the young man to restrain him. The drunk swung the bottle at Mike, who was able to push the man away, knocking him off balance. Bill lunged forward and tackled the dude. The bottle flew from his unsteady hand and smashed right at the entrance.

By now, all the women had started screaming. By the time the security guards showed up, all the ADP brothers were on the scene. The guards spent more time pulling ADP brothers off the drunk than anything else.

Just as the scene by the front entrance was calming down, Danny bolted out the kitchen in hysterics screaming, "We just got robbed! We got robbed. We gotta catch 'em!" The brothers instantly left the drunk and ran into the kitchen.

"They came in through the kitchen emergency exit," said Danny. "Look, there they go!" He pointed through the open kitchen emergency exit door towards a couple of men walking near 12th Street. "You all go on foot. Me and Samuel will try and catch them in my car."

"Why they ain't running?" asked Mike.

"What, man? They trying not to be noticed," Danny shot back. "Samuel, let's go." They jumped into Danny's car and sped away, while about seven of the brothers pursued the would-be robbers on foot. Mike ran back inside the hall to let the others know what had gone down outside. "How the fuck did Danny get robbed that quick?" Luke asked, pacing back and forth.

"He said they came in through the emergency exit door in the kitchen," Mike explained. The security guards proceeded to the door where Danny claimed the robbers came in. They examined it and both said there was no forced entry. "These doors haven't been tampered with."

"See, that's bullshit. It's bullshit, man," said Luke. Where's that nigger that caused all the goddamn commotion?"

"I escorted him out. He's gone," said Bill.

While Bill retrieved the empty safe, the brothers who stayed behind gathered their coats and hats, and the DJ finished loading his equipment. Luke put his sawed-off shotgun in his gym bag, neatly wrapped beside his bottle.

"Luke, your mom and my mom told me to move the money and that Danny had been checking it like every five minutes. They had a feeling something might happen. We had too much money," said Mike.

Luke said nothing, but his face tightened. On the ride home, Luke exploded. "They stole the money, man! Danny and Samuel stole it to cop some blow. That's what they want to do. And, oh yeah, Samuel want to pimp too. Ever since you took him to meet your old paper route customer, Sweet-Daddy Long Leg, he be talking about pimpin'.'"

"Pimpin'? Samuel pimpin. You crazy. He must be stupid."

"Man, that's all that fool talk about to me. Sellin' P and pimpin' hos."

"Then dammit, Luke, how come you didn't see this comin'?"

"I didn't think that fool was serious. I couldn't believe that shit, just because he met Sweet-Daddy from Texas and read Iceberg Slim's book. Be for real, Mike. That weak ass chump, please."

"They got the whole kitty except for maybe three or four hundred dollars. They got over nine G's. Don't let me find those fools first." Mike just looked at Luke who had a crazed look on his face.

Later that Sunday, the ADP met at Bill's, where they gathered in the basement. All of the members showed up, with the conspicuous exception of Danny and Samuel. Everyone knew what had gone down, but nobody agreed on what to do about it.

Bill looked all tensed up in his chair, legs pressed tightly together, armpits dripping wet, as he struggled to find the words. His brother, Mel, looked on as the group advisor, and shook his head in agreement as Bill spoke. Bill led off by suggesting that the two be barred from the frat and frat activities, and that the ADP move on.

Mike interrupted him as he was starting to explain his position. "They can't get away with that, we got to at least report it to the police," said Mike.

"Already done that, after y'all left this morning," Bill retorted. "The security guards insisted we report it because of Local 75 rules. If we want to operate there again or at any other local in Detroit, we got to play by the rules. The cops are looking for them as we meet."

"They better hope the cops find 'em first because they got a good ass kickin' comin' from me," said Luke. Bill's brother, perched on a high bar chair in his basement overlooking the group, hopped down waving his arms furiously.

Mel said, "Retaliation is not the way to go. Not with those two idiots. If we stomp them, we only hurt ourselves and our families. We don't want to stir this pot because they on a one-way ticket to hell anyway. Let the police handle it. If you hurt them the police will be out for you. You'll be the one in jail."

"This should've never happened," interrupted Mike, "Some of y'all knew they wanted to deal P; some of y'all seen it comin'. Luke said he knew. Bill, you ain't never heard them talking about dealin' . . . ?"

"Yeah, talking," Bill said. "Everybody's talking . . . "

"You knew Danny should've never held the money," Mike said, and stood up.

Mel walked over to closer to the group, and said, "You brothers are gonna kill each other. This shit don't work like this, Mike. Sit down."

"Sit down! I ain't your dog now. Man, I got practice, man. What don't work is this ADP shit."

"Yeah, ADP," said Luke looking at the letters on his sweater. Then as he pointed to each letter he said, "Asses Done-got Punked. Yeah, done-got is one word." Luke then hastily took the sweater off and flung it to the ground and stated emphatically, "I'm through wit' this shit!" He followed Mike out the door.

~ ~ ~ ~ ~ ~ ~

After about a week of long and hard basketball practices, Mike nearly forgot that the rip-off had even happened. The ADP was already a distant memory. He was back in his sports groove.

Two weeks later, Bill confronted Mike one day after school, and asked him to attend an emergency ADP meeting. Mike couldn't believe his bad timing. Basketball practice started in thirty minutes and he still had to get dressed.

Mike thought. *Maybe there's word about the whereabouts on Samuel and Danny.* The two hadn't been seen since their heist of the organization's bank. Mike checked his watch for the time. It was already 3:12 and people were still coming in. Bill showed up at about 3:15. He took a seat at the classroom teacher's desk. He kept his head down when he spoke.

"Thank you all for showing up at this meeting. I have some shocking news, and I wanted to be able to tell you all at once." He paused for emphasis, then continued. "Danny and Samuel were found dead. They were murdered."

"Say what?" Mike responded. A few in the group let out gasps of emotion, but there seemed to be more anger than sadness among the brothers.

"The police found Samuel and Danny bound and gagged, shot full of holes in the trunk of a stolen car, parked at Belle Isle." Bill finally lifted his head. "That's fucked up. Whewwww," Bill let out all his breath.

"Drug deal gone bad, or what?" Mike remarked sullenly.

"Drug deal gone fucked up, is what the police say. I think it's them Jamaican dudes they met in Toronto. They were lookin' for a Detroit connection," said Bill.

"Damn. How we gonna retaliate against that?" asked Luke.

"We ain't. At least, I ain't." said Bill. "I can't speak for y'all, but I don't think there's much we can do. We really don't know who did it. All this has got their families in terror. They want to leave the state, I heard."

Mike left the group as they were still debating who did it. "I got practice."

CHAPTER 48 –
Jon-Jon's Drums on Belle Isle -
Fall 1970

MIKE WAITED FOR JON-JON AFTER PRACTICE. Mike knew he had to get his head back in the game after learning of the tragic death of his former frat brothers. But things with the basketball team were looking up. Coach Freddie Ray had finally given him more playing time at strong forward, and the team had the talent to take state-Mike knew it.

Waiting outside the school, he saw Jon-Jon coming out from the side exit, after he and Bongo Bob had been rehearsing some routines with the cheerleaders. Ever since Jon-Jon had joined Bongo Bob's troupe in the eighth grade, Bongo Bob had been grooming Jon-Jon to lead a group of his own one day. Besides carrying his conga, he clutched a handful of fliers. He passed out the fliers about the gatherings at Belle Isle to cheerleaders and ball players after practice, though the coach had already warned the team not to get involved in "all that stuff."

Both headed outside with their coats on. The temperature had dropped below forty degrees. Jon-Jon shivered and zipped his jacket up to his neck.

"Before it gets too cold I want you and your boys to come out to our drummin' jam sessions at Belle Isle," he said to Mike as he approached. "Been out there with Bongo Bob and the troupe every Sunday since school started. You ain't came out yet."

"Ain't that a jam just for y'all drummers?" Mike said, looking for an excuse. Jon-Jon pulled his new black hood over his head, saying, "Now that feels good. And the answer is no. All kinda people show up just to listen, sometimes dance. You know Bongo Bob is playing more of the African drum now. He's lovin' it, and I'm trying to learn from him. We gonna start bringing more African drummers and dancers to the games for half-time shows to work with the cheerleaders."

Mike just looked at Jon-Jon, and didn't know what to say but "No shit." He admired the way Jon-Jon ventured out on his own. He loved music and that's what he went after. Mike also admired the way Jon-Jon focused on school and his "movement politics" as he put it. Jon-Jon's natural stood twice the height of Mike's. And when Mike looked at his little brother he saw the regalness-he saw a brother going somewhere. His little brother walked with confidence and whenever he cried out "black power!" or talked movement politics at home Mike knew he meant it.

He wasn't nearly as tall as Mike, who stood 6'3", but rather a slim 5'10". He had eyes like his mother's - marble-shaped and penetrating, like he could quickly see through the BS. Mike felt that his pursuit of sports stardom didn't give him the time for the movement that Jon-Jon had become so immersed in. And Mike knew that none of the coaches could stand the movement politics. Mike wondered if Jon-Jon had gotten too close to Uncle John and his African Research Center (ARC) brothers or Bongo Bob and his African drumming troupe, always spouting black power messages.

Jon-Jon asked again, "Maybe you and your boys on the team can come out to Belle Isle this weekend to see what this black power movement is all about. We're having a poetry-fest."

"A poetry fest, uh? Yeah, well, that's cool, but I live on the field, the court, the track. Know what I'm sayin'? I'm doin' something year-round. I ain't got time, and besides, the coaches don't like it. But I'll come this Sunday, really." Mike felt that he needed to do something different. "

"What about your boys, though? Do they know what's happenin' out here?"

"Dig Jon-Jon, everybody know something, even if they don't read nothing. People ain't like you—they ain't studying this shit. We ain't thinkin' about it the way you, Uncle John, or the Panthers thinking." Mike glanced at Jon-Jon as they walked in stride. "You probably got somethin' in your back pocket right now, knowin' you." Jon-Jon gave up a wide grin, then reached for his back pocket and produced a book titled *The Wretched of the Earth*, by Frantz Fanon.

"Damn straight," he said, still smiling and waving the book in the air. "This is part of a revolutionary's toolkit. I'm reading it with Uncle John's ARC Study Circle at the City Club. The brothers know what they're talking about."

"Oh, yeah? What's this book about?" Mike snatched it from Jon-Jon's hand.

"'Bout the revolutionary struggles in Africa. This dude's a psychiatrist.

Born in the Caribbean, then moved to France where he hooked up with some revolutionaries from the continent."

"There you go with that African shit, boy. You gonna end up in the jungle, as much as you talk about it. I can see you now, playin' your tom-toms and carryin' on."

"Man, gimme my book back." Jon-Jon snatched it from Mike's hands and promptly shoved it back into his back pocket.

The next evening the boys sat on the front porch as Bongo Bob pulled up in his 1963 Chevy Impala station wagon, which was perfect for hauling drums and equipment. Jon-Jon hauled his two congas to the rear of the car and gently laid them on top of the thick layer of carpet Bongo Bob had lined the back of his wagon with. Mike hopped in the front as Jon-Jon settled into the back seat, where he wasn't used to riding. But he always deferred to his older brother.

"Here comes Luke," said Mike, watching him saunter up to the car. Luke hopped in the back and Bongo Bob took off. The boys slapped palms and greeted each other with the usual "What's happenin'?" Bongo Bob's pat response was always "Everything is everything."

Luke said, "We digging your half-time show, man, and what y'all putting down during the game."

Bongo Bob said simply, "Thanks" as he got on the John C. Lodge Freeway heading to Belle Isle. He edged his wagon up to a cruising 75 mph, and glided into downtown Detroit in less than fifteen minutes. As they stayed on Jefferson Ave. through the downtown area, Mike couldn't help but notice how deserted the streets were as the sun began to set. The sky mellowed into a blue-purple hue. The night was unusually warm.

"So how does this thing work tonight?" Luke asked.

"Well, after the Brotherhood play for awhile and a few people read, we'll ask for newcomers and what y'all got. We say 'Habari Gani,' and then whoever wants to read will shout back the name of their poem, song, or story and come to the front of the group. What you gonna read, Luke?" asked Bongo Bob.

"'Signifyin' Monkey.' I'm gonna entertain y'all with 'The Signifyin' Monkey.'"

Mike often described Belle Isle as heaven on earth—an oasis of peace in a tumultuous city. He visited Belle Isle on many occasions with his family, on his bike, and lately driving the family car.

At the gathering of drummers, Jon-Jon appeared to be the youngest of the group of young adults. Most of the men looked like they were in their early twenties, except for Bongo Bob who was eighteen. Jon-Jon looked intense, and beads of sweat seemed to be stuck on his forehead as he played his drum, his dashiki already dripping wet.

But Mike couldn't focus on the music. He walked towards the huge fountain, his mind kept shifting back to the horror of dying on the streets of Detroit. He still couldn't get over how Samuel and Danny had ended up dead over some stupid shit. *Who did they think they were? Who did they think they were fucking with? This was not some TV game show: "Let's Make A Deal" or something. The real hard-cold world turned them inside out*, Mike thought. And Duane killed over some little gambling debt. The drug scene just taking people down to nothing. The white stuff was everywhere all the time – like snow blowing in July.

Mike did an about-face. Facing the drummers, Mike saw about two dozen people had gathered around the drummers. Luke bobbed and bounced his body to the rhythm, then moved up to the music to give his rendition of an African dance. The boy could dance. Then suddenly the drumming ceased. One of the drummers called for the new poets: "Habari Gani, Habari Gani."

A young brother stepped up. The drummer said, "You read, and we play. We'll follow your lead." That first poet started a black-power chant to the soft background drumming.

"Black power, black power. What do we want?"

"Black power!" the crowd chanted back.

"When do we want it?"

"Now!"

This call and response went on for a few minutes. Then another brother went before the group and talked about his Queen. "Mother, sister, Queen of the universe, oh so lovely, so lovely with your blue-black beauty, darkened by the penetrating sun . . . shine up from the earth, spread your arms around us . . . nurturing, comforting, compassionate, Mother Africa, my African sister, you are my Queen." He went on and on. A brother jumped up from a seated position off to the side and began to rail against what he called the capitalistic, cannibalistic system of oppression in America.

"America lusts for your blood," he said. "Blood lust. The pigs got blood on their hands, the blood lustful pigs, they got the blood of my mother, my father, the capitalistic pigs with her capitalistic fangs are sucking the blood out of America . . . "

People from the audience cheered him on. They clapped and some broke out in shrill sounds, whistles. Others cried out, "Teach, brother!" and "Tell it like it is."

All the while, Luke danced. Then, just as suddenly as the others, Luke made his way to the front.

"Habari Gani," said one of the drummers.

"Yeah, I got me a little something off the Rudy Ray Moore album. It's called 'The Signifyin' Monkey.' I'm gonna do my rendition of it and it goes a little something like this: 'Deep down in the jungle . . . '"

The drummers kept time. The drums seemed to carry away Mike's feeling of loss and hopelessness. He thought, Damn, *look at Luke. He act like he ain't got a worry in the world. Gotta get past it. Basketball season is on me now. We starting off against class A schools!* Mike knew he had to bury his grief deep, the bottom of the ocean floor deep.

The drumming felt intoxicating. "I'm getting high on drums," Mike hollered to Luke. Luke had just finished his Signifyin' Monkey poem to light applause and had walked back towards Mike.

"Better than herr-ron, my brother," said Luke. The two slapped palms. Mike knew that Luke was qualified to make that judgment, and the two cracked up. Bongo Bob, Jon-Jon, and the others formed a semi-circle on the grass.

In that moment, Belle Isle looked more beautiful than ever to Mike.

CHAPTER 49 –
White Castle

A WEEK LATER, AFTER COMING FROM a Saturday-night party, Mike decided he would hang out with Jon-Jon, Bongo Bob, and several other drummers again, this time at the White Castle. Mike parked his dad's car on a street nearby, then headed straight for the line to order burgers. He ordered two ten-packs of the small patties, enough for him and his friends. When Mike came back outside into the parking lot, he spotted Jon-Jon and Bongo Bob exactly where they had planned to meet. Mike made his way through the boisterous late-night revelers in the parking lot, noticing that, among some who were dressed as if they had been working on their hot-rods all day, many people at the White Castle were dressed in nice threads like they had just left a party.

This White Castle was *The Spot* to gather for those who wanted to extend the party. People came to the White Castle from everywhere to watch the show of "muscle cars" being towed or driven in preparation for street racing that would take place in the early hours of the morning at a "secret" location.

"What's happenin', little brother?" said Mike, approaching Jon-Jon. "What's up Bongo Bob?" They all gave each other dap. "They're towing cars down here?" Mike asked in amazement.

"Yeah, they can't drive some of these cars on the street," said Bongo Bob. Mike checked out the range of high-powered muscle cars rolling down the street circling the White Castle, drivers revving up their engines.

"Y'all play down here in all of this? Man, I don't believe it."

"Brother, we add to the excitement. We use the drums to help build up the intensity for the races," said Jon-Jon.

Four more brothers in dashikis drove up in a Ford station wagon. They parked in a nearby alley and got out, carrying their drums, and walked over to the group. The drummers formed a semi-circle on the corner. Bongo Bob led the group with some slow and easy beats, and the others quickly joined in. And while the drummers drummed, Mike stuffed himself with White Castle burgers.

Just as he was getting into the rhythm of the music, Mike spied a souped-up '63 Chevy Impala cruising around the lot, then saw a '66 Barracuda fastback on a flatbed tow truck, followed by a '68 Chevelle and '68 Camero.

Talking with his mouth full, Mike asked, "How do y'all compete with all this? I mean, people blasting the radios over there, and look, here comes the Corvette Club."

Mike could see a long line of 'vettes going by a throng of women, whose faces lit up. "Look at that, y'all, a bunch a 'vettes go by and all the women at full attention."

One of the older drummers named Abdul, whom Mike remembered from Belle Isle as the oldest of the group at 22, peered over his spectacles and said, "We're not here to compete, brother. We're just part of the whole vibe out here. This is a collaboration, you know. Sometime we draw the people to us, sometime we're drawn to the people, the masses. Look at all these brothers and sisters out here man, and hardly no police in sight. Everybody's doing fine. We ain't trying to dominate the scene, we're just adding to it. But I'm gonna' tell ya, these rhythms penetrate, my brother. Look at 'em," Abdul said, pointing to a group of sisters. "They act like they don't see us or hear us as they step over to the 'vette boys, but they sure feelin' us. You see how they walkin'?"

The drummers kept up the drumming, and Abdul went on. "You see that bounce? That's the African comin' out. Yeah! Man, we all in this stew together."

Yeah, Mike thought. *Like the Compact: Dad trying to get people at the compact schools together.* Then he said, "Yeah, I can dig it. Hey, anybody want burgers? Man, these burgers are good."

Abdul laughed, "Naw, no sawdust burgers for me."

Mike waved him off and said, "White Castle's da bomb." Polishing off the last few, he got back in a long line for more burgers, taking some time to admire all the good-looking and decked out women.

"What's up, Mike?" he heard from behind.

Mike recognized the voice as that of Big G, a brother he played baseball with before the riot. They slapped palms, then gave each other a big hug. Mike had never felt so happy to see someone. While standing in line Big G and Mike reminisced about old times. Big G told Mike that he played baseball for Northern High School and that he might get picked up by a farm team. He said he was batting over .400 and snagging everything in sight at first base.

"Yeah, I remember," Mike said. "You had a helluva glove and bat." He was about to start filling Big G in on recent happenings when they were distracted by the big uproar they heard outside. People were clapping. Mike looked out the window to see someone driving down the street with a Plymouth Fury on a flatbed, the words "Detroit Muscle" artistically painted on the side.

"Who's that?" Mike asked.

Big G said, "Man, that dude be down here winning all the time. He races at Detroit Dragway, too. His ride smokes. Believe me, if you see the race . . . You ever seen a race, man?"

"Naw."

"Man, you got to see this shit, brother. These cats be flyin', and I ain't lyin'." He cracked a huge grin.

Despite the uproar outside, Mike could still feel the sounds of the drums. At the front of the line at last, he ordered another ten-pack of burgers with cheese and onions.

"So what happened to you, man? We never heard from you after the riot," he said, turning back to Big G as he waited for his burgers.

"Well, you know the house is gone. It caught fire, being so close to 12th Street. Man, we had like minutes to try to grab everything we could and haul ass. 12th Street was burning like crazy and we started loading stuff into my Uncle's pickup." Big G started waving his hands wildly as his story picked up pace. "Then our crib caught on fire and my dad and uncle still trying to save the furniture and I'm watching my little brothers and sisters in my dad's car watching everything. Man, the whole house just went up, and my ol' man ran back in one more time, said he left a wad on bills in the kitchen cabinet. Mom tripped out and started screaming, then my little brother and sister started screaming. Uncle Jerry ran in after my pops. Man the shit was wild. Then here he come with a jar full of bills. We copped a hat, real quick. I mean, we was gone." Mike and Big G slapped palms. "Shit, it was crazy. We stayed with my Uncle Jerry over on the Northend. We finally got our own place on Westminster Street, around the corner from Unc. And it's been good, man. I'm five minutes from school . . . "

Their food ready, Big G and Mike grabbed their bags and headed back outside to join the others.

By three in the morning several hundred people spilled out into the streets around the White Castle. The Vette Club brothers lay back against their rides and entertained whomever seemed interested. Mike and Big G walked through all the bustling energy back to Jon-Jon. Mike leaned against a lamppost where he and Big G bobbed their heads to the music, and he and Big G talked it up while they both wolfed down the burgers.

The drummers paused. Then Jon-Jon said, "It's about that time, brothers."

"Dig that," replied Bongo Bob.

Abdul said, "The sound of Mother Africa is infectious. It gets inside your soul, travels to your heart, then pumps all that spirit to your brain, down your spine and out through your funky toes, baby. And before you know what hit you, you got soul. Remember, Mike . . . " Mike looked over at him, and he nodded, "We're all in this stew together."

Mike nodded back, and thought for a moment before speaking. "Where do they go from here?" he asked Jon-Jon.

"Over to Holbrook, back up there by the Chrysler Freeway. There's a strip over a mile long, no lights, no stop signs. It's perfect for street racing."

"Me and G will meet y'all over there. I'll call dad and let him know we want to stay out a little later tonight." Mike glanced at his watch. "Shoot! It's already three o'clock in the morning."

CHAPTER 50 -
At the Hop -
March 1971

MIKE HAD BEEN THINKING ABOUT THE big dance all week. The St. Martin DePorres Senior Class of 1971 organized their big "Spring Thing" dance for late March. It was their last hurrah. For this year's big dance, the student council president, Al Kerry, successfully got the R&B band Parliament/ Funkadelic to play, because Al's father had been a sound engineer for the group at United Sound Studio. This year's party theme, "Let's Go to the Hop," would feature music of the late 1950s and early 1960s in between the live music sets that would be played by Parliament/Funkadelic. To complete the scene, the senior class organizers asked that the hostesses wear roller skates to serve food and drinks — just like hostesses had done at the old A&W drive-ins.

Before Mike left home for the party, he got a call from Lola. She started talking about how she had dumped her boyfriend, saying that they could no longer see eye-to-eye.

Mike listened with fascination. He knew that her college-ball- playing, now ex-boyfriend, was having a field day with women at Ferris State. At least that's what he had heard. Steve had gotten the nickname 'Da Wabbit' because he spent more time jumping from hole to hole than anything else. Mike heard that if there was a female nearby, he'd be sure to mention that he'd like to be her wabbit and tunnel under. Mike believed the stories he heard. And Mike knew Lola had heard the same stories.

"I cut him loose, Mike," she explained. "He expected me to just sit at home after school and on the weekends and wait for his call, if he called at all, or wait 'til he came home before I could do anything. I told him, 'I ain't in no jail.' He wanted to lock me up and throw away the key. How can he? My father told me to do whatever I wanted to do because don't no man own me."

Then Lola said that she looked forward to seeing Mike at the dance. Mike felt that maybe now he could talk to Lola but he also knew he was interested in other girls now, from Mumford, Henry Ford, and Immaculata High Schools. And at least a couple were coming to the dance tonight.

Mike rode to the dance with his old friends, Luke and Brother Bear. Luke drove his '68 Torino. When he and his buddies arrived, the first thing Mike did once inside was check out the huge posters of old cars — '57 Chevy, '59 T-Bird, '56 Fleetwood and a couple of dozen assorted muscle cars like the Barracuda and GTO and pictures of Jackie Wilson, The Platters, Chuck Berry and Little Richard. A blue and gold banner hung over the stage that read "Let's Go to the Hop". Mike loved the theme, but of course the biggest draw was the live entertainment — The Parliament/Funkadelic. Everybody knew they would blow the place up. Mike still loved listening to The Parliament's hit song *Testify* from 1967; he had dug their music ever since. *Maggot Brain* and *I Bet You* were among his favorites. Mike had not yet seen them perform live, but he'd heard from classmates that one of the musicians would appear in a diaper. He was looking forward to the spectacle.

Before the show, Bongo Bob, the DJ, blended some 1950s and early 60s music in with some hot new Motown hits. Jackie Wilson's *Reet Petite* was blaring over the sound system when Mike and his partners arrived. Then Bongo Bob played Jackie Wilson's *Baby Workout*. Partygoers were dancing through the door as they came in.

Not far away, Mike spotted his former frat brother, Bill, who came through the doors with a wide grin.

"Mike, what's happenin', my man?" he said, coming up to Mike. "Man, I got a contingent of girls coming here tonight - Immaculata's finest are on their way."

"I can dig that." Mike knew that Bill's motive had always been to seek the best of both worlds. He had told Mike once, "Yeah, we got superstar women here but there's a whole world of superstars out there, especially at Immaculata. And besides, once our girls get to know them, we might still pull off a united sisters sorority for our fraternity."

Mike didn't care to hear any more of this fantasy fraternity stuff, especially since Samuel and Danny were murdered, and he wasn't surprised when Luke walked away before giving Bill a chance to get into it again. Mike knew that everything boiled down to booty for his former fraternity. "Bill, you must want to start some stuff," said Mike. "Luke, you hear that man? A united sisterhood!" Mike tried to call Luke to come back, but Luke threw both arms in the air with his back to Mike and Bill.

Turning back to Bill, Mike went on, "These women don't want no parts of each other. Remember our parties? Remember they sat at the opposite ends of the dance hall that night at the Local 75? Bill, you still fantasizing, man. You don't know when to quit."

Mike turned around to check out a long-legged, golden-brown, girl named Ronnie who skated up to the brothers to take their orders. Mike used the distraction as an opportunity to say goodbye to Bill, and hurriedly copped a table in the back corner with Luke where he could sit down and keep a good view of everything that was going on.

Mike saw about a dozen girls from Immaculata arrive in a bunch. Julie, an aggressive young lady who Mike had met a year ago after a football game, quickly eased her way over to the table where Mike and Luke sat. Without further greeting, she sat down and put her legs across Mike's lap, closed her eyes, leaned her head back, and said "Aaahhh, feel like I'm home in bed."

Before Mike could respond, she sprung up looking more animated and asked Mike, "Do you like bike riding?"

Mike gave her a surprised look and raised his eyebrows. *That sure came out of left field*, he thought. Mike couldn't tell if she was serious or not, but he decided to give her a serious answer.

"Yeah, I have a 10-speed. I ride in the summer. Why? You ride too?"

"Oh yes, I love to ride," she said matter-of-factly. "Do you ride fast or slow?"

"I'm a speed demon,. It's more fun."

"Well, if you ride with me, you got to go slow. You got to slow down. You wouldn't want to lose me."

Mike laughed, "You a trip, girl. If you ride with me, I promise I won't lose you. Hey, maybe we can ride to Canada together."

"Yes, maaaay—be," Julie said, very slowly drawing out each syllable. "We can ride in Canada, Belle Isle . . . yes, Belle Isle. It's a lot closer and very convenient. I'm excited already." Julie glanced down at her breasts, then touched her nipples and said "Oops! My nipples are all firm."

Mike looked at her and laughed, then led her to the dance floor for the next song.

Mike never danced as much as he did during that year's Spring Thing. Mike felt fully engaged in the dance. Julie from Immaculata danced her ass off — she barely took a break.

During the bands intermission, when Bongo Bob played *Mickey's Monkey* by Smokey Robinson and the Miracles, Mike checked out the band members, who moved to the beat while they left the stage to start partying with the students. The Brides of Funkenstein had been singing with the group all evening and they came down from the stage still fired up. It was one big party.

Mike felt like going outside for some fresh air. At the door, Mike suddenly caught sight of Lola. He also noticed the cold-hard stares he received from Lola and her girlfriends.

As he approached, Lola pointed to Julie who was still inside and asked icily, "Is that your girlfriend, Mike?"

"Yep, for now."

"What, tonight? And what about later?"

"And what *about* later?" Mike fired back.

Lola looked Mike up and down and said, "Well? What about it?"

Mike didn't know what to think since Lola had been with Steve for darn near the past three years. He was still searching for a retort when he heard the sounds of Jimi Hendrix's – *Who Knows* coming over the speakers. So Mike shrugged and said simply, "Who knows?"

"Who knows?" Lola asked.

"Yeah, who knows? I mean, really, who knows about later?" And Mike kept walking. He couldn't help wondering if he blew it, but he shrugged off the feeling. *Lola's feeling jealous here at the dance and what am I supposed to do, jump? Yeah, she's fine, but I ain't jumpin just yet,* he thought. Mike stepped outside into the beginning of a late winter snowstorm. He felt the heavy wet snowflakes blowing into his face. After about five minutes, he retreated back inside to the tune, *Going to a Go-Go.*

After the thirty-minute intermission, George Clinton grabbed the mike and said in a deep bass voice, "What is soul?" Another voice from the group chimed in: "Hamhocks in your cornflakes." Mike took that as his cue to head back to the dance floor and find Julie again.

The band started playing the soulful song *All Your Goodies Are Gone.* Then the Brides of Funkenstein cut loose on a couple of hot dance numbers. Mike and Julie kept dancing. When the group began to sing "Goodnight sweetheart, it's time to go . . . ," Mike knew the finale had begun.

But the band left the stage at the completion of the song –- for only about a minute. Then they returned to play "Whole Lotta Shakin'." And when the Parliament/Funkadelic played "Whole Lotta Shakin'," a train-line formed right away. Julie grabbed Mike's hand and led him to the front of the line, pulling him in as they snaked their way around the dance hall and onto the stage.

The band played for twenty minutes, and by the end of the number Mike's shirt was soaked with sweat. Just before limping off the dance floor, Mike asked Julie if he could drop her off after the party. She nodded her head "yes" enthusiastically.

Before they left the party, Mike asked Luke to drive to Belle Isle. Luke agreed, and he and Brother Bear pulled the car around front. Mike and Julie climbed in the back seat, sitting close. The snow had been falling all night and the visibility was bad, so Luke drove slowly. Mike was in no rush. On the way to Belle Isle, he began to work his hand inside Julie's panties. He felt her warmth. She put her hand on top of his which kept his hand firmly inside her loose-fitting jeans. As the car swerved slightly on some snow, she leaned her head back and held her mouth agape, moaning. Mike caught Luke glancing in the rear-view mirror, but ignored him. Mike kissed her on the neck, then placed his long tongue into her ear. He found her hot spot.

"Oh, Mike!" She started unbuttoning her shirt. He kept kissing her, and she kissed back with force, sticking her tongue half-way down Mike's throat.

Sooner than he would have thought, Mike noticed they were on Belle Isle. Luke pulled over after the first curve on the island, which faced the Detroit River and Windsor, Canada and, turning to Brother Bear, spoke up for the first time since they had gotten in the car.

"We got to go out in this blizzard so Mike can get his rocks off."

"Let's go," said Brother Bear, laughing. "We'll be back." Mike and Julie stopped kissing for a moment to let the two exit the vehicle.

"Oh, it's so cold out there," Julie said.

"I'll keep you warm, baby," Mike said, moving in closer to Julie.

Thankfully, Luke left the car running. Julie slipped off her shirt, pulled down her jeans and tights, then unsnapped her bra — all in less than ten seconds. Mike watched in disbelief, wondering, *Is this it? Is it really happening?* He got harder than he'd ever been. He stared at the voluptuous naked body of this beautiful coco chocolate young woman in the back seat of Luke's Torino.

"What am I waiting for?" he said, softly but audibly.

Julie paused and said, "I have no idea." Mike stripped off everything with Julie's help, then reached into his pants pocket for his rubber johnnies. He waved them in front of Julie. "Da da."

"Negro, I know you're not putting that thing on." Julie ever so gently began to massage him.

Mike started to protest, but Julie stopped him with a finger on his lips and said, "But I want the real thing. I want to feel it in me." Mike immediately got on top of Julie and kissed her all over. She squeezed his butt. Mike had never felt so sexual. His entire body vibrated. He moved delicately, like he would inside a shop of fine china.

My rubber, where is it? Mike wondered, feeling overwhelmed. He had learned from his Uncle John always to use a rubber if he were to have sex. He thought, *She's probably clean, right? Right?* It felt too good for Mike to stop now.

The windows steamed up so thickly that Mike couldn't tell what the weather was like outside the car. He felt extra warm. Julie turned Mike over and got on top. She started bouncing up and down, sweat running down her bare chest, and leaned her head back before falling forward on his chest. All Mike could say was, "Whew." He grabbed Julie's butt tight with both hands and said louder, "Whew, I feel good."

"Oooh, Mike. We got to do this again." Julie giggled. Then, as if on cue, Brother Bear and Luke rapped on the windows, acting like the police.

"Get out of the car." Mike almost fell for it as he searched for his pants and cleared a spot on the window, only to see Brother Bear and Luke standing outside laughing.

"Where are my drawers?" said Mike as he kept on looking. "Where are my drawers?" Mike demanded.

Julie got dressed fast without saying one word. Luke and Bear rapped on the window again, "Come on, now. We freezing out here." Then, seconds later, they started bombing the car with snowballs. When still no response came from inside the car, Luke came up to the car again, pressed his face against the window and said, "Goddamn, boy! Get dressed. Open the door 'fore we really call the police. Shit." Julie giggled, then reached under the front seat and pulled Mike's underwear out.

"I guess your boys don't want to see your naked butt."

They all piled back into the car and Luke drove around the island once more, despite the near-blizzard conditions.

"Y'all wanna stop and have a snow ball fight or something?" Luke asked.

"Naw," said Mike. "We want to play like Houdini and jump into the Detroit River. Man, let's get up outta here. Julie got to be home." Julie didn't seem to care. She laid her head in Mike's lap. Luke cautiously rounded the final curve at Belle Isle before heading back to the mainland in the near-blinding snowstorm.

After letting Julie out and while waiting for her to let herself in the house, Luke couldn't help himself. "So y'all been biking, huh? Biking through the snow?" he asked with a wide grin.

"Yep, all the way to China." They slapped palms and laughed.

CHAPTER 51 -
Jim Dunham Gets Recognition - May 1971

OFFICIALS FROM THE STATE DEPARTMENT OF Education toured St. Martin DePorres one day in late 1970, then returned the next day to hold a news conference. Mr. Dunham had been nominated by his peers to receive the *Detroit Free Press*'s "Michigan Educator of the Year" Award. The newspaper ran a front page story the next day. The headlines read: "Like A Phoenix Rising, St. Martin DePorres Stands Tall on 12ᵗʰ Street and Webb. Principal, Mr. Dunham Named Michigan Educator of the Year." There was a photo of Mr. Dunham standing outside the school.

An award ceremony was scheduled for the first Saturday in May 1971, during the annual dinner fundraiser. The ceremony and dinner fundraiser would be held at Cobo Hall in downtown Detroit and, as always, sponsored by the automotive industry. This was the school's third annual fundraiser and Mike heard from his father that it would be a great idea to combine the recognition award with the dinner, and that this dinner could bring in the "biggest haul yet, maybe $50,000." Mike heard that the dining hall was set up for one thousand people, but that night, it seemed to Mike that more than a thousand people showed up. The room was packed. This was the first time Mike had seen the school's faculty out with their spouses. They were *clean to the bone*. Mike's siblings were at the dinner, too, as were his parents, Mama E, Luke and Sharon. They were all seated at the Waterman table.

A huge banner hung in front of the large rectangular stage: "Congratulations, Mr. Jim Dunham – You are Michigan's Educator of the Year 1970-71." Stevie Wonder's song *Fingertips* blared over the speakers. The atmosphere was festive. Mike checked out the waitresses serving, noticing a waitress for every table, all of whom were busy pouring water. There were several student tables set up near the front. The three National Honors Society and honor student tables were nearest to the stage. The athlete's table featured Mike, two of his football buddies, two basketball players, a baseball player, and two track stars, and was situated in between a table of student musicians to the left and artists to the right. About 40 students in all were seated near the front.

When Mr. Dunham entered the room he received a standing ovation. The crowd quieted when Kim Weston sang, acapella, "Lift Every Voice and Sing." The audience remained standing until she finished, then clapped and cheered wildly. When the audience quieted, she began to sing, "To Be Young, Gifted, and Black." She asked all the students to stand up, then asked everyone who knew the lyrics to join in. The sound was tremendous as hundreds of voices sang with her.

After the song, Kim Weston congratulated the students and Mr. Dunham to another standing ovation. Mr. Dunham accepted his award graciously, thanking his staff profusely, as well as his assistant principal Sister JoAnna who, Mr. Dunham said, "taught me everything I know about running the school." He thanked Father O'Malley for turning over the "keys to the castle," then thanked the school board for supporting his vision. He gave out a special thanks to his "two confidants" Frank Waterman and Ted Wilson. Then he turned towards Mr. Carl 'Curly' Cornell and said, "And yes, Curly, we have risen out of the ashes of 12th Street."

Mr. Dunham then faced the audience. After pausing reflectively for a moment, he continued, "These young brothers and sisters seated around this room are being prepared to lead this country to a better place. These young men and women have risen to the occasion. Our family here at St. Martin DePorres has grown together over these past three years. And you have shown me that we can do whatever we want, once we set our minds to it. The proof is in the pudding. And look at all this pudding in this audience. Beautiful chocolate pudding." Everybody in the hall cracked up with laughter. As the laughter subsided, Mr. Dunham continued, "I have seen you grow. You have shown me and our brilliant faculty that you can truly become whatever you set your hearts and minds to. We have raised over $30,000 each year for the past two years at this annual dinner, and this year I hear we may get over $50,000 thanks to your generosity." The applause was thunderous.

By the time the night was over Mike felt a natural high, a high he had never felt before that night. He felt proud of his school and his principal.

CHAPTER 52 -
Ceceliaville, Detroit -
Summer 1971

EARLY THAT SUMMER, MIKE WAS HANGING out with his dad when Frank met with Sammy Washington (aka "Wash") about his intention to start a top tier summer basketball league in Detroit at the old St. Cecelia gymnasium on Livernois Ave. Sammy called it Ceceliaville, USA, and explained that the summer league would feature talent from Michigan high schools, area colleges, and professional and non-professional adults. Sammy told Frank, "This league will bring the very best together. And we'll run it first class. I want Detroit to become a magnet for summer basketball. Father Ellis gave me the green light a few weeks ago."

Frank replied, "This will be different than what we put together here at City Club over the past few summers."

"Ceceliaville will give Michigan youth a chance to really hone their skills," Sammy said.

And Frank said to Sammy, "Brother, I'm behind you one hundred percent."

Two years earlier Wash had started a new Pop Warner football program in Detroit at the former Catholic parish, to compete with the much-respected West Side Cubs for metro-Detroit dominance..

During the summer of 1971, Mike started thinking more about taking his school to the state championship in all three sports in which he competed successfully: basketball, football and track. Mike felt that his time had come, and said to his dad, "I'd like to play summer league ball, then football in August. I want to work with Hunt and Darnell and Uncle John on the youth power summit they're planning. They told me they want it to jump off just as school starts in September."

"We'll have to see what your time allows for, son," was all Frank had said at the time.

That summer, the football team voted Mike captain. Still feeling inspired by the recognition awards ceremony he attended in June, Mike pitched an idea to the team. Mike's big idea for the football team was to try to get some of the players on the honor roll — finally. During his first three years at DePorres, not one athlete in any sport had made the honor roll. At a team meeting during the off-season, Mike shared his goal with the team, saying, "One of y'all, at least *one* got to make the honor roll. We got to get rid of the dumb-jock-strap mentality because not only do we have to graduate and get into college, we got to get *through* college. Then do something with ourselves. And we best know how to read. Yeah, I know that's a challenge for many, but we gots to do it. Basically, what I'm sayin' is I want us to be the smartest football team in Michigan –- on the field and off."

Coach Taylor had been hanging in the background but stepped up and said, "Shit, boy. You sayin' something here. I've been around the game all my life, but ain't never heard nothing like that come from a player."

Turning to his team, Coach Taylor continued, "Y'all ready for Mike's challenge?"

The locker room got quiet. No one responded.

"I'll ask again. Are y'all ready for Mike's challenge?"

The players belted out a resounding, "Yes, Coach Taylor. Yes, Coach Taylor!"

"Now that's music to my ears."

But Mike had no idea how he would get his project going. Over the summer he shared his ideas with his mother.

"Mom, we could ask the teachers for extra help after school or something or maybe look for tutors to come in to the school, or maybe we can do it on the weekend in the off-season."

Rose said to Mike, "Your grades are good Mike, but you can do better. Your Dad tells you to aim high, reach for the stars. Aim high, Mike. You want to show that you can be good in sports and in school at the same time." She tilted her head down, eyes open wide. "And ain't nobody at St. Martin DePorres criticizing anyone for being smart."

"Dig that. I mean, you're right."

"Listen to this," Rose said. "I think you might want to ask the honor roll students for help. The smart kids. Set aside your study hall to meet with honor roll students, either for group sessions or one-on-one sessions. I bet that'll go over well. And I bet those honor roll students will feel mighty proud if they get some of the athletes on the honor roll. I hear that a lot of the honor students want to teach. They love their teachers and want to be just like them," Rose said with authority. "And here it is: they can start with you all. What do you call yourselves, jocks?"

Mike smiled widely. Mike appreciated his mother's interest because she'd been pushing him hard to keep his grades up. He couldn't help but give his mother a big hug.

"Mom, you're the greatest. I love you."

Still lost in thought, Mike continued, "And once we get this thing going we can share it with the other compact schools."

Rose said, "Some schools already got this going on. A lot of teachers realized that high school students were graduating without knowing how to read past the third-grade level. And many couldn't even read at that level. They've set up remedial reading programs, and at the same time they encourage honor students to help other classmates. Check with Central High School. I believe their National Honors Society set up something similar. You know, I heard from our neighbor, Tonya Roberson, she graduated from Central two years ago and by the way she's now attending University of Michigan. She said that it was mandatory for all ball players to attend study hall at Central."

But then Rose changed the subject. "Do you still need help making the picnic basket for you and Julie this Sunday?"

"I sure do, Mom."

~ ~ ~ ~ ~ ~ ~

Mike had been enjoying his regular outings with Julie since the *Spring Thing* dance. He took her to the movies, to Cedar Point amusement park with a group of friends, and canoeing at Belle Isle, but Mike felt that this date on Sunday evening would be something special. The week before, Mike had read an article in the *Detroit Free Press* about Windsor's Jackson Park. Along with the article, pictures painted an idyllic portrait of the Park as a picturesque flower garden. Mike craved a romantic afternoon with Julie in Jackson Park. He planned for a picnic at the park, and packed a picnic basket borrowed from the family pantry.

Mike decided not to sneak a bottle of Cold Duck with him because of the tricky drive over the Ambassador Bridge. *What if I get popped driving under the influence in Canada? How embarrassed would I be?* Mike thought. *What if the border guards don't let me back in the United States?*

Sunday felt perfect in every way: the cloudless sky, light traffic on the bridge, and Julie looked like a perfect ten with icing on top. When Mike picked her up, she wore a pink summer dress with a big white bow tied in the back. *Yes,* Mike thought, *she is quite a package.*

Once inside the park they both walked around, admiring the rows and rows of colorful flowers and the fountains in the pools. Everything seemed to shine under the warm summer sun. Julie carried a large pink bag over her shoulder, while Mike carried the picnic basket.

"Ooh, look at the couple getting married over there!" Julie exclaimed, pointing to the small gathering of people near the entrance to the park. "That's beautiful! That is just so nice. Everyone is so dressed up," she continued. She stared for another minute without saying a word, just watching as the couple took their vows.

Mike said, "Yeah, real nice." Then he took her hand and led her in the opposite direction.

As they walked away, Julie stared at Mike with a big smile on her face. "I want to be married one day. What about you?" she asked.

"Ha! I haven't even thought about it."

"Not at all?"

"Nope, not yet. It just seems like a long ways off. I mean, we're still in high school. How could we be thinking about something like that?"

"I think about it a lot. Be like Ozzie and Harriet."

"Yeah, right. Like Leave it to Beaver."

Julie laughed and squeezed Mike's hand, then said, "Yeah, right."

"You know what, Julie? You're just like this sunshine — warm and beautiful."

"And you're just like the sunshine, too. I'll be yours if you'll be mine — sunshine."

They both giggled. Julie stopped then and looked like she was trying to get her bearings. "Hey," she said, "let's eat here near these bushes."

"Looks good to me." Mike spread out the blanket, and presented Julie with a chicken salad sandwich. "Compliments of my mother. She helped me prepare all this good food."

"I'll have to thank her myself."

The two ate chicken salad sandwiches and drank lemonade, then lay down beside one another and dropped grapes in each others' mouths. After a while, Julie sat up, grabbed her handbag and, while reaching inside for something, asked, "Are you ready for dessert?"

"Yes, as a matter of fact I have Mama E's famous pecan cake."

But Julie stood up and walked closer to the bushes, holding what looked like two sheets, one white and one black. "I'm talking about me, silly." Then she lifted up her summer dress to show off her naked and beautiful dark brown body. "See? No panties."

"Yes, I see no panties."

Julie laid out the sheets and said, "See this one on the bottom and this one for cover, as she laughed. Then proceeded to undress herself. It was dusk and the park was nearly empty. Mike thought, *Isn't this a surprise!* But he had a rubber in his wallet for surprises like this. *This time I'm putting it on before I get started*, he said to himself, as he thought about the signs of his zodiac chart under his bed at home.

CHAPTER 53 -
Youth Summit -
Summer 1971

FRANK ORGANIZED A MEETING AT HIS house to plan a city-wide youth summit that the youth at City Club spearheaded. Kwame had spent hours at City Club talking with the young men about the African liberation struggles: Jomo Kenyatta and the Mau-Mau in Kenya, Patrice Lumumba in the Congo, and Kwame Nkruhmah in Ghana. He had also been sharing his photography skills with Frank's brother John. Frank invited over his brother John, and Mike's friends George and Darren. Kwame, Sekou, Malik, Hunt, and Darnell all from City Club planned to attend. Frank prepared a large pot of his famous chili.

"I put some hog-head cheese in there," Mike said, teasing Jon-Jon about his new no-pork diet.

Jon-Jon protested immediately. "Dad," said Jon-Jon, "you let Mike put hog-head cheese in the chili! You know I don't eat pork."

"Mike better stay away from that chili," Frank said. "Of course he didn't put any hog-head cheese in the chili. Not in my chili. That would be an insult to every cow in America, as if they weren't good enough."

Mike laughed. "Psych! Boy, I can't believe you told Dad. You gonna change your name to Muhammad?"

"I might."

Just then, the doorbell rang to quiet the banter. Frank ran up the stairs to open the door. From downstairs, Mike could see his dad greet more of the planners.

"Come on in," Frank said jovially. "Everybody's downstairs. Help yourself to some chili."

Mike went upstairs and greeted the two men in the kitchen, giving each one a black power handshake, then went outside for some air. From outside on the porch, Mike watched Uncle John park his '66 Mustang convertible. Uncle John rode alone. Mike walked back inside with him, and they gave each other a strong black power handshake. Uncle John beamed at his brother's chili.

"Just like dad used to make. Boy, that's some good stuff."

"Thanks! Grab a bowl - we're gonna get started real soon. Kwame's coming later."

The doorbell rang again. Mike went to the door. "Father Thom! Father Akoji! I didn't know y'all were coming."

As he squeezed through the narrow doorframe, Father Thom said simply, "We want to help."

"Well, help yourself to some chili and head downstairs," Frank responded.

Hunt, the meeting's chair, opened the meeting. "Thanks for coming, everyone. As y'all know, things are getting more and more out-of-control with the heroin situation, all over Detroit. The heroin is everywhere, and that's how the pigs want it. Young brothers are dealin' and usin', and we see what's happenin' to them. Our brothers and sisters getting strung out, ODin', gettin' kilt, or goin' to jail. Just like that. What we talked about doin' is bringing all the compact schools together into a united front and put an end to this. My boys versus your boys. Central against Mackenzie. Mackenzie against the big N.O. I want this summit to deal with us coming together to get these drugs outta the schools. Then we can look the real enemy straight in the eye, and you know who I'm talking about –- the pigs."

Frank cut Hunt off. "Hold up, hold up! This is not a war against the police! No, no, no, no — this is about justice. We want more blacks on the police force. We need an unbiased oversight commission in place to investigate police misconduct. And we must insist that the city investigate the homicides in our community, just like they would in their own community. And investigate with the same vigor."

Darnell said, "Or the African Peoples' Council will put the police on trial."

Frank said, "Okay, dig brothers. I think there's at least three fundamental things going on: we got the drug problem — a heroin problem. We want to stop the flow. We got to stop the police brutality, and we demand an oversight board or commission. And we must stop killing each other. Most of the killing is over foolishness."

Hunt said, "We want the students at the compact schools to sign a peace pact. The summit will lay out what's gonna go into the pact."

At that point, about half-way through the meeting, Kwame and two other men came in. They sat down and listened while Hunt and Darnell continued to run the meeting.

Father Akojie jumped into the conversation. "We think we can help. Father Thom Kelly and myself would like to go door to door telling people in the various neighbors around DePorres and Central in particular about the youth summit and the peace pact. We both think you all have a wonderful idea."

The group set the Youth Summit for September 30, 1971, to give the organizers time to spread the word throughout the high schools.

Father Thom said, "Blessed are the peacemakers."

At the end of the meeting, as Mike and Jon-Jon helped their dad clean up and put away the extra chili, Mike thought about Duane. Turning suddenly to his dad, he said, "What happened to Duane made no sense. He was killed, man . . . " Mike threw up his arms, feeling emotional, his voice cracking. "It made no sense, no sense at all." Frank patted his shoulder. "The elders said it's a minefield out here," Mike continued, "and that's true dad."

"But Mike, Jon-Jon, listen up, we still got to keep pushing, keep flowing like a river to the sea. We can reach our goal because, what, Detroit's got soul . . . "

"Yeah, dad, with 'the power of soul, anything is possible'," said Jon-Jon quoting Jimi Hendrix.

CHAPTER 54 -
Death at City Club

MIKE TRANSITIONED FROM SUMMER LEAGUE BASKETBALL at Ceceliaville to football rather easily. Teams from Flint, Lansing, Saginaw, Ann Arbor, and Jackson - all smaller cities in Michigan - traveled to Detroit for summer league basketball at Ceceliaville. Mike had spent the past six weeks banging it up with college all-stars, professional ball players, and the best left behind in the street. Mike played with one of the compact school teams that featured players who attended Northwestern, Central, Mackenzie, and St. Martin DePorres. He felt he raised his game to new heights, trading elbows and attitude with many of the state's best players.

On the first day of football practice, he sought out the junior quarterback, Leon, who had earned the starting position for the upcoming season.

"Hey, Leon." Mike looked Leon up and down, then laughed and said, "Looks like you're all grown up now." Leon stood about six feet, two inches tall, about an inch shorter than Mike. His body was chiseled from his weightlifting in the off-season.

"Yeah, almost past you," said Leon, raising a hand to compare his height with Mike's.

"Man, we're gonna need to get together after practice, just like I did last year with Bobby. Know what I mean?" Leon nodded yes but didn't say anything. He even looked a little perplexed.

Mike said, "Maybe you don't remember. Bobby and I got together after practice three weeks straight, every day, including weekends. He'd throw me at least fifty passes every day, at least. So dig this. This year I want to double that. I want us to do a hundred passes every day for the next three weeks. Yep, seven days a week, baby. We're gonna really eat, drink, and sleep football.

Man, I want you and me to be in-sync. I want to catch everything you put up there."

"Dig that." The two slapped palms hard three times, then gave each other a black power shake.

Mike said, with an overconfident tone, "Man, we're going to state this year." Then Mike gave Leon a hard look and asked slowly, "We are going to state, right?"

On cue, Leon stuck out his chest and said, "Damn straight, we goin' to state." Mike laughed at the inadvertent rhyme, and he and Leon repeated it together about a half-dozen times: "Damn straight, we goin' to state." Then they burst out laughing again.

Mike thought about the logistics of this extra practice. "Looky here," Mike said. "We can stay right up here at Sacred Heart, It's the school's new practice facility, thanks to my dad and Mr. Dunham. We can come up here on the weekends too. They leave the gates open."

Mike thought back to his preteen years, when he and the neighborhood boys would climb the fence to Sacred Heart Seminary to play football on their huge field, only to be chased away by some old white security guard. Mike remembered how he and his buddies would return hours later, then again the next day. Not long before the riot in 1967, Mike and his buddies had decided not to run but rather confront this old man and ask if they could have a certain amount of time on the field each week since nobody seemed to use it much.

Mike remembered Brother Bear saying, "All we want is one hour every Saturday, just one hour."

"Now, I'll have to ask the people in charge and let you know. Come back next Saturday and I'll have an answer for you."

The security guard must have been tired of playing cat and mouse with us, Mike thought.

A week later the security guard had told them "Yes," and explained that the authorities had granted them one hour a week. They would all have to show up at the same time and be let in the Linwood Ave. entrance at a specified time. They were more than happy to comply. After the rebellion Frank Waterman and several block club captains in the neighborhood convinced the Seminary to open up the facilities to the neighborhood. Summer day camps were organized and the gymnasium was open six days a week during the summer.

Leon agreed to work with Mike seven days a week for the next three weeks, just as Mike suggested. Mike and Leon kept working on the post-corner pattern, over and over. Mike knew that when his team got within the twenty yard line, near the goal line, he could beat anybody to the corner of the end zone after a good fake post pattern. Mike would hold his hand up going inside, Leon would give a good fake pass, and then Mike would turn towards the corner of the end zone while Leon passed the ball perfectly over Mike's right or left shoulder.

"This is for touchdowns and extra points," Mike told Leon. You put the ball up there, and I'm catching it. They call me Deep Ball. They call me Deep Water. Pick one - just put it deep, baby, deep." Leon and Mike became as close as brothers as they spent the night over each others house and would pass out together in Mike's family room during breaks in football practice.

On one evening after practice and after catching over a hundred passes in his post-practice session, Mike walked over to City Club to sit in on a Youth Summit planning meeting with Hunt, Darnell, and several others. By the time Mike got there, the meeting was nearly over. Labor Day was approaching fast. There were fewer than thirty days left to pull off the Youth Black Power Summit.

Mike stepped into the meeting room where several of the organizers were meeting.

"What it is, black?" Hunt greeted Mike.

Hunt had insisted that the word black be a part of the headline: "Without 'black,' it's just another summit. We got to stay on the Black to remind people what the hell this struggle is all about."

"Everything's cool," Mike responded. "How's everything coming along, my man?"

"Check this out," said Hunt, handing Mike a flyer. Mike read it aloud.

Youth Black Power Summit
Let's organize to stop police brutality, drug warfare,
and Black-on-Black violence.
September 30, 1971
City Club (Collingwood at Petoskey)
Free Admission
African Name Ceremony Follows Summit

"We decided not to charge," said Darnell. "We're gonna pass the hat."

Mr. Waterman said, "And we got us a small grant from the city."

The small group ended the meeting not long after Mike arrived, and hung out in the City Club lobby talking about the Ali-Frazier fight, Ali's first loss as a professional. "I'd like to get Ali here to talk at the summit. He'd be perfect."

Hunt said, "But we got Stokley Carmichael for the main speaker. Look

234

at this lineup. Just what we talked about. We're just waiting for people to respond before we put their names on the final flier."

Mike read the flier and asked, "What's this African name ceremony all about?"

Hunt said, "We can elect to take an African name instead of keeping our slave name. We are given a name by a distinguished elder or we can choose a name. Like, I'm taking the name Jomo and Darnell is taking the name Kenyatta. Dig it, Jomo Kenyatta, the great Mau-Mau revolutionary. Me and my brother Darnell will be united forever."

"That's too deep for me," Mike responded. Mike then noticed that Hunt was looking past him through the door, which had been opened. Through the opening, Mike could hear what sounded like an argument coming from the front of the building. The small group remaining inside stepped to the door and saw a cab driver and a customer, both white men, arguing about something. The customer was carrying a gas can and began staggering away from the cab, shouting back all sorts of profanities.

Hunt nodded to Darnell to go outside with him. "Let's go check this dude out, see what his problem is."

The two left and followed the man around the corner. Gun shots rang out. Mike hollered, "What the . . . ," then took off running to the corner, with everyone else in the club, including Frank, following close behind. Before they could even get to the corner, a half-dozen police cars were speeding to the scene. Mike saw Hunt and Darnell sprawled out on their backs in a pool of blood. Several officers still had their guns drawn. A hunting knife was in Hunt's hand.

Frank ran up, screaming, "What the hell's going on?"

The white man, who'd pretended to be drunk with the gas can still in one hand, held a gun in the other hand and shouted back, "They tried to rob me."

"Bullshit!" Frank yelled.

Kwame put a hand on his shoulder and said quietly, "Be cool, Frank. This pig got his finger on the trigger. Just be cool, man."

Over a dozen plainclothes police wearing black vests, who were all in unmarked cars, stepped out of their vehicles with their guns drawn. Mike could see the tension growing, as the police looked back and forth from the man with the gas can to his friends' bodies.

Then Carr approached the scene, yelling, "This is bullshit, man! Hunt never carried a knife and don't nobody I know carry no hunting knives. They put a knife in his hand. This shit's a set-up."

Mike felt a knot in his stomach. His adrenaline was still flowing. More police arrived — more unmarked cars and several marked police cars. Mike began tensing up, balling his fists and getting ready for a fight.

But Kwame and Frank pulled Mike aside. Kwame said gently, "You got to cool down brother. You and Carr. Carr, come over here. We all know this was a set-up. We know that, but these pigs will shoot all of our behinds without a second thought." Mike felt like he wanted to tackle the plainclothes cop who held the gas can.

"Mike," Frank said, "We don't know what the hell this was all about. Our young brothers are lying here dead. And we got half of the city's police force down here ready for a massacre. They don't care who we are. Stay back here, Mike." Frank began to whistle softly.

Kwame turned to face the group and said, "The best thing we can do is head back to the Club and decide what we're going to do about it. That's the best thing we can do. They'll shoot us and won't even blink. We don't need any martyrs right now." Kwame spoke up loudly. "No martyrs! Someone needs to stay here with the bodies."

On the walk back to the club, Mike saw Uncle John nearly a block away taking pictures with a telephoto lens. Mike didn't say anything, but kept walking with his dad. Frank asked Mr. Carr and Mr. Blue to stay back and witness the police activity and report back to him. "I need to notify their parents." Back at the Club, the scene was explosive. Kwame didn't offer any guidance; he seemed to be too stunned. But he did herd everybody back inside the Club.

Mike flashed back to the day Malcolm X was killed and his neighbor, in tears, kept asking the boys, "What y'all gonna do?" Nearly in tears himself, Mike said in a shrill voice, "What we gonna do now, huh? What? What we gonna do now?"

Someone hollered out, "Retaliate. Off the pigs."

"Hold up everyone, just hold up," Frank said loudly. "Don't even think about it. You and what army? What you gonna do, start another riot?"

"A rebellion . . . Frank," said Kwame.

"We ain't going that route. Show up Monday morning. We're gonna march from here to the mayor's office downtown. Let's all show up at the mayor's office at 11 and find out what's going on. If you want to march from here, be here at 8 o'clock." Frank knew he had to decide quickly on a course of action because of the spontaneous outrage in the neighborhood.

CHAPTER 55 -
Drums across Detroit

THE WATERMAN HOUSEHOLD WAS DEVASTATED WHEN Frank and Mike broke the news. Pounding the door, Frank said, "This is a terrible loss to all of us. It hurts to see these two outstanding young men die this way. This is just too much."

Mike said, "And someone's got to pay . . . "

"Mike," Frank said, cutting him off, "I think it's best you stay focused on your school and your football right now. We're not seeking revenge. We want justice."

Mike stayed quiet, but wondered if getting involved in planning the youth summit had been a bad idea.

Frank turned to the rest of the family and said, "We barely have time to grieve. A group of us plan to show up Monday morning at the mayor's office and demand some answers."

Several heads nodded gravely. A few tears fell. All exchanged hugs and words of comfort.

Early Sunday morning Jon-Jon asked his dad whether his team of African drummers could lead the march. "We talked last night, Dad. We want to have drummers stationed at different points along the march route and elsewhere in the city. It's like we're going to let people in the neighborhoods know we're coming. We want to attract attention to the march and the problem of police brutality."

"That sounds really positive, but I think you need to go to school," Frank said, with a tone of fatherly authority. But Frank knew that Jon-Jon would be there in the march, and let it go at that.

People in the neighborhood began to assemble at City Club early Monday morning. Everyone Frank talked to wanted to march from City Club to the mayor's office in downtown Detroit. Frank got word that Mackenzie High School called for a walkout, and heard from staff that other schools might follow suit.

Frank wasn't surprised when he saw Jon-Jon, Bongo Bob, and a group of African drummers show up. Two volunteers arrived to drive the City Club vans behind the marchers in case people tired or needed food, water, or assistance.

By ten o'clock Monday morning, Frank, Carr, and Kwame led over one thousand people through the streets of Detroit south down Dexter Boulevard to West Grand Boulevard, then east towards Woodward Avenue before turning south to head downtown. Because Frank hadn't secured a permit to march, there had been no time, he needed to keep his group on the sidewalks. But they crowded the streets all the same.

The drummers were stationed all along the route, signaling to each other when the marchers were coming. The marchers chanted.

"WE WANT JUSTICE! WE WANT JUSTICE!"

Frank and Carr picked up on the mood and kept it rolling. Holding bullhorns, they called out, "What do we want?"

The crowd responded, "Justice!"

"When do we want it?"

"Now!"

The march continued, and the shouts got louder and louder.

As they marched, Frank walked up and down the line to check with his brother John who, along with about a dozen brothers and sisters from Wayne State University, served as marshals. John warned Frank to be on the lookout for agent provocateurs among the marchers and for the potential for police provocation from patrol officers. But the march continued to go smoothly as they rounded West Grand Boulevard and headed south down Woodward. Frank heard drumming from the east and from the west, and felt its intensity as it pulsed up and down Woodward Avenue.

Just before the marchers got to city hall, John shouted to Frank over the noise of the marchers, "I'll be taking pictures like I always do. I'm watching them just like they're watching us. Know what I mean, brother?"

The brothers slapped palms and said "Right on," as if on cue.

"They know we're coming," Frank said. "I talked to the mayor's aide this morning and he said the mayor will see a small group of us in his office. And Councilman Eric Byrd will meet us at Detroit City Hall and escort us up to the mayor's office."

John left the group. Frank wondered what John was going to be doing with his pictures, and what kind of pictures he had been taking. Frank hadn't yet seen any of them.

As promised, Frank and the several hundred protesters were greeted by Councilman Eric Byrd outside city hall. Frank and the councilman greeted each other with a warm hug and handshake.

"Frank," the councilman said reassuringly, "we can take about ten people up. The rest can continue to protest outside. I made arrangements for a permit for the protest outside. It's okay. How's that sound?"

"That's fine, and thank you. Carr, round up a few brothers." Carr hurried off, then returned just as quickly with about a dozen brothers. Frank noticed that Kwame stayed outside with the marchers. The rest entered through the revolving doors.

A couple of the brothers who had been selected to go meet with the mayor started to show-out.

"These honkies better watch out, coming in the hood and shit," said one of the protesters named Kenyatta.

But Frank intervened immediately. "Be cool, Kenyatta. We're going to ask the mayor some questions. Just be cool."

At the end of a long corridor, Councilman Byrd turned back to Frank. Pulling him gently aside, he said, "Frank, I want to brief you before we see the mayor. The mayor created this new police undercover unit called STRESS: Stop the Robberies, Enjoy Safe Streets. Look, forget the fancy name. We know what they want to do. They're decoys posing as drunks, sometimes with money hanging out of their pockets. A similar police shooting on the eastside of Detroit was reported to us last week."

"Yeah. Well, we've seen it first hand."

"And I'm very sorry for the loss of those two young men. I want to send their families my condolences."

"Sure, sure." Frank was eager to get in to see the mayor as quickly as possible. He could sense that those around him were growing impatient.

After a brief elevator ride, they arrived on the twelfth floor under bright lights and heavy police security.

Kenyatta called out, "Where the hell's the mayor? We didn't come all this way to see your jive asses. The whole thing Saturday was a set up."

The police looked on edge; some had their hands on their holsters. Councilman Byrd spoke up, "These gentleman here are outraged at what happened to the two boys on Saturday. Everybody, just be cool."

Pointing to Kenyatta, one of the police officers added, "And especially you with the black jacket on."

"I ain't gotta do shit. I didn't come down here to play games with you . . ."

But he was interrupted by the sound of the mayor's office door buzzing to let the group in. One of the guards opened the door and motioned to the group to enter.

"Welcome," said Mayor Roy Grubbs.

The men filed in, standing along the back wall of the room. Frank and Carr sat down in the two leather seats facing the mayor's desk.

Frank had barely taken his seat when he started the dialogue.

"Mr. Grubbs, we got a problem in the neighborhood. Tell me, on what planet can you have white men walking around in the black community like they're drunk, carrying an empty gas can and with money hanging out of their pockets? Tell me, where?"

"Mr. Byrd, Mr. Waterman," Mayor Grubbs said patiently, his eyes level, "we've had reports of heightened crime activity, assaults, even rape, in certain areas of the city. Our officers, I am told, responded appropriately—"

"Mr. Grubbs, there was nothing to respond to. Those two young men were inside the Club. They went out to see what was going on. And they don't even carry knives, you know, like the ones that your officers said they found."

Carr spoke up, "And those that do carry knives don't carry hunting knives."

The mayor said, "There's a routine investigation taking place."

"What on earth are your undercover agents doing in the neighborhood posing as drunks? Then they gun down two of the community's stars for nothing. We need to know what the hell is going on here."

"Again, Mr. Waterman, the current circumstances require extreme measures. Hell, we live in a dangerous world. What do you want?"

Mr. Byrd said, "Roy, these decoy tactics you're using may be entrapment. You must know that."

The mayor leaned back and laughed. "Entrapment my ass. You must be kidding me." He leaned forward again, glanced at his guards at the front door, then scratched his head.

Frank said coolly, "Mr. Grubbs, we want you to disband this STRESS unit immediately. And we asking for a Council-led investigation into these shootings."

"I can't promise you anything, but I do want to say, I appreciate you and your people coming down to air your concerns. This is what makes our democracy the greatest on earth." He rose and motioned toward the door. The interview was over — the entire exchange between the mayor and Frank Waterman's group had lasted less than fifteen minutes.

On their way out of the office, Carr couldn't stop himself from reacting. "That son-of–a bitch acted like he don't give a damn!" he spat out.

The group crowded on the elevator. Frank could feel their restlessness as they jostled against one another in the tight space.

Going down, Frank said, "Eric, any chance you could get the Council to approve an independent investigation?"

"I'm going to put that on the agenda tomorrow. I believe we need a permanent commission to investigate any police shooting. It doesn't make sense that some people are more afraid of the police than the criminals. Makes no damn sense."

At the ground floor, Councilman Eric Byrd shook hands with each of the gentleman. The protesters were still outside, chanting, "NO JUSTICE, NO PEACE!" They had formed a line around city hall.

Kwame came up to Frank at the steps of city hall and said, "I think we got their attention. Frank, we got to follow-up with the councilman."

"Yeah, and we got to also let people know about this STRESS unit. We should go out to the schools and let the kids know about this."

"Yeah! Come on, a white man stumbling through the neighborhood with money hanging out his pocket," said Carr.

"They're out to kill our youth," said Kwame.

Frank only nodded. Then he entered the crowd, and began to circulate among the protesters the news that City Club vans were available to shuttle people home or that he could provide bus fare for those that needed it.

When Frank got home he immediately began to loosen his clothes. He asked Rose, "Where's Mike?" Rose greeted Frank with a warm embrace. Frank kissed her softly on the lips, then looked her in the eyes, and leaned his forehead against hers. "I love you baby."

Rose flashed a broad smile.

"How did it go downtown?"

"I feel that downtown isn't going to be much help to us. We got to let these kids know what's going on."

"What is going on, Frank?"

"What's going on is that the city got this new undercover police unit called STRESS — Stop the Robberies, Enjoy Safe Streets — and what they're doing is using decoy officers posing as drunks in black neighborhoods, with money hanging out their pockets. If our young men even get close to them, they'll open fire and claim self-defense. Councilman Byrd thinks it's already happened on the eastside last week."

"Oh, my God," Rose gasped. "Frank, this is wrong, very wrong."

"Where's Denise and Jon-Jon? They have to know about this." Frank looked dazed.

"Are you all right, Frank? Is something wrong, Frank?"

Frank felt a strain in his brain. "My vision's blurry."

"Frank, are you okay? Look at me." Frank shook his head yes, then rolled his head in a circle.

"Oh no, no, no, no, no. Sorry baby, I felt dazed for a second. I'm fine." He blinked a few times, and rubbed his temples. "We just need to discuss this with the kids. That's all."

"Frank, I think you need to see a doctor, you might have high blood pressure."

"Naw, I'll be okay. Where are the children?"

"Jon-Jon's at rehearsal. I heard his drummers led the demonstration through the city."

"They did a fantastic thing. Never seen anything like it, ever."

"And Denise, she's down the street at Sharon's. Mike's downstairs lifting weights."

"I'm worried, Rose. I'm worried for the kids. Those cops executed Darnell and Hunt."

"I can't even think about it. I'm still devastated. "

Frank took off his shirt and shoes.

"I'm going downstairs to talk to Mike."

Once in the basement, Frank saw Mike straining to bench press two hundred ninety pounds. "I'll spot ya," he said, striding over to his son's side. Mike grunted as he pushed the weight up and rested the bar on the rack above him.

Mike sat up and said, "I'm just about done, Dad, but thanks anyway." Mike had once lifted weights with his dad regularly, but hadn't done so in months.

Frank emptied his pockets, then lay back on the bench and looked up at the weights, wrapping his hands around the barbell. He looked at Mike and let out a hearty laugh.

"Boy, if you don't take some of these weights off this thing . . . ! Keep on about a hundred and eighty pounds for your ol' man."

Frank did three sets of five reps. Mike looked on while he did curls with the dumbbells. In no time at all, Frank was winded and sweating heavily. He was more exhausted from the day's events than he had anticipated.

"Hand me a towel, son." Mike reached behind him for a small towel in a clothes basket and handed it to his dad.

Frank sat up straight and wiped his forehead dry. Then he turned solemn eyes towards his son.

"Mike, you got to be careful out there. The police will shoot first and ask questions later."

"Dad, what about Darnell and Hunt? When's the funeral?"

"Don't know about the funeral yet. What we're trying to do is have the city council request an independent investigation. But we really don't know if that's going anywhere. We don't know what's going to happen. The city is already calling it justifiable self-defense."

"That's a lie and they know it. That's a lie!" Mike began pacing, his fists curling and uncurling.

"We know it too, Mike."

"And what about the summit, Dad"?

"Postponed for now. We'll do it in the spring."

"Why?"

"It'll be better organized after we take this issue on. We need to deal with the STRESS unit right away. We're going to plan more rallies to ask the city to disband this decoy unit they call STRESS immediately. The police are posing as drunks and walking through the black community with money hanging out their pockets. Now what do you call that but a set-up?"

"When in the spring can we have the summit, Dad?"

"Don't worry about the summit right now. This is your last year of high school. You're college bound — you're All-American bound. Don't get side-tracked." He paused and shook his head. "Yeah, I thought working with Darnell and Hunt would be cool and you would get some community organizing experience, but look at where we are. I want you to focus on your ball and school. Scouts are looking at you. And believe me, they are looking at everything: your attitude, how you treat your teammates, how you talk, everything. I should have never asked you to get involved . . . "

"Dad, what am I supposed to do? My friends, my schoolmates getting jumped and killed . . . What am I supposed to do?" Mike slapped his own forehead.

Frank stood up and said, "I understand, Mike, but the best thing you can do is get your school work. All this struggle stuff, leave that to us adults. Things could get out of hand."

"Dad, I'm not a baby."

"Never said you were. I just think you getting an education is more important right now than you getting all involved in this mess."

"I'm already in it, Dad. Just like I heard you tell Mom — when you had Hunt and Darnell over to the house – we're all in this stew together. Abdul said the same thing. We're all in it."

"We're paving the way for you, your sister, and brother, and the rest of these kids in the neighborhood. We don't want y'all to go through this type of disrespect like what's going on. Just go to school and keep up the good grades."

"And that's it?"

"Right now, that's it. Dig it, your mother is worried about you kids all the time. You see her praying the rosary, don't you? Who you think she's praying for? That's right — Y-O-U, Denise, Jon-Jon, and the neighborhood kids." Frank said as he pointed his finger at Mike.

Mike shrugged in frustrated silence, then slipped three hundred ten pounds on the barbell for another bench press.

He lay down and said, "Can you spot me Dad?"

"Sure, son." Mike got a firm grip on the barbell and let out a huge sigh when he hoisted the barbell off the rack.

"I'm doing five."

CHAPTER 56 –
John and the ARC Study Circle

ABOUT A WEEK LATER, MIKE HEADED for the City Club to see Uncle John after football practice. He wanted to share with him some news he had gotten in the mail. Mike didn't know much about Uncle John and his Study Circle that met two or three times a week at City Club, except that the group read and discussed books on politics, world history, and community issues. Usually, the meeting would be open to the community. Occasionally, Jon-Jon would sit in on the sessions, as would Hunt and Darnell. Mike carried a letter in his hand. He rapped on the door where the ARC Study Circle met, and he heard the sound of a chair scraping the floor as Uncle John rose to open the door.

When he saw Mike he said, "Boy, what are you doing here?"

"Jon-Jon's here, isn't he?"

"Yeah, but Jon-Jon's a regular. What the hell you doing? You never showed any interest."

"Well, there's something I need to talk to you about. Can I come in?"

"Well, brother, we're not meeting tonight to talk about your worries. If you can sit and listen to the discussion at hand, you're welcome to come in. Can you dig that?"

Mike nodded yes and slid through the doorway, taking a seat against the wall. Mike saw only about three or four of Uncle John's brothers from Wayne State University at the meeting and noticed two large maps of Detroit taped on the wall and several photos of people, some of whom looked like police officers.

"What you're looking at is our urban combat strategy for dealing with STRESS and the heroin epidemic in the city. None of this leaves the room."

Mike felt like walking out. He felt intimidated, and unsure of what he was stepping into. But his curiosity got the better of him, and besides, he needed to speak with his Uncle.

"Okay, brothers, pay attention," said Uncle John, who walked up to the maps on the wall. "These red dots are what?"

"Major dope houses in Detroit," said one of three older men in the room.

"The orange dots are . . . ?"

"STRESS units that are known to escort the drugs to the major dope houses," another man responded.

"Right. This is where we have spotted them during major drug deliveries. Over on this wall, we have pictures of the officers who are involved in this dope-running operation. Below their pictures, what do we have?"

"Names and home addresses."

Mike was feeling increasingly uneasy, and blurted out, "What are you going to do with—"

But Uncle John cut him off.

"Mike, just hold up. You can't just waltz in here for the first time and start asking questions. Let's say something goes down and the FBI or some Grand Jury starts asking you questions. What's your rap?"

"I tell them nothing, right?"

"Naw, that's not right," said Uncle John. "That's not your rap. You tell them exactly how many times you joined our ARC Study Circle and you tell them we were reading a great historical book right here called *Before the Mayflower*, by Lerone Bennet, Jr." Uncle John tossed the book at Mike, who caught it. "Just make sure you read it so you know what's in it."

Uncle John then walked up to a world map and used a classroom pointer to point out what he called, "The heroin drug trade." He went on for another thirty minutes about what all their research showed.

As the meeting broke up, Mike waited for Uncle John outside the Club near his car. When he saw Uncle John and Jon-Jon approaching he said, "Uncle John, I need to talk to you about something."

"What's that, Mike?"

"About my girl Julie. I got this letter today and I damn near freaked out but wanted to talk with you about it. Read it. Man, I feel like going off on Julie and my boy Leon." Mike gave the letter to Uncle John, who read it aloud.

"Dear Mike, You have been a very nice young man and I like you very much. We had some good times together. Remember Belle Isle? I just wanted to say that I hope there are no hard feelings but I must move on. You are so preoccupied with football and basketball and all your sports stuff, I don't think you will ever have much time for me. And I hope you are not mad at Leon for going out with me. We go together now anyway. He said he wants to marry me one day. Don't be mad at me, Mike. We can always be friends. Truly Yours, Julie"

Uncle John rubbed his forehead, then said, "Have you talked to Leon yet?"

"No, not yet. I haven't told anyone but you."

The trio started moving toward Uncle John's car. As they piled in, Uncle John continued.

"Cool. Tell you what — after reading this, brother, the first thing you got to do is talk to your boy Leon. He's your team quarterback, right? Act like you don't even care, man. In fact, congratulate him and wish him well. Y'all can't let anything destroy y'all's chemistry on the field, especially some female who's trying to play you and him both."

"This ain't that easy. I mean, we had a good thing going . . . "

"Come on Mike. Just because she was your first don't mean she's your last. I hate to tell you this, but your girl Julie just took you for a ride and it's best to just get her out your system."

Jon-Jon interrupted, "Mike, man, I can't believe you let her get your nose all wide-open like that. Mean like, we got so much else goin' on out here and you worried about some piece . . . "

"Jon-Jon, be cool man," said Uncle John. "Mike's got a legit concern, and he ain't feelin' too good about it. All relationships mean something, Jon-Jon. Sometimes they drive people over the edge. Mike and Leon could get to fighting and shit and guess what, they whole season's over. Naw, man. We got to talk about it."

Uncle John seemed to look more at Mike than he looked at the road. "So look at it like this Mike. Julie is an annual, not a perennial, using the metaphor your daddy like to use. She ain't comin' back, and you probably don't want her back. Annuals can be real nice. They can look beautiful and you should enjoy that beauty while it lasts, but at some point it leaves. Whereas your perennial, she comes back. She's different; she got a different character. Now, your girl, my sister, Renee, now she's your hardy perennial . . . "

Mike laughed, "Yeah, I like Renee, but she got that boyfriend."

"Uh . . . ah, well . . . her boyfriend," said Uncle John, "I heard he was leaving town, going to Oakland to be at the Black Panther Party headquarters. And I don't think she's going with him."

"I don't know about Renee. I might start dealing with Lola, see how she is," said Mike.

"There you go. See there? You already casting out your net."

"Lola's a big catch, she's the finest girl in the school, like fine china."

"Mike, don't always get hung up on the finest, boy, shit, that's what got you in too deep as it is. Man, look for the one with heart, with personality, one that digs you for you."

John parked in front of the Waterman house on Atkinson Avenue, and the three continued to talk without making any move to get out of the vehicle.

"I've seen Lola, she's an unknown."

"She went with Steve. You remember I told you, they went together for three years."

"Yeah. So now you picking her up on the rebound, like we used to say."

"So what? I been trying to get with her from the giddy-up, from the night we met anyway. Maybe now's my chance."

"Yeah, but don't get hung up on her body . . . "

"You mean her booty," said Jon-Jon.

"Body, booty, you know what I'm sayin'. Check out her head, Mike. See where the girl's head's at. Get inside her head and you might steal her heart. But Renee, boy — I'm tellin' you, she's a perennial. I think she's just waiting for you to turn 18, and bam . . . "

They all burst out laughing. Mike was feeling better already.

Uncle John checked his watch. He said, "I got a quick run to make. I want y'all to see something anyway. Game?"

"Yeah we're game," said Mike. He looked back at Jon-Jon who nodded yes.

Uncle John drove to the corner of Hazelwood and the Lodge Freeway service drive, and parked on the service drive.

"See that house right there?" he asked, pointing. "I've been casing the place lately because I heard from Denise that Sharon had been showing up there with a known drug dealer."

Mike said, "We've all been wondering what's been up with Sharon."

"Sharon's on that P, that's what's up."

"How you know that?"

"Denise know, she know."

"She ain't told me about it."

"Look, my man, Denise know, your mama know, and Sharon's mama know. They been quietly trying to get her in rehab."

Mike looked puzzled. "Damn," he said. "How did we let that happen?"

Avoiding the question, Uncle John pointed again in the direction of a young man ambling across the street, and said, "there goes the dude right there. His name is Sonny Tyler. He's the baby boy in the Tyler family drug business."

"I've seen him before," said Mike. "Up at the school."

"Sharon believes he's a banker visiting his clients."

"I don't believe Sharon would fall for that line," said Mike.

"Shit boy, people believe anything for that P." After the group sat and watched for about ten minutes they drove off.

CHAPTER 57 –
Sister Sharon's Hooked Up

DENISE, ABRUPTLY STOPPED RUNNING WITH HER best friend Sharon after the latest incident she had with her. Sharon wasn't making cheerteam practices on time, if at all. When she did arrive she was on P, always wiping her nose. The thing that hurt Denise the most was that Sharon thought that she was now cooler than the coolest cat in town. She wouldn't even hide it.

Denise told her mother about Sharon's new coolness. Rose said that she too noticed it. Rose tried to intervene by talking directly to her. She began offering her rides to practice. When Sharon continued to miss practice, Denise and her mother called Sharon's mother, Delli.

With Denise looking on, Rose told Delli, "I'm a bit concerned about your baby, she's not looking well."

"Honey," Delli replied, "that makes two of us. We've been trying to get her away from that idiot, Sonny, for the longest. He's got her brainwashed. She thinks he's a hot-shot banker downtown. That boy ain't nothing but a two-bit dope pusher."

"Why can't she see through all that nonsense?" Rose asked.

"She don't want to. The girl don't do her homework anymore. And the child ain't eating much these days either.

"Have you tried to put her in rehab?"

"Rehab? Yeah, we tried rehab, Rose. But rehab is the last thing on her mind. This is much more than she is used to dealing with."

"She's a beautiful girl, Delli. You'd best watch out before something worse happens to her."

Denise threw her hands up in despair and said, "She's with him all the time." Denise sunk down in the sofa and started to cry.

The women talked for about an hour before Rose said she should head home. Rose was not feeling any more at ease, and was still concerned about how to protect Denise and Sharon.

~ ~ ~ ~ ~ ~ ~

The next day Sonny pulled up in a Lincoln Continental as cheerleading practice ended.

"Come to Daddy, you pretty, sweet thang," he called from the window of his car. Sharon dropped her conversation with Denise like a brick, grabbed her school bag, and took off. She didn't say bye until she was half-way to the car.

Over her shoulder, almost as an afterthought, she shouted back, "Oh, bye-bye. See y'all tomorrow."

"No girl, I'm going with you," Denise shouted.

"Can you give Denise a ride home?" Sharon asked.

"Yeah, but I need to see a couple of my clients first."

Denise got in the front next to Sharon. Sonny occasionally took Sharon on his dope drops and pickups. He called his group's dope houses his clients; he told Sharon he was servicing his clients. She would rarely get out of the car to go in with Sonny, and would wait patiently in the car while he did his work.

That afternoon, however, when they stopped at a two-family flat on Hazelwood near the Lodge Freeway, he asked Sharon and Denise to come in with him. When they entered, Denise could see people gathered in small groups. Four were in the dining room, with scales visible, and another group was in the kitchen. Sharon could see plastic baggies, red caps, and other paraphernalia used for drug making and distribution. Coming from the basement was an odor like something was burning. The drapes were drawn, and once inside someone bolted the door, then placed two heavy steel bars across the door. Sonny strutted through the place like he owned it.

"Come down here with me, baby," Sonny cooed. He reached out for Sharon's hand and she gently gave it to him. Denise followed. The basement was all lit up in red lights and black lights, with beautiful black light posters on the wall. As the trio passed through the main area they opened a door, passing a couple of people asleep on the sofa. They made their way into the back room.

Money was piled two feet deep on the table. People were stationed at different tables, counting and wrapping the wads of bills.

"Sonny," a voice called out angrily. "Whatcha doin', man?"

"What you mean?"

"Man, you know what the fuck I mean. I run this shit down here and we don't allow visitors," said a tall, older-looking man. He looked at Sonny with a vicious scowl on his face.

Sonny threw his bag on the table.

"Take this shit and count it and leave me the fuck alone."

"Sonny, step over here for a minute my brother," the tall man said. "Daddy can't cover your fuck-ups forever. Now get those friends of yours outta here. Do it now. Don't have me embarrass your motherfuckin ass."

Sonny smirked, rolled his eyes, and said haughtily, "Can't leave until the bag is counted. Me and my girls will be outside."

He took Sharon and Denise out on the basement patio and pulled out three caps of P.

"Baby, let me show you how the big boys do it," he said.

Sonny demonstrated how to cook the P in a bottle cap, then use a rubber hose to tie around his arm as he searched for the best vein. He drew up the P in the needle, then injected it effortlessly.

"Try it," he suggested to Sharon.

"Why not? You can see my veins easily. Which one do I stick it in?"

"Sharon, we got to go," Denise said as she stood up anxiously.

"Just calm down Denise," Sharon told her.

Sonny said, "Here, try that one there by your armpit. Nobody'll notice. There we go. Perfect." It didn't take long for both to be in a nod.

Sharon was in such awe of everything she barely said two words. All she said before nodding off was, "This is some good shit, Sonny. Your banker friends . . . " She fell into a nod, bent over the table, looking nearly frozen.

After about ten minutes, Sonny got up, pulled himself together and took a slip of paper from the man who had counted the money.

"Don't do it again," the man hissed at him. "And look at you getting high on the job. Nigger, you ought to be fired."

Sonny just laughed as he led the girls back upstairs and outside. Denise shoved Sharon up the stairs and out the front door.

This was not Sharon's last hit with the needle. In fact, she would insist Sonny take her back to see his banker friends. Denise noticed that Sharon's view became more and more distorted. She was getting higher and higher. One afternoon at school, Denise found Sharon in the toilet stall throwing up, heaving over the toilet. Her shirt was off, exposing her bra, and the jumper was down around her knees.

She turned around and gave Denise a crazy look, drooling out of one side of her mouth. Her eyes were bloodshot and a rubber tube was tied around her arm.

"Oh my God," cried Denise. "Oh God, help!" Denise moved in closer towards Sharon. "You need help! Look at you – you ain't the same!" Denise put her hands to her face and started crying.

"Don't cry for me, baby," Sharon drooled. "I'm feeling like I'm in seventh heaven." Sharon lay her face on the cool tile of the floor.

Trying not to panic, Denise ran down the hall to the principal's office and called Uncle John from the office to help take Sharon home. He helped her get Sharon to her feet, and without school officials knowing what had gone down, they left the building.

CHAPTER 58 –
Close the school

FRANK ANSWERED THE PHONE. IT WAS Jim Dunham on the other end.

"Are you coming with me?" he asked.

"Of course I'm riding with you. I'm ready."

Not long thereafter, once inside the spacious downtown headquarters of the Archdiocese of Detroit, the two men were met by Father Richard and ushered into Cardinal Beardum's office. Curly Cornell was already seated at the right side of the Cardinal. Father Richard seated the men, but remained standing, and offered everyone water. Frank and Jim accepted. The cardinal sat behind his expansive desk, and didn't waste anytime getting to the point.

"Mr. Dunham, there are too many non-Catholics attending the school," he said, in an accusing tone. "You can't recruit the kids just to play basketball and football. That tends to water down the religious significance, not to mention the academic excellence." The cardinal reclined in his plush red leather chair.

Jim knew that the school board had met with Father Richard last week, and that the very same point had been raised.

Exercising his role as school board chairman, Curly Cornell jumped into the conversation before Jim had a chance to respond.

"You see, Jim, there's this technicality about schools in the Detroit Diocese that have less than 50 percent Catholic students attending at any given time."

"Now, Curly," Jim said, "in our own constitution we have a clause that reads that as long as the kids show progress towards becoming Catholic, they would be listed as Catholic."

"*Progress* is the key word," said Curly. "Progress. Have these kids and their families made progress during the past school years?" asked Curly.

"It's only our third year, Cardinal Beardum. You can't expect these families to just leap into the religion after years of being Baptist, Methodist, or whatever they are. These families are looking for a good school, a safe school, and we need them to stay afloat. Why would you put this kind of pressure on us when all we are trying to do is survive as a school?" Jim asked.

"Because, Mr. Dunham, it's more than a school. You see, I have to answer to the Council of Bishops. It's part of the rules. It's not me. Mr. Dunham, you and I know we have too many kids who are just looking to play sports. I'm told that almost the entire football team is non-Catholic - the same with the basketball team. We want to put the emphasis on academic competitiveness," the cardinal said sternly.

"What more do you want? We already send eighty-five to ninety percent of our kids to college. What the hell do you want?" retorted Jim, raising his voice and standing up as if to challenge Cardinal Beardum to a brawl.

Curly jumped up between Jim and the cardinal as if to protect the cardinal.

Frank interjected, with a hand on Jim's elbow. "Sit down, Jim." Then Frank said to the cardinal, "And you recall Jim was named Michigan Educator of the Year last year."

With both hands still raised, looking like a human shield, Curly said defensively, "We want to send our students to the best colleges . . . "

"For crying out loud, Curly! What are you talking about? These kids are going to schools that offer them financial assistance, schools close to home. Come off your high-horse, man," said Jim.

"No, Jim! Look at the stats. The students today have to be prepared to compete with the best and the brightest. We're talking about students at Brother Rice, Country Day, Cranbrook, and—"

"And what . . . ?" interrupted Jim, "I get it, you want DePorres to—"

But Curly cut him off. "It's Saint Martin DePorres, not DePorres. You sound as bad as the students — in fact they probably get it from you. Now, the cardinal went out on a limb to get the school named after a black saint and here you go using only the last name." Curly threw up his hands in disgust.

"Let me finish, please," said Jim. "You want some high-falutin' preppie-like school reserved for the elite, the well-to-do. You think your kids are better than the rest, don't you?"

"Wait a minute, Mr. Dunham. Don't get personal. All we want is high academic achievement, not some watered-down curriculum with all this Afro American lit jazz," said Curly.

"The longer I sit here and listen to this bull-crap—"

"Now, Mr. Dunham—"

"Shut up, Curly. The longer I listen to this bull-crap, the more I'm convinced you all are not in this for the kids. You got some hidden agenda," Jim finished.

The cardinal sat up and pulled himself close to the desk and leaned forward toward Jim. "The archdiocese wants to pull the plug on this little experiment. They are not all that happy with the results."

"Results. The results — you mean converts, that's what you mean," Jim said, raising his voice again. "Let me tell both of you something. My people are not a bunch of heathens, as you high and mighty folks seem to think of our brothers and sisters in the community. We are not savages that need to be tamed by you missionaries, as you might think."

"Now, Jim," Curly interrupted. "Watch your tone! You're talking to the cardinal." Curly again stood between Jim and the cardinal as if he was expecting Jim to punch the man.

"Cardinal Beardum, how is it that are you ready to pull the plug when the parents and the community have fought hard and long to get the school renovated, raising the school fund — thousands of dollars?"

"The school may still be a go, for now, Mr. Dunham, but we want a different type of school," said the cardinal.

"We want to de-emphasize athletics," said Curly.

"Over my dead body," said Jim.

"That's the only way we could sell it to the Bishop's Council, or they pull the plug," said Curly.

"You just wait until the parents find out what's going on up here, they'll be all over this place. You just watch!" Jim hollered, losing his composure.

The cardinal stood up and pointed his wrinkled finger. "Don't you threaten me or the archdiocese, Mr. Dunham. Don't do it, or you'll be looking for a new job, real soon. I think this meeting is over."

CHAPTER 59 –
What's Going On?

AFTER THE MEETING, FRANK AND JIM agreed to go for drinks at the Collingwood Bar on 12th Street, their favorite watering hole.

On the ride over, Jim said rather calmly, his voice low and almost hoarse, "Frank, I'm calling for a retreat next weekend among the administration and board. Things are getting a bit overwhelming, trying to comply with the Diocese's financial requirements. We need to develop some new strategies for taking the school forward." He paused as if waiting for Frank's reaction and, seeing none, continued. "Father Kelly's been talking about this liberation theology and using non-violent direct action techniques in Latin America against Military Juntas and all. We might need to apply some of that right here."

"You mean what Martin Luther King was doing."

"Right."

"Against who?" Frank asked.

"The Archdiocese of Detroit. Cardinal Beardum really wants to close the school after this year. Enrollments have been declining at the school and as you are well aware, Visitation Parish is in a severe decline in membership."

"Yeah, I know. We're down to one mass on Sunday. We used to have three."

"They're playing Curly with all this B.S. about a prep-school. They want to shut us down."

"Some reward, huh, Jim?"

"Yeah. Well look, Frank, what we need to do is to talk over some tactics and strategies with you, Rose, Ted, and the rest of the bunch. I'm mailing out the letters tonight asking for participation from the board and staff in a retreat."

From his conversation with Jim, Frank knew that they were going to have some discussions on the record, and some off the record, about how to keep the school open. Frank and Jim stayed at the bar until about midnight talking about the upcoming retreat.

A week later, Frank and Rose left Detroit early Saturday morning for the Farm and Retreat Center owned by the Detroit Catholic Diocese. It was located fifty miles northwest of Detroit in Howell, Michigan. They pulled into the sprawling two hundred-and-twenty-acre retreat center at about eight o'clock in the morning. The soybean crop had been harvested, and there were smaller plots for vegetables and about ten acres of cherry trees.

A beautiful log cabin lodge had been built about five years earlier, replacing the historic but deteriorating farmhouse to serve as the main building. Male and female dormitories were built nearby. Married couples had the option of staying in one of the five bedrooms in the main lodge, either in the old farmhouse or in the separate dorm facilities. The lodge was equipped with a stove, refrigerator, color television and fireplace.

After covering important issues before dinner such as fundraising for the school and internships for the students at some of Michigan's most prestigious firms, Frank felt the positive emotional support for the school among the board and school administration. To perpetuate the warm mood, after dinner Frank took advantage of the lodge's fireplace to start a nice fire. The birch logs were stacked nicely in a nearby shed outside. Frank hauled in about a dozen logs along with a bunch of kindling.

Frank and Rose were joined at the fireside by Ted, Jim, and Sister JoAnna. Ted casually started talking about the pressing problem of heroin use among the areas teenagers while Frank, on one knee, stoked the fire.

"Heroin is taking the best of us," said Ted.

"And it doesn't discriminate," added Frank. "You all have heard James Brown's poem, 'King Heroin,' haven't you? He says, 'it'll make a good man forsake his wife, sell his kids and give up his life.'"

Jim nodded and said, "Yes. And what are we going to do about it, brothers and sisters?"

Sister JoAnna spoke up. "It's too big for us, Jim. We can't address this alone. We have to get the police involved. We know the kids in the school who are using and dealing."

Ted looked quickly at Jim, surprised at what he'd just heard. He then turned towards Sister JoAnna and said slowly, "We do?"

Ted looked back at Jim. "Jim, is that right?"

Frank cut in on the exchange. "It's much bigger than us at DePorres. We got high-quality heroin coming in, we got more guns than the city can handle, and rogue cops getting paid off. We got a program at City Club. We just started this collaborative effort with the Northend Family Center. They have a 24-hour hotline for anyone who wants to quit or who needs to start the methadone treatment. See this card?"

Frank stood up and handed Jim a card with a phone number to a 24-hour drug rehabilitation program and counseling service, with a dime taped to the back.

"We're passing the card out to people — users, non-users, anyone who knows someone who might need help."

Sister Jo continued to press her point. "We need to get the police involved. A heroin addict is capable of doing anything."

"Now Sister JoAnna," said Jim, "I'll expel a student in a heartbeat if I think he's a danger to anyone at the school. And you know that. But these kids need help –- a different kind of help. Some treatment. We can't just run to the police, who by the way haven't exactly been our friends for the past three hundred years. This has got to be a community and family thing."

"That is a reckless approach, Mr. Dunham. Some of these students are regular users. We can't turn a blind eye," said Sister JoAnna.

"We're not turning a blind eye. We've counseled many kids and parents when we know there's a problem of drug abuse in the home."

"And what about the dealers in the school? Do you think they're too petty to be concerned about?" asked Ted.

"The two major troublemakers are gone. They graduated last year. And besides, they were small potatoes."

"But you let it go on for three years, thinking you could help them," said Sister JoAnna.

"Sister JoAnna, what's getting at you? We did help them, we did. They quit using their own drugs. We saved their lives."

"You mean you paid off the neighborhood dealers. With school funds."

Jim leaned forward quickly and said to Sister JoAnna, "Now that's a truckload of donkey doo-doo! The money came out of my pocket, dammit. If that gets out of here, Sister Jo, I'm going to charge you with slander and you will resign as my assistant principal."

"Mr. Dunham, you can't make me resign, and you can't fire me."

"Father O'Malley can, and he'll do it if I ask him to. You're accusing me of misappropriating school funds and that's an outright lie. How dare you bring that up while we're here trying to solve the school's financial problems!"

"Mr. Dunham, you refuse to work with the police, and that is not going over too well downtown."

Jim countered, "The police have refused to work with us. Right now we're asking the city to dismantle STRESS and back off their confrontational approach when it comes to black people. Sister, you think there's a police solution for everything. But that just isn't so!"

Sister JoAnna opened her mouth as if to say more, but found herself cut off by a sharp reprimand.

"Sister Jo!" Rose shouted suddenly, as if she couldn't take the quarreling any more.

Sister Jo got up and stormed out of the lodge.

"Yeah," Jim said sullenly, in the silence that followed, "I paid off Captain Z and his boys three grand just before last year's graduation. Man, Frank, that's why I too was looking forward for this Youth Summit - to try and get some of these cats to work together under a big tent for peace strategy involving all the compact schools." He shook his head.

They all stood quietly around the fire, gathering their thoughts and pondering the next steps.

Rose decided to go to bed. "I'm fatigued. I been up since five o'clock this morning."

"Good night, baby," said Frank, kissing her on the cheek as she went by. When Rose was out of earshot, Jim spoke up once again.

"That's part of the story, anyway. Later I met with Captain Z's old man at the Collingwood Bar. My favorite waitress, Bonnie, who's rapidly become my favorite person these days . . . "

"You sweet on Bonnie?" asked Ted.

"Very sweet, my brother, very sweet. But let me finish. I told her what was going on with Curtis and Norm owing some drug dealers several thousand dollars and how their parents had asked me to intervene. So, I'm telling this to Bonnie and how I paid Captain Z three grand, and she tells me how Captain Z's father been laid off from Chrysler because he's an alcoholic. Chrysler put him on leave while he's supposed to be getting help. Bonnie knows him and his wife well. I asked Bonnie to set me up a meeting with this cat.

Make a long story short, we met and he starts to plead with me about not going to the police about his son. Well, you know I was never going to, but I didn't tell him that. I told him that we want Captain Z and his boys to become part of our compact and sign a peace-pact. I told the old man I want him to deliver Captain Z and his top lieutenants to the Youth Summit. Shoot, the man went on babbling - he was drunk - about how he would pay me back. I told him that we needed to meet again, minus the inebriation. I wanted to talk to him when he could listen and maybe remember a few things. And we did. The next time we met he carried a notebook and a pen to take notes. He told me that his kids run the house. He and his wife live in fear. He told me that Captain Z bragged once about getting paid by some white people who said they were downtown businessmen, but that Captain Z smelled a rat – he figured they were undercover officers. He took the money and did the job anyway."

"Jesus Christ," said Ted.

"Holy Mother Mary," said Frank.

"You mean more like, 'what the hell is going on?'" said Jim.

"Right-on," said Ted. The trio slapped palms.

After a moment's pause, Frank said, "Mike told me that the thugs were mercenaries and would hit anybody if they were paid. It's usually black-on-black and the police aren't going to investigate."

Jim turned to Frank. "So Frank, when it's time to redo the Youth Summit, call Captain Z's ol' man, Mr. Moore. He said he would pull together a few of the parents and bring those thugs to the summit."

Jim, Ted, and Frank stayed up half the night talking tactics and strategies on how to save the school. Frank added more logs to the fire as they plotted. Jim said, "You know the archdiocese thinks it's my job to proselytize. But that's not my job or my interest. That's what the priests are here for."

"Yeah, but the church expects more from the laity in the community these days," said Ted.

"Sure, I know all about the new direction under Synod '69. We've all heard about it," said Jim in a dismissive tone. He began to explain to Frank and Ted that an all-student fundraiser during the holiday season might demonstrate just how committed the entire St. Martin DePorres community is to keeping the school open. He said that the students could solicit donations the same way Reverend Cleage's congregation does for his Shrine of the Black Madonna Church —fanning out with donation cans. Jim explained that a 3-week campaign between Thanksgiving and Christmas would be perfect.

It didn't take much time to convince Frank or Ted. Jim said he would make a formal presentation to the board at their monthly meeting the following week. Jim insisted that he had the support of the black lay Catholics and the folks at the Office of Black Catholic Affairs within the Detroit Archdiocese.

Finally, Ted interjected. "And what if none of this works?"

"Yeah, I wondered about that too, Ted. I got a backup but it'll require some courage and strength."

"To do what, Jim?" asked Frank.

"Close the church –- on Sunday morning. Close Visitation."

"Why not Blessed Sacrament? Now that would make a statement," said Ted.

"No we'll stick with Visitation for now Ted. "Here's the point –- what's more important in this community right here, right now? We're battling for the hearts and minds of our young people. And they need this school — we all do –- right here, right now."

CHAPTER 60 -
Getting Through -
Fall 1971/ early Winter 1972

By HOMECOMING, MIKE'S TUTORIAL PLAN BEGAN to pay off. Two of the offensive lineman and a running back were on their way to becoming honor roll students. Several others had shown improvement over the course of the last year. Julius, a junior, jumped from C average to an A average going into the first marking period. He told Mike after practice one day that he'd always had it in him; the tutors just helped him focus and complete his assignments. It was clear to Mike that Julius felt good about his accomplishments. Mike's own grade average teetered around a B. His strong subjects were math and science, so Mike signed up for physics and calculus his senior year to keep up his grades.

An undefeated football season, however, was not possible. The DePorres Eagles were 6-1 going into the last game. But Mike had forty-three catches (averaging about six per game) and averaged eighteen yards per catch. His stats looked good and college letters poured in. Most were letters expressing interest, but three big-named schools — Michigan State University, Arizona State University, and University of Colorado — made very good offers: a full scholarship for four years. Mike told his family and friends that he would decide after the season.

Mike kept his left middle three fingers taped tightly during the season, just like he'd done for the past two years. Mike was getting used to the excruciating pain during the game, though he felt more pain than ever, especially after games when all the adrenaline wore off. He continued to use over-the-counter pain relievers that never lasted long, if they worked at all. He took every over-the-counter pain killer and reliever he could get his hands on. He continued to ignore the advice from his coach and parents to see a doctor. He lied, telling them that it wasn't so bad. He kept telling himself, *after basketball season, that's it.* But Mike could not stand the pain and had to sit out the final game. DePorres lost and would not be in the playoffs. Mike told his teammates that he felt more pain watching from the sideline than playing.

Not long after football season, Mike visited the family doctor to have his finger examined. Doctor Washington recommended surgery before basketball season, but Mike refused to do anything until after basketball season even though the pain was becoming unbearable.

"Can you give me a painkiller, Doc?" asked Mike. "Just enough to get me through basketball season."

"If you had seen me a year ago, it's possible we wouldn't need to operate. But it's gone too far. In good conscience, I must do something. But you have got to take care of this real soon, or we may need to amputate. I'm going to give you a one-time prescription, no refills. This stuff can be addictive, Mike. You understand? I'll give you enough to last through the season, but you must take it only as directed." He handed the prescription to Mike, who read it, then stuffed it into his shirt pocket.

"And I'll need to see you once a month until you get the surgery. You got that?"

"Got it, Doc." *Got doggit, yes,* Mike said to himself. He finally might get a little relief.

Cruising through the city with Mike later that night in Luke's Torino, Luke said that he quit snorting P - cold turkey. He told Mike that the brothers at the Northend Family Center had stayed up with him for several days as he went through withdrawals. Luke told Mike that if he quit then maybe he could save Sharon. Luke had seen that his sister had started mainlining, and that he couldn't stop her. He said that it took several weeks to prove to Sharon that he was clean, but then Sharon asked him how he did it.

"And she seemed truly interested," Luke said to Mike.

~ ~ ~ ~ ~ ~ ~

Luke went on to tell Mike that Brother Bear did not want to put down the P. He told his band partners that the P made him play better. Sometimes he'd mix it up with cocaine and smoke it. Brother Bear became a hardcore user by the time he'd graduated from high school. "Ain't no turning back," he said to his boys during a game of pool. During pool games at his home, Brother Bear and DeAngelo would always split for a few minutes and come back fucked up.

Luke reminded Mike about how Brother Bear played a mean sax. "The boy was so good he was bad," said Luke. Brother Bear graduated from Northwestern High school in 1971 and played in a local band called "Made in Detroit." And he'd back up many notable local musicians and recording artists, including Aretha Franklin and Kenny Burrell. He accompanied George Benson once at Baker's Keyboard Lounge. He wanted to start his own jazz band to include female vocalists.

~ ~ ~ ~ ~ ~ ~

Rose took over as varsity cheerleading coach after football season, and she spent her free time working on various fundraisers with Mama E. They had hoped to break ground on the health clinic at City Club in the spring of 1972, but by December 1971 they were still about $20,000 short of their goal. Visitation had cancelled its Bingo nights a year previously and the relationship they had started with Blessed Sacrament wasn't working well. Even though Rose and Mama E knew several families at Blessed Sacrament, they were treated as outsiders trying to cash in. Without Bingo nights, Rose and Mama E had to come up with a new strategy. Where else could they sell bean pies and fish dinners?

Rose and Mama E had pretty much burned out on the fundraising. To take her mind off the fundraising efforts, Mama E spent hours in the garden tending the flowers, and often just sitting in her lounge chair gazing at all the natural beauty around her.

But Rose had a harder time relaxing. In the backyard, she would start in: "Mama, we got enough flowers back here to make floral arrangements and—"

"And don't even think about it," Mama E would interrupt her. "These are precious gifts for people, especially our seniors. These flowers bring so much joy to people, I couldn't even put a price on these if I had to. So we'll just keep on giving these away."

The Waterman backyard became so beautiful and bountiful that they began to give tours to neighbors and strangers who heard about the flower garden. Some folks would stop by to ask for a flower or two for a girlfriend, a mother, or a sick relative.

One warm afternoon, Mama E said, "Rose, this year we gave floral arrangements to over 150 families, and the yard gets more bountiful every year."

~ ~ ~ ~ ~ ~ ~

Later that night Mike overheard his mother, father, and Mr. Dunham discuss their plans for the school's fundraiser. They said they'd talked about the logistics with Sister JoAnna, and the entire school board backed the plan, even Curly. Mr. Dunham said that the students and staff were eager, and had gathered hundreds of collection cans.

But one frosty night in January, after a successful fundraising campaign, Frank caught up with Jim in his office after playing handball with Father O'Malley. Hearing the office door click open, Jim turned his swivel chair around to greet Frank. He looked at Frank solemnly, and said softly, "Frank, they say it's not enough." Jim shook his head side-to-side then buried his face in his hands.

"Great day in the morning," said Frank.

"Yeah, let's prepare for plan B."

CHAPTER 61 -
To The Wine Store -
Winter 1972

St. Martin DePorres made it to the Catholic school basketball finals. The winner would go on to play the Public School League (PSL) Champion in the renewed matchup – the Friendship Game. DePorres played their cross-town rival, St. Augustine, for the Catholic school championship. Mike was psyched, and so was Jon-Jon.

At the start of the new year, Jon-Jon promised everyone a big surprise performance if they went to the Catholic school basketball finals. He had choreographed the show for months in anticipation of the big game. Jon-Jon put together what he called the "first-ever African drumming half-time special." Jon-Jon learned from Bongo Bob that in the absence of an official school band, the drummers and dancers were to fill those shoes with the same level of seriousness. He would stay long hours after school working with the cheerleaders and with Amen-Ra, the African dancers and drummers collective he helped form with Rahim and Malik, two older brothers who attended Wayne State University.

Integrating the African dancers and drummers with the cheerleaders was one of his biggest challenges. Typically they performed separately, but Jon-Jon was determined to blend together the half-time performance. Most of the cheerleaders had limited exposure to African drumming, and getting everyone in sync took hours.

On that cold, late-February night, Jon-Jon staged a mini-parade a block away from the Visitation Recreation Center, where the game was being played. The drummers and dancers thundered through the streets, along the parade route lined with students, parents, and neighborhood residents. The cheerleaders intermixed with the African dancers, and cart-wheeled, twirled batons, and danced their way down the street. Jon-Jon led his drummers, dancers, and cheerleaders down the center of the street and into the recreation center.

Once inside the jammed-packed center, Jon-Jon led the group into the gymnasium to wild cheering among the crowd. The stilt-man who walked in the parade had to dismount to get inside the gym. Once inside, he towered over everyone, standing over twelve feet high. His long, intricately designed African mask looked life-like. The stilt-man's eyes glowed underneath the mask.

Inside the gym, the fans reeked with enthusiasm. The standing-room-only crowd rocked to the rhythms. The DePorres crowd stood on its feet, chanting its favorite cheer: "Are the Eagles Gonna Win It?" "Hell Yeah!!"

After a few minutes a group of seniors at one end of the gym started one of its latest chants:

"When I was one – hey! I had some fun – hey!
When I was 2 – hey! I did the do – hey!
When I was three – hey! I did some P – hey!
When I was four – hey! I did some more – hey!"

This went on for some time. The drummers waited until the raucous DePorres crowd finished before they started drumming to the entry of both teams.

At the sound of the half-time buzzer, DePorres led by ten points. After about fifteen minutes, during which the crowd chatted idly and enjoyed the first part of the half-time break, all the lights were turned off for a dance routine. Carlos Santana's "Black Magic Woman" blasted over the loudspeakers, and under the spotlight a young man and woman performed a short skit. When the lights returned, the drummers, dancers and cheerleaders paraded around the gym then headed for the center of the floor, where the entire group formed a circle with a couple of drummers in the center. Cheerleaders cart-wheeled inside and outside the circle, while dancers took turns performing in the center. After ten minutes, Jon-Jon led his group to the lobby doors to thunderous applause.

St. Martin DePorres's won the game and was on its way to the City Championship. In two weeks they would face Central High School, the Public School League Champion. The students broke out into a wild frenzy chanting, "To the wine store, to the wine store." Then the students chanted "To the big house . . . " This went on for several minutes.

CHAPTER 62 -
Plan B - Shut the Church, Not the School

ROSE AND MAMA E WERE IN the living room discussing their next steps to raise money. Frank sensed that things were coming to a head. Rose said she'd heard about the conflicts between Curly, Jim, and the church over issues like the lack of conversion to Catholicism by the families, drug abuse in the neighborhood and in the school, and "rowdy" behavior at the games. Jim told Rose and Frank that the real reason he thought he was beginning to catch hell was the strong influx of Afro-centrism at the school.

"What else do they want?" Jim said heatedly. "We sent the students canvassing all over downtown Detroit, our teachers took a pay cut, and our annual fundraiser keeps getting bigger. And the cardinal tells us we're still not in the black."

Rose said, "You're too black Jim."

"Jim," Frank said, "he's accusing you of giving out too many scholarships and not collecting tuition."

"You all know the story. I'm sure everybody just don't have it to give. They get in a financial strain and we're the first they let go. Enrollment is down. Every year it gets lower. We calculated that enrollment would rise from 600 to 900 in four years. Instead, we're down to 400 students. Then, here's the cardinal: '*Where are my new black Catholics?*' Well, here's his black Catholics . . . " They continued their conversation as Frank drove Rose and Jim to the church to prepare for "Plan B." Frank went back home while Rose stayed.

Earlier in the week, Jim secured the church hall meeting space from Father O'Malley under the guise of making plans for a fundraiser. But when his volunteers arrived, Jim turned to his team of ten volunteers to go over the details of the takeover of the church sanctuary. They were planning to barricade themselves inside the church and prevent Sunday service from taking place.

"Is everybody ready?" Jim asked his team of volunteers. "Our request is simple: no school closures!" .

"This is going to be a long one-nighter," Rose told the group.

Rose helped lead the group of volunteers, which had been instructed by Jim to chain each entrance and lock it from the inside. Earlier in the week, Rose had purchased several long link chains. Rose counted ten possible entry points into the church, either from the outside or from the church hall below. Jim called the action a *"strong dose of our faith."*

This was the first time Rose had participated in anything this serious — she had never thought she would buck up against the Catholic church. But she reasoned that this uprising was long overdue. Sweat beaded up on her forehead. She checked her handbag for tissues.

"I'm actually sweating, y'all. Does anyone have a Kleenex?" she asked to no one in particular. Then she lifted her head and flashed the group a wide grin. "No, I'm not nervous."

"Yeah, you are," said Jim "We're going to do one more check to be sure all the potential entrances are locked. We'll do one bathroom run at six in the morning. Then after that we're here until one o'clock tomorrow afternoon."

"Unless they have the Big-Four storm the doors," said Dorothy, a volunteer.

"There'll be no storming the doors, no tear-gassing the church, no smoke bombs to get us out. Cardinal Beardum isn't crazy. He ain't gonna have the police tear his property down just to get us out. We're calling Father O'Malley at six-thirty in the morning to let him know that Sunday Mass is cancelled. Remember, Father Thom already knows the plan and he agreed to say mass and offer communion outside."

"Right," Rose nodded in assent. "And no matter what, we're here until one o'clock."

Sunday morning Father Thom greeted many of the parishioners outside the church's locked doors. Inside, Rose and a few others walked over to the door to hear what was going on outside.

"No, we are not going to call the police," they heard Father Thom assuring the parishioners. "We don't know how the police will behave. They might get excited and storm the place with tear gas and assault weapons. We cannot control the police. I don't want our church destroyed or the people inside abused. I would rather wait it out."

"Father Thom knows we're leaving at one," said Rose reassuringly.

Father Thom continued to speak with the group outside, as those inside continued to listen at the door. "Jim and those inside decided to go about this in a peaceful non-violent way. They are not inside destroying the church. They want to make a point."

"And that point is . . . ?" came a loudly voiced complaint.

But Father Thom was on a roll. "The point is that the archdiocese must become a participant in this community. They've got to be a part of the long-term solution of rebuilding this community, rebuilding Detroit. They should get more involved in helping to find the resources to keep St. Martin DePorres open and not abandon it. Our children are coming back from college telling us how well we prepared them not just for college but for the world. How we gave them the skills and confidence to compete. Let's not lose that. Yes, we want more families to be part of our church community. But the archdiocese wants to throw the baby out with the bath water. Let us pray, Dear Heavenly Father . . . "

Inside, Rose looked at Judith, another DePorres parent, and said, "Can you believe it? Father Thom got our back, girl."

After the prayer, Father Thom continued without offering an opportunity for any further interruption. "We can honor the Sabbath right here," he said firmly. Then he went on to offer communion to all those in attendance. "Having church in a nice plush environment is not always possible. Ask Father Akojie, ask him what he has to deal with in Nigeria. Ask Father Escobar down in Guatemala. We said the mass in the jungle and in the slums, we were outside for weeks. We built a church from scratch. It was the will of the people and the will of God."

Father Akojie said as he laughed, "I said mass in a wrecked bus once. We had 50 people crammed in there."

Father Thom continued, "It's not where you pray, but how you pray — not where we live, but how we live, not what we have but what we give."

Rose heard that and tears began to flow down her cheeks. She led Judith and a few others back inside the sanctuary and towards the altar, where she instructed the group of volunteers to hold hands and sing.

"*We shall overcome . . .*" Their voices reached the rooftop, and soared over the crowd gathered outside.

After news of the Sunday protest, donations from across the country and around the world began to pour in for the school. Checks from Catholics in Ireland, France, and Lebanon rained down on St. Martin DePorres. Because of the pressure from the world Catholic community and many parents, Father Richard convened several meetings with the school board to resolve the crisis. The Archdiocese of Detroit relented and agreed to keep the school open on a five-year plan on one condition - Jim Dunham had to resign.

After fighting his emotions for a few days, Jim received a call from Father

Richard who made it a little clearer to Jim - either resign or be fired. Jim sent a letter of resignation effective at the end of the school year. But after overwhelming support from the parents Jim changed his mind within the week. He sent another letter to Cardinal Beardum, accompanied by a letter from the Board, insisting that he be reinstated in spite of Curly's objections. But Jim received from the Detroit Archdiocese a firm denial.

Rose Waterman followed this chain of events closely. She talked about another protest. She told members of the parish, school parents, and anyone else interested in reinstating Jim as principal that they would launch a twenty-four hour round-the-clock sit-in at the Cardinal Beardum's residence in Sherwood Forest, Detroit's plushest neighborhood.

Over the phone, Rose told people to "bring tents, sleeping bags, and a change of clothes. We'll stay until he's rehired."

On the first night of the campout, a group of about thirty parents and parishioners were expecting Jim to stop by to thank them and give them a pep-talk. Instead, the only person Rose saw come to greet them was Father Thom, running from his car to the group. He said, "Jim just had a heart attack! He's at Henry Ford Hospital, in serious but stable condition." Rose and everyone else just looked stunned. After a few moments and some hurried exchanges, Rose led a small group down to the hospital, while the others remained vigilant in their protest.

Jim Dunham didn't say much other than thanks for going through with the protest and having the courage to stand up to the cardinal once again. Later in the week and after five days of protest, Jim told the group that he would resign instead of 'dragging everyone into the quicksand.' He told them that the Catholic Church behaves worse than donkeys at times.

CHAPTER 63 –
Winter in America

SHARON HADN'T BEEN TO SCHOOL IN three days. More importantly, no one at the Waterman household had heard from her or knew where she was. John had tailed Sonny T, her boyfriend, for the last several weeks. He watched deals go down between Sonny and his suppliers. He watched the police get paid off. In fact, John and his study group had gotten so obsessed with Sonny and the two agents getting paid off that he had lost sight of Sharon. One afternoon Luke and Mike were talking on the porch of the Waterman home when they saw Sonny T and Sharon speed past in Sonny's car. He barely stopped at 14th Street where he skidded as he turned right. Seconds later, another car sped past and peeled right on 14th Street. The boys could see Luke's mother Delli running up the street towards them. She screamed "they after that fool. Some dealers out of New York. I gave Sharon the money he owed them, about ten grand and he kept it. They want their money."

"Let's try to catch them." Luke said. Luke had his Torino-GT parked in the driveway. Luke burnt rubber rounding the corner in pursuit.

Mike said, "We have no idea which way they went, go down Hazelwood up to the freeway." After two hours of searching, there were no signs of Sharon or Sonny T. The boys called it off.

Two days later, Sharon and Sonny T were both found dead in an abandoned apartment building on Linwood Ave. used by drug addicts. Both deaths were officially classified as an overdose of heroin.

After the funeral for Sharon, Frank drove his family out to Belle Isle to meet up with John and Mama E who drove separately. They pulled into a spot at the west end of the island facing the downtown Detroit skyline. The

Detroit river waters were choppy as iron ore freighters made their way between Detroit and Windsor.

John embraced Frank and said, "Someone murdered Sharon. We got a copy of the coroner's report. The needle was inserted into the back of her legs. Her wrists were bound. We don't know who did it but the police are covering this shit up."

CHAPTER 64 –
Dope house raids

JOHN AND THREE OF HIS ARC comrades had scoped out the targeted dope house for several days after Sharon's death. They looked like ordinary houses on Detroit's west side, along tree-lined streets and inhabited by working class families — people coming and going to work, like most hardworking families.

But the targeted two—story houses acted almost as drug warehouses. John and his crew had identified four heroin supply centers throughout the west side of Detroit . His late night planning involved only three other people, though Jon-Jon sat in on a couple of these sessions. John told his group "We're making targeted hits, one after another. One each day for four days, then we disappear." Under John's plan, two of them would disperse to Libya and two would go to Cuba. Everyone swore to keep the secret.

"We have to commit everything to memory brothers, no paper trail," John told the brothers.

Plainclothes STRESS officers would roll by regularly in an unmarked Plymouth Fury. There were several officers involved, maybe a dozen. They would drive slowly but would never stop.

John's big black book contained the names and addresses of the officers they photographed who were involved in the drug trafficking. John also obtained the names and addresses of their relatives and girlfriends.

From an unnamed source, John learned the code for the day needed to gain entry to the drug houses. The drug dealers changed the code everyday, sometimes twice a day. Knowing the pass code meant that he was a new customer who could be trusted. Someone would then let him in. That was the preferred method of operation: deal with only those they know or who sent over by someone they could trust.

When the doorman opened the door for John, John quickly placed the barrel of his .38 revolver against the doorman's temple.

"Shut up and take me back," said John. Two of John's partners followed behind wearing ski masks. They caught everyone by surprise. All three had their guns drawn. John had two — one he kept at the doorman's temple and the other aimed at others in the room. There were four dealers in the house.

John stayed on the main floor while the other two went upstairs, then downstairs looking for dope and money. After they collected all the dope throughout the house, they slung the bags onto the table. "Open it," said John. Before the man could even grab the bag, John picked it up and flung it across the room. Then John picked another large bag of heroin and began to beat one of the dealers across the head.

"This shit's the shit that's killing us, fool," he shouted as the powder flew around the man's head.

As he calmed down and moved away from that dealer, John saw near the back of the house a card table piled up with heroin. He promptly kicked the table over, then pushed another dealer to the floor. Scanning the room again, John eyed the loot piled high on the dining room table.

"Tie these clowns up and take the money. We giving this money to the poor. Let's go!" The group removed their masks and walked out to the getaway car parked not far from the house.

Back at the safe house, they counted over two hundred thousand dollars.

And they hit again the next day after learning the password from their inside source. John carried a sawed-off double barrel shotgun inside his trench coat. There was a backup doorman, so this time John waited until he got close enough to pull his weapon.

"Go back slowly and open the door," John told him. Both doormen went back to the front door to let John and his two partners in. Once inside, they drew their guns. They taped the first doorman's mouth shut, then tied his hands behind their backs. In what seemed like seconds, they tied the second doorman's hands behind his back., then escorted the two towards the back of the house.

"Oh, shit," said the second doormen.

"'Oh, shit' is right," John said. "The game is over. Where's the dough?" The brothers found it under the sofa. They secured three men and two women inside their second target, and duct-taped all of them to the chairs.

Once in the car Stewart asked, "How much we get here?"

"Two hundred and sixty thousand," said John.

"Man. What are they doing making that kind of loot?"

"Think it's two days' worth. I heard some of the dope houses starting to move their money every two to three hours now."

"And they still paying off the heat."

"Yeah."

"Brothers, listen up," said John. "One more hit and that's it. I think they had lookouts posted on the corner tonight and maybe got a look at us. They'll be hip to what we drive now. First, we need a new car and we might need disguises."

The next day news reports in the paper ran an article headlined:

Robin Hood Bandits Strike Again

That evening John let the brothers know where they'd be going in a few hours.

"We'll hit Hazelwood tonight."

But later that night John still hadn't heard from his source. They waited outside Esquire Deli on Dexter Boulevard, parked in a 1964 T-bird that John had purchased from a friend earlier that day. John spotted his source going inside.

"Y'all sit tight," he told his brothers. "I'll be right back."

His own team didn't even know his source, and John was determined to maintain secrecy, so he stood in line and ordered his favorite corned beef sandwich and peach cobbler, then sat in one of the empty booths behind his source. His source and a woman he was with were chatting back and forth as usual while he sat quietly waiting for his clues. The source threw up his arms as if to emphasize a point he was making to the woman, then provided John with the clues.

"Ain't nothing baby, nothing," he said. "The only ones getting in are those they know. Ya hear that, baby?" The source pretended to be talking to the woman about an after-hours club nearby.

John had heard enough. He'd have to take his team to the next target without an easy way in or decide to scrap it. He finished his peach cobbler quickly before he exited the deli. He had decided to go through with it anyway.

"There's no password, my brothers," he said, as he slid into the seat.

"How do we get in?"

"We lay in the bushes until the next person is let in, then we bust in behind him."

With ski masks as disguises, the three entered exactly that way. John knew they didn't have much time, so he moved quickly. Guns drawn, they taped up two of the doorman and three others inside. Again John smacked one of the dealers with a big bag of P. Heroin flew everywhere.

"This money over here would be better spent feeding the hungry," he shouted. "Where's the rest of it?"

John spotted another batch of money in an open cabinet. As he went to retrieve it he saw Darren, his source, hiding in the kitchen. They nodded at each other. John threw in his bag whatever bundles he could quickly get his hands on, then said to his team, "Let's get the hell outta here."

They ran for the car several doors away. As they raced to the getaway car, John said, "Something's not right." No sooner had they climbed in the car, two unmarked police cars sped up the street to the dope house.

"It's the police, they're 4-deep. Shit, I saw my source in the kitchen. He was watching. Man, we got to roll. But take off slow. We can't let them see us leave too fast."

John saw three of the officers rush up to the door of the house and kick the door in, while one officer stayed behind. John told Herman, the group's driver, that it was clear for them to pull out, but just as they began to take off they heard shots.

"Shit! Let's roll!" yelled John. "Keep the headlights off."

John looked back and saw Darren jumping through the side window, shattering glass, then running towards the alley behind the house. Within a minute, Herman noticed that they were being followed by an unmarked police car. A flashing red light came on.

John said, "Pull over and put the guns under the seat just like we practiced."

While some of the brothers began sliding their guns into hidden compartments under their seats, Herman declined.

"Bullshit, I'm sitting on mine in case we need to off one of these pigs."

John was about to argue when two police officers got out with their guns drawn and approached the car.

Herman slowly rolled down the window as they approached. He was about to utter the standard line — "Is there a problem, officer?" — when he was cut off by the cop.

"I want all four of you niggers to get out the car. And where's my money, you low-life motherfuckers?" shouted the officer. "You niggers been hitting my houses. Now where's my money?" the officer asked again.

The officer drove his gun into the driver's window, and grabbed Herman by the neck and tried to pull him out through the window. He had Herman in a choke hold. As Jamal started to get out from the back seat, the other officer opened fire. Jamal hit the ground like he'd been shot. Stewart, who had two pistols, took this as his cue and opened fire on the officers while still inside the car. As the officers' firing tapered off, John picked up Jamal, who was grazed and not injured too badly, and threw him back into the car. Herman stepped on the gas.

They sped off. Behind them, lying still on the ground, both officers were down, maybe dead.

With a shake of his head, John turned and spoke to Stewart. "Man, you blasted two of the most notorious STRESS pigs. They're the heroes at the police department. They're getting paid from everybody. They're the same ones who secure the drug routes as they come in from Canada. You saw the pictures. We got to ditch the car," John continued.

Herman snaked the car through the neighborhood without being followed by the police. All four brothers jumped out the car as soon as Herman parked it. Taking everything out of the car, they left it behind at the curb.

They walked around the corner, where they spotted a Ford Maverick.

"This one's easy," Herman said. It took him all of thirty seconds to hotwire the car. They shed their ski masks and over-clothes into a large plastic bag that John carried with him, and dumped it in an alley.

"Plan C," said John. The brothers would not utter another word to anyone unless absolutely necessary. They drove to the "honey pot," their secret location, to bury some of the money and retrieve their pre-packed bags of loot from the previous days' dope bust-ups. John tended to Jamal's bullet wound, and was able to stop the bleeding.

They went in separate directions. Herman kept the stolen car. Stewart didn't seem to want to leave Jamal, so they split together. John was headed for Cuba. On his way out of Detroit he would drop a bag of money at Frank's with a note that simply read *She Hit*. He had decided to go through Canada to London, Ontario first, then take a flight out of Toronto to Mexico City, and on to Cuba.

John got into a disguise using clothes he had stashed in an alley trash can, near where the money was buried at City Club. He transformed himself into a drag queen, and hailed a taxi on Dexter Blvd., directing the driver to take him down to the Female Impersonators Club on Woodward not far from the Fox Theatre.

Arriving at the club, John hurried inside to rendezvous with an old high school friend Melvinia, formerly known as Melvin, who had turned from a boy basketball star to a drag queen homosexual. Melvinia, also earned a black belt in karate and would teach his fellow drag queens how to defend themselves in the streets. John threw up two fingers like a peace sign to Melvinia.

Through the smoke, Melvinia eyed John. He didn't recognize John, but knew the signal. John flashed him again. Melvinia then knew what she had to do — meet John out back.

Once outside, she said, "I know those eyes. You've got those beautiful eyes."

"Thanks, girl. I need to get across the bridge to Windsor. Gotta go now."

"I'll get a couple of the girls and we can all go together."

"No, just us," said John. "We need to go."

Melvinia nodded, then turned her eyes downward. "Um, you look good in drag, Johnny."

John didn't say another word, but remembered when Melvinia was a young man in high school and thought about how he had been able to pull girls like it wasn't nothing. He'd always been surrounded by women. Little did he know that one day he would become one: Melvinia, King of the Drag Queens. But at any rate Melvinia was taking a high risk taking him across the bridge and he would never forget that.

John felt exhausted during the ride across the border –- on his way to freedom. At the border, the two faced the standard questions:

"Citizens of what country?"

"United States," the two responded in unison.

"Where are you going?"

"To Windsor."

"How long will you be in Canada?"

"Just a few hours," said Melvinia.

The border security let them through. John breathed a sigh of relief.

"Whew, shit, holy moly!" John said. "Hey man, I need you to take me to London."

"Look, John, I'm ready. You told me you might need my help and I knew this day would come, I just knew it."

John and Melvinia headed towards a safe house in London, Ontario. John would stay there only one night before heading to Toronto, Mexico City, then Cuba.

The next day's papers in London read:

"Robin Hood Bandits Kill 2 Police Officers in Detroit and 5 Massacred at Suspected Drug House on Hazelwood Ave. Gunmen Still at Large."

Chapter 65 -
Jon-Jon's walk home

Sister JoAnna and Father Thom were in charge of the school while Jim recovered. After nearly a week at home on bed rest, Jim advised the parents to call off the protest, telling them that he was weighing his options. He needed time to think about what to do next. He realized that the Catholic Church would not budge on their position, and thought maybe it was best for his own health to move on.

No one had heard from John in nearly two weeks. Everyone suspected the worst and feared that it was just a matter of time before he turned up dead. As if in divine foreshadowing, during his flight to Cuba, Abdul and Stewart were killed in a shoot-out with police in St. Louis, apparently on their way to Mexico, and Herman was caught trying to outrace the police in the stolen car and got beaten to a bloody pulp before being tossed in the city jail. People in Detroit wondered collectively: *was John Waterman still out there, alive?*

Jon-Jon kept himself busy preparing for the half-time show for the City Championship game. He also was waiting at the recreation center to hear from Bongo Bob on whether Bongo Bob's African Drumming troupe would be invited to the upcoming Pan-African Music Festival in Lagos, Nigeria, this summer. Jon-Jon would play as part of Bongo Bob's group. Thursday evening, after a long practice the day before the big game, Jon-Jon told Denise that he would catch up with her on her walk home after practice because he needed to talk to Bongo Bob, who was on his way.

As Bongo Bob pulled up in front of the Visitation Recreation Center to a waiting Jon-Jon, he screamed to him from the car.

"We're in, we're in! We're going to Lagos. We'll open for Fela Kuti."

He parked the car and got out, waving a letter in his hand. "We're gonna open for Fela Kuti. Man, can you believe it?"

"I can't wait to tell my mom and everybody, man. I been praying for this." Jon-Jon couldn't help grinning.

Bongo Bob handed Jon-Jon a copy of the letter. "Here's your copy, brother. Show 'em that." Jon-Jon took the letter with a beaming smile.

"Hey, Bongo Bob, I need to catch up with Denise. She's about a block or two away on 12th Street." Jon-Jon punched Bongo Bob playfully in the arm, then clutched his drum in one hand and the letter in the other and took off down the street to catch up with Denise. After a short jog of just a few blocks, Jon-Jon saw Denise heading towards a small crowd of boys at the corner of 12th Street and Calvert. He hollered and waved the letter.

"Wait up, Denise, wait up! We're going to Lagos!" Denise kept walking, evidently not having heard him. Jon-Jon noticed that she seemed to be marching straight ahead, and shouted to her again. "Denise!"

When some boys on the corner blocked Denise's path, Jon-Jon finally caught her. He breathed in deeply then let it out.

"We're going to Lagos," he announced happily.

Denise smiled at Jon-Jon but checked out her surrounding –- the boys continued to block her path.

"Excuse us, please," she said politely. "We're going to Lagos." But the boys did not move, and Jon-Jon quickly refocused his energy.

"What's up, what's up? We trying to get through, brothers. Let us through. Can y'all brothers step aside?"

"Who you think you is?" asked one of the boys.

"Y'all besta get ready to run," said another one of the boys.

It was only then that Jon-Jon recognized several of the boys as part of Captain Z's boys. Trying not to let his surprise show on his face, Jon-Jon said, "Y'all know who I am and y'all know Denise too. Quit fucking around and let us through."

"Like I said, y'all besta run when I say run," said one of the boys, laughing.

Denise said emphatically, "We ain't running nowhere," as she tried to push her way through the crowd.

"We ain't fucking around with you. Jon-Jon, we know you got some of that dope money."

Another one said, "We heard you was in on the shit."

Slowly, Jon-Jon put his drum down and said, "Now hold up, just wait a second. Y'all brothers think I was in on that . . . ?"

"Nigger, we *know* you was in on it."

Denise acted like she'd heard enough and plowed forward.

"Get out the way," she said.

Someone said, "Hold it, bitch," and grabbed her by the arm.

Denise shrieked, "What did you call me?" She didn't wait for an answer as she slapped one of the boys across the face and threw her book at another, hitting him in the nose. Blood instantly started to trickle down his lips and chin. Jon-Jon took advantage of the momentary distraction and hit one of the boys with his drum. As Jon-Jon moved in closer to help, someone jabbed a knife into his side. He pulled the blade out and stuck Jon-Jon again.

"Now how you like that?" he shouted at him as Jon-Jon's hands fell to his sides. Then the boys turned and ran. Jon-Jon fell to the pavement, bleeding heavily, and the letter fell by his side into the pool of blood. Denise quickly ran to his aid, screaming for help.

At the sound of her voice, a few neighbors came out of their homes. An elderly woman near the corner brought some fresh towels and, coming to Denise's side, said calmingly, "Honey, we can use these towels to stop the bleeding. I called the ambulance, they coming."

Denise followed her instruction. Tears flowed like a river. Through her tears, she spoke softly to Jon-Jon.

"Don't leave me little brother. Don't leave me." The police and ambulance arrived at the scene simultaneously. The medical team lifted Jon-Jon into the ambulance with the blood-soaked towel at his side.

"We'll take him to Henry Ford Hospital."

Denise picked up the blood-soaked letter and said, "I'll ride to the hospital with him." She thanked the woman and boarded the ambulance.

In the ambulance, Jon-Jon's vision went blurry, then he fell unconscious.

Several hours later he woke up to a room full of people. He couldn't remember what happened after he slammed one of the thugs with his drum.

Seeing Jon-Jon's eyelids flutter, Rose leaned over the side of the bed. "Jon-Jon, we love you baby. You're going to be fine," said Rose in a soft voice. "It was a close call, son, but the knife didn't puncture any organs. You're just now waking up from the surgery. Everyone's down here. Ah, and yes, we heard the good news from Denise. We are all very proud of you. You earned it, baby. The doctors said you will need to take it easy and let this wound heal. You'll have to lay off the drum for about two months."

The Waterman family and friends spilled out from the room into the hospital hallway. Renee, who had been working at Henry Ford Hospital for a couple of years now, led the group of nurses overseeing Jon-Jon's recovery after the surgery. She stepped in closer to Rose and Jon-Jon to let them know it was time for his medication, and to clear out some of the visitors so that he could rest.

CHAPTER 66 –
The Chase

THAT DAY'S INCIDENT WAS A PAINFUL reminder of the neighborhood rivalry often between those attending public schools and Catholic schools. And the game that night – the Renewed PSL-Catholic School Championship, or the Friendship Game — would be intense. .

"Dad", Mike called out, "The archdiocese wants to postpone the game, maybe cancel the whole thing. I think the whole school is walking out."

"And do what?" Frank asked.

"Everybody's just walking out." Mike knew more. He knew they were going to be looking for the boys that jumped Jon-Jon. He and Luke were even going to pack a "piece." "And I do know one thing: they better not cancel the game tonight or we might shut the school down indefinitely."

"Now hey, boy, don't get cocky. I don't think they'll cancel, but we're going to need a whole lot of parent volunteers for security. That way we can watch the police who might get carried away."

"This whole thing makes me sick, Dad. Jon-Jon in critical condition and everything. Shoot, it makes me sick. I want some payback."

"He's getting better, son, don't get caught up in revenge. It's a dead-end street, a ticket to hell . . . "

"Dad, the whole school's in on it. It's time for a showdown, I'm outta here." Mike flew out the door with his letter jacket open and his sweater exposed. Before he got far, he spotted Luke running to catch up. Luke hollered for Mike to wait.

"You got your shit?" asked Luke. "I got mine right here," said Luke pointing to the pistol in his waistband above his side pocket. Luke always seemed to have a pistol when things got tight. "This thing could get messy."

"This 'unity in the community' shit is dead. Denise said they stomped Jon-Jon, they damn near killed him, just like they killed Duane. This shit got to end - now." The two took off running down 14th Street towards their school.

Mama E came running down the stairs after overhearing the conversation between Mike and his father. "One of my pistols is missing," she exclaimed. Mike knew where she stashed her small cache of guns that her father had given to her years ago. A terrifying thought came to Mama E and she bolted out of the house after Mike and Luke. "Mike!" she screamed.

Mike heard Mama E's voice, and unconsciously slowed his pace. He turned around and saw Mama E sprinting towards him. He couldn't believe how fast she was running to close the gap, and he stood on the corner of 14th Street and Boston Blvd. next to Luke in stunned silence. She caught up quickly; they hadn't had a chance to go far.

Her voice winded, she reached her hand out and said firmly, "Give me the gun. Give it to me now, Mike." Mike just looked at her in disbelief. "GIVE-ME-THE-GUN," she said again in a more authoritative voice. Unsure what else to do, Mike reached inside his waistband and handed her the pistol.

"Dammit, these white folks got us fighting like cats and dogs. Don't fall for this. This is all STRESS," Mama E exhorted. "Give me yours too, Luke," Mama E continued in the same tone. "C'mon, give it here."

Luke and Mike looked at each other. Luke said in a low tone, "Shhhit naw, now Mama."

"Don't cuss me boy. I ought to wash your mouth out right here. This ain't no time to act a fool. Give me your gun, Luke. I'm not gonna ask you again." Mama E squared her stance and reached out her hand once more.

Luke turned around in a circle as if he wanted to run, then looked at Mike again. He wore a dejected expression. "Man, we got nothing."

"Just give it to her, Luke."

Defeated, Luke pulled out the .38 snub nose revolver he had taken from his mother and gave it to Mama E. She continued to glare at them, so without another word, they turned and ran towards school.

By the time they arrived there, the parking lot was full of people. Nobody seemed to be going inside. As the boys approached, many of the students asked Mike how Jon-Jon was doing.

"We know who did it," were the first words out of Luke's mouth. "Some go to Durfee, some are at Central, some are at that youth home up the street. Denise saw 'em real good, and she scratched the shit out of one of 'em. So, we know what they look like. We did our own art sketch."

Looking at the sketch that Luke pulled from his pocket, one of the boys looked surprised. "This is that little punk-ass motherfucker. He did it? He's one of Captain Z's boys. We can find this fool up on Calvert near Woodrow Wilson."

Teachers gathered outside the back door and then, en masse, they fanned out into the parking lot trying to entice the students inside the school. Jim Dunham stood at the top of the stairway to the backdoor entrance with a bullhorn in his hand.

"All students please go to your homeroom. If you are not a student at St. Martin DePorres," and there were plenty in attendance who weren't, "leave the premises now."

The students rejected the teachers and the Jim's polite overtures.

"No thanks! We're just here for on-Jon," one student called out.

Another said, as she gestured to all her friends around her, "We're having a prayer vigil. We're praying for his recovery. That's all we're doing."

Mr. Jurowski, the language arts teacher, glanced around looking concerned and said, "But can't we do that inside?"

"But we want to do it out here," said another student.

Mike noticed that the teachers were not being too aggressive. Mr. Jurowski soon moved on to other students, talking with them, sympathizing with them.

The crowd continued to mix and mingle. Mike heard a familiar voice somewhere by his left shoulder, and turned.

"How are you holding up, Mike?" asked Sister Mary Ellen, Mike's Physics teacher.

Mike looked down at the ground for a moment, then held his head up and said, "I'm doing fine, Sister Mary, fine."

"Forgive them, Mike, Don't seek revenge."

Mike didn't feel like making small talk. He'd been up all night at the hospital and had a big game tonight. Sister Mary seemed to take the hint and moved on.

Denise hadn't come to school at all, but had stayed with Jon-Jon. She told Mike that a couple of city detectives were stopping by the hospital to talk with her and to take down her version of what happened. Jon-Jon was still unable to talk.

Looking around, Mike saw a patrol car circle the block. He walked slowly around to the front, where he saw the patrol car parked on the sidewalk in front of the church. One tall heavy-set officer stepped out the car with a donut in one hand and a coffee cup in the other, and was greeted eagerly by Sister JoAnna. Mike had heard that Sister JoAnna had called the police and reported the incident, and that she believed all of DePorres students might be in danger. After watching this exchange, Mike returned to the noisy crowd in the parking lot behind the school.

Students were chanting: "Fired up! Won't take no more." This went on for several minutes. Jim stood and watched as no one responded to his calls to come inside. He was content to watch, so long as the crowd stayed controlled.

Suddenly, someone in the crowd roared, "There they go!" Mike looked in the direction that a student pointed and saw about a dozen young men half a block away. Some students took off after them, and Mike joined in the chase.

Luke had a megaphone in his hand, and shouted into it. "Those that are staying back, we're going up to Central. We gonna let them know we tired of this bullshit. Let's march to Central."

Jim hurried back inside the school.

Mike kept up the chase. The dozen or so young men scattered in all directions. The DePorres students scattered in their pursuit.

A wave of people stampeded around the corner at Calvert and 12th Street. The thugs kept running. They hopped fences and cut through a neighbor's property.

Before he took off in hot pursuit, Mike said, "Some of y'all go back to 12th Street - we'll try to chase them back to y'all." Then Mike and about a fifty others tore through the yards and into the alleys in hot pursuit, Mike out front. He led his group back to Collingwood and 12th Street, where they met up with another group of about fifty students. They still had not found the twelve boys they had been chasing.

"Shit, they got away," said Mike, breathing heavily. "Let's go up to Central and Durfee with the rest of 'em." They ran to catch up with the group led by Luke. As Mike and a large contingent of students crossed 14th Street, they came across a large group of DePorres students standing on Burlingame between 14th Street and LaSalle Blvd.

Mike made his way to the front of the crowd, from where he could see what looked like several hundred teachers and parents blocking the path of the students who were descending on Central High School. Jim stood in the front of this group of parents and teachers.

In a much more assertive tone than he had used previously, Jim said, "Return to the school immediately, right now. If you attend St. Martin DePorres, return to the school immediately, and get to your class, or you will be expelled. There will be no game tonight. And if I hear another word outta anybody, I'll see you in my office — me, you, and the 'Board of Education'," he said, referring to his trademark paddle with several holes drilled through it for maximum efficiency. He held his paddle high and the parents cheered Jim on. Mike noticed coach Freddie Ray pointing his finger towards him mouthing for him to *turn around, turn around or no game.*

"This is fucked up." said Mike. He felt a knot in his stomach.

"Ain't nothing we can do but turn around," Luke said. Mike agreed.

"Let's go, coach Ray up there looking all crazy." he said.

"Well," Luke said, "at least we ain't running away."

Mike said, "Ain't nowhere to run. We ain't no runaway slaves. What we gonna do, part the Detroit River and escape to Canada?"

Luke said, "Hell naw."

CHAPTER 67 -
To The Big House II -
Spring 1972

THE GIANT BANNER READ, "OPERATION FRIENDSHIP City Basketball Championship: St. Martin DePorres High versus Central High."

Frank walked into the field house to the thunderous sounds of Central fans singing along with James Brown's song *Payback*, which was blaring from the public address system. The lower-level bleachers were filled on both sides of the gym. Frank felt the tension in the air. He checked out the Central cheerleaders doing a routine on the gym floor while the DePorres cheerleaders and Rose looked on along the sidelines. Then Frank saw Rose coming his way.

She walked up to him and, standing close by his side, said quietly, "They won't even let our girls on the floor, Frank."

"Yeah, and it looks like they're having a good time."

Rose gave Frank a stern look.

"Rose, let it go. Just seize the floor at half-time. They probably know y'all a got a big show coming up."

"We do. Jon-Jon put together a terrific show. I am so sad too, for what happened to him. Frank, I can barely do this." Her eyes began to brim with tears.

"I know, baby, but that's what makes it so much more special." Frank put an arm around Rose's shoulders. Pulling her close, he said, "Jon-Jon's going to be fine. You just keep praying for him. I heard that Jon-Jon was sitting up and that he and Renee plan to watch the game on Channel 50. It's a miracle he's still alive."

"Yes," said Rose with a deep sigh. "And you know I believe in miracles."

"And we're sure gonna need another one to get through this."

Frank didn't want to tell Rose about the call he'd got from Captain Z's father Mr. Moore, as he'd closed up City Club about an hour ago to head for the game. All in a panic, Mr. Moore had said to Frank, "They say they comin' down there tonight. I heard 'em talkin' 'bout lockin' and loadin', seeking revenge for being chased through the neighborhood today."

"You gotta be kidding me, man," Frank had responded. "Only person got hurt yesterday was Jon-Jon. He's barely conscious. What the hell are they talking about?"

"It's about a hundred of 'em, Frank. Heard them fools say they were gonna step to the field house and make what happened nine years ago look like a picnic."

"Dig this my man," Frank had said, "I need you to get down to the field house with their parents right now. You hear me? Right now!"

"Hey, Frank," Mr. Moore had said right before hanging up. "I'm sorry about your son."

"Thanks, man. We got to stop what's about to go down."

Frank thought that what they really needed was the entire school community down there. As soon as he had got off the phone with Mr. Moore, he'd called about a dozen compact school parents asking them to come down to the field house and to put their phone tree to work asking as many able-bodied men as possible to come to the field house to prevent a repeat of what happened nine years ago. Frank vowed that there would be no bloody Friday after this championship game, and would rely on the parents of DePorres, Central, and the other compact schools to help keep the peace.

After talking with Rose, Frank slipped outside to scope-out the situation around the building. As he scouted around the facility, surprisingly, he saw only two patrol cars. The police officers parked their cars near the front of the building, then stood outside and looked quite bored, sipping coffee and munching donuts. Frank was alarmed at the lack of police presence. The city knew of the rivalry between the two schools and had to know this was going to be a very big and volatile event.

His anger growing, Frank walked a few blocks away to place a call on the pay phone on the University of Detroit campus. He called police headquarters, identified himself, and wrote down the desk captain's name, then asked, "Where are the police for the championship basketball game tonight? I see two patrol cars here and the officers act like they're on vacation."

Captain Smith responded, "Well, as you know, the mayor is having his big reception tonight. We've got dignitaries from all over the world coming in to celebrate the renovation of the Detroit-Windsor tunnel. We're doing our level best, what else do you want? Tell you what, we'll send a couple more squad cars down."

Frank held his voice steady. "Captain, you're full of it."

"Hey," said Captain Smith, raising his voice, "my hands are tied."

Frank slammed the phone down. *We'll just have to do it ourselves.*

Frank then called a neighbor and friend, Abdullah, who had joined the Nation of Islam several years ago and had become a Captain in the Fruit of Islam, the Nation of Islam security unit.

Without hesitation, Abdullah said, "I'll be there and I'll bring some brothers with me."

When parents starting showing up outside the field house, Frank told the parents, "We are going to lock arms around the field house. And we're going to prevent these kids from going to war with each other."

Frank stepped back inside to catch the beginning of the game. "Ladies and gentlemen," the announcer said, "our national anthem." The crowd rose to its feet. After the National Anthem, Detroit's own Kim Weston sang the black national anthem, *Lift Every Voice and Sing.* Frank felt the electricity in the air as the fans sang along with her. As the fans remained standing, cheering Kim Weston as she finished, someone on the St. Martin DePorres side shouted "DePorres." And someone shouted back "DePorres" pulsating throughout the field house. Then on the sidelines the cheerleaders flowed with the crowd with their riveting line, "Are the Eagles gonna win it?" And the Deporres fans roared back "Hell yeah!" This eruption of emotion went on for a minute or two as both teams huddled among themselves getting final instructions from the coaches.

Just before tip-off, Frank asked Coach Ray if he could have a word with his son. Frank said, "It's about his brother, Coach."

"Sure thing, Frank. But make it quick – we've got a game to play."

"Thanks." Frank hurried over to Mike and leaned close to his ear. "Son, nine years ago when I brought you down here for the city championship, you remember what happened? You remember and I remember, we couldn't do anything to stop those kids from getting killed. I don't want to see that happen ever again. So you have to dig deep inside yourself, son. Forget about what happened to Jon-Jon. He's going to be okay, he's going to pull through."

Mike turned his head away and looked at the floor, saying nothing.

"Son, there's something much bigger than this game. There's the game of life. I want you say something to this crowd before the game is over. Say something that's going to help bring peace to the streets."

Frank put one hand on Mike's shoulder. Then, without waiting for a response, he turned and headed back to the sidelines next to Rose to watch the tip-off.

Frank watched DePorres struggle near the end of the first half. He walked back over towards the bench as Coach Ray called his team over the side.

Coach Ray said to Mike, "Listen, man, there is nothing but tension in the air. You guys got to take it easy out there, you got to slow down and play your game."

Frank clapped and shouted as the team went back to the court. They continued to play hard, but they still struggled. DePorres looked tight, and a little bit on edge. They were down ten points, and Central controlled the tempo of the game. At half-time, Central led by a score of 45 to 32.

Frank stuck around for the half-time show.

The DePorres cheerleaders lined up and took the floor. The cheerleaders ran around the perimeter of the gym floor screaming *"Here come the Africans! Here come the Africans!* Several drummers, dancers, and martial artists entered the gym and followed the cheerleaders around the floor doing cart-wheels and back flips, and generally dancing their way around the court. The African-masked stilt man came through the door.

Frank looked over at the DePorres fans and could see them become more energized during the performance. He let loose a guttural holler, throwing his fist in the air "DePorres!" he shouted.

Everyone moved with rhythm to the beat.

After the half-time show, Frank returned outside to check on the situation. There were about two dozen members of the NOI and what looked like about 500 parents and friends standing in front of the field house. Frank overheard a news reporter standing near the entrance of the field house.

We are down here at the University of Detroit Field House reporting live. There is a great deal of tension in the wake of yesterday's stabbing of a St. Martin DePorres student, Jon Waterman, brother of all-star center Mike Waterman. It remains to be seen if the two schools can play this game without any violence. We are told by many of the parents and students down here that there will be peace between the two schools.

However, these two schools are right in the heart of Detroit, dubbed Murder Capital of the United States, right where the riots took place in 1967. This is a troubled community rife with drug overdoses, high crime, and a high murder rate. Will they be able to prevent this time bomb from exploding . . . ?

Frank, Jim, Ted, and Abdullah stood together discussing their strategic plan.

Abdullah said, "We got our own scout cars watching those thugs. They aren't close yet. I believe they want to arrive near the end of the game. We'll line up out front here. The parents can show their support by locking arms behind us. We're simply going to talk with the young brothers and ask that they drop their weapons. Ted, why don't you lead a group of parents inside? Keep the gym floor secure, and check the restrooms and vending areas for signs of possible trouble."

Ted asked, "You Nation of Islam brothers don't use weapons, do you?"

"We don't need weapons. We've got the force of Allah with us. All praise be to Allah."

"Brother," said Frank, "we're going to need Allah and all his angels to keep the peace tonight."

Abdullah nodded, then held his walkie-talkie to his ear to hear an incoming call from a member of his security team. After about a minute he said, "I just got word we got a couple of hundred thugs headed this way. Yeah, this Captain Z and his crazy so-called hoodlums. All of this is being provoked by STRESS. We're going to meet them right here. We're going to stop them right here, and ask for peace. Ask them to put down their weapons."

By the end of the third quarter, several hundred more parents had shown up to support the cause. Frank estimated that there were now nearly a thousand parents in attendance. Jim led them in a practice run.

"Okay, let's lock arms," he said. "Shoulder-to-shoulder, everybody tighten up."

Frank just stood in awe. "We got about a thousand parents ready to encircle the Big House. This is nothing but love, baby," he shouted.

Frank wondered if and when Mike would talk to the crowd. He went back inside and watched the last few minutes of the third quarter. Before the beginning of the fourth quarter, Frank saw Mike with a microphone in his hand, talking with Coach Ray. Seconds later Mike walked to the center of the court holding the mike up to his mouth.

"Good evening ladies and gentlemen, brothers and sisters. *Asalaam aleikum. Habari gani?* What's happenin'? We are a beautiful people. We are a beautiful African people." He paused, his eyes scanning the crowd. "Hey look, I don't have a speech or nothing like that. I'm just a ball player. But my brother Jon-Jon got stabbed yesterday - he's doing all right. He's in critical condition, but he's gonna make it." The crowd erupted into applause and cheers. As the noise died down, Mike continued, "Here's the thing. All this violence, it's bigger than Jon-Jon, bigger than me, bigger than any one of us in the field house. And it's got to stop. It kills me to see us dying for nothing - at the hands of the police, from heroin, and from killing each other – for what? For nothing. Let's stop it! Just stop the killing. Let's stop it right now. Stop the dope using, stop the dope dealing. Shoot, I ain't got a speech. All I know is that we need some peace. So after this game is over tonight, let's all be dignified, no matter who wins. Let's go in peace."

The crowd cheered wildly and gave Mike a standing ovation.

"In three weeks," Mike continued, shouting over the noise of the crowd, "in three weeks, my Dad, Mr. Waterman, and his staff at the City Club are hosting a Youth Black Power Summit. It's gonna be da' bomb and I want to see all y'all there, especially y'all ball players." Mike looked over to both benches of players. "Cause everybody thinks we don't stand for anything. So now we got to make a stand too. We all got to do something, something. Everybody's got to do something. See, we're all in this soup together. We're gonna rise up together, or we go down together."

Central High's captain, Tyrone Brown, walked over to Mike, raised his fist in the air and whooped up the crowd.

"That's right," he said, taking the mike. "And make that bean soup." The fans went crazy with laughter. "We all in this soup together. We all in it together. You might be the carrot, you over there, the onion, and me, I'm the celery, you over there, the beans. We all in it together. Mix it up right and we got something to nourish us for a lifetime." The crowd got back on the feet and cheered like they would for a Jackson 5 concert. He passed the microphone back to Mike.

"Let's stop the madness and act like we supposed to act," Mike said. "Like a family, the human family." The two players gave each other a strong black power grip and half hug.

The cheers continued as they ran back to join their teams. A whistle blew, and the final quarter began.

As the game wound down, Central remained in the lead by two points with about sixty seconds left. DePorres put on a successful full court press, stole the ball, and made a basket to tie the game. Central inbounded the ball, made it past mid-court, but could not get a pass off. DePorres played excellent defense. The referees called Central for a five-second violation. DePorres got the ball back.

With twenty-five seconds left in the game Mike tried to catch a hard pass with his left hand. He dropped the ball, grimaced, and held his left finger with his right hand. Frank thought Mike might keel over right there on the floor.

"Take me out," he shouted to his coach. "I can't do anything right now. My finger feels like it's going to fall off." Frank noticed Mike looking up at him, and looked the other way.

Coach Ray said, "Sit down, Mike." With twenty seconds left DePorres took the ball inbounds and passed it around, seeking the last shot. With fifteen seconds remaining, Al passed the ball to Ron at the top of the key. They ran a pick and roll for Al down low. The point guard Ron threw it up to Al who caught the ball and makes an alley-oop lay up; DePorres was up by two points.

With eight seconds left and DePorres up by two points, the DP crowd began to shout, "Aw we beat, bang, bang, . . . Aw we beat."

On the inbound play Central wasted no time breaking the press going coast to coast down the floor with a lay up at the buzzer. The Central crowd sang, "It ain't over, it ain't over, this shit ain't over . . . ." The game went into overtime.

~ ~ ~ ~ ~ ~ ~

Meanwhile, outside, Abdullah and two dozen of the Fruit of Islam (FOI) were greeting Captain Z and his thugs. Another couple of dozen Black Christian Nationalists from Rev. Cleage's church were also up front. Frank hustled his way back up to the front next to Abdullah, who greeted the young thugs. Kwame and members of the African Council joined Frank and Abdullah at the front.

"My brothers," said Abdullah, "we've got a thousand parents down here and we want peace. These parents, your parents, are concerned about their children, and are not about to let this mess go down like this. We want you to put your weapons down."

"What do we get out of this?" Captain Z said. "What do we get out of this if we walk away?"

"Brother, if you walk away, there will be no bloodshed. You will help bring our community together instead of tearing it apart. We've been at war with each other and it's not because we hate each other. It's because we have been provoked, played. We've been set up, and we know it's STRESS doing this. They want to see us fight and kill each other. We end up dead, in jail, or on drugs. That's their master plan. Don't you understand, my brother? And that shouldn't be our plan. You and your boys can do better than this."

Father Thom Kelly led about fifty Seminary student priests near the front of the circle near the FOI.

Abdullah said to Captain Z, "Brother, put your guns down. Please, put you guns down." The priests took a knee and started to pray. Frank stood shoulder-to-shoulder with Abdullah, wondering what might happen next.

The parents shouted, "Put the guns down, put the guns down." They kept up the demand for about a minute or two. Then, everyone went quiet for what seemed like hours. Captain Z laid his gun down. His boys followed. They all laid their weapons down.

Abdullah said, "All praise be to Allah."

Father Thom said, "May God bless each and every one of you."

Captain Z and his boys turned back and turned away. Abdullah said, "Asalaam aleikum."

Captain Z, in retreat, turned around and said, "Wai leikum asalaam."

The crowd outside cheered for joy.

Father Thom commented, "I counted over 30 guns, where did they get all that weaponry?"

Abdullah replied, "Where do you think?"

~ ~ ~ ~ ~ ~ ~

Back inside, Frank watched the last few seconds of the overtime period. Frank noticed that Mike sat on the bench in what looked like excruciating pain. The trainer was hunched over him, tending to his finger. DePorres was leading by four points as time ran down. But Central forced back-to-back turnovers, and DePorres could not break Central's full court press. Central tied the game with three seconds remaining. Coach Ray called time out for DePorres.

Frank stood behind the bench to listen in. Mike got up to huddle with the team.

He said, "Coach, they're pressing but leaving nobody in the backcourt. It's wide open for a bomb."

"Okay, okay, I see what you're saying, Mike. We'll do a stack inbound. Then one of you take off full speed to the hoop, and Ron, you got the best arm, you hit . . . "

Ron said, "Hit who?" Then everyone looked at Mike. The coach looked at Mike and said, "Mike?"

"I'll do it," said Mike. "But you got to throw it over my head. Just throw it as far as you can. I'll get it. They don't call me deep-ball for nothing." He smiled warmly.

On the in-bound play, Mike sprinted to the hoop while Ron lobbed the ball beyond the mid-court line ahead of Mike.

Frank shouted, "Catch it, Mike." Mike caught the ball with his good hand, took one bounce and soared over the rim for an uncontested lay in at the sound of the buzzer. DePorres fans erupted like a volcano. The fans spilled out of the stands and onto the court.

Frank felt a strong surge of emotion and tried to find Mike on the crowded floor.

"Mike! Mike!" Frank hollered as he jumped up and down along with the hundreds of other fans from St. Martin DePorres. The teams somehow found each other and shook hands. Central's team held up its arms to get a cheer from its fans, who gave up a hugely warm applause. The players invited all the fans to the floor to the sounds of Bongo Bob and his conga players who remained in the stands.

Frank and Rose embraced at the family car.

"We did it," said Frank. "We did it. Yes, peace prevailed, peace prevailed. Thank God almighty, peace prevailed."

"Thank the Lord," said Rose.

CHAPTER 68 –
The Aftermath II

FRANK WOKE TO THE PHONE RINGING. He checked the clock as he got up to answer it. *Who the hell's calling here at five in the morning?* he thought. Frank hurried downstairs to the kitchen to answer it before the ringing woke the entire household.

"Hello?"

"Who won?" asked the voice on the other end. Frank didn't hear what was said because of all the static in the phone.

"What?"

"Who won?" Frank paused for a few seconds to make out the voice. Suddenly Frank knew. "God bless you, boy! How the hell are you?"

John laughed on the other end, then said, "Fine, Frank. But you still didn't tell me who won the game."

"We won it! Mike made the winning shot –- in overtime."

"That's fantastic. Tell Mike I said congratulations. Hey, brother, I'm in Cuba. I'm safe and everything's all right. Been working at a sugar cane cooperative. Got room, board, health care, and a few pesos on the side. The government even gave me a small plot to grow fruits and vegetables, man."

"Hey, brother, I'm glad to hear you're fine. But there's some bad news on this end: Jon-Jon's in the hospital. He and Denise got jumped just two days ago and someone stabbed Jon-Jon. One of them thugs around the school did it, but we think STRESS had a hand in it. The thugs asked Jon-Jon about some dope money."

"Oh shit, Frank, I'm sorry about Jon-Jon. Damn, that's my main man. How's is he?"

"Better, he's going to pull through. But detectives are asking Denise about what Jon-Jon might know about the dope-house raids."

"He don't know a thing Frank. And your phone is probably bugged."

"Dig, John, I know what's in the package for Mama E. I'm not sure if I should give it to her or not. She may not want the money if she knew where it came from." Frank knew for certain that if Mama E found out the money John left for her came from John's dope-house raids, she would not accept it.

"Well, think about it, Frank. If you don't give it to her, get it back to me. I'll have someone contact you with the details."

Before Frank could tell John about everything else that had happened since his disappearance, John said abruptly, "Frank, I got to go. Just wanted to let you know I'm alive and well." Then he hung up.

Frank had opened the package that his brother left for him to give to Mama E, but hadn't bothered to count the money. He decided to count it after he got off the phone with John. He counted $40,000 — twice as much as the remaining money Mama E and Rose needed for the community contribution for the health clinic. Frank stuffed the money into a couple of empty shoeboxes and tucked it into the top shelf corner of his closet.

Later that morning, unsure what to do with the money, he walked around the block to the Williams' house, home of the neighborhood numbers man.

Justice 'Big Man' Williams, who was always formal and friendly, said, "Good morning, Mr. Waterman. Come in, come in, and sit down." He had the morning *Free Press* newspaper paper spread out on the coffee table.

After exchanging brief pleasantries, Frank turned serious.

I got a dilemma here," said Frank.

"I already know your dilemma. Mama E is short, right. I've been hearing all about this fundraising activity for years now. And guess what, Mr. Waterman?"

"What's that?"

"Mama E hit the number yesterday. We called it late last night. She hit big."

"How big?" Frank asked.

"Twenty grand big."

"No kidding. That's about how much she's short."

"What a coincidence. Haven't called her yet, but she'll know before you get home."

"A helluva coincidence, I'll say."

~ ~ ~ ~ ~ ~ ~

That same morning, Mike got up about eight o'clock, ate a couple of his favorite glazed chocolate donuts, downed a quart of orange juice, and went straight to the hospital to see Jon-Jon. Renee greeted him as he came through the double doors that led to Jon-Jon's room. Mike smiled broadly when he saw Renee. He hugged her tightly. She hugged him back, just as tightly. They stood for a minute looking like they were glued together. Then Renee stepped back and said softly, "Jon-Jon's sleep." She pointed down to his room and said, "He's right down the hall. We can go inside and see him. He still not talking though, even when he's awake. I believe it hurts for him to do anything. But Mike, believe me, he's gonna make it."

"Under your care, I know he's gonna be fine."

Mike followed Renee down the hall, watching her sway and noticing her hips in her tightly-fitted uniform. Her curly afro hairstyle had grown since Mike last had seen her. Renee looked as fine as ever, and Mike couldn't keep his mind off her.

She turned to him as they entered the room and said, "And congratulations, big boy. You won the game for your Eagles last night. We saw you. Jon-Jon passed out after your speech. My African people . . . since when did you become an African? What, last night?"

Mike laughed and then said, "Yep, it just came out. I didn't know what I was going to say. The words just flowed out."

She laughed gently. "Speaking of Africa, I'm going to Ghana in August. Yes, I've been accepted into the Peace Corps. I'll do two years in Ghana, then come back home and maybe go to graduate school."

Mike felt nervous, stunned. He hadn't even had time to bask in the glory of victory. He watched Renee move around the room, checking the instruments and equipment. Then she turned back to Mike.

"He's doing fine," she said reassuringly. "He's getting most of his nourishment from this tube. He should start eating regular food tomorrow," she said. As Jon-Jon lay there, motionless, Mike felt that Jon-Jon would really be fine. His thoughts turned towards Renee. He wanted to see how far he could go with her.

"Well, if you're going to Africa, I'm coming to visit. Can I stay with you?"

"Of course you can," she replied in a delightful tone. Mike couldn't believe it.

"Will you need a permission slip?" Renee laughed.

"Girl, please. I'll be grown in two months, and I'll be able to make my own decisions, dig it?"

"Yeah, I can dig it, big boy. We'll see."

"Know what? I'm gonna go with Jon-Jon to Lagos. He's going in August too . . . "

"I thought you had football practice . . . "

"No football for me next year. I'll be red-shirted. That's when the college puts you on a five-year program. You don't play the first year."

"Really?"

"Really. Anyways, I'm getting my finger operation on Monday. My doctor told me that I might not be able to play again."

"But Mike, how does he know now if you'll ever play again? I know that's hard to hear and you have all this doubt now, just wait and see. Go through the therapy, then see how well you can play."

"Doc said it could take a year or two, maybe longer, to rebuild."

"Ahh, Mike, you worry too much. Go through the therapy first, and don't worry."

"I could lose my scholarship?"

"You won't Mike, but if you do, if it comes to that, then maybe you'll do something else other than become a professional athlete.

"Yeah, that's right, I'm still gonna finish college, with or without the scholarship."

Renee hugged Mike, put her head on his chest, and said smoothly, "Big boy, you'll be fine."

Renee slipped out of the room to check on other patients, leaving him alone with Jon-Jon to mull over his prospects.

After sitting for about an hour watching Jon-Jon sleep and looking at all the colorful get-well cards people had left for him, Mike got up. To Renee, who had just drifted back into the room, he said resolutely, "I'll come back tomorrow or after the operation Monday. Thank you for taking such good care of little brother. It makes me want to take good care of you." He wrapped his arms around Renee, pulled her close, and gave her a big wet kiss. She opened her mouth and kissed him back. Mike felt the passion inside. They hugged tightly. The two kept on kissing like they were at home alone. "I don't want to stop," he said, fully aroused.

Renee took a step back and with a wide grin on her face, she said, "I think we better. I'm still on duty."

Mike couldn't help but bring up the past. "Yeah, remember when you were still on duty at the bakery?" Mike pretended to be dancing. "And you gave me dancing lessons to Smokey's *Second That Emotion*. Since then, I've come a long way baby. Renee, that kiss . . . Your lips are honey sweet, a tasty treat."

Renee blushed, then cracked up laughing.

"Boy, you are something else."

"Yeah, think I better go before I get carried away."

Mike looked once again at Jon-Jon, shook his head and said, "We all going to Lagos, Jon-Jon. Renee, I want you to go to Lagos too, see Jon-Jon play, before you go to Ghana. Let's all go to Lagos." Mike did an African dance impression as he exited Jon-Jon's room and made his way through the double doors.

Behind him, Renee whispered, "Maybe I will, my African big boy."

The Waterman family came to visit Jon-Jon again after Sunday Mass. Jon-Jon was smiling and sitting up with his eyes open, but he still did not talk. When asked questions, he would nod yes or no. He indicated that he felt better but still weak.

After a few minutes he picked up a pen and wrote, *I love you all for all your support. I'm healing my soul with two weeks of silence.*

Frank nodded. As everyone fell silent in response, Mike decided to bring up the idea of the family going to Lagos to see Jon-Jon play at the Pan African Arts and Music Festival in August. Frank looked surprised to hear Mike's request.

Frank said, "Boy, I don't know what's come over you lately, but that's a great idea."

He turned to Jon-Jon, who was sitting up and sipping on a bowl of soup, and said, "We'll all go to Lagos, son. I really want to see you perform." Jon-Jon smiled broadly as he continued to sip on his soup.

~ ~ ~ ~ ~ ~ ~

Mike arrived for surgery on his finger at Mercy Hospital early Monday morning. Rose and Mama E joined him. The nurses told Mike that the surgery would last over an hour. When Mike woke up he saw his mother and Mama E in the room with him. He noticed that another patient shared the room. The cast on his left hand felt heavy. He couldn't move his middle finger at all, though his other fingers were free.

"Thank God, it's done," Mike said.

Rose shook her head slowly, then told Mike that she'd had to insist that the doctors stick with their plan to rebuild his finger. "One of those doctors, I believe he's a rookie, he had the nerve to ask me if they had to remove your finger would I grant permission. I said, son, if it comes to that, we'll find another doctor first. It's always good to have two or three opinions on something as important as this."

Mike felt butterflies in his belly. "They wanted to amputate? Mom, they wanted to cut it off? Then I could never play ball again."

"Cool down. I said they wanted to know what I thought, that's all.

Anyway, I asked if they could stay positive and focus on the repair. They saved your poor middle finger."

"Doggit, I told Lola last night that they might amputate my finger, but I wasn't serious. Then again, I didn't think Doc was serious when he told me about a possible amputation a few months ago. I thought he was just trying to scare me into surgery. I really wasn't serious . . . "

"What were you saying to that beautiful girl, crying wolf?" asked Mama E. "Don't go crying wolf. What else did you tell her?" quizzed Mama E.

"Well, I told her that I'd get red-shirted and probably play after one or two years after rebuilding my finger. But she kept saying that I needed to play now because I was the star. And then she asked how could I make it to the pros if I didn't play."

Mama E said, "Lola said that? I'm surprised. That don't sound like Lola."

"Mama E, she started all this stuff about her being my queen and I'm her king and that we were destined to be together, me in the NFL or the NBA. I don't think it made no difference to her. It took me by surprise too. I told her that I might not play again. I said that the pain had been so great over the past four years, I never wanted to feel that kind of pain again. I couldn't take it."

"Then what, did she get soft and show some compassion for you?" asked Rose.

"Sorta, yeah," said Mike.

"And that's it?"

"Yeah, that's it."

"Really."

Mike thought there was no way he could spill the beans about his sex life to his mother and grandmother. And tell them that Lola said she had even been thinking about giving him some. Then Mike said, "All I got to say is that I got upset, Lola got upset, and she hung up on me. She made me madder than a mug. But I'm still gonna ask her to the prom.

"Mike, your story don't add up. You're trying to jive us old folks," said Mama E. "We might be old but we ain't dumb. We sure ain't senile." She paused reflectively. "Mike, Lola's a beautiful girl."

Well, she's still my moonbow – the quintessence of beauty."

"Really, but Mike, I think the love bug done bit you with Renee."

"Dag, how y'all know so much?"

Rose and Mama E looked at each other and gave an obvious wink. Then Rose said, "We just know."

Mike just thought about Lola for a minute - *His blue-black African violet, dark as the midnight sky, like mysterious dark matter, and as rare as a moonbow . . .* he once told her.

~ ~ ~ ~ ~ ~ ~

The groundbreaking for the Health and Fitness wing of City Club was scheduled to begin at 9 AM, and the Youth Black Power Summit was to start immediately following the groundbreaking. There would be a moment of silence to honor Dr. Martin Luther King, Jr., who had been assassinated four years earlier.

Rose placed a phone call to confirm the attendance of State Senator Coleman Young, the only mayoral candidate who vowed to get rid of STRESS. "He will be there," said Rose with a sigh of relief.

Rose turned around towards Frank and Mama E and said, "We need a man like Coleman who stands up for his people. And I know someone else just like him." She turned to Mike with a wink and said, "You got to stand for what you believe or you will fall for anything."

Rose and Mama E embraced Frank tightly.

"We got your health wing, Mama," said Rose. The family formed a huddle. Mike got down on one knee and said, "Okay Mama E, you go long, Mom you go short, ready . . ."

"Hold it, hold it," Rose jumped in. "I'm the quarterback of this show. Son, you just hike the ball. I'm throwing Mama E the bomb. Ready, break."

Then Rose laughed and said affectionately, "Look at my walking wounded, all my men. Frank with his high-blood pressure, Mike's middle finger, and my poor baby Jon-Jon . . ."

Luke, DeAngelo, and Darren showed up at the Waterman's house to ride with them to the groundbreaking and youth summit. When DeAngelo and Darren arrived, they were suited and booted, wore bow ties, and carried *Muhammad Speaks* newspapers. Mama E welcomed them into the house. "What have we here?" she greeted them. "Come on in, brothers."

"Hi, Mama E," DeAngelo said. "You can call me DeAngelo X now . . ."

"And call me Darren X," said Darren.

"You brothers look great this morning. Mike," she called up the stairs, "your friends are here."

Mike came into the living room where they had taken a seat.

"Hey, brother, me and Darren joined the Nation of Islam," DeAngelo said proudly.

Mike didn't know what to think. *What a surprise*, he thought. "You bring us some bean pies?" asked Mike jokingly.

"Sure did, for Mama E. And brought y'all a *Muhammad Speaks*, newspaper," said DeAngelo.

Mike gave him three dollars for the pie and the paper. DeAngelo handed Mama E the pie and gave Mike the paper.

"Be sure you read what the Messenger has to say in the center section of the paper. That's the most important part."

"Yes sir," said Mike. "I want you to tell mom and dad what y'all's doing."

After a few minutes of small talk about DeAngelo and Darren's new-found identity, Rose asked Luke what he planned to do after high school.

He said, without hesitation, "Join the police academy. We need more blacks on the force."

Then Frank strode into the room. "Are we ready to go?" he asked. Everyone nodded yes.

"We better take two cars. There's nine of us. You take the Ninety-Eight, I'll drive the Fury."

Frank and the other organizers had invited the entire city, and people started to gather early. The groundbreaking of the Darnell Watkins-Hunt Ward Community Health Clinic was to be a community-wide event.

Jim arrived early with Bonnie, whom he introduced as his fiance, saying he wouldn't miss it for the world. Mayoral candidate Coleman Young arrived before nine and began to shake hands with the crowd. By nine o'clock over two hundred people had shown up.

The parents of Duane, Darnell, and Hunt were on hand to actually dig the first shovel of dirt. Darnell's mom, Mrs. Watkins, spoke as a parent who had lost her son to police brutality. Then came Hunt's dad, Mr. Ward, who gave his pitch for working together, and remarked how thankful he was that there had been no bloodshed after the championship basketball game. He spoke at length about how his son had been cut down before his time, and told the crowd that he was so thankful the center was named for his son and Darnell. With tears in his eyes, he went on to explain that this was a big moment for him after losing his wife to cancer, then his son to the violence in the streets. He was thankful his son's name would be remembered.

Frank took the mike and said, "We moved a mountain and weathered the storm to get here. And we'll continue to weather the storm and move mountains. We thank God for our strength, the strength to keep on pushing."

After the groundbreaking ceremony, but before the start of the Youth Black Power Summit, the Watermans and several others formed a small circle outside on the grass around the site of the groundbreaking. Frank had music playing from inside the City Club. He turned up the speakers.

Bongo Bob and several African drummers and dancers arrived and joined in the circle.

Bongo Bob said, "Now, you know once we have the circle, everybody gets a turn at center stage. He played his congas softly at first, then got louder as he stayed in rhythm with Curtis Mayfield's song *Move on Up* playing on the turntable inside.

Hearing the sounds of the drums, more people arrived who wanted to join the circle others came from inside the club. Mike said, "Let's make the circle bigger. Everybody spread out."

Pretty soon, Mike recognized a lot of familiar faces in the circle. He spotted Leon and Julie. Luke nudged him, "You know Julie's 5 months pregnant."

"What?"

"Yeah, sure nuff. Mike, remember that Hare Krishna chick Miss Lilly invited to our class. Remember she said see with your third eye, listen with your third ear. Well man, it looks like your boy Leon was only thinking with his third leg." Luke laughed at his own joke.

Mike chuckled then said, "Yeah, I'm still wondering what she meant by the sound of silence . . . "

"Yeah like the sound of one hand clapping . . . " Luke held up his hand as if to clap.

Mike thought, *Wow, this sure is a different kind of circle.* The drumming became louder. Renee stood between Denise and Rose. Denise jumped into the center first, dancing. She cut loose as she broke it down to the ground. Then Rose, Renee, and Mama E danced into the circle. Frank went in next as the women left. Frank looked like he was trying to do the limbo. Then Mike jumped in and said, "Dad, I'll show you how it's done. Mike got low. Frank quit and left the ring, grinning. Mike kept going. Mike checked out Jon-Jon as he watched with intensity in his eyes. Then, Father Akojie and Jim and Bonnie jumped in the circle. Bonnie pulled in Curly, who resisted at first but then joined in, doing some kind of karate-chop dance. Everyone laughed. Renee clapped her hands to the beat. Others joined in.

Father Akojie shook his hips like a pro. He pointed to the crowd watching, and said, "See, you didn't think a priest could dance. In Africa, everybody dances." Then he continued to move with the wind, shaking his booty around and around. He called Father Thom to join him. Father Thom complied, but only for a few seconds. Everyone in the circle clapped.

Captain Z and a few of his thugs, including Petey Bones, strolled near the circle.

Seeing them approach, Mike said, "Make the circle bigger, everyone. Get in!"

Captain Z and his boys joined in. Petey Bones walked over to Mike, looked him square in the eyes, and offered his hand to shake. Mike and Petey Bones gave each other a strong black power hand shake. Mike cried.

Father Akojie looked like he was in a different world, still dancing, like he was floating on a cloud, moving effortlessly to the rhythms. When the music stopped, he said, "All of you must come to Africa, so you can learn how to dance like this. We're all African, even you Father Thom, you're African too, you just don't know it yet."

Everybody clapped and laughed. Jon-Jon couldn't stop laughing.